SIMON PHILIPE

SIMON PHILIPE
BY JOHN BRUHWILER

Simon Philipe

A Kerlak Publications Book
Published by Kerlak Enterprises, Inc.
Memphis, TN

www.kerlak.com

ISBN: 0-9660744-4-0
ISBN13: 978-0-966074-44-4
Library of Congress Control Number: 2005938596
First Edition: January 2006

This book is printed on acid-free paper.

Printed in the United States of America

For my Sons

CONTENTS

INTRODUCTION

Simon Philipe is the story of a man and the women and horses that he loves. Simon copes with a job that has become routine, and struggles with divorce, finding release and strength in his horses. A new woman, lovely, intelligent, and independent, challenges Simon's outlook that seems old-fashioned in a rapidly changing world. Several years younger and of a different race, she causes him to explore his past, from abandonment as a child to the youthful adventures in the harsh world of the Canadian wilderness. Simon will learn that caring for a woman, for children, even for a horse, demands sacrifice.

John Bruhwiler writes about the challenges of the modern man with ease and authority. He illustrates the complexity of family relationships, and brings to life a gallery of unforgettable characters. His writing about horses is some of the best you will find.

Allan Gilbreath

PREFACE

Low on the western sky, the April moon illumined the horses grazing in the dew-wet pasture. Jesse, the big-bellied red mare, was circling the herd, now and then cropping grass, easing toward the shadows in the fence line. Par Three, her four-year-old colt, lifted his head and watched his mother, wondering what she saw in the shadows. Then he lowered his head again, giving his full attention to the sweet clover. The next time he looked up, the big mare was gone.

~~~~~

Simon Philipe woke up with a start. Not wanting to disturb Ellen, he slid out of bed and pulled on the shorts and shirt and jeans he'd dropped into the dirty laundry basket.

Ellen switched on the lamp.

"Go back to sleep," Simon whispered. "I'm heading to the barn."

"At three a.m.?"

"I'm uneasy about Jesse."

"You said she wasn't due until next week."

"I know." Reaching across the queen-sized bed, Simon kissed Ellen's cheek. She wrapped the sheet more tightly around her face. "Don't forget your eight o'clock lecture."

Simon had no reasonable cause to worry about Jesse's giving birth. She wasn't due for another ten days. Besides, it was more common for horses to be late than premature. Nevertheless, something had alerted him.

Rather than cranking the old pickup in the driveway and waking his children and the next-door neighbors, Simon let the vehicle roll down the hill, starting the motor in the street. Even in heavy traffic, from midtown Memphis north to the barn on James Road, the drive took less than fifteen minutes. Cutting through the empty streets of a rough neighborhood that he usually avoided during the day, Simon made it to the barn gate in half the time.

In the soybean field beyond the tracks, a couple of coyotes babbled, and a grey haze gave the place a magical air. When he found the dozen horses grazing peacefully in the back pasture, he felt foolish for having wasted precious sleep. But since he was there, he strode through the widely scattered herd to check on Jesse. He immediately found Par Three, his son Stefan's bay gelding, but not his own hunt horse. After checking the stalls and crisscrossing both the front and back pastures in the rising mist, he remembered the panther that had leapt on a lame old gelding the year before and torn his back to shreds.

Now with some concern, Simon started the search anew. This time, he found the mare. She lay in the deep shadows of the farthest corner, groaning, a foal's leg sticking out of her rear.

At his approach the tall horse jumped to her feet, swinging her butt against him. "Cool it, girl," he said, pretending to be calm. "You're in trouble. I'm here to help." As if she'd understood, the mare plopped down again. He knelt in the wet grass behind her and took hold of the foal's leg, praying it wasn't a back leg, or she'd really be in a mess. It was a front leg, which meant the foal was positioned correctly. But with the other leg stuck inside, the mare couldn't squeeze the foal out. To make the birth possible, Simon had to free the other leg, and in order to do that, he had to push the outside leg nearly back into the womb. Firmly he pushed it in until only the tiny black hoof with its soft leaves remained out, then inserted his hand through the torn placenta, feeling for the other, jammed foot. He was in a sweat, and almost in despair, before he found it on the leg bent at the knee and managed to straighten and ease it through the vagina. Both feet were out now, and with each contraction the foal slid toward him, its head resting on the legs, its eyes closed, unmoving. He folded the torn placenta back, and the eyelashes moved. When the mare groaned again, he just barely evaded the flood as the foal slithered onto the grass. The mare rose to her feet, breaking the navel cord, leaving the placenta on the ground.

Simon rubbed the foal's dark wet sides, neck, legs, scraggly mane, and touched the brush of a tail. Before long, the baby horse tried to get to her feet but collapsed into a heap of tangled legs. After long minutes and several more attempts to stand, she tumbled back into the slimy placenta. Simon picked her up and moved her a dozen paces away. Again she plunged forward and fell. In the next attempt, the foal spread her front legs, lifting her chest, but her hooves slipped. Again and again she tried. Finally, she kept her head up and chest and stood. The foal took three steps, wobbled, stayed on her feet.

Then Par Three discovered the new addition to the herd. Whinnying, he approached at a high-stepping trot, drawing the other horses after him. Neck arched and ears pointed, he pranced around them in a circle, the others in tow, blowing, not sure whether to attack or to run. The new mother swung her rear end left and right and all the way around, snorting and kicking at her impertinent mates.

Finally, the mare placed a violent kick on Par's hip, drawing blood, and the leader of the mob decided to keep his distance. The others followed, staying thirty feet away, heads still high, ears pointed, whickering into the rising dawn.

The foal slung out a long tongue, almost offensively pink, flinging it at her mother's belly. She suckled, tentatively at first, then vigorously. Now she was safe. The colostrum in the first draft of milk would make her immune to foalhood diseases.

Letting go of the udder, the skinny baby horse turned her eyes toward Simon, permitting him to touch her head and rub her ears. He stroked her back and belly, careful to avoid the stub of the navel cord, reminding himself to splash it with alcohol, and rubbed her legs all the way down to the hooves. He lifted her legs one after another and tapped the hooves with his open hand, desensitizing them for the farrier who would clean and trim and eventually shoe them. A few moments later the filly ran a circle around the mare, bucking, then, spreading her forelegs wide, lowered her head to the ground, and, as if she had done it a thousand times before, she tore a few leaves of grass. The long-legged filly, hardly out of the womb, was a finished creature, bold and bright-eyed, accepting the world as her due.

John Bruhwiler

CHAPTER 1

When Simon stepped out into the quad at Brinkman College, a red Frisbee came sailing toward him knee-high, making him jump.

"Good catch," he complimented the student who caught the missile just inches off the grass.

As he crossed the open space, the saucer passed over his head and sailed on an even keel ahead of him toward the corner of Lawler Hall, too high for the girl there to reach it. It bounced against the wall above the door and dropped down, rolled, and came to rest at Simon's feet. Flashing a smile, the student picked it up and launched the saucer to a third player some hundred feet across the square.

Simon entered the building and ran up the stairs three steps at a time rather than taking the elevator to his third floor office. He laid his books on a shelf, plugged in the electric kettle, and plunked down in the creaking swivel chair. Placing his feet on the desk, he rested his eyes on a Leopard Appaloosa pictured on the 1978 calendar advertising Nutrena feeds. The horse stood on a promontory overlooking a desert under a cloudy September sky.

The scene made him think of Southern New Mexico, where he'd found his hunt mare Jesse, the horse he was preparing for the Preliminary level at the Nashville trials. Lately, though, he'd been spending more time on the back of Jesse's dappled gray filly, Snow Goose. He'd surely hit the jackpot with the Arabian stud that bred Jesse. In size and conformation, the three-and-a-half-year-old was already almost her mother's equal. And sweeter. Truer. More willing.

With a bang Ludwig Stoppelfeld strode into the office. Simon took his legs off the desk and rose.

"Thinking about Snow Goose again?" He said it with a slight sneer, never having understood his friend's attachment to horses.

"I thought you were the cleaning woman."

The German professor bent over the table, shaking Nescafé into a cup and pouring water from the steaming kettle. "You get up for the maids?"

"I get up for any female. Blame the nuns."

"Don't tell me you used to get up for Ellen?"

Simon reached for his cup and made himself some instant coffee, too. When Ellen had asked why Simon, a Quebecois French professor, was becoming friends with Ludwig Stoppelfeld, who was a Boche, he'd shrugged his shoulders. As a child, he'd replied, the only foreign nation he hadn't cared for was the British, Quebec's old enemy. Besides, he liked the German. Who was honest. Even his bullshit contained a grain of truth.

"Ellen came by the house last night to see Elsa. She

was sharp. You know, it's been two years since your divorce. Time to snap out of it, my friend, don't you think? Ellen has."

This comment from the man who'd told him "to throw the bitch into the street" when Ellen demanded he leave the house.

"You're right," Simon said, grinning. "Time for a new woman."

"You're kidding?" Ludwig stared at his friend open-mouthed. "Who is she? A divorcee?"

"I don't think so. As far as I know she hasn't been married."

"Is it that horsewoman you introduced me to at Alex's the other night? Sassy ass?"

Alex's was a midtown bar that was neither a faculty nor a student hangout but where either could be found among the regulars any time of the day or night.

Simon shook his head. "That was Patricia Dupont. She fox hunts with me. Like most good women, she's married."

Sometimes, even when he'd lived with Ellen, Simon wondered what would have happened if he'd met Patricia in his single days. As a fellow whipper-in on the hunt, Pat rode like a Cossack. And she excelled in dressage. What Simon admired even more than her riding skills was her bright and subtle mind and, yes, to give Ludwig his due, an alluring ass.

"So, who is this new female?"

"A woman I met at a Catholic study group. I'm not

sure it'll work out."

"Hell," Ludwig said retreating toward the door, "you're too damn particular. If I were in your shoes, I'd screw a different broad every night." He guffawed. "Every weekend, anyway." His expression turned serious. "Not that I don't have respect for your grief. If Elsa left me, I'd go bonkers. I have to run. Don't forget! The party after the faculty meeting is at my house. A couple of drinks may just be what the doctor ordered."

His German friend rushed out, slamming the door.

Grief? Grief wasn't exactly the term for Simon's feelings. Frustration, yes. Anger. Regrets. Guilt?

More sadness. Sadness for the loss of a love that had never bored him.

Yes, grief, too. Grief for the fate of three children whose home was split now into arrangements with single parents dealing with new partners. Well, Ellen anyway. So far, his own efforts were nothing to boast about. Maybe now, with a little luck, things might change.

~~~~~

From habit, Simon sat in the back row reading papers during the faculty meeting until an important vote came up or a colleague needed support. Preoccupied with the woman he'd met at a Matthew discussion group, he paid little attention to the president of the college who opened the meeting by calling on Hamilton Studdard of the religion department for an invocation. Along with his colleagues Simon rose, bowing his head while Professor Studdard recited a prayer, asking for excellence in teaching, guidance in research, and wisdom for the powers that be.

The president thanked Studdard for his thoughtful words and congratulated various professors for their latest publications. Then he announced the prospect of a multimillion-dollar grant to the department of religion for the development of freshman Bible studies. Applause by the assembly, and the president departed, handing the chair to Associate Dean Hopkins, a shy, introverted professor who also taught history. Hopkins began with the monthly routine agenda, committee reports, approval of honors proposals, student requests. The boring details made it easy for Simon to lose himself completely in his thoughts: Of all places, he'd met her at the last meeting of a gospel study group that he'd volunteered to facilitate Monday nights.

A few minutes before seven he had hopped from the cab of his pickup, crossed Peabody, and climbed the three lighted steps between the pillars. The door was unlocked and he walked in. As usual, people were scattered on easy chairs and couches in the entrance hall that doubled as a den, and they were staring at a cabinet TV going full blast. Simon looked for Bernie Mohan, the owner of the mansion on the old Midtown street. His wife, a gracious lady in her fifties, was a contrast to her loud and outspoken husband who'd made his fortune as a real estate developer. She approached Simon from a doorway behind the staircase, stretching out her arm and holding his hand with both of hers.

"So sad this is the last meeting, Simon. We'll have to wait for Bernie who ought to arrive any minute. He doesn't want to miss it."

With the comfortable seats taken, he pulled a chair out from under the table and sat down near the door where he could see the screen, yet be far enough away from the others to avoid small talk. The show was an I Love Lucy rerun. As a Quebecois, Simon found it easy to empathize with a Cuban coping with an Anglo-Saxon wife, though Ellen had been the very opposite of scatterbrained Lucy.

As he checked his watch, a light draft touched his neck, and over the canned laughter blaring from the set, Simon felt rather than heard the front door shut. Two women, a blonde in jeans and a black woman in a sweater and skirt, her hair nearly as short as his own, passed his chair, stopping in front of him. From her shoulder hung a woven sack, probably African, and she wore sandals.

Intrigued, Simon rose, about to offer her his chair and get another for the blonde. At that moment, big Bernie stepped through the front door, shutting it hard, and the two women turned around. The black girl's eyes met Simon's, holding them with a steady look.

Bernie led the group to the den, and the members introduced themselves to the two new arrivals. The black woman's name was Sybil. Obviously, it wasn't just the intensity of her eyes, large and luminous, that caused a tumult, or the long legs, and wide, animate mouth. The aura about her was so vibrant and bright that Simon felt sluggish. If he hadn't been used to taking charge of a class, he couldn't have talked and answered questions. He didn't relax until Bernie announced that it was time for a break, and the folks rose, stretching and smiling, forming groups of twos and threes.

Armed with a full paper cup of coffee in one hand and a plate with a piece of chocolate cake in the other, Simon faced Sybil squarely and said, "I haven't seen you at St. Patrick's, Sybil."

"I don't go to St. Patrick's," the woman said, regarding him with a smile. A mocking smile, Simon thought, making him feel awkward. "I came here to support a friend who was too shy to come by herself."

He now noticed that she had hips, that her eyes were hazel, her face about the color of his own tan. "I know your first name is Sybil," he said. "I didn't get your last."

"McLellan."

"I like that. My first saddle was a McLellan. It once belonged to a cavalryman in the Indian wars. There's a cut high in the left flap, probably from an arrow, and a bullet hole in the cantle, also on the left side. It must have killed the trooper's horse."

Sybil looked amused but didn't comment. Simon took a bite from his cake and chewed it, annoyed at his bullshit and wondering how best to tell her he wanted to go out with her. He swallowed and said, "I would really like to get to know you. Could we meet for a drink sometime?"

Looking him full in the eyes, she shook her head. "I

don't think that's a good idea, Professor Philipe."

"My name is Simon. If I call you Sybil, you can call me Simon. You're not a student at Brinkman, are you?"

"I graduated from Tulane, four years ago. I'm an architect."

A degree in architecture took five or six years. That made her about twenty-six, maybe twenty-seven. Twelve or thirteen years younger than his own thirty-nine. Her words said no, but he knew that he'd struck a cord in her, as she had in him. She turned away, taking the seat next to her blond companion.

At the end of the session, Simon followed the young women outside and offered them a ride home. Sybil's companion claimed that her boyfriend was to pick them up. Simon said goodnight and strode across the street to his vehicle. He looked back to find Sybil following him, and she started to run as a pair of headlights approached.

Laughing, Simon held out his hand. He opened the door, supporting her elbow while she stepped into the high cab, parking her sack on the floor.

"I'm glad you changed your mind."

"This is a neat truck. What is it?"

"A fifty-six Ford. I'm restoring it. Where do you live?"

"On Reese, off Central."

"I know the area. It's not too far from Memphis State."

Pressing the starter button with his foot, he fired the

engine and made a U-turn, heading east. The girl was quiet, her presence warming the cold space. "How about some coffee?"

"How about some heat?"

"Good point, but the heater doesn't work yet. Hold the wheel, and I'll take off my jacket." He let go of the steering wheel and she grabbed it. When his arms were free, he pulled them out of the leather jacket and laid it over her knees.

"Where are we heading?" the girl asked without alarm, Simon was pleased to note, as he turned left on McLean driving north in the direction of the barn.

"Force of habit. It's the way to my horses. I'll circle the block and head toward Reece. Unless you would like to see some pretty horses?"

"I love horses, but in the dark?"

"The moon's out."

"You're determined, aren't you? How many horses do you have?"

"Three."

The woman didn't comment, so Simon asked, "What inspired you to become an architect? Doll houses?"

"I didn't play with dolls. I played with Doberman puppies. If I had my druthers, I'd be an artist. I like to draw, and being good in math, architecture was a natural choice."

"I'd like to see some of your creations."

Sybil shook her head, explaining that there weren't any creations of hers out there yet, that the firm specialized in industrial plants, and she, as a newcomer, mainly clarified and finalized details.

When Simon parked at the pasture gate and the inside handle wouldn't work, she simply rolled down the window and opened the door from the outside. A practical person. Self-sufficient. His fingers supporting her elbow lightly, he led the way into the pasture, liking her long stride.

Some of the horses silhouetted in the moonlight were cropping grass; others were browsing in the shadows near the woods. If Simon hadn't asked Mr. Crumb to feed them earlier, they would have trotted up to him, expecting to be led to their stalls. Now Par Three just raised his head looking toward the two humans. Simon pointed him out to Sybil.

"My stepfather would like that name. He plays golf."

Behind Par, Jesse laid back her ears and plunged sideways into a bunch of horses, telling them in no uncertain terms to keep a respectful distance.

"That's Jesse, my hunt horse. She rules the herd."

"Bossy, isn't she?"

"Yeah. Mares have opinions. That's why I like them. Snow Goose, my three-year-old filly, must be grazing in the back pasture."

"A three-year-old filly? When does a filly become a mare?"

"I call her filly because she's so young and beautiful. The word mare doesn't fit her. Once she has a foal, then I'll call her mare."

"So you're going to have her bred?"

"Maybe. Maybe in two, three years when she's well trained and physically mature. She's put together nearly perfectly; she's feminine, yet athletic; she has the floating trot of a warmblood and the ground-eating canter of a thoroughbred. Her best feature may be her disposition: she's as gentle as a Golden. You know," he added, laughing, "except for her color, the filly's a lot like you."

"Oh my! True, I'm sort of athletic, but I'd better warn you. Disposition-wise I'm more a Dobe than a retriever."

They wandered through the dew-wet grass trying to locate Snow Goose. "The filly knows wer're here," Simon explained. "I think she's playing games. Maybe she just knows that I forgot the carrots. As a rule, Snow Goose comes trotting up to me whenever I come, day or night. When I'm alone, that is. She probably won't show while you're here. She's the jealous type."

"A jealous horse?"

"You're not a horsewoman, are you?"

"In my teens, I've ridden trails."

Suddenly out of the shadows a horse hurtled toward them, braking to a skidding stop a foot from Simon, and stood, neck arched, a pale statue in the moonlight.

"Snow Goose, you bum!" Simon scolded. "Mind your manners!"

Apparently totally unafraid of the powerful creature, Sybil said, "What a magnificent animal. Her name is all wrong. She's nothing like a goose."

"Neither was the girl I named her after."

"A girl called Snow Goose? What was she? A native American?"

"A native Canadian."

"I have never met a North American native. You must tell me about her sometime."

"I don't think so. It's a pretty boring tale for a woman."

Sybil swallowed her response and remained silent. Snow Goose had relaxed, lowering her neck. Putting his hand around the animal's nose, Simon pressed his lips against the softness behind a flared nostril, and the filly stayed very still.

"I'm beginning to understand the Roman Emperor Caligula," Sybil said. "He let his horse eat at his table."

Simon stroked the filly's silken neck. "A man who loves horses can't be all bad."

"Like Caligula?"

"No, like me."

This sounded like a joke, but the failure of his marriage had left a residue in his system that, always at the wrong moment, rose like acid from his stomach, making him feel inadequate.

~~~~~

Ludwig nudged Simon. Apparently Meyer Tyson, an assistant professor in classics, had made a motion that the college abandon need-based stipends, a move that would surely decrease the already negligent number of minority students.

"Not again," Simon muttered. For once, he'd thought, they'd get through a faculty meeting without having to listen to Tyson, who seemed to make motions just to hear himself talk. And there was no subject under discussion, ever, that he didn't comment on, regardless of his lack of expertise. The guy was an embarrassment to the language department.

Lowering his glasses, Associate Dean Hopkins looked over the rims at the dozen or so raised hands evenly distributed among the assembled men and women, most of them on the edge of their seats, ready to leave. The dean was bouncing back and forth on his toes, making the locks on the points of his forehead wiggle, then called on Whelan "Fats" Herrington, the overweight chairman of the history department. Slowly, deliberately, Whelan pushed himself to his feet. The big man never made a mean remark but played a mean game of tennis, standing centered behind the baseline, forcing his opponents to chase the ball at their end of the court.

"It seems to me," Fats declared as firmly as he hit a backhand, "we should aspire to the exact opposite of what Professor Tyson is suggesting. With no minority instructors among ninety-three full-time faculty, and just one black administrative assistant among a hundred and fifty-one office staff, and only thirteen non-white students in a body of a thousand and four, we look more like a segregation academy than one of the better liberal arts colleges in the South."

"That's not quite accurate, Mr. Dean," Tyson pointed out. "The college does employ nearly two dozen blacks."

"If Professor Tyson is referring to the grounds crew and the housekeeping staff," the history professor stated, "I rest my case."

"Hear, hear!" several voices shouted and, there being no new business, the faculty was dismissed.

CHAPTER 2

Simon had already crossed Jackson Avenue driving north, thinking of how his involvement with Sybil—if it was an involvement and not just a passing acquaintance—might affect his attitude toward black concerns in Memphis, when he remembered Ludwig Stoppelfeld's invitation to the party. Having changed to his barn clothes at the office, he wasn't dressed to mingle, but since he could do with a drink, he made a U-turn.

In Hein Park Simon slowed the pickup. Even at night he was aware of the stately homes, well-kept lawns and gardens, and possibly the tallest, most beautiful old oaks in the city. This is where they should have bought a home ten years ago, he reflected, parking behind a line of cars half a block from Ludwig's house. Not that it would have made a difference. Today, Ellen would own it.

At the door, Simon could tell the party was already in full swing. On hearing the men's laughter, probably at the latest of Jonah Brown's jokes, he hesitated before he rang the bell. Even after ten years he still was more at ease with his horses than his colleagues, although for the most part he enjoyed their company.

Ludwig opened the door. "Monsieur Philipe, I'm honored."

Simon followed the host to the kitchen where half the clan, glass in one hand, cigar in the other, were helping themselves to the appetizers. He joined them, amused at the attention his colleagues paid to his boots and worn Levis. With a plate of Brie, strawberries, and smoked salmon, he checked the selection of liquor on the counter. At home, he restricted his alcohol intake mostly to a beer or two with dinner in the warm season, a glass of wine in the cold. He took a bottle of tequila and poured generously of the golden liquid.

"Cheers," said Sid Fettucci, the chairman of the art department. His caricatures in bronze could be found in banks and hotel lobbies across the city, but his claim to fame, at least among the college faculty, was his collection of dildos. Simon thought the man was cheering him, but Sid was drinking to a voodoo doll carved supposedly in the likeness of "Thumper" Lee, the college president. It was a caricature with a swollen head, wide shoulders and big arms, huge, bloated bags for testicles, with an erection to match, but standing on spindly legs. Could be anybody, Simon thought, including the artist himself. Sticking a pin in the belly of the cedar wood doll, the art professor declared, "It's not the dean who freezes salaries. It's the prez. The dean, poor sonofabitch, only sucks his cock."

"Exactly," said W. W. Kingsley, the power in the psych department, pouring Beefeater into a tumbler, and adding a fistful of olives. "Sid's right. Thumper makes his whole staff suck cock."

W. W., who habitually inbibed martinis at his office, was already deep in his cups, scaring Magnus Dilworth, the brilliant but somewhat naïve botany professor who looked at the speaker in dismay. Beside the tall, lion-headed Kingsley, Magnus was so delicate in stature he looked like another species.

"W. W. didn't mean it literally," Simon explained, touching gentle Dilworth's arm, hardly believing he was saying this to a world authority on ferns with a Ph.D. from Harvard and three or four honorary doctorates. Simon was about to add that Kingsley meant that the president's underlings were yes-men, but decided that would be insulting.

"Well," said Jonah Brown, a senior English professor, an uncut fingernail scratching the doll's proud member, "looks like somebody ought to suck it."

Not to worry about Thumper, Fats declared. He was sure that Cora, a fiftyish blonde with a Dolly Parton hairdo and a former homecoming queen at Texas Christian, took care of her hubby.

"I wouldn't trust that hard-mouthed bitch with my equipment," complained Meyer Tyson.

"I doubt if you'll ever have to worry about that," quipped Fettucci, and the men chuckled. Before Tyson had a chance to respond, Mitch Rountree burst into the house, slamming the door and shouting, "You guys won't believe this, but I just walked in on Hamilton Studdard and Megan Coolidge in his office."

Mitch, an assistant professor in the department of anthropology who'd spent some summers in the jungles of Ecuador and the mid-term breaks canoeing in the Ozarks with Jonah, Ludwig, and Simon, poured himself a tumbler of Crown Royal, enjoying the suspense he'd created.

Hamilton Studdard was a specialist on the Book of Revelation, on which he had published several papers. At present he was working on a monograph, "Redemption in the Apocalypse," that had apparently already been accepted for publication by St. Bartholomew Press, an enterprise located in the city. Everybody was familiar with Megan Coolidge and her miniskirts. Simon appreciated her legs, too, but he was wary of women who too obviously displayed their physical assets.

"Old Ham had Megan spread over his desk," Kingsley guessed.

Yeah," Fettucci wheezed, "eating at the Y."

"Bull's eye!" Mitch yelled. "Hamilton was working so hard, I tell you, he didn't even hear me open the door."

The professors roared. When the laughter subsided, Jonah mumbled, "Studdard always was a hard worker." Another roar.

Simon, thinking of Hamilton's wife whom he liked, refilled his glass, poured some salt into the palm of his hand, and took a stroll through the house, examining the paintings hung on the walls in the hallway and every room. Life in the South, folks resting under Spanish moss, black women tearing greens, roses hugging a tomb. Paintings Ludwig's wife, Elsa, had done as a student in New Orleans.

In the glass-enclosed den, where in the daylight he would have seen Elsa's garden, he settled in a rattan rocker, leaned back under the leaves of a weeping fig, and stretched his legs.

Soon Ludwig joined him, setting the tequila and a salt shaker on the coffee table. Behind his host, Jonah Brown appeared, puffing on a fresh cigar, and in the open double-doorway, shyly coughing, stood the botany professor. Ludwig waved his arm, and the two men stepped down into the den, sitting down. Magnus Dilworth was nursing a tall drink but looked very sober. Cola with a drop of rum, most likely. With his feet crossed, he wiggled his knees back and forth. A nervous habit he had when something was on his mind. It was obvious to Simon the man wanted to talk. Sensible talk. A discourse worthy of his fame. After all, the shy fern specialist, together with botanist Arlo Smith from Southwestern College, another harmless-looking professor, had been instrumental in preventing the State of Tennessee from carving Interstate 40 through Overton Park. Smith and Dilworth hadn't fought the highway project to save the playgrounds for the midtown folks, but to conserve the trees as well as some insignificant plants, like the ubiquitous ferns he was an expert on. The power of science, Simon thought, curious about what Magnus was going to say in his verbose fashion.

"Simon," Magnus began, clearing his throat politely, "I understand you raise horses."

"I don't raise them, exactly," Simon said, surprised at Magnus' opening. Always ready for horse talk, he elaborated. "I have three horses. The oldest is Jesse, a twelve-year-old thoroughbred mare. She's the one I ride on the foxhunt. My son Stefan hunts Par Three, Jesse's seven-year-old colt by a quarter horse stallion. Then there is Jesse's second foal, Snow Goose. She's a three-year-old Anglo-Arabian filly. Snow Goose may turn out to be the best of the lot. Why do you ask?"

"This teenage niece of mine who lives near Pantherburn, Mississippi, is a horse nut. She's also my godchild. Unwisely, I gather, I bought her a paint horse for her confirmation. A pretty mare, I must confess, although, as it turned out, it would have been smarter to get her a gelding, because now, according to the vet, the mare's in foal, due, she thinks, later this month."

"Fall is an odd time of year for a horse to give birth. The usual season is early spring to early summer. But it happens. Horses can conceive year round, like women."

"Ah. Well, the vet's clinic is thirty miles away, and my godchild is worried."

"Tell her not to worry. Par Three—Jesse's first colt—was in the pasture when I got there in the morning, suckling, running about. Jesse'd done it all on her own. That's normal. It's what happens in nature." He was about to tell him about the complications at Snow Goose's birth, but decided that wouldn't ease the professor's mind.

A roar from the kitchen made the men turn their heads.

"The jokes must be getting raunchier," Ludwig observed, refilling the glasses.

With another burst of laughter rolling into the study, Ludwig and Magnus rose, aiming for the kitchen to join the fun. Jonah, apparently asleep, didn't budge. Simon sat back stretching his legs, sipping tequila. Against his will, he found himself trying to catch the words that caused the hilarity but couldn't, and when he tried to get out of his chair he found it easier to stay put. Just as well. Ludwig and Mitch stepped down into the den, not too steady on their feet, falling heavily into a seat. Jonah dropped the glass. It rolled across the rug and came to rest against Simon's foot. The English professor opened his eyes. "No doubt that Hamilton Studdard is an asshole and ought to be sacked, but I tell ya," he pronounced, staring each of his colleagues in the eye and sounding almost sober, "pussy is good."

~~~~~

By a quarter to eleven Simon was outside leaning against the back of the pickup. "I've got to feed my horses."

"Let them eat cake."

Despite his near nausea, his friend's remark made him laugh. Ludwig, spreading his legs for balance, said, "Spend the night at my house."

Noticing Meyer Tyson striding down the path, Simon

straightened up. The assistant professor had once called Simon "a savage from the North, probably half Injun," passing it off as a joke.

"Great party," he said to Ludwig, shaking his hand. To Simon's surprise, Meyer offered him a lift, and he was tempted to accept it but didn't want to confirm his colleague's opinion of him by throwing up in his car. Claiming he needed fresh air, Simon pulled his faded Yankees' cap deeper over his forehead and started walking. At the end of the street, he turned west on North Parkway and continued along the quiet campus of Southwestern at Memphis, wondering what it would be like to teach at a college whose architecture was modeled after that of an Ivy League university which had itself been modeled after some medieval English college. An imitation of an imitation. It made him feel good about Brinkman. Concrete and steel. An honest kind of beauty.

Meyer Tyson wasn't entirely wrong about Simon's lack of polish. Now and then he'd park his twenty-two-year-old pickup with a two-horse trailer on the campus, where the horses might stomp or whinny, or even leak urine on the sacred grounds. What annoyed some of his colleagues more had been Simon's involvement with the neighborhood association in '69 and '70 that was trying to persuade white families not to move to the suburbs. His editorials in the newsletter praising the charms of the neighborhood and pointing out the advantages of living in midtown failed in the end anyway.

With some amusement he remembered the call he

got during dinner one night. She had friends in the Ku Klux Klan, a woman's voice warned, and if he wouldn't stop welcoming colored folks to the neighborhood, they would burn a cross on his lawn.

Too bad, Simon thought, with an effort keeping himself from falling off the curb waiting for the light to turn green, the Klan hadn't burnt a cross. That would have been an incident to remember. A tale for his children to tell their children.

No, the difference between himself and his colleagues had little to do with his concern for the community. Or academics. It was more subtle. An air about his person. As if part of him had never left the wilderness. And now that he was about to date a black woman, the difference would be obvious. If he'd have sex with her, he'd be a criminal. At least in Virginia he would. Probably other states, too. He imagined dancing with Sybil at the faculty ball. Although he was barely able to keep his balance on the curb while waiting for the light to turn, this prospect made him grin.

On the other side of the street he decided to stop before falling into the oncoming traffic. His fingers gripped the chain-link fence that separated the zoo from the sidewalk. Being loose at the top, it swayed toward him. He focused on the shadows in the zoo, hoping to regain his equilibrium. In the paddock beyond the fence, one of the water buffalos defecated with loud splats, and suddenly Simon lost control and threw up. There seemed to be no end to this release. It was as if he were losing not only the contents of his stomach but, judging by his throbbing head, his brains.

When the attack was over, he kept shaking with dry heaves. He stared at a puddle of hors d'oeuvres pickled in tequila at his feet, and wondered what on earth had made him drink so much. He hadn't been drunk in years, not since his single days in fact, nearly twenty years ago. Odd that was, he thought, now that he'd met this promising woman, he ought to be up, not down.

Simon let go of the fence and started walking again, trying to stay in the center of the narrow sidewalk. As he reached the apartment, a wolf howled. The howl was low and long, rising with a quiver. Then it stopped. He stood, listening. No other howl.

He'd probably imagined it.

CHAPTER 3

Except for the yellow light from a floor lamp in the dining room, the apartment was dark. On the cleared table lay two index cards. Simon picked one up, a thank-you note for dinner from Mark, the eldest, who was living with Ellen this semester. Mark preferred staying at his mother's house. At nearly seventeen, the young man was establishing his own space, and of the two parents Ellen showed more tolerance. At the bottom of the card Simon deciphered the signatures of Victor Blankenship and Antowayne Williams, two of his children's black friends.

He'd forgotten he'd invited Mark to Friday dinner. Ellen must have been fuming when the boy called her to come and pick him up. And he didn't blame her. She'd had to take the friends home, too.

Idiotic to waste hours making himself sick when he could have shared a meal with all of his three children, a rare occasion these days, holding hands to say grace, listening to their adventures, remaining neutral in their competitive squabbles, being the proud father.

In the garbage can under the sink he discovered three

large frozen pizza cartons, neatly folded, some onion peels, and a crushed gallon jug of milk. The bucket of ice cream in the freezer compartment was also nearly empty. The dishes had been washed and stacked in the cupboard except for the large iron skillet. Just as he did, the kids had spread sautéed onions and grated cheese on the pizzas before heating them.

Instead of worrying, he should count his blessings. He'd lost a wife and a house, but the two-bedroom apartment was beginning to feel like home. The children had accepted the second-hand furniture, and the bean-bags in the den where they watched cartoons Saturday mornings on a thirteen-inch, black and white set with rabbit ears. They seldom complained, and Simon was starting to wonder what the fuss was about with single parenting.

Across the hall, a child cried out. Simon tiptoed into the room. Little Carolyn lay on her back in the bed along the inner wall. She was the youngest of the three, and so lovely it almost hurt. Every time the girl smiled at him with her clear, blue eyes, Simon had to pinch himself. Neither he nor Ellen had blue eyes. If it weren't for the cut of Carolyn's face, he'd be tempted to think the child had sprung from a cuckoo's egg. The fifth grader lived in a world of her own, seeing what she wanted to, ignoring the rest, reminding Simon of himself when he was that age. Bending over the bed, he laid his cheek against the girl's forehead. Her temperature seemed all right. Definitely not hot.

It must have been Stefan who'd cried out. At fourteen, Stefan had become the boy he relied on most. More so than on Mark, who was three years older but didn't share his father's interests. Stefan, playing host, had done the cooking. And probably the cleaning up as well. Perhaps the boy found it harder than his siblings to feel loyal to either parent. Simon sat down on the edge of the bed and for a moment stroked his son's hair.

When he stepped into the shower, the hot water rushed over his tired bones, steam filled the bathroom, and his thoughts embraced the woman he'd taken home from the Matthew discussion Monday night. Sybil. A charming female. More than that. Enchanting.

A black woman. Black. Half? A quarter, an eighth? A thoroughbred crossed with a quarter horse, judging by her easy disposition. The thought made him smile. What part was the thoroughbred, the Caucasian or the African? Absurd musings, because the world, even with one eighth black, nay, one sixteenth black, considered her black. He, too, considered her black, and although he was all for treating people of color civilly and granting them equal rights, he'd never met one he wanted to be close friends with, much less lovers. Except for Mahalia. That had been a long time ago. And different. Up to this moment he'd never realized that his children, who enjoyed the friendship of two or three black children, were more civilized than he himself.

Even in bed his mind wouldn't let go of the woman. Why had he promised to call her? Simple: because he'd liked her. What he'd liked most—besides her long legs—was her eyes. The intelligence in them. The humor. Yes, he wanted to see her again. The desire to be with her became so overwhelming it nearly cured his nausea. Tossing this way and that, he suddenly remembered the other note. Relieved to get his mind off the woman, he strode to the dining room.

What Stefan had written on the index card with strong but irregular lines didn't make sense: At four-thirty Mr. Crumb called. He said Par and Jesse disappeared this afternoon. Par came back, but Jesse didn't. Snow Goose is okay. What about the cub hunt in the morning? Please wake me if we go. Stefan.

Disappeared? Even if Jesse were chased from the barn with whips, she'd return. Mares didn't disappear. They were like homing pigeons. Unless she'd been stolen. Which was absurd. He read the note once more: At four-thirty…So it'd happened before the faculty party. Before he would have fed them. Small consolation, but it made him feel a little less guilty.

The kitchen clock showed a quarter to twelve. Too late to call Mr. Crumb. He stretched out again but still couldn't sleep. Something was wrong. If Par had returned, his mother would also. If she hadn't been tied up somewhere, if she had a choice, she'd come home. She probably leaned over the gate already, trying to push it open, or grazed along the fence, talking to the horses inside. Without another thought Simon pulled on jeans and sweat shirt, grabbed some carrots, and jogged to

Ludwig's place. Perfectly sober now, he climbed into his pickup and drove to the barn.

Jesse was not at the gate. The other horses, including Snow Goose and Par Three, were plucking the short grass in the front pasture. The gelding seemed to be all right except for some burrs Simon felt in his mane and tail. It looked as if the horse had been down by the river. Picking burrs from Par's short mane, he said, "You're a tiger, getting away from your captor and coming home through the traffic. You've made Stefan a happy boy." The quarter horse rubbed his head against Simon's shoulder, and Simon stroked his neck.

Next Simon checked out the stalls and stomped through the weeds along the fences, stirring up the neighbors' dogs. By the time he returned to the barn, the herd had drifted to the back pasture except for his own two horses, who advanced toward him, ears pointed. The gelding examined Simon's pockets, looking for a carrot, and the filly pushed her head under his right arm. He rubbed her forehead and hugged her long neck until she pulled her head out, also nosing his pocket.

"Sorry guys, I left the carrots in the truck."

Pointing her nose at the half moon now visible in the sky, the Goose rolled back her upper lip. Simon laughed. "You're a spoiled brat." It was nearly an hour past midnight, yet the night was almost bright enough to read by. Putting a hand on Par Three's crest, he led him to the barn, closing the paddock gate to lock out the filly. A few minutes later, he'd removed the burrs in his mane and tail, brushed his back, and saddled him. After circling the five-acre back pasture at a trot, with Snow Goose following and now and then dashing ahead, then falling behind again, Simon halted next to the pole gate in the board fence where the field met the woods.

The gate was built of four cedar rails to prevent any adventurous equine from leaving the pasture. Not that a high gate was necessary. None of the horses had ever shown an inclination to explore the woods that in the summer hummed with stinging bugs and now, even in the light of the moon, loomed dark and forbidding. About to lift one end of the top rail and drop it to the ground, Simon changed his mind. Snow Goose was liable to jump the three poles and follow. Trotting a circle, he steered the gelding toward the moonlit gate. Par eased to a canter and floated over the four rails, landing softly in the dark.

"Good boy," he said, patting the horse's neck, bending low to avoid the branches that he knew crossed the path. Behind him a rustle and a whinny, and Snow Goose pushed by, hitting Simon's leg, whinnying again, blocking his way. "Move, smartass!" He hit her butt with his boot, and the horse leapt forward. Out on the dirt track that led to the river, he slid off Par, dropping the reins, and reached for the filly, whose shape was now illumined by the moon. "Three-year-olds don't jump four-foot fences in the middle of the night," Simon scolded the Goose, trying to hide his pride in her boldness. Since she was okay, it seemed a waste of time to hustle her back into the pasture and put her up in the stall. "Stay behind me, you hear?" Like a willing but mischievous youngster, Snow Goose listened, tapping his chest with her nose. "Stop that. We're not out here for fun. We're looking for Jesse. Listen, and keep your eyes peeled."

While they trotted between the hard, dry ruts, Snow Goose followed, but as soon as they turned into a field, she dashed ahead, zigzagging through the chest-high sage and ten-foot reeds. Worried about her hurting herself on her wild runs over ground where rabbit and woodchuck built their dens, Simon slowed the gelding to a walk, and Snow Goose settled down. It was a beautiful night, spurts of wind bending the sage, leaves blowing across the dirt.

The unusually blustery, late September night reminded Simon of his own birth, which he must have imagined a thousand times, though never quite sure of the facts. All he knew for certain was that the April night his mother set him out in a Quaker State oil box was cool and windy, much like this one. That she had laid him on his back, wrapped in a towel and covered by a blanket she'd taken from the rooming house, and had set the box on the front step of the Petites Soeurs des Pauvres across the street. She or an accomplice, maybe even his father, had cut one narrow end of the box down with a knife to let the baby stretch his legs.

At daybreak, he woke up and screamed. Maybe he screamed as soon as they put the box down. Maybe he hadn't slept at all. Maybe the gum wrappers, scraps of paper and dirt the wind had swept over him during the night, kept him entertained, and he didn't holler until he wet the towel. Sister Elisabeth told him with pride that he made some loud noises at daybreak. He didn't cry continuously, but off and on, like a rooster, she said, not only waking the street, but causing the neighborhood dogs to respond. A newborn's lungs, he guessed, wouldn't be strong enough to wake the neighborhood. Her story gave substance to his theory that he wasn't a newborn on the second of April, but at least one day old. That he was born on April Fool's Day. Not that he cared about the exact date of his birth, but if he had been born on the first, his mother must have nursed him. Given him the colostrum in her milk. What Simon really hoped was that she'd touched him. He wanted to believe that for one moment, his mother had cared.

When Sister Elisabeth, the nun in charge of the Sisters of the Poor, came out of the house in her wool robe to check on the crying of a child and bent over the surprise on her steps, the baby stopped bawling, his dark eyes focusing on her. She touched his face, feeling, she told him later, like Pharaoh's sister when she discovered the basket with Moses in the reeds. Holding her garment together at the throat, she looked up and down the deserted street, glancing at the several open windows with a head or two silhouetted against the light behind them. The nun lifted the box off the step and, acknowledging the comments from the windows with a nod, took the baby inside. Used to taking care of infants as were all four sisters living in the house, Sister Marie-Joséf opened a can of goat's milk, and Sister Elisabeth fed him.

She fed him and burped him and changed him and cuddled him for three months. For the first few days, the nuns made inquiries, but they couldn't discover the identity of the boy's mother. A trio of musicians, two men and a woman, had stayed at the rooming house, paying in advance for a week, but they'd left after four days late at night in an old Ford. The woman had strummed a guitar and softly sung ballads in her room, the landlady claimed, singing in English like an *anglaise*. She was young, with gray or green eyes, her hair dark and wavy. Still in her teens, definitely less than twenty years old, she was pregnant but didn't look full term, the landlady also told the sisters. Attractive, but nobody heard her name. The man who paid the bill was a violin player named Trudeau. No first name, no address, just Trudeau. The third musician, also a Frenchman, played the accordion, as well as the piano and the drums, another of the boarders reported. When the mother hadn't materialized within a week, Father Lebas baptized the boy Simon Pièrre, the name Sister Elisabeth, his godmother, insisted on. Simon Pièrre had been her father's name.

If it had been up to Sister, she wouldn't have given up the child when foster parents were found. In spirit she never did. But the house wasn't a proper orphanage. Rarely did it harbor more than three or four children, only occasionally an infant. It was a last rather than a first resort. Foster parents usually took over the children until they were adopted. For two years, various people took Simon in. It was 1939, near the end of the Depression; few could afford to feed an extra mouth, including the sisters, and the families who could, wouldn't think of adopting a boy of unknown origin. Sister took him back regularly, happy to keep him for a few weeks that sometimes stretched into months.

These return visits upset some members of the order, but never Sister Elisabeth. Every time Simon came "home," he was radiant, no matter how morose he'd been with the foster family. Simon loved Sister Elisabeth with enthusiasm, convinced that despite his often willful and rebellious behavior this aristocratic woman from Belgium with her lustrous, dark eyes, her precise, yet soothing language, her warm embrace, loved him equally.

Besides Sister Elisabeth, he couldn't remember much about his early childhood. Except for the saints whose pictures decorated the whitewashed walls of the house. And he could remember the bell the nuns rang at mealtime. A gentle bell. Like wind chimes. When he listened, he could still hear them.

In front of him, Snow Goose stopped. The gelding bumped her, then backed up a step, snorting. Both horses lowered their heads, stretching them forward to examine the pile of objects that blocked the dirt road half overgrown with weeds. Simon advanced Par to get a closer look. Reluctantly, he moved forward a foot, retreating two. Snow Goose, on the other hand, boldly approached the mystery, shaming the gelding into following. A huge pile of flat metal containers stacked every which way. Someone had dumped a truckload of old gas tanks. On Jesse, Simon simply jumped smaller obstructions like stoves and refrigerators. This pile, however, was too high. Nor could he circumvent it, not with a trench on one side, thickets on the other. Turning Par about-face, he retraced his steps for a hundred yards and entered the woods, heading west now instead of east. Among the trees, the gelding quickened his stride, despite, or because of, the almost total darkness, as if he sensed Simon's thoughts. While he patted the horse's neck, slowing the eager animal, the filly pushed forward, nudging the rider's leg, demanding attention, too.

Perhaps he should be riding the paths he and Jesse used most often, like circling the big lake, or up and down the sandy shore along the river. But if she'd been on any of the familiar routes, she'd be home now. Unless she'd broken a limb or got stuck in quicksand—God forbid—her absence made no sense.

The horses stepped out of the woods into moonlight, staring at a ditch half-filled with water. Par balked, then jumped, landing with his front feet on the opposite bank, his hind feet in the water, scrambling up to the dirt road that paralleled the high embankment of the railroad tracks. Behind him, Snow Goose had stuck her head into a patch of fescue, tearing it vigorously.

Shouting over his shoulder to the filly, "Come, Goose!" Simon grabbed Par's mane, and the gelding leapt up the bank. Crossing the first set of tracks at the top, Simon heard a splash, and before he had crossed the second pair of tracks, Snow Goose was on top of the dam, tiptoeing on her bare hooves over the hard-edged rocks around and between the ties.

Three quarters of a mile north, where the tracks crossed a thoroughfare over a concrete structure, one of the signal lights showed green, the other red. Around the bend toward the south, the rails ran on elevated wooden beams toward the river and an old-fashioned wooden bridge.

The iron tracks shimmered in the moonlight. The Goose stood at the edge on the west side, her neck lowered, staring into the black unknown below the bank. From around the bend, a low rumble broke the silence of the night. Any minute now, the headlights of a freight train would flood the tracks.

"Let's go," Simon shouted, slapping the filly's rump, then spurring the gelding down the steep wall to the swampy ground at the bottom of the embankment. Par Three half stepped, half slid down, plowing through the muck. Simon turned his head, calling Snow Goose, who stood on the dam, transfixed like a deer in the hunter's spotlight. Turning the horse, he again called the Goose, who hadn't yet moved, still facing the approaching flood of light, the increasing roar of the train.

Kicking Par, Simon forced him back through the mire, making him climb to the top of the embankment. With the locomotive barely fifty feet away, blasting its whistle, the filly awoke from her trance, reared and swung about, banging Par in the head. The gelding's hind feet slipped over the edge, but Simon managed to yank him about-face, hanging on while the horse leapt again down the bank, hitting bottom and falling to his knees, his nostrils buried in the ooze, knocking Simon down onto his neck. Holding on, scrambling back into the saddle while Par rose to his feet, Simon got just a glance of the terrified filly spurting ahead of the approaching monster.

Again the engineer blew the whistle, and all Simon could do was watch the train rolling by, pulled by three locomotives, with lights in the rear cabs. Then came Cargill grain cars.

"Shit!" Simon hissed. "Shit! Shit! Shit!" he repeated loud enough to make Par's ears twitch, despite the roar of the train. Nothing but Cargill cars rumbling by. Empty grain containers traveling to the elevators of the prairies for a new load. And up ahead, impossible for him to see through the trees, the sweet young horse running for her life, approaching the bridge, a death trap with its open gaps between the narrow concrete slabs. Or maybe she had already fallen and been hit, or jumped down the bank and broken a limb. Driving the gelding out of the mud into a soybean field, he galloped through the leafy stalks, circling a wood bordered by a ditch, racing around a lake, riding like a demon.

The train was still rolling by, out of sight, but not out of hearing, behind a stand of hardwood trees, mainly gum and oak. By now, the engines had reached the bridge, and the engineer hadn't blown the whistle again. Simon steadied his mount, stood up in the stirrups, and peered across the strip of field bordering the woods. If he was lucky, Snow Goose would trot out of there, head up, calling out to him.

She didn't. Looking for one horse, he'd lost another.

The red light of the caboose disappeared over the bridge, and the night became quiet. Not even the sound of a frog.

Dead silence.

Approaching the tracks, Par Three suddenly turned his head, standing stiff, ears pointed. Behind him, muffled hoof beats approached, becoming louder. The dark form of the filly appeared out of the shadows and raced by, making a wide circle, then came close at a trot, eyes bright. Snow Goose stood in the moonlight and whinnied with exuberance.

CHAPTER 4

Stefan who woke up first, wanting to help his father search for Jesse. Simon thanked him but shook his head. He made a thermos of tea and a sandwich, and as the dawn broke, drove to the barn.

Mr. Crumb, a retired maintenance worker who managed the fifteen-acre property in a rather casual fashion, mainly interested in collecting the board money, met him at the pickup. He dropped tobacco juice between his boots and mumbled an apology for the disappearance of the two horses. Handing Simon a yellow plastic rope with knots and a loop in the middle, he said, "This was tied around the gelding's head."

Simon pulled the rope across the gravel. A homemade bridle! The kind he'd seen on an Indian's pony in Wyoming. It almost made him smile. But it wasn't funny. Par Three had returned through Friday afternoon traffic. Paling at the lawsuits he would have faced if the gelding had crashed into a car, he tossed the rope into the truck bed and followed the old man into the house where he called the north precinct, reporting the theft, and was told an officer would be at the barn within the hour.

Rather than wait for a policeman who might or might not show, Simon climbed into his truck and drove off, merging at the end of the driveway with the traffic Par Three had faced returning to the barn. It was barely seven o'clock on a Saturday morning, yet the thorough-fare was already heavily traveled. At the partially finished access road to the elevated expressway, he stopped the truck, got out, and looked for tracks. There were none. The dirt was hard as rock, even on the unleveled part of the road bed. He drove several miles east, moving slowly, searching the overgrown fields and the edge of the woods to the north, then turned around, driving west, peering into the even wilder landscape that lay between the high-way and the river.

Back on James once more he entered the black neigh-borhood that bordered the fields north of the future expressway, inching his way past cluttered yards, noisy children, and scruffy dogs. In the middle of a dozen young men tossing a football, he stopped.

"Did you happen to see a red horse coming this way yesterday afternoon? Probably from the direction of the freeway site?"

They shook their heads, laughing, making him grin, too.

On his return to the barn, Mr. Crumb told him a Sergeant Pryor had come and gone, getting the descrip-tion of the mare from him. Almost immediately, Simon left again, now driving north, cruising slowly, stopping and getting out of the truck every few minutes. He entered half-deserted lanes with dilapidated houses, walked down overgrown alleys, peered into backyards with leaning sheds, all the while expecting a splash of red behind an untrimmed hedge. He listened for hooves hitting a wall or kicking up gravel, pounding packed ground, the whinny of a horse coming home.

He did find horses, all sizes and shapes, but only one was a chestnut mare without markings, an animal with a long, dirt-caked coat not thick enough to hide her ribs. Her scraggly mane and tail were a far cry from Jesse's pride. Mainly he came across cans and bottles, old mattresses and chairs, stoves and refrigerators, stripped cars, even a school bus turned upside down.

When he got back to the barn at four o'clock, three pickups had parked by the gate. The red, white, and blue Ford with an oversized camper was Ike's, owner of a carpet and tile laying business. The turquoise, four-wheel-drive Dodge with spotlights on the roll bar belonged to Jamie, a welder's apprentice, and the maroon step-side Chevrolet to Thelma-Lise, an anesthetist's assistant at Baptist Memorial, who sometimes fed Simon's animals when he or Mr. Crumb couldn't. Simon found the three saddling their horses in their paddocks.

"I know who took your horses," Thelma-Lise greeted Simon.

"Who?" he asked, trying to meet her eyes that were shaded by a black Stetson while he helped her tighten the girth on her long-skirted racking saddle.

"The two nigger boys I caught in the back pasture

during lunch hour a couple of days ago. They were riding Jesse and Par, with no reins or nothing. I went after them, but they jumped off and hightailed it over the pole gate into the woods."

Simon bit his upper lip. After ten years in Memphis he was still disconcerted by the n-word.

"You actually saw two black boys ride Jesse and Par?" he asked, letting go of the girth.

"Yes. I still can't figure how the one little bugger climbed on Jesse."

"I wouldn't worry yet," Ike said. "They can't sell a beautiful horse like that without people asking questions."

"Sure they can." Simon had to contradict the overweight, cheerful carpet layer. You didn't need a bill of sale or any other proof of ownership to sell a horse.

"It's a damn good thing they didn't take mine!" Jamie said. "I'da blowed their heads off."

The lanky boy nodded toward his truck where he kept a double-barreled Smith and Wesson on the gun rack. The three riders volunteered to search for the missing chestnut in the bottoms. They mounted and walked their horses toward the front, Simon on foot ahead of them, opening the gate and thanking them for looking.

Thelma-Lise on her skittish, black Tennessee Walker took the lead, followed by Jamie on his broad, lumbering palomino. Ike brought up the rear on a white Arab gelding so small his boots almost touched the ground. They turned left at the end of the driveway and jogged along the fence against the oncoming traffic. For a few seconds, the house hid the riders from his view. At the northwest corner they turned left again, following the fence south, still in the same order but now loping their horses.

Touched by their willingness to help, Simon watched them disappear into the woods. From behind, Snow Goose nudged his shoulder. Facing the filly, Simon said, "You dodged a bullet. If I were a horse thief, I would have taken you." The Goose spun about and galloped away, raising a thin trail of dust. Simon started the truck and took off, spinning his wheels, scattering the chickens in the driveway.

Chapter 5

In the middle of a bridge over the Wolf River, he stopped next to a beat-up Oldsmobile that belonged to two black men fishing and gazed down the river toward the west where the setting sun was blinding. Crossing to the other side, he looked east. No horse. Next he drove past a field where an old black man worked in a garden plot. Simon made a U-turn, parked, and walked across the grass. The man straightened up, holding a cardboard box filled with turnip greens against his coveralls.

"You have a nice garden," Simon said.

Wiping his brow with his shirt sleeve, the man nodded, pushing a yellow, sweat-stained baseball cap with a Firestone emblem back over his short-cropped, white hair.

"My name's Philipe. I lost a horse yesterday, north of the river, a sorrel mare. You didn't see a red horse on the other side of the river, did you? Yesterday before dark?"

"Hmm," he said. "Lost her on the other side of the river?" He shook his head. "That's bad. Holes in the bottoms. Fox dens. Quicksand. Fallen trees and logs. People goes back there and cuts timber. A pile o'logs can get a horse's foot broke."

Simon enjoyed the old man's easy-flowing language, although he had to listen carefully to understand what he said, and he wondered whether Sybil had relatives who still talked like that. The old man looked at Simon, expecting an answer. There were no log piles in the bottoms anymore for horses to break a leg on. In fact, there weren't any trees anymore, at least no trees that could be split for firewood. All the oaks had been felled, cut up, and hauled away in four-wheel-drives, small Datsun pickups, Ford Rangers.

"These days, the men who cut trees for firewood don't leave any logs on the ground for long."

"They still a bunch of fallen trees from the ice storm in 'seventy-four. They pretty bad too."

Simon wasn't worried about a few rotting logs. They were no more dangerous for a loose horse than the dismembered crowns of the young oaks barring the footpaths, the stumps and jagged remains the amateur loggers left behind along with the beer cans and the broken bottles. The old man went on talking, telling Simon that it was the summer before Dr. King was killed when some kids took his horse out of the shed while he was at work at the Firestone plant. "They stoled my gray mare in the middle of the day, and the bridle and the saddle, too."

"Did you get the horse back?"

"I look for two days before I find her. She standing in a grassy spot, behind briar bushes. She still wear the saddle and the bridle. The reins was caught between her feet. She whinny at me when she see me, but not much, and she don't move. She stand on three legs and jus' look at me. You know why she don't move? Because her left hind leg is broke, right above the foot. Her foot's all twisted. Them boys done rode her over a pile o'logs. One of them tell me couple years later."

The old man looked past Simon toward the river.

"I take the saddle offa her and the bridle, and then goes down there with my rabbit gun. I draw a line in my head from the mare's left ear to the right eye and from the right ear to the left eye. Where the lines cross, you find the brain. Hosses don't have no big brain, you know. I shoot, an' she drop like a sack o'potatoes."

The man was right. A horse's brain was small, about the size of a man's fist. "What did you do with the carcass?"

"Left it for the foxes. I like the little mare." He turned toward Simon. "I still have the saddle. You wan' buy a racking saddle?"

The sun was now a red balloon squatting on the horizon.

"No, thanks," Simon said, shivering in the air that had suddenly turned cold.

CHAPTER 6

At Montesi's supermarket, where the words of some of the young, black employees sounded as strange to Simon as his French accent did to them, he dwelled on the old man's sad tale. Well, that wasn't going to happen to Jesse. If she had ever been in the river bottoms in the first place, she'd have returned with Par Three.

Driving the pickup home, he wondered why Sybil spoke a neutral language like his own children who went to school with kids from all sorts of backgrounds, and why the language of other children—black or white— remained so heavily "Southern" it sometimes sounded like they were speaking with a mouthful of glue. His children hadn't adopted Ellen's subtle Canadian speech. Certainly not his. Nor had the language of their black teachers or the Memphis twang of an occasional white teacher affected their accent. Was it due to television? Too bad he hadn't studied linguistics.

As he parked the truck loaded with the groceries at the rear of the apartment building, Stefan and Carolyn were taking turns tossing the ball into the basket hung on the garage roof. When Simon called them they came over to help lug the paper sacks through the backdoor into the kitchen.

"You didn't find Jesse, did you?" Stefan said.

"Does it show?"

Stefan nodded. "I wouldn't despair yet, Daddy. The policeman who called this afternoon sounded pretty positive."

"What'd he say?"

"Not to worry. He'll find the horse."

It would take more than a cop to find Jesse. It would take a miracle.

"Well," Simon said, "I'm hungry. How about spaghetti?"

"Yes!" was the unanimous verdict.

"You can help me cut up stuff for the sauce."

While they sliced onions and bell peppers, Stefan told his father that Victor had joined him as a part-time sacker at the Pic Pac grocery, and Simon told him about his futile search. When the aroma of the sautéed onions filled the kitchen, Simon spooned them into a steel pot, adding a can each of sliced tomatoes and tomato sauce, heaping spoonfuls of basil and oregano, sea salt, garlic and black pepper. In the iron skillet he now fried ground chuck. When the meat turned brown, he poured the hot fat from the pan into an empty can, then dumped the hamburger into the simmering pot.

Changing his clothes, he tripped with his left clog and fell against the stack of cardboard boxes piled high along the wall at the foot of his bed. Of the boxes that tumbled, the top one hit the edge of the mattress, which broke its fall, before landing squarely on the rug. The other fell directly to the floor. The muffled sound of breaking glass provoked a mild curse. With some reluctance he opened the box with the broken glass. Sandwiched between notebooks from graduate school were pictures, some loose, some in frames, snapshots from Ungava Bay, the Baffin Strait. At the bottom was a brittle, wooden frame, shards disfiguring the face of St. Francis.

He lifted the old picture out of the box and dropped the broken glass into the wastebasket. He'd forgotten about St. Francis, an antique he'd found in New Mexico. The saint would like the birds in Memphis, especially the female cardinal in the front yard. She was a softer, warmer red than the scarlet male. He'd like the bluebird, too, that sometimes showed at the barn, a modest little fellow, almost as elusive as the partridge in the pasture who kept calling "bobwhite" to his girlfriends in regular intervals, all summer long. He wondered if St. Francis had ever seen a turkey buzzard, circling in the sky, dark and beautiful.

But Simon didn't need the birdman. He needed St. Anthony, the saint who helped you find lost treasures. If he didn't have Jesse back at the barn within a week, he'd have to cancel his entry to the Middle Tennessee Pony Club horse trials in Nashville. And he would have to call Hector Hollenbach, who relied on Simon's truck and trailer to transport him and his mount. The two men competed in horse trials all over the Mid-South, from Little Rock to Knoxville, from Tuscaloosa to Lexington. Simon hated to do this to Hector, the creative owner of an ad agency and a fellow fox hunter, who had recently been divorced from his wife. Hector was good company.

Simon dwelled on the dressage clinic at the Rutland estate in Birmingham he and Hector had attended June a year ago. The first night of the two-day affair, a sweltering Saturday night, the men, still in their breeches and boots, had stuffed themselves with steak and lobster claws and fries. After cream tortes and coffee, Hector suggested they buy some Scotch, return to their room, and watch a movie on cable. Simon welcomed the suggestion. Dressage classes with an instructor observing your every move were stressful, especially in ninety-five degree temperature with humidity to match. In the liquor store he was about to pay for a fifth of Black Label when a voice behind him said, "If I were you, I'd make it Wild Turkey."

Simon didn't recognize the young woman who seemed to know him. She was short, with an enterprising glint in her eyes.

"I'm Lauralee Moore. You gave a guest lecture at Southwestern when I was a freshman. Afterwards you and I talked."

He remembered. In Buchanan's class, three years ago. A lecture on François Villon.

The girl introduced her friend, a dainty blonde named Sissy. The girls were both from Jonesboro, Arkansas, attending a summer course at the University of Alabama at Birmingham. Simon introduced Hector, and Hector immediately invited the two students for a drink back at the motel. Simon exchanged the Scotch for Wild Turkey, then Lauralee gave her friend the keys to her BMW and climbed into the pickup with Simon.

Cooling their drinks with ice from the machine in the hall, they made themselves comfortable in the room, talking about doings in Jonesboro and Memphis. An hour later, Sissy proposed to show Hector the night sights of the city using the BMW, if Lauralee didn't mind, and his buddy jumped at the chance. On the way out the door, the girl winked at Simon.

"For such an innocent-looking creature," Simon said to Lauralee, "your friend seems to know the score."

"Sissy may look like a virgin, but she'll give Hector a run for his money."

At a loss for an answer, Simon swallowed a mouthful of bourbon.

"Don't worry," Lauralee assured him, "Sissy's a nice girl. She's taking this accounting course at UAB because her boyfriend lives in Birmingham." She laughed. "I'm taking it because I need it. Lucky for Hector, her boyfriend's out of town for the weekend. Hector's not gay, is he?"

Hector was just pretty, not gay, with regular features and fine manners. With his blond curls, he looked like St. Exupéry's little prince grown up and gaining pounds. Then it occurred to Simon that Hector had left still wearing his Vogel boots. "I hope," he said, chuckling, "Beatrice can hustle up a bootjack. Hector's custom-made riding boots won't come off without one."

"Really?" Lauralee said, grinning. "That won't bother Bea. She'll find a way to turn it to her advantage. She's fun."

No point in worrying about his friend. Hector would take care of himself. That was more than Simon could say. There was no way he could resist this sexpot sitting on the queen-sized bed, her back against the headboard, skirt pulled up over her thighs.

The girl flicked her lighter. She'd been smoking cigarettes from a green pack of Salems, but the hand-rolled paper she'd tucked between her lips was no Salem. Inhaling deeply, she patted the spread, inviting him to squat beside her. With his muscular, almost muscle-bound legs he preferred stretching out. Lying across the foot of the bed, supporting his chin on his left elbow, he wondered if she would offer him a drag, and whether, if she did, he'd take it.

Already too tipsy to get up for a refill, Simon reached for the bottle and by doing so nearly touched the girl's legs. Lauralee laughed, undid the buttons of her blouse, and tucked the stub of her joint between his lips.

It should have remained a one-night bout, but when Sissy's boyfriend called to tell her he wouldn't be back until Monday, the girls easily persuaded the two men to extend their stay another night. On his return to Memphis, Simon thought, that was the end of that and spent much of his time during the summer working on a paper about the erosion of French dialects. But in the last week of August when Lauralee arrived in the city to register for her fourth year, she showed up at his apartment, peeling off her clothes even before checking whether the children were in bed.

Out by her car at dawn, while Simon insisted—once again—that they couldn't see each other anymore, she cried. Confused, Simon stood on the sidewalk, reaching through the window, wiping her tears.

He'd liked the uninhibited girl. At times he'd regretted breaking up with her so quickly. He had much preferred her to the Kimberly-Clark executive he'd met at one of Erica Hopper's singles parties. She was a thrice-divorced colleague in the sociology department, and the women gathered in her house said little besides bad-mouthing men. Some come-on, Simon thought, nevertheless making a date with the platinum blonde who invited him for a nightcap at her condo, then reached into her purse, tossed a handful of rubbers on the bed, and started taking off her clothes. Pick your color, she'd said, like an aunt telling a child to choose a candy. If you want me to kiss you, use the green. Mint's my flavor.

After this ridiculous incident he'd stopped dating. He cycled with his sons through the woods in Overton Park and, on occasional weekends, camped and hiked with them in the Ozarks. He tried to cook more nourishing meals, vacuumed the rugs, washed clothes at the laundromat. And every night he spent an hour or two with his horses.

Still, he didn't like being the odd man out. Couples that used to regularly invite Ellen and him ceased calling. When New Year's Eve came around, always a happy night when they'd drop in at people's houses or had friends cheer the New Year at their own place, nobody called him suggesting he come by, and nobody took his invitations seriously. Simon stayed home, working, watching the arrival of the New Year on TV. He opened a bottle of champagne and drank it with the children living with him.

And now, after more than a year of celibacy, he might be getting involved again. Maybe was involved already. Yet Simon asked himself why he hadn't called up Sybil yet. Being too busy to go on dates had never stopped him in the past. Was it her "color" that slowed him down?

God, he needed a woman! Rising with a grunt, he dropped the picture of St. Francis to the floor and broke the frame. "Damn," he muttered. Pressing the gold-colored frame together, he stood it against the camping equipment on the top shelf. "Sorry I broke your picture, birdman. And I have no business asking you, as horny as I feel, but I'm going to ask you anyway. I know you're not St. Anthony, and you're certainly no horseman, but if you find my mare, who's never harmed a soul, I promise to stay celibate, I swear."

As he dropped to his knees, affirming his vow, Carolyn knocked on the door to tell him the spaghetti was ready.

CHAPTER 7

Sheila Walker, a warm and attractive woman from suburban Germantown, gave him a hug at St. Patrick's Church during the peace offering. Then, holding on to his arms and leaning back to face him, she said, "So sorry about your horse, Simon."

Wondering where she had heard about the loss of Jesse, he nodded absently. If he really wanted to find the mare, Sheila continued, he should join the prayer group that met at eight o'clock Sunday nights in the basement of the diocesan headquarters. There was power in prayer, she assured him. She could practically guarantee the horse's recovery. Simon nodded again, thanking her. And at a quarter to eight, surprising not only his children but himself, he was on his way to the meeting. Only three days had passed since Jesse's disappearance, yet it seemed like she'd been gone a month. Although he didn't believe in praying for favors, he was willing to give it a try. If it didn't bring the mare back, it might help him. Even physicians claimed that prayer had a healing effect. Besides, what was there to lose?

As he stepped from the truck onto the parking lot,

he felt weighed down, stuck, like a horse in the clay of a sodden bean field. He longed for a dry place. The Sisters' chapel in Northern Quebec, with wooden pews smoothed by the knees of the faithful. A silent, peaceful room with flickering candles where he could kneel, as he had as a child, shutting out the world, asking the Father to hear his *Domine non sum dignus*, and maybe having the spirit touch his unworthy soul.

Reaching the diocesan headquarters, he entered a long, low basement room to find men and women, white but for a couple of blacks and one Asian, standing in a half-circle around three leaders who faced them. Instead of folding their hands, they held out open palms, their heads tilted at various angles, eyes closed, some swaying their hips, others, including two of the men, slow-moving their groins, Elvis fashion. Simon expected them to burst out into "Love Me Tender," but they weren't singing, nor were they talking. They made babbling noises, much as his children had as toddlers when they played with Tonka trucks. Although he had never heard such babble before, he immediately knew that these folks were speaking in tongues. Or pretending to, like the one very loud man repeating the exact same series of rolling sounds over and over.

Simon had expected to find Sheila among them; she'd have greeted him and made him feel more at ease. She wasn't there, and he found himself among a group of strangers, many of them younger than he, some with small children. Simon didn't know how to hold his hands, or where. Keeping his eyes open, surveying the spectacle, he eventually crossed them over his crotch. After a few minutes, the leaders ceased speaking, and the circle followed suit. One of the three in front, a fellow in his twenties, confessed how he and his wife had been in despair for weeks after his employer's business went bankrupt and he'd lost his job. They hadn't known where to find the next meal for themselves and their three children, none in school yet, when a miracle saved them. One of their long-time friends who'd owed them a hundred dollars paid his debt although he, too, had been without a job. "Praise Jesus!"

"Praise Jesus," the circle repeated, clapping their hands.

"Well, as always, we gave ten percent to the Lord, and then we all went to Wal-Mart." More clapping.

The woman among the three shouldered her guitar, tightened some strings, and started picking. She began singing a tune nobody seemed to know, but they all swayed to the rhythm. Then the other front man, bigger and older than the rest, recounted how for years he had wandered the country, east to west and west to east, often jobless, always homeless, ignoring the love of Jesus, denying it, fighting it. But Jesus never abandoned him. "Praise Jesus," he said and "Praise Jesus," the group responded. He worked at Montesi's now, stocking shelves, and rented a warm room, "Praise Jesus." And "Praise Jesus," the circle chanted.

It became clear to Simon that many members of the

prayer group had service jobs in markets, fast food places, hospitals. They were paid by the hour, hardly more than minimum wage, living from hand to mouth. And at this moment, being strapped for money himself, he couldn't help feeling some empathy for these Christians. From sixteen to nineteen, Simon had tasted some hard times, too, gone hungry, been homeless himself, though he'd never realized it. Not until the morning he left the family home in Memphis. The loneliness of his youth paled against the despair he'd felt that day, moving into the dump he'd found some hours earlier.

Embarrassed for letting his thoughts wander, he looked up. There was a break in the action. The elderly lady to his left wiped her glasses and stretched her neck while blinking at him, probably through cataracts that distorted her vision.

"I don't know why I clean my glasses," she said with a smile, coming so close her frizzy orange hair touched his shoulder. "I can't see anyway."

Simon nodded, tempted to tell her she should have her cataracts removed before it was too late. Perhaps that's why she was there, to pray for courage to have it done, to pray for Medicaid to foot the bill. Her flowery dress seemed too threadbare even for this overheated basement.

The big fellow on his right, about his own age, with a beaver haircut and a protruding stomach not totally covered by a white, V-necked T-shirt was fighting an attack of rumbling burps and took the opportunity to loosen his belt.

"It's stuffy in here," Simon said in an attempt not to appear standoffish, but the man didn't respond. The fellow reminded him of the Korean War veteran who had sat on the porch when Simon moved into the duplex on Cooper, a beautiful Friday afternoon in October, two years before.

Why on earth couldn't he get over that day? No jury in the world would have condemned him for capitulating, for giving up resisting Ellen's relentless efforts to get him out of the house. "If I have to look at you one more day," she yelled after the kids had left for school, "I'll scream so hard the neighbors will call the cops."

My God, Simon thought, his temper rising, what had happened to the decision they'd arrived at the night before, to stay together till the first of January? It would allow them to celebrate one more Thanksgiving as a family, and one more Christmas, with gifts and friends and love and laughter.

"Christ!" she yelled. "Get out! Get out! Get ooo-ouuuuuut!"

Unfortunately, Simon thought, he had obeyed her wish and left. If Ellen hated his guts with such a passion, he'd thought sadly, there was no point in trying anymore. That was then. Now, two years later, he wasn't so sure. Maybe he'd given up too easily. He could have tried harder . . .

Again the woman in front began picking. Now an easy tune Simon had heard before, but he couldn't bring himself to sing along. His thoughts were stuck on the day when he'd left his home. He'd used his office to check the rental ads and found an apartment in a duplex on Cooper just north of Madison, close to Overton Square. Trusting the female realtor's assurance that the place was fit to live in, he took it sight unseen. After school, Carolyn and Stefan, who volunteered to go with him, packed their suitcases and tossed them into the back of the pickup along with Simon's. In, too, went some boxes quickly filled with odd dishes and his reference books. The boys jumped into the back, and he drove the load to Cooper Street, curious about his new digs, though not as excited as his children.

From the outside, the gray clapboard bungalow didn't look too bad. Rocking in a wobbly chair on the landing, an unshaven man, his white undershirt too short to cover his bulging stomach, greeted them with a belch. Simon introduced himself, and the man answered without removing the cigarette from his mouth. Simon couldn't understand him, but since the building was divided into two apartments, sharing the same hallway, he guessed he was the occupant of the other flat. Inside, the children, who understood and spoke any Southern idiom, informed him that the man's name was Clyde, and that he was a disabled veteran. Simon, recalling the realtor's description, walked through the three-bedroom apartment, glancing at the kitchen stove and refrigerator, the electric heaters attached to a wall in each room, not liking the rough, wooden floor or the tall windows without curtains. At least the lock on the front door worked, as did the one at the rear.

They unloaded their gear and went back to pick up the beds. As soon as they had carried the last load past the veteran, who watched them without comment, Carolyn opened the old-fashioned icebox. It didn't work. Stefan turned on the electric heaters, none of which started to glow. "At least one of the wall sockets works," the girl commented, plugging in the floor lamp she'd brought from her own room. Stefan, regarding the bare windows, suggested they undress in the dark.

While Carolyn and Stefan put the dishes away and got the kitchen functioning, Simon stood on one of the folding chairs they'd brought and nailed a bed sheet over the front window, at least keeping the neighbor's nose out. Then Simon set up the card table in the room next to the kitchen where Carolyn would sleep. Stefan informed him that none of the four burners on top of the electric stove got hot, only one of the two elements in the oven. Carolyn pointed into the drawer in the cabinet next to the sink. It was full of dead roaches, a layer almost half an inch thick. Simon asked her to empty the drawer in the yard, but not to put the plastic container with the silver in the drawer before he had washed it with soap and hot water. When there was no hot water, he pulled the Coleman stove out of its worn cardboard box, pumped the gas tank, and lit a burner with a match. He filled a saucepan with water and put the pan on the blue flame.

In retrospect, the move with the two children as sidekicks had been more like camping than a disaster. They had assembled their beds and made them with the sheets Ellen had let them take, added blankets and pillows, and then fried hot dogs on the Coleman stove. They ate dinner wearing shoes and sweaters, and they talked.

"Have you ever lived in a derelict place like this?" Carolyn asked, her blue eyes bright in the beam of her lamp that they had moved near the table, the only light in the apartment.

Simon laughed. "Derelict? Where did you pick up a word like that?"

"That's what you said."

"I exaggerated. In the developing countries, people dream about living in a spacious apartment like this."

Before they'd finished their hot dogs, a party started on the second floor of the adjacent building, and the rock music that blasted through the shut windows made talking impossible. The children rolled their eyes, laughing. In the morning, Carolyn picked up the empty aluminum cans, filling a plastic garbage bag.

Although they didn't know that their father had already decided to move to a better place, the two children weren't in the least upset about their shabby surroundings. On the contrary. They welcomed the change from their clean street, the neat homes, backyard trees, shrubs and flowers. Stefan and Carolyn were intrigued by having moved to within a block and a half of Overton Square, which, with all its restaurants and stores and nightly crowds, resembled a miniature downtown. On their trip to the laundromat at Cooper and Madison, Stefan and Carolyn watched a mangy dog leave a puddle on the already filthy floor, and overheard a brown-skinned blonde in a miniskirt offer their father a blowjob. When he ignored her, the woman shouted, "What's wrong with you, bud? Don't you like blowjobs?" Embarrassed for his children, Simon turned away, but everybody else, including the prostitute, had a good laugh.

The new neighborhood made little difference to Simon's routine. Regardless of where he lived, he had his office, classes and lectures, the nightly trip to the barn. From September to March, he had his Saturdays, the weekly high point, when he and Stefan loaded the horses into the trailer and drove to the hunt. Four or five hours he was oblivious to all but horses and hounds, and to the clever beast, fox or coyote, who offered the riders an earth-pounding chase.

~~~~~

Another round of prayer in tongues was over. The sudden silence brought Simon back to the present. The name "Jesus" kept dropping all around him, as softly as the beer cans had dropped into the grassy alley. Silently he joined in.

CHAPTER 8

Monday morning started badly. First, the alarm didn't go off. Both he and the children slept in and he had to drive them to school. Mr. Crumb, whom he'd called while Stefan and Carolyn were gulping down bowls of raisin bran, informed him that his mare had not returned, but he promised to keep an eye out during the day. In his lecture on Balzac Simon found the biographical pages of his notes missing. And then he got a memo from Dean Pettit stating he couldn't accept his students' evaluation of his teaching skills. It was too high. Why make rules for a merit system, Simon wondered, if you didn't adhere to them? He remembered Fettucci's doll at the faculty party. Maybe Fettucci was right. Maybe it was the prez with his quarter million income who squeezed the faculty's salaries.

Simon picked up the phone, and for the second time called the north precinct. Again he was told that Sergeant Pryor wasn't available. Frustrated, he put the receiver down, and suddenly he had an idea where he might find some clues to Jesse's whereabouts. Instead of eating lunch at his desk, he changed to his jogging suit and drove to the barn. The horses, who were combing the ground for edible roughage, raised their heads. Only Snow Goose walked toward the gate. Simon scratched her between the eyes, then shook the persimmon tree on the fence line, and fed some of the acrid fruit to the filly.

A few bending and stretching movements, then he jogged down the driveway and along the blacktop till he reached the access road to the expressway construction. If Par Three had returned that way, the mare might have, too. Running in place, he examined the street for traces of a horse's fall, scratches on the pavement or hair, or—God forbid—dried blood.

Discovering nothing, he turned onto the packed dirt, picking up speed. He wouldn't find tracks here either, but perhaps some of the workers had seen the horses. On top he ran east, crossing two bridges, but there were no vehicles, no workers, no equipment anywhere. As far as he could see, the expressway project had been abandoned.

Back on James, Simon noticed a fellow on a lawn across the road digging with a shovel. If he'd been doing that Friday afternoon, he might have seen something. Simon waited for the line of traffic to pass and dashed to the other side.

"Hey," the man old enough to be retired said, wiping his forehead with the back of his hand, "you been jogging."

Simon nodded, regarding the broken end of a fence

post the man was unearthing. Treated pine. Two other broken pieces that he had already dug up lay on the stone walk.

"Jogging is the rage these days, I guess, but it ain't for me. A man ought to stir his blood working."

"Running's easier than digging in this dry ground, that's for sure," Simon said, suddenly afraid to ask the question he'd crossed the road for. "What happened to your fence?" he asked, speaking up to be heard over the whooshing noise of new columns of vehicles whizzing by in each direction.

"Used to keep a pony for my grandson. Should have took the wire down long ago. Well, a loose horse done the work for me. Dragged the fence through my neighbor's yard and out to the road yonder."

Simon followed the man's glance but did not comment. He listened to his description of what happened on the road in front of his house the afternoon Simon's horses had disappeared. Stripping some of the wildly exaggerated details from the story, Simon reconstructed the following scene: Galloping on the packed dirt strip that met James Road head-on, barefoot Par Three had managed to turn when he raced onto the asphalt, but Jesse, shod for the horse trial, fell, sending sparks flying. She slid into the nearest of the four traffic lanes and just missed getting hit by a pickup braking hard that, in turn, was rammed from behind. Terrified by the screeching of brakes and the smashing of metal, the mare jumped to her feet, lurched forward and slipped again, now falling in the fast lane, landing on the hood of a VW Beetle. Shoved from behind by a station wagon, the little car carried the big animal into the intersection before coming to an abrupt halt and dumping the load onto the pavement.

Skinned bloody, Jesse scrambled to her feet for the third time. She stood, legs spread, mouth open, showing the whites of her eyes, then half-reared and shot forward into the path of a glass company truck sliding sideways from the right. Just before crashing into the escaping horse, the truck came to a stop, but the display window strapped to its side broke loose, landing on the mare broadside, splintering with a great clamor. Glass falling off her like rain, she lunged over the curb and into the front lawn of the old man's bungalow. She ran through his barbed wire fence as if it were made of rubber bands and, dragging wire and posts, disappeared into the yard behind and raced north.

The driver of the glass truck jumped from the cab and rushed over to the VW with the crushed hood whose occupant was trying to open the door. Men and women stood around the vehicles that pointed every which way as a result of rear-end crashes. No one seemed to be seriously hurt. Nor did anyone pay attention to Par Three who had galloped west and turned into the driveway to the barn and out of sight.

Pointing to the curb, the man said, "Only yesterday they finally swept up the broken glass out there on the road, where the display window come off of the truck.

That breaking glass musta frightened him outta his mind."

"Him? Was it a gelding?"

"Stud more likely. That's what my neighbor says. A big red stud horse skinned bloody on the pavement. I ain't no horseman, but I can't see no gelding tearing down a barbed wire fence and running off with it. Takes a stud to do that."

"Do you know who the red horse belongs to?" he asked.

"Somebody north o' here, or he wouldn't have crossed. I mean there's horses everywhere north o' here." He laughed. "The son of a gun pulled my barbed wire fence through Riley's gazebo. I won't have to look at that eyesore no more."

"Anybody hurt?"

"Couple ambulances showed up, but they took away one lady only. Whiplash. A VW the horse fell on was totaled."

"What did the police do?

"What they always do. Write reports."

"Well," Simon said, "got to go back to work."

"Good talking to you."

Nodding, Simon waited for the traffic to lighten, then crossed the road. Returning to the barn, he wondered why Sergeant Pryor didn't know about this chain-reaction disaster caused by a loose horse. Or if he did, why he hadn't connected Jesse with it. On the other hand, if the horse was gone, there was no evidence, and insurance companies would find it difficult proving a case against him. Simon had a hard time himself believing the red horse that had crossed the road and torn down the fence was his Jesse. Not unless he found her, and touched her wounds.

CHAPTER 9

Some of the leaves on the gum tree outside Simon's office were turning yellow. Now and then a leaf fell. He was depressed, and he didn't know why. Whatever the reason, he hadn't felt so low since the Sunday morning the children were informed about the divorce. Then too he had watched the odd leaf of a yellowing tree twirl to the ground. And all he'd managed to do was suggest they build a couple of side-by-side hot wheel tracks from the dining room through the living room and race their cars.

Together they'd constructed the tracks and in no time started the races, the three children excited about the fast cars that mastered the curves and inclines without falling off. When Ellen called him to the kitchen, Carolyn hung on to his leg, refusing to let him go. He wanted to tell her he'd be right back, but he couldn't. After their mother's revelation, he would never recapture this moment.

"I can't do it," Simon said, shutting the kitchen door that had rarely if ever been shut before, leaning his back on it and pressing his palms against the smooth wood.

"You have to," Ellen said, outwardly as cool as if they

were about to tell the children that Simon was going on a camping trip.

"I'm a good father, and a good husband. Without my consent, you can't get a divorce," he said, keeping his voice low, though the excited children made so much noise they wouldn't have heard if he'd shouted.

"Christ!" Ellen said just as quietly but with an edge. "If you refuse to give me a divorce, I swear I'll make your life so miserable you'll beg me on bended knees!"

There was nothing, absolutely nothing that his wife could do to make his life any more miserable than it already was.

"They've got to hear it from both of us. You can't make me look like the bad egg."

Simon opened the door, and Ellen went through it. He stayed another moment in the kitchen, watching a scarlet cardinal flitting through the barren branches of the sycamore in the backyard; then reluctantly he followed his wife.

"Children," she said, "stop playing for a minute. Your father and I have an announcement to make."

"What announcement?" Carolyn asked, her eyes lighting up. Stefan was spinning the tires of a black Maserati in his palm. Intuitively expecting bad news, he gravely glanced from his mother to his father. Mark, playing it cool, straightened a support pillar on the near track.

"This may come as a surprise to you," she continued in a measured voice, "but your father and I have decided to separate. As soon as your father finds a place, he'll move out."

A moment of stunned silence. Then Mark, clear-voiced, said, "This sure is a surprise!"

"Sure is!" the smaller children echoed.

Simon, losing his composure, turned and retreated to the kitchen porch, sitting down on the step outside the screen door. The cardinal had perched on the near corner of the garage roof, preening its wings.

In the living room, Ellen held center stage, reciting her speech, not missing a beat, to the three she'd born and raised, the oldest of whom hadn't reached his fourteenth birthday. Carolyn had just turned eight. She assured them that the separation had nothing to do with them, that both she and their father would continue to love them, and they each would, part of the time, share their father's new domicile, wherever that might be.

Ellen didn't need to raise her voice for Simon to hear her. It easily carried through the house to the backyard. A beautiful voice, soft yet firm, it had carried to the farthest pews in the Roman Catholic church of St. Vincent-de-Paul in Ottawa, promising faith and love and trust, for better or for worse, until death do us part, witnessed by her parents, Mr. and Mrs. Trevor H. Jones, ambassador on leave, and witnessed by a festive congregation of prominent friends, Protestants all except for the honorable Judge Joseph W. Byrd, retired, and Father Bergerac, a Capuchin monk, who solemnized the marriage. And last but not least, it was a union witnessed by the Host in whose hands they had laid the promise.

For the first time since his childhood, Simon lost it. He closed the porch door, sat down on the back step and bawled, shaking helplessly, facing the cardinal, now a blood-colored blur.

In the living room, Ellen had reached the end of her monolog. "Oh my God," Simon grunted, rising from the step, wiping his eyes on his sleeves. He headed toward his children, wanting to protect them with his strong arms. But it was too late. Mark had rushed to his room, slamming the door, and Stefan hurried out the front door, leaving it wide open.

Only little Carolyn stayed in the room, looking puzzled. "Did Mummy say you're going to leave us?"

"No," Simon said, looking at her with puffy eyes, "I'm not leaving you. I'll never leave you." He would deny it to himself, of course, but he had already been spun out of his children's orbit.

And he was spinning still, judging by this sudden depression. How could his wonderful Ellen have done this? Or had she? Jesus. Enough is enough. Where was that Sybil girl's number?

CHAPTER 10

And before leaving the office and driving to the barn, Simon called Sybil. The phone rang once, twice, three times. A quarter to six. Maybe she wasn't home from work yet and he wouldn't be making a fool of himself. Barely eight days had passed since the Sunday night he'd met her and shown her his horses, yet so much had stirred his daily routine he found it difficult to remember her exact reaction when he'd promised to give her a call sometime. Sometime. A vague promise, if a promise at all.

"Yes," a throaty female voice answered.

"Simon Philipe. I'd like to speak to Sybil McLellan."

"This is she."

He cleared his throat. "How are you?"

"Okay. I thought you'd forgotten about me."

"Hardly, although I've had all kinds of stuff going on. Being busy is a teacher's fate, I guess."

She laughed. "Certainly for one who spends half his time with his horses. What are you up to?"

"I thought you might like to go out for a drink."

"I guess I could do that. I'm not much of a drinker,

though."

"I'll pick you up at eight. That okay?"

"I'm afraid not. Not tonight."

Disappointed, Simon muttered, "You have a date?"

Again she laughed. "I'm afraid so."

More bad news. "I thought you were unattached."

"I am unattached."

Feeling better, Simon said, "How about tomorrow?"

"How about Friday? Friday would be better. Do you mind?"

Of course he minded but he couldn't say so. Come to think of it, Friday was a more convenient night for him, too.

"Friday's good. Around seven?"

"Seven is fine."

Simon wanted to shout but only said, "Okay, see you Friday at seven."

She hung up and Simon called Ellen at home and asked her to meet with him for a drink. It concerned a matter he couldn't discuss over the phone, and he'd appreciate her coming. How about six-thirty at the Bicycle Club? She said she'd rather talk to him at Trader Dick's where she was to meet some friends around seven.

Simon agreed, although Trader Dick's wasn't his favorite watering hole. It wasn't only a Freudian slip when he called it Trader's Dick. With the early night pushing through the windows, and the smell of beer mixing with the rankness of fried fish, he wished he were elsewhere. He stopped at the bar, ordered a martini, and found a seat by the window along the rear wall, watching the barman mix his drink and bring it to his table on a tray with a couple of paper coasters and a glass of ice water.

Sipping his martini, he watched the entrance. Several people came through the door, singles and couples. Among them was a black woman who gave him a nod, and for an instant he mistook her for the counselor at Family Services. She had insisted that he knew why his wife wanted a divorce.

He didn't know. In his own opinion it might be because he'd been too controlling. But Ellen had never accused him of that. In fact, she had never accused him of anything. And she had never told him what it was that depressed her, just said, "It's not you, it's me." After a long moment of silence, Simon had said to the counselor, "My wife believes her father doesn't love her. She's convinced that I, having come into her life as a stranger, couldn't possibly love her either."

"Doubting a father's love is a common phenomena in women, especially when the man is domineering. I wouldn't attribute much significance to that."

Annoyed with himself for inwardly sneering at her using "phenomena" instead of the singular, "phenomenon," Simon said, "It may not be significant for my wife, but it is for me."

"You're wrong. Yesterday, when Ellen and I were one on one, I got the impression that your wife was abused as a child."

Maybe that's what had happened to the overweight

therapist, Simon thought, shaking his head. Then he said, "I told Ellen I would sell my horses if she stayed with me. She said she wouldn't ask that of me."

The woman smiled. "Ellen is correct. If you stopped riding horseback, would you spend more time with her? Anyway, I believe your wife's depression has a physical cause. She needs to be in therapy with a psychiatrist. A man who is able to dispense drugs."

Good luck! he'd thought. Ellen didn't even take aspirins.

He'd missed Ellen's arrival, didn't notice her until she hung her maroon leather coat on the back of the chair and sat down before Simon had a chance to rise. She also ordered a martini. Simon moved his water glass toward her.

"Tough day?"

"My supervisor just promoted another guy I trained ahead of me. That's the second one in less than two years."

If she were still smoking, she'd be blowing smoke out of the corner of her mouth. Now she just opened the corner of her still unpainted lips from old habit.

Simon had met her boss. A fellow in snakeskin boots, wearing a Stetson even in the lab where he sat behind his desk, legs on top, drinking coffee, reading crime magazines and shooting the bull with the young men he hired, while two middle-aged women, Ellen and a Hungarian refugee, did the work.

She looked him in the eyes. "What is it that's so important you couldn't tell me over the phone?"

The waiter put a napkin on the table and the martini on it. Ellen nodded toward the young man, her smile pulling the corners of her mouth upward. Creepy, Simon thought, how daughters adopted the mannerisms of their mothers by the time they were forty. Or thirty-eight, as in Ellen's case. He probably simply hadn't noticed before.

"I asked you this last year," he began. "It may not be important to you, and I know it's of no consequence to the world, but I have to ask you a final time. Have you given any thought to getting back together?"

Stripping the first of two olives off the plastic spear with her teeth, she nodded. "I have. I've given it a lot of thought."

At a table near the entrance, a burst of laughter broke the relative quiet in the place, and suddenly almost everybody in the restaurant was laughing. Ellen stared at the glass she was slowly turning with both hands, unaware of the general hilarity. "As miserable as my life has been in divorce," she said, without looking up, "I've learned to value my freedom."

"The word freedom has a lot of meanings. For me, being with you set me free."

"That's because while you carved out a life for yourself, I bore and raised your children. For fifteen years I shopped and cooked and washed and cleaned. Now it's my turn to live."

Working for a man she hated? At a loss, Simon wanted

to tell her that the children paid a hell of a price for her freedom, but he didn't feel like rehashing an argument when it was too late, anyway. Tapping the table with her fingers, Ellen turned toward the front, obviously hoping her friends would show up soon and rescue her. Across the street, a neon sign with missing letters was flashing some unreadable come-on message. Ellen's attention seemed to be captivated by it, the way it had been by the northern lights they'd watched from his bed in Ottawa, wet from their love-making.

"Let's get married," he'd said, gently kissing her still swollen nipples.

"Look!" Ellen said, sitting up. "Northern lights!"

The horizon was flashing with dancing colors. Red, green, blue, yellow. The colors of the rainbow. Playful. Wild. Ever changing. For a while they watched, fascinated, then Ellen wiped her face and body with the sheet and grabbed his penis, amused at his new erection. Holding it, she said, "I think it would be wonderful to be married to you." That's what she'd said. Words etched on his mind, northern lights swirling about the sky.

"Do you remember the night we watched the northern lights from my room?"

"What northern lights?"

"Never mind," Simon said, regarding the large fishnet on the wall behind the bar. "Before I get involved with another woman, I wanted to know if there is still a chance for us."

Without answering, Ellen turned her head toward the

door. At least she didn't get up and walk away. Although he hadn't seen her without clothes for several years now, her body looked as fit and feminine as it had that night. Her face, except for the fine wrinkles and an expression in her eyes that wavered between desperate and fey, was the same. Her eyes were indeed almost too much to bear. He was glad that her friends showed up just then, two women and three men, waving. As she rose, a smile crossed her face, and she sailed through the room like a queen.

CHAPTER 11

Annoyed with himself for wasting feelings on a lost cause, Simon drove to the barn, planning to work Snow Goose. The pasture, though still green, had become as hard as rock in the recent weeks without rain. Not conducive to flat work, especially with a young horse like Snow Goose, who hadn't yet learned to appreciate the benefits of dressage. What he needed was an arena covered with sand. Soft, safe footing.

What he really needed of course was the return of Jesse. Not only because the Nashville trials were to be her last at the Preliminary level before he moved her up to Three-Day and Intermediate, but because he missed the mare. Jesse was his creation. In the eleven years he'd worked and grown with that character, she'd become as much a part of his life as Ellen.

Getting a horse of his own had been a strong reason for accepting the job at New Mexico State University in Las Cruces. As soon as they were settled out in the valley, and before all his books were unpacked at the office, Simon asked around and started checking the ads. What he wanted wasn't just any old cow pony, although he'd loved the Quarter horses he'd ridden in his teens on a ranch in Wyoming. What he was looking for was a horse with size and looks and spirit. Something like the thoroughbreds he'd learned to love on the horse farms in Lexington, where he spent three years as a graduate student. He wanted a horse suitable for the trail, roping, jumping, dressage, whatever, an all around athlete like himself, only better. Any chance he got, and on weekends with Ellen and the children, Simon drove to isolated ranches and farms, checking out a variety of horseflesh and meeting men and women eking out an existence from the harsh, dry land.

The first horse that he'd liked was a two-year-old sorrel filly that belonged to a peach farmer near Cloudcroft in the mountains above Tularosa. An April frost, the man explained, had killed his fruit crop; otherwise, he wouldn't be selling his registered quarter horse. Simon, respecting the farmer's ability to hang on to his place after losing his income for the year, was tempted to help him out and buy the youngster despite her swayback. He liked her eye, her calmness, her apparently sweet disposition. Ellen and the children were enchanted by the filly's pretty head, but in the end, he wasn't willing to buy a horse with an odd conformation.

Then, in the mountains west of Truth or Consequences, he bargained for a blue roan with a rancher who raised bucking horses. The two-year-old he and his wrangler had gelded earlier in the day, apparently without anesthetic, was still a little wobbly on its feet and looked so pitiful he felt sorry for it. But he couldn't buy a horse out of pity. He needed to covet it.

Sunday he saw a handwritten note stapled to the church bulletin board, advertising Arabians for sale. The lady who lived in a trailer on the edge of a thirteen-acre sand lot explained that due to the drought she was willing to part with a three-year-old gelding. A gray, she announced proudly, with ancestors going back to Mohammed. She could let him have him for fifteen hundred. Of the ten horses picking on widely scattered brown cactuses, only a dappled gray mare didn't show all of her ribs. The gelding with the royal family tree stood about thirteen-two hands, showing his ribs under the pale skin and a bloated belly. The lady, noticing Simon's shock, assured him that they'd get rain soon, and in no time the desert would bloom. He listened to her but kept eyeing the dappled gray that now came prancing toward them, shaking a proud head. The horse stopped in front of him, nudging his chest with her mouth. Simon rubbed the head and patted the neck of the sleek animal. Although the filly wasn't as tall as the average thoroughbred, she was well muscled and her gaits were those of a big striding horse.

"This is the one I want," he said.

The woman regarded the sand at her feet, saying she'd turned down five thousand. Which happened to be more than half Simon's annual income, and that included three months of teaching summer school.

"How much would it take?"

The lady bit her lips. "I don't know." As if speaking to herself, she added, "They're my children."

That night he sat enjoying the breeze in the yard with Ellen, who was breast-feeding Carolyn, wishing he knew how to do a rain dance to save the innocent horses. It wouldn't rain a single drop for another five months. He would think about those horses all winter long, but didn't go back to the barren desert patch.

"You'll find a horse," Ellen said, squeezing his knee.

He put his hand on hers. "How about you? You're not sorry we moved to the valley?"

"Mark and Stefan love it, but for me it's a little lonely."

Taking Carolyn from her arms to burp her, he said, "Look at the stars. They're so close you'd think you'd hear them move."

The following day he decided to take his chairman's advice and check out the ranch that was part of the experimental farm where the Ag professors did research. The university wouldn't sell him a horse, but old Hokus McGann, the cowpoke who was in charge of the livestock, might find him one. The afternoon was as sunny and hot as every afternoon had been for three weeks since the start of the semester. He drove slowly on the bumpy road, watching the cloud of dust that hovered behind, announcing his coming for miles. He crossed the cattle guard at the gate and stopped in the middle of the yard.

Facing him was a large shed, some outbuildings, a circular stallion pen, ten-foot-tall, boarded up with heavy planks, and a square corral built of split cedar poles. The horses in the corral raised their heads as Simon shut the door of the Chevy wagon. Simon's eyes were immediately drawn to a sorrel with a red mane and tail, taller than the rest of the horses milling in the corral. Even with the late afternoon sun obscuring his vision, he could see the horse's ribs, but the mare carried her head proudly.

In the barn, several horses nickered, probably expecting to be fed. He walked into the shade of the hallway, calling hello, but got no answer. In one of the box stalls a paint stallion pawed the shavings on the dirt floor, and in another, a bay yearling pushed its nose through the bars.

After inspecting every animal in the barn and petting them all, Simon went back outside and sat in the car with the door open, listening to a mariachi band and correcting a batch of first year French tests. When he was through with them, pleased that they weren't as bad as he had feared, he turned the music off, got out, and climbed on the pole fence of the corral watching the red mare.

It was past five o'clock. If McGann had been out on the range, he should be returning soon. The view from the top of the fence wasn't much better than from the front seat of the car. Beyond the buildings nothing but desert, pale sand and cactuses and a few grasses whose names he didn't know. At a distant water tank, a turkey buzzard circled low. Either some little critter had died in the sand or the bird was thirsty.

Simon had to smile. Like the buzzard, he was thirsty. Every day all day long he thirsted for water. In the classroom, in his office, in the living room at home, even in bed at night. The lush, irrigated fields that surrounded their house in the valley made very little difference. On days like this, it seemed the air held no humidity at all.

Hokus McGann rode into the yard from the side of the barn, unnoticed by Simon until he heard the muffled steps of a horse in the dust. The man riding out of the sun was a dark silhouette, looking neither young nor old. Not until he halted the pony before him did Simon see the wrinkles around the gray eyes and the leathery skin of his face under a straw Stetson. He looked fifty but could have been forty or sixty. As he stepped down from his appaloosa, slapping dust off his denim shirt and fringed chaps, Simon noticed the man's scuffed boots and the coiled lariat on his plain roping saddle.

"I'm Simon Philipe," Simon said, holding out his hand. The cowboy shook it, squinting against the bright sky. "I teach French at the university. I would like you to find me a horse."

McGann glanced at Simon's loafers, beige gabardine trousers, and blue polo shirt. "What kind of a horse?"

"I like the skinny sorrel in the corral."

Laughing, the man loosened the saddle cinch. "That mare ain't broke to ride."

"I spent a summer working on a cattle ranch in Wyoming." He smiled sheepishly. "I did some roping and bronc riding at the rodeo. Of course, that was a dozen years ago." He'd also taken jumping lessons on a thoroughbred while in graduate school, but he didn't think that would impress a cowhand.

The cowboy led his horse to the barn, dropped the saddle on a bale of hay, took off the Hackamore bridle, and the appaloosa walked into its stall. Closing the door, McGann said, "Wyoming, ha? Never been that far north myself. We used to work cattle here, too. These days the profs just do research. Now and then I move some steers for them. Sometimes sheep. I mainly keep the place in shape."

The horseman hung a halter with a lead rope over his shoulder and took the lariat off his saddle.

"If you're interested in that mare, let's have a look at her. She's a two-year-old thoroughbred off the track. This sonovabitch dealer in El Paso first beat her, then starved her. Walker from the Humane Society trailered her up here." He dropped the lariat on the sand and slunk through the throng of horses, hiding the halter with the lead rope behind his back. But as soon as he got near the mare, she swung her rear end about, pointing it at him, whichever way he went. The cowboy cursed and came outside, tossing the halter to Simon. "You want to try?"

Simon dropped the halter and picked up the lariat and entered the corral, twirling the rope, following the mare. She immediately sensed his intention and moved faster, trying to hide behind the smaller horses. Simon pursued her slowly, taking his time. When he finally swished the rope over the other horses' heads, he lassoed the mare's neck, and braced his loafers in the sand. The mare pulled just enough to stretch the rope tight, then swung around and backed, making Simon hop along. Trapped in the far corner, all by herself now, she raised her head, showing the whites of her eyes. While Simon moved closer, slowly, sliding his bare hands along the lariat, McGann joined him with the halter and lead rope.

The horse pointed her nose at the sky, too high for the cowboy to reach. When Simon tried to pull her neck down, she reared, lifting him a foot off the ground. The moment the mare dropped to her feet, the cowboy swung the halter high, catching her nose, then slipped the strap over her poll, closing the buckle. Clicking his tongue, he started to jog, making the horse trot. Then he unsnapped the lead rope and slapped her on the butt, and she cantered, leading the half-wild ponies in a run around the corral.

"You can count her ribs," Simon commented disappointed.

"When she first got here, the mare looked so bad I didn't think she'd make it. You can't tell about a racehorse, of course. They pull tendons, fracture bones, get arthritis, but this mare's conformation is nearly perfect. When she's fit, she'll be one heck of a horse. If she wasn't so tall, for sixty-five bucks I'd buy her myself.

"Sixty-five dollars?"

"Nobody in these parts wants a sixteen-hand horse.

But you don't have to work cattle with her, and for pleasure, a tall horse is no disadvantage, I'm told. Me personally, I don't wanna sit no higher than fifteen hands. You
ever break a horse?"

Remembering the ranch horses in Wyoming, Simon
was about to nod. Instead, he said, "I've trained a dog."

"Not quite the same thing. Both take patience, that's
true, but a dog will work for you because he loves you.
A horse don't give a darn about you. You have to be very
consistent. Develop training patterns. Repeat the moves
twenty times or more if you have to. If she don't get it
after twenty times, start over again the next day. And
keep your cool. Always keep your cool."

~~~~~

A week later, when Simon had built a paddock and
shed in the back yard that bordered the neighbor's
plowed cotton field, Hokus McGann delivered the
red mare in his one-horse trailer, and sold him his old
McLellan cavalry saddle plus a girth and bridle. As soon
as the dust cloud from the departing rig had cleared,
Simon tacked up his new possession. To his surprise,
the mare fidgeted little while he tightened the girth, and
even kept her ears pointed. Then grabbing the reins, he
stepped into the English stirrups, swinging his right leg
over her back. Even before he found the other stirrup, the
young horse bucked in twists and circles, slowly bouncing away from the paddock into the vast, fallow cotton
field. Simon hung on to the saddle, bouncing with the
horse, and gradually the jumps diminished both in fre-

quency and height. Triumphantly, he waved to Ellen and the watching children. Suddenly, without any warning, the mare threw her rear end straight up, tossing him into the air where he flipped and, disoriented, piled head-first into the black adobe clods. As he tried to sit up, the mare reared, front hooves bearing down on the fallen rider. She would have stomped on his head if he hadn't rolled away. Again she raised her chest and came down, forcing him to roll again, and again, and again.

How he eventually struggled to his feet, Simon couldn't tell afterward. Every muscle in his body ached, and breathing caused a stinging pain, but he threw the reins over her head, and mounted, and she stood still. When he turned a heel against her side, she moved forward, and Simon rode the lathered mare back to the paddock.

"You'd better return that horse, don't you think," Ellen said, pushing Carolyn in the stroller.

"That horse is an outlaw, Daddy," Mark exclaimed, bright-eyed. "We should call her Jesse."

Simon laughed and quoted the old cowboy adage, "Ain't no horse that can't be rode, ain't no man that can't be throwed." And indeed, Jesse—as he called her from that moment on—obeyed his seat, walking out of the backyard toward the gravel road where he made her stay on the edge of the plowed field, just in case. After a while, he touched her with both heels, and she switched to a big trot. He soon came to the sand dunes, passing a pile of bleached cattle bones, and reaching the tunnel under the freeway. Bending low over the mare's shoulder, Simon guided her through the semi-dark where she carefully climbed over loose rocks and chunks of concrete. On the other side, he slapped her rump and cantered into the wide-open desert.

"Oh, Jesse, wonderful Jesse, where art thou?"

CHAPTER 12

"Good girl," Simon said, lifting his right leg over the horse's neck and sliding to the ground. The young, inexperienced filly was no Jesse, but she was no cart horse either. The daily work sessions had done wonders for her performance on the flat. She now flexed her head at the trot, stretched it out at the walk, cantered circles with a bend, even came to a square halt, at least with her front feet.

He changed saddles, mounted, trotted over the crossbar, and eased into a canter, heading toward the four-rail gate. The Goose raised her head, pointing her ears. For a second, Simon considered dropping one end of the top rail, even though the filly had jumped the gate when she'd followed Par Three in the dark. "Fly, Goose!" he said, getting a hold of her. And the Goose flew, with no hesitation, a foot higher than she needed to. It took practice to gauge fences correctly. Anyway, the Pre-Training fences were much lower, barely three feet high.

"Good horse, gooood horse!" Simon almost shouted, moving on at a canter, stroking her neck with both hands, ducking and bending away from vicious branches. On the dirt road Snow Goose extended her stride, running south between the hard tracks. Then, in a wild scramble, they scaled the nearly vertical ascent to the expressway construction. On the packed dirt they galloped east, crossing three bridges, and working their way back west at an easy canter, and cooled off, facing the heavy traffic back to the barn.

If Jesse didn't return in time for the Nashville event, he'd take Snow Goose. She was ready for the cross-country. All he had to do was work her some more on the flat and let her see some stadium jumps.

Earlier he had planned to start grading the French papers for his seventeenth century class after the ride, but the mare's performance had given Simon such a boost that he decided to call on Sybil instead, even though it was the night before their first official date. The papers could wait for the weekend.

A gleaming, black Acura sat in the driveway of the house on Reese. The night he'd taken Sybil home from the discussion group, a large, beat-up Sixties sedan had stood on the curb, a white station wagon in front of it. This evening, neither car was there.

Simon liked the man who answered the door. Tall, hair parted in the middle, loose tie, gentle eyes behind oval glasses. A professional of some sort, quite likely the owner of the shiny sedan. He informed Simon politely that Sybil wasn't home. Simon introduced himself and shook hands with Justin Pott who thought that Sybil might have stopped in at her mother's house. Her mother's name, he said, was Sorenson. The number was under T. Sorenson, on Walnut Grove. If he wanted to, Simon could use their phone. Potts opened the door into a large living room furnished with a Persian carpet, a couple of leather love seats, designer easy chairs and teak end tables, and lamps throwing blue moons against the ceiling. Pointing at a door in the far corner, he said the directory was under the phone in the kitchen. Simon had to excuse him, he was in the middle of solving a problem, but to go ahead and make himself at home. The man waved, retreating toward the back of the house, and Simon stepped into a brightly lit kitchen that gleamed with chrome, steel, and polished granite.

As Justin Potts had promised, the phone hung on the wall inside the door, the city directory on the counter beneath. Sorenson. Several of them. No T. Sorenson. But higher on the page, among the Sorensens with an e, he found a T. Sorensen on Walnut Grove. That had to be it. Simon hesitated. The decor in this house didn't fit the woman he'd judged Sybil to be. Though on second thought, like a rose, the girl would be the focal point of any house.

And now, what will she think of him who couldn't wait just one more day to see her? Oh hell! Since he wanted to be with her so badly, maybe she wanted, too. If she didn't, she might as well learn at the beginning that French Canadians weren't as couth as Southern gentry. He dialed the number.

"Yes?" the same throaty female voice said.

"Simon Philipe. How are you, Sybil?"

"I'm afraid this is not Sybil. One moment, please."

A pause, then Sybil's laughter. "That was my mom. Are you canceling our date?"

"No. Adding one. I had a good day. I'd like to share it with you. Can you join me for a pastry dessert at the Danube Café?"

"I haven't had dinner yet."

"Neither have my kids. I can pick you up about eight, eight-thirty."

"What about your children? Don't they want dessert, too?"

"They'll have frozen yogurt."

"That doesn't seem fair."

"Life's not fair."

Again she laughed. A low, friendly laughter. "I love pastry."

She gave him directions to her mother's house and hung up.

Simon could hardly believe how smoothly he'd been able to arrange a spontaneous date with this desirable woman. In the empty living room he shouted, "Thank you, Justin," and from somewhere in the spacious house a "you're welcome" echoed back.

Chapter 13

The strains of a piano étude greeted Simon through the closed windows. When Sybil answered the door, wearing a skirt and blouse, he looked into her eyes and the doubts he'd had about this spontaneous encounter vanished. Inside, her mother, white as the Queen of Sweden, sat behind a baby grand, her fingers doing magic. After a minute the pianist raised her eyes, nodding slightly, and rose from the bench and approached with a smile.

"Simon Philipe," Simon said, charmed by the good-looking woman who probably wasn't too many years his senior. "You play Chopin beautifully."

"Libby Sorensen," she said, holding out a hand with long fingers. Simon took them gently, tempted to touch the cool, firm skin with his lips.

"You must have musical training to recognize this piece."

He shook his head. "Just a lucky guess."

"We'd better go," Sybil said, saving Simon from an inevitable faux pas. She grabbed a jacket from the clothes tree in the hall and shouldered the same sack again.

"What about your car?" her mother asked, forcing a smile. "You won't leave it on the street all night?"

"I'll pick it up later."

"We won't be gone long," Simon assured Mrs. Sorensen. Sensing the woman's concern about her pretty daughter, he suppressed a smile and offered her his hand with his most sincere expression. "It was nice meeting you."

Outside, the evening was still warm, and silent. It seemed that despite the many trees along the street the cicadas had stopped singing. As Simon opened the door of the pickup, helping Sybil into the cab, the piano music started again, drifting across the lawn, less melodious now and jerky, in a minor key. Simon hurried around the front of the truck, joining the girl in the cab. Nodding toward the white Ford station wagon in the driveway, he asked if it belonged to her. As an amateur painter, she told him, she loved the room in its rear that carried her easel and paintings and junk.

With the windows open and starting off in first gear, conversation stalled. They were driving down Central before Simon spoke again.

"Your mother is charming," he said. "That means you'll be just as charming when you reach her age."

"You're saying it'll take me twenty-five years to become as charming as my mother is now?

He laughed. "I'm French. My English isn't always as precise as it could be." Which wasn't true. He'd translated his French dissertation into English for publication, and the white lie annoyed him. "You are not only very charming," he said, "but very beautiful. What I meant was . . ."

"I know what you meant, but I doubt it. I'm more like my father."

"What's he like?"

"A Masai warrior."

She had to be kidding. Most black Americans originated from the Western part of Africa, not from Kenya or Tanzania where, to his knowledge, the Masai raised cattle. "Did your father come to this country as an immigrant?"

"No. He's the descendant of a slave in Georgia. He just looks like an East African. Tall and athletic. If he were a horse, he'd be a thoroughbred." She laughed. "A black thoroughbred."

"There are no black thoroughbreds. Dark bay or brown. Why do you call him a thoroughbred?"

"Daddy's a triathlete. He also runs marathons. He moves like a race horse, I swear."

"What's he do for a living?"

"He's a pediatrician. He and his partners have their own clinic. Daddy's second wife is also white."

The daughter of a black physician and a white pianist. An interesting cross. Intelligent, sensitive, sensuous. And artistic, and athletic? Who seemed to like horses.

"Where is your dad's clinic?"

"Lexington, Kentucky."

"Really? I went to graduate school at the University

of Kentucky. Took my first jumping lessons there. And in my third year I also taught French at Transylvania University." Stefan and Carolyn were born in Lexington. But this wasn't the moment to be distracted by a place so rich with memories. "I love Lexington. Bluegrass country. Horse farms. Do you ever go to a horse farm when you visit your dad?"

"All the time. My two half-sisters do hunter shows. Probably the only black girls in the state of Kentucky." Sybil turned toward him with an amused look. "Don't get any ideas. There's no obsession with horses in my genes. My sisters inherited that from my step mom. She rides, too. I prefer dogs to horses. Dogs don't step on your toes."

Simon thought of the young hounds he'd fooled with in his backyard for the hunt club over the years. "Being a dog person is good," he said. "In the spring, you can help me socialize a pair of foxhound puppies. It's easier with two people. Foxhound puppies are the sweetest things. You'll love them. And once you get to know my horses, you'll love them, too."

"I like them already. In fact, I wouldn't mind riding Par Three."

Elated, Simon slapped her knee. "So you shall!"

They had arrived at the Danube Café. The ambiance at the establishment, where he and Ellen used to take the children for dessert as a reward for good report cards, was more that of a fast food restaurant than a Viennese coffee house. But the warmth of Frau Sperber, who welcomed and seated every guest herself, waitresses in folk costumes, good coffee, and a variety of rich Austrian pastries, made the place popular. Squeezed into a corner and surrounded by a group of babbling high school students, they both dug into their chocolate tortes. Unusual for a school night, the noise was too loud to converse or encourage romance. Romance? Yes, it was indeed romance he desired. Maybe even love. Again he laughed. He hadn't been in such a laughing mood in anyone's company for a long time.

"What's so funny?"

"When I took you home after that discussion group and then the light came on in the room on the east side—your bedroom, I guess—I felt like pulling myself up onto the sill and knocking on the window. I hated the thought of leaving you and going home alone. Absurd for a grown man."

"Not really. That night I felt the same way. If you had knocked on the window, I would have let you in."

"Through the window?"

Now she laughed. "Through the front door. The windows are painted shut. It's because I was attracted to you that I told you I didn't want to go out with you. It was strictly self-preservation."

"When did you realize that I'm a kind and harmless soul?"

"You're kind, but certainly not harmless. You know the old saying, it's kindness that conquers."

"You *are* a Catholic."

"I'm afraid not. I come from a long line of Baptists on my father's side, except for my dad, who doesn't think much of organized religion, and dyed-in-the-wool Episcopalians on my mother's side."

This came as a surprise. He'd always wondered if the marriage with Ellen might have lasted if she'd shared his faith. He'd underestimated the difference in religion between them. Or, to be more accurate, his traditional beliefs and her free spirit. But what the hell, he wasn't about to marry this girl. "I don't know much about Baptists, but Episcopalians, in my experience, are a lot like well-heeled Catholics."

"I don't vote Republican, if that's what you mean. I'm really quite religious. Almost Catholic. At Little Flower school I joined my fellow pupils at mass every morning and took Communion with them, went to confession, too, even though the nuns knew perfectly well I was a Protestant." She paused, then said, "The nuns at Little Flower taught me that kindness is a positive force. That's probably why they were so successful in the classroom."

Simon nodded. His nuns in Chicoutimi had succeeded in the same manner. And how could he forget Sister Elisabeth's command to always be kind. That was one of her absolutes. If kind proved too difficult, she elaborated, at least be civil. He usually managed that, certainly with his students. Being civil, making an effort to treat them with equanimity, he'd learned, showed better results than kindness.

"It wasn't the nuns, though, who inspired you to study

architecture, was it?"

"No, the art teacher at Central High. Drawing and geometry, math of any kind really, were my favorite subjects. If there were a future in art, I mean for an amateur like me, I might have tried to become an artist." She smiled. "I've become a good draftsman, anyway, and that's more than my folks expected during my wild teens."

He suggested they have another pastry, but Sybil shook her head, patting her belly. On the drive back to her mother's place, his pleasant thoughts mixed with the memory of the meeting with Ellen at Trader Dick's, the apparent finality of their split, and what it meant for the future of the children, and his own future.

"Before you get out," Simon said, as Sybil rolled down the window to open the door of the pickup, "there's something I ought to tell you. I like you a lot, and I don't want you to get the wrong idea about me. After I met you at the gospel group and took you to the barn and knew I wanted to see you again, I asked my wife—ex-wife—if she'd considered getting back together with me."

Sybil, who'd been digging in her sack, looked up. "I assume she said no, or you wouldn't be here."

"Yes. There's no doubt in my mind now that the divorce is final."

"In your mind. What about in your heart?"

"There is a residue."

"I guess that's normal," she muttered, now dangling a bundle of keys. "I recently broke up with a man who turns mean when he has a couple of drinks. And guess what? I still have feelings for him."

Wondering about her taste in men, and about his own judgment, Simon walked her to the door. He wanted to tell her that her affair was hardly comparable to a marriage with three kids, but he didn't. He also checked his curiosity about the race of the fellow she'd dated.

"The guy I had dinner with this week is a Brinkman graduate who minored in French. I asked him about you and your wife."

"What did he say?"

"He said that Ellen was friendly, good-looking, and smart."

Simon tried to recall the students who had minored in French during his ten-year tenure, especially the exchange students from Africa, all of whom had been at his home at one time or another, loving Ellen's cooking, as had all French minors, domestic or foreign. When Sybil mentioned neither name nor race, and he felt too awkward to ask, he cleared his throat and said, "Good for him."

"About you he wasn't so complimentary. He claimed you were an all right professor, but he didn't like the way you looked at women." Grinning, she kissed Simon on the cheek. "I told him I like the way you look at me."

CHAPTER 14

Friday afternoon Hector Hollenbach called Simon at the office, telling him that Nashville had accepted his entry in the Pre-Training division and would Simon mind giving him some pointers for the dressage test. Othello, Hector's old gelding had fox hunted for the larger part of his twenty-six years and resented the restrictions of an arena, but he was a bold and honest jumper who did well at horse trials even with mediocre dressage scores. Simon said that Hector didn't need pointers. But yes, he would work with him after the cub hunt Saturday.

When he hung up, it hit him that if Jesse wasn't found within the next few days there'd be no horse trial for either of them, unless he took Par Three at Training level or Snow Goose at Pre-Training. Taking Par meant not only a step down from Jesse and the Preliminary level but practically a routine victory, not a very challenging prospect. Pre-Training, on the other hand, was two levels lower than Prelim, but on an inexperienced horse definitely a bigger challenge. The plan to event the Goose so intrigued Simon that he tacked a note to the door, canceling his three o'clock office hour, and drove home.

"Stefan," he addressed his son who had already spread his books on the dining room table, "let's go to the barn!" Obviously not pleased by the interruption, the boy muttered something Simon didn't understand, but he disappeared to his room and, like his father, changed his clothes.

In the pickup, Stefan said, "I just started a paper. I don't see why you need me today."

"I'd like your help with Snow Goose. There isn't a snowball's chance in hell of finding Jesse in time for Nashville. I have definitely decided to take the Goose in Jesse's place."

"In Preliminary? Daddy! She's only three and a half years old!"

"Not Preliminary. Pre-Training."

"You could ride Par in Preliminary. He could do it."

"He probably could, but I'm embarrassed to put two hundred pounds on a fifteen-one-hand mount over those big fences. You'd never forgive me if I hurt that sweet horse."

"Well then, take him Training. He can win Training."

"I know he can, but it's more of a challenge to do Pre-training on Snow Goose. All I need is some pointers about my posture on the flat."

"Pointers isn't enough. Not in Nashville. The place is jinxed."

At Stefan's Pony Club rally they'd made the youngsters jump an airy hay feeder without hay, eliminating half the competitors; and on Simon's first Training event on Jesse he had broken a stirrup leather buckle at the third fence and eventually completed the cross-country course without stirrups, giving him the most painful experience in his riding career.

"Snow Goose is too inexperienced," Stefan said. "And too young. Even Bruce Davidson wouldn't ride her."

His son had a point, though the filly wasn't too young. The vet had x-rayed her knees at the age of three and declared her ready to jump. And she was fit. And in her mental attitude, Snow Goose bettered any other horse he'd known.

"Well, how about it?"

Stefan grinned. "If you really want me to, I'll be glad to tell you how you're messing up."

CHAPTER 15

On their first official date, Simon took Sybil to the Bicycle Club, a midtown restaurant. While they sipped their drinks—Sybil a glass of Cabernet and Simon a martini—he expected another exchange of light-hearted banter, but Sybil was in a more somber mood, asking his views on local politics, white flight, black crime, pollution. Her main concern seemed to be the increase of teenage pregnancies, funding for Head Start, drug babies, the decay of parental care in the black community, the apparently unstoppable cycle of poverty. Simon wondered whether this kind of involvement in the ailments of city life was a black thing or whether she was just another Ellen, who volunteered for Head Start and let abused women and children stay at her house. When halfway through the third glass, with her reserve in retreat, Sybil made a remark about his divorce, he was almost relieved.

"My mother," she said, "who calls me two or three times a week, declared that a wife wouldn't desert a man with a 'prestigious' job like yours." She laughed. "I find that a really funny statement from the woman who'd divorced my dad. My dad's clinic grosses a couple of mil a year. She must know that in our society the status of an M.D., even that of a black doctor, is loftier than that of a foreign language professor. Still, I think my mother has a point."

Simon recalled Ludwig Stoppelfeld's description of Ellen's divorce hearing, where his wife Elsa had appeared as a witness. Ludwig had given him an account with German precision, neither adding nor omitting a word.

"Unhappy?" Judge Belzen, a sour-faced old man had spat. "I see nothing in this document about a negligent or abusive husband. Exactly how does he make her un-happy?"

"I don't know how he makes her unhappy," Elsa had responded, "but I can testify that she is unhappy. If Ms. Philipe says it's her husband who makes her unhappy, it's true. I have known Ms. Philipe for seven years. She's a truthful person."

"Not good enough. I need facts! Don't he provide for the chil'ren?"

"Yes," Elsa said, "but Ms. Philipe contributes, too."

"Is he a drunk?"

"No."

"Does he fool around with other women?"

"Not to my knowledge."

"Does he beat his wife?"

"No."

"Why, exactly, is she unhappy, Miss . . . uh . . . Miss?"

"Ms. Stoppelfeld. I just know she is, your honor."

"Ever'body's unhappy," the judge bellowed and coughed. "I'm unhappy. This case makes me very unhappy."

"Your Honor," her lawyer called out, but the judge raised his hand, shaking his head. "All right, since the perfessor isn't contesting this case, I have no choice but to grant a divo'ce. Nex'!"

Judge Belzen, Simon thought, may have been an old chauvinist, but a total ass he wasn't. He suddenly wished he hadn't given up tobacco. He wished he could stuff his pipe and blow a cloud of smoke, obscuring himself. Instead of answering Sybil's question, he reached across the table and touched her fingers. Then withdrawing his hand, he lifted his glass and drained it. Obviously he'd made mistakes. Serious mistakes. All thirty-nine years of his life he'd made mistakes. But he'd loved Ellen. Loved her with all his being.

Sybil dug into her sack, extracting a small tube of Vaseline, and squeezed some on her unpainted lips. "It must be awfully hard to remain faithful to a spouse. I'm not sure I could."

Simon nodded. "Sure is." He'd been faithful to Ellen, though. At least in fact if not in thought. He'd lusted plenty after other women. Probably always would. It was man's nature, Uncle Baptiste had declared.

Sybil laughed. A gentle, almost wise laugh. "Sorry to bring up my mother. I should have told you first that my roommates are happy for me. Cat Morrison, who's a public defender, says she can't wait to meet you. And Justin Potts likes you. He's the very conservative corporate lawyer whom you met. He thinks our difference in age is 'inconsequential.' I think so, too." She paused and finished her wine. "In my opinion, age is a state of mind."

"Race isn't."

"Says who?"

Simon laughed. "Maybe you're right. And I appreciate your friends' endorsement. I wish your mother felt the same. What kind of man does she expect you to date?"

"A man of wealth. She believes that wealth guarantees happiness. Frankly, I don't care about my mother's opinion of you. Let me warn you, though. If you get involved with me, you don't know what you're getting into, and not just because I'm black."

That should have been his line, Simon thought. "What about you?" he asked. "Don't you care what you're getting into? Aren't you curious why I didn't answer your question?"

"You mean why you got a divorce? It was a dumb question. How can you tell in a few words why fifteen years of marriage went kaputt?"

"Your mother is right. Wealth is a blessing. All through my youth I had to fight for survival. Shave pennies through college and graduate school. So much so that doing with little became a way of life. To do with necessities became a point of honor long after the need had gone. A man who's hard on himself is hard on others."

"You're not hard on yourself anymore, are you?"

"I'm afraid so. It's either in my genes, or the nuns drummed it into me."

She laughed gently. "Yes, the nuns. I know what you went through. The nuns kept me on the straight and narrow, too. With love. Love can be a killer."

CHAPTER 16

Despite the many differences, Sybil reminded Simon of Sister Elisabeth, the woman he had loved more than any other. He couldn't tell exactly why. Something to do with a certain spark in her eye, and the cut of her face resembled Sister's in her picture as a young horsewoman on her parents' estate. Maybe it was Sybil's friendly, non-judgmental disposition. She seemed to have Sister's certainty about who she was, and that he, Simon, had become part of her life.

Ah, Sister. She never had Sybil's good looks but was always good to look at. As she grew older, the wrinkles about her eyes hightened their luster, and a couple of wavy grooves across her forehead complimented the curve of her lips. There was an air of kindness about her, and often it only took the timbre of her voice to soothe the beast in the boy.

The early morning Madeleine pulled her panties down in the empty kitchen, for instance, asking him to mouth her bijoux. When the girl tattled, Sister didn't clobber him over the head as some of the foster parents did just for dropping crumbs. She never made a scene.

If a child had caused trouble, she'd come down to the common room where the three or four orphans spent their days. She would usher the sinners upstairs to her office about the size that Simon imagined a hermit's cell to be. An austere place, but the bookshelves that covered the left wall and the ever-present flowering plants on the windowsill lent warmth to the room.

In this office Sister made the two children sit on the one upholstered seat. She turned her own desk chair around and sat down, keeping as much distance as was possible between them so that they wouldn't feel threatened. And while she talked, her voice remained matter-of-fact.

"What have you got to say for yourself, Simon Pièrre?"

That's what she called him when he was in trouble. Normally, it was *mon enfant*.

He lowered his eyes, looking at Sister's worn shoes, always shined, and the gray cotton stockings about her ankles. "I'm ashamed, *ma soeur*."

"Ashamed? Why are you ashamed?"

"Because I kissed the evil bijoux."

"Evil?" the Sister said almost angrily. "Where did you hear such nonsense? The human body isn't evil."

"Father Lebas says it is," Madeleine piped up.

Children were like puppies, she explained, and if they didn't go to school and learn the catechism, they would act like dogs for the rest of their lives. The flesh was weak, not bad. One's body was God's gift. A vessel for the soul. That was why they shouldn't fool with it, and should wait until they were married. In marriage, the two bodies became one.

The children looked puzzled.

"That means," Sister continued, "the wife's body belongs to the husband, and the husband's body belongs to the wife. The wish of the one becomes the command of the other."

Neither Madeleine nor Simon understood these words, but he never forgot them. At fourteen, when he sat in the same chair again, feeling guilty about his erotic dreams, he still wasn't sure he understood Sister's words.

"*Mon enfant*," she said, "your body is blossoming like a flower." A smile crossed her face when Simon cringed at the metaphor. "Your dreams are natural, not sinful. Nature isn't sinful."

"Maybe," he complained dejectedly, again regarding Sister's shoes, probably still the same pair, the same gray stockings. But it wasn't only his dreams. His daytime thoughts, too, were so sinful that God couldn't forgive him.

"Simon Pièrre," Sister declared, without a trace of a smile, "everybody has sinful thoughts. We're all sinners. Even the saints. When you're young and the juices flow, it's hard to see reason. Let me tell you how the ancient Greeks looked at love. Maybe this will help you. The Greeks defined four types of love.

"Our raw sex drive they called *Epithelia*. Without it, the animal kingdom, including us, wouldn't survive. It's one of God's greatest gifts. Without it, *Eros*, the love that binds in marriage, wouldn't stand a chance. Don't let the sins of the flesh get you down, Simon. We are made of flesh. You might say it's our purpose to become lovers. Jesus never got angry at the sins of the flesh.

"It's the sins of the spirit that make life miserable. Dishonesty and greed. Dishonesty prevents you from finding yourself, and greed hardens the heart."

Simon regarded the floor at Sister's feet.

"*Mon enfant*, don't look so shocked. I'm not condoning sinful ways. Remember how Jesus also told us not to throw pearls to pigs. Don't waste passion outside the bond of love.

"We must cultivate *Philia*, too. Brotherly love. The way we love Jesus. And we must pray for the gift of *Agape*. Unselfish love. The way parents love children, often sacrificing just to feed them. The way Jesus loves us, and, I hope, the way I love you."

It had taken years for Simon to comprehend Sister's types of love. And never fully, at that, except perhaps for *Epithelia*, common lust. He was very familiar with that. But with Sybil now, it wasn't the promise of celibacy he'd made to St. Francis that reined in his lust. It was a touch of *Agape* that stopped him cold.

CHAPTER 17

As Simon stepped into the pasture, the horses, throwing long shadows, looked up, ears pointed. Snow Goose approached him immediately, nudging his chest, followed by Par. He opened the paddock gate, and they marched through, each entering its stall. Out of habit he patted their necks, checking hides and legs, then cut the strings on a bale of hay and tossed a square into a corner of each stall.

Snow Goose was caked in mud. Using two rough brushes, he cleaned her tail, squeezing the black and gray hair between the bristles, and with an aluminum comb he broke the hard dirt in her mane. Then, curry comb in one hand, a brush in the other, he scraped the dried clay off her body, following the toothy steel tool with the soft brush, soothing the area he'd scraped, keeping the animal content. With the rough dirt gone, he exchanged the comb for a second brush, stroking the Goose's back and sides and chest and neck with both, imagining he was cleaning a half-ton pussycat. There seemed to be no end to the fine dust that kept rising after each stroke, but her skin was clean enough for a schooling session.

Inserting the snaffle bit between the filly's teeth, he pulled the bridle over her ears, grabbed mane and swung himself onto her bare back. "It's you and me now," he said to Snow Goose who pricked her ears as he pointed her through the paddock gate, bending low to close it. "Just me and you." At the edge of the field he changed her walk to a trot, soon extending her gait, posting from his thighs, just in case he lost another stirrup in Nashville. The filly tossed her head but moved up another gear into her great, ground-covering stride. Simon couldn't even completely circle the five-acre back pasture before his thighs started to ache. Realizing that his muscles were pitifully out of shape, he asked the filly to canter, which allowed him to relax his legs. The second time he approached the pole gate, Simon pointed the Goose at it and jumped her into the woods.

Snow Goose galloped easily, dodging trees and hopping ditches, running with the exuberance of the three-year-old youngster she was. She would have run for an hour if Simon had let her, but when they reached the river he turned her toward home, slowing to a sitting trot, then within a half-mile from the barn to a walk.

When Simon slid to the ground at the gate, Snow Goose's chest was dry. Only where his jeans had touched, her hair felt damp, and despite the coolness of the late September night, he hosed her down. Par, who loved water, whickered and pushed close, wanting a bath, too. Simon obliged.

After scraping the water off the horses with his hands

and arms, he shared a carrot with them, then slapped them on their rumps, watching them gallop around the barn, stirring the herd into a run.

His friend Ludwig couldn't understand why he spent a good hour a day fooling with these giants who were liable to fracture your toes when they stomped on them. Working with his horses, Simon had tried to tell him, cleansed his mind. On a bad day, mucking out a stall would do it. When hurried, the feeding routine was enough. At times just watching the horses prance through the paddock, whinny and gallop out into the night, boosted Simon's sense of freedom.

In the pickup, Sybil again entered his mind. Some of his energy spent, Simon felt relaxed now, and he welcomed her presence. Come Sunday, he thought, he'd give her a lesson. If a skinny student like young Elisabeth du Soulier could handle a thoroughbred, agile, athletic Sybil could ride Par Three. After dinner, he thought, he'd find Sister's horse picture and hang it up. He should have done it years ago.

CHAPTER 18

Sunday morning rose bright and cool as Simon arrived at the barn to feed the horses and get them ready for Sybil's first lesson. To his surprise, she showed up fifteen minutes early, dressed in a burgundy sweater and black jeans. From Thelma-Lise's trunk they borrowed chaps that hung loose from Sybil's hips, unlike Simon's helmet, from which he pulled the pads to make it fit her head.

"You've got a brain and a half."

"Before I was one year old, my mom tells me, my head was so big I used to tip over."

She grabbed Par Three's reins and boldly stepped into the stirrup, throwing her leg over the saddle, clicked her tongue, and the little gelding moved out, showing off his easy walk. After twenty minutes of instruction, Sybil felt comfortable enough to sit a running walk and, in a fashion, post the trot. Delighted with the woman's talent as a rider, Simon saddled Snow Goose and took the only too willing student out on the trail. Along a grassy path between two bean fields, Simon eased the Goose into a canter, and Sybil uttered a cry, but she hung on as Par Three lunged out, too.

"You're doing super," Simon shouted, turning around in the saddle. "Don't lean forward, relax with the motion."

Moments later he slowed the Goose to a walk.

"My heart was in my throat," Sybil confessed, beaming with excitement.

"Pat him. He's a sweetheart the way he takes care of you."

"He sure is. He's coming home with me!"

"If you take Par, you'll have to take Stefan, too. He loves his horse."

"Actually, if I had a choice, I'd take the Goose. I've been watching her. She's maaagnificent."

"If you take her you'll have to take me."

Sybil laughed, then concentrated on her seat as the horses walked to the end of the fields, crossed a wide ditch and entered the woods, a thicket of sumac, sweet gum, briars, poison oak, wild roses. The path was well-trodden, leading in a roundabout way to the shore of the river where they dismounted and sat in the sand, holding the horses by the reins to let them nibble on a patch of grass.

"What a peaceful spot."

"Deceptive. Behind the bend on the left traffic runs over a bridge, and around the bend on the right, the railroad crosses the water on a wooden structure. Next time we'll ride down there. It's like a scene out of the Old West. I come here a lot. There's always a treat. Turkeys. A blue heron. Once I watched a hawk-like hunter catch a fish. Critters don't run from Jesse and me." Although he immediately realized he'd meant to say Snow Goose, not Jesse, he didn't bother to correct his mistake.

Suddenly Snow Goose swung her rear end, head raised, still as a statue. A young buck walked down to the edge of the water. He drank three, four drafts, then raised his head toward them, paused, and casually ambled back the way he'd entered the clearing. Snow Goose started grazing again.

"Funny," Sybil said. "Snow Goose seemed ready to run. Why not Par?"

"Par's older, and he's male. By nature, mares are more sensitive to danger."

"Well," Sybil said, stretching, then getting to her feet, "I'm glad you brought me here. I never dreamed there was such a peaceful spot practically in the middle of the city."

Simon rose too, checking his watch. If they wanted to attend the eleven o'clock mass at St. Patrick's, they'd have to hustle. Again Sybil mounted Par on her own. Without incident they made it back to the barn where Simon took off saddles and bridles, storing them in the tack room. Sybil unzipped her chaps and Simon returned them to Thelma-Lise's box. As they headed to the pickup truck, the horses bunched, trotting off into the back pasture. Only Snow Goose stayed behind, following the couple to the gate.

"I think she wants to come with us," Sybil said. "How sweet."

Simon shook his head. "She wants a carrot. I forgot them."

"I'll make sure to have carrots next time."

Simon said nothing, happy that Sybil planned to ride again.

CHAPTER 19

The white summer dress contrasted markedly with the shadow that dimmed Sybil's face when he picked her up for church. For a block or two they drove without speaking. Simon, recalling his visits to St. Patrick's with Ellen, usually after a Saturday night party and hours of making love, glanced at Sybil's legs. They were long and elegant and, like Ellen's, in pantyhose and medium-heeled pumps. If it were ten years earlier—or was it fifteen?—she might be wearing stockings. Too bad. Gone was the challenge of a fellow groping with a girlfriend's straps and girdle.

Sybil looked distracted and kept rubbing her thighs, now and then twitching her feet. She seemed to have been more comfortable in the jeans and chaps she'd worn a couple of hours earlier.

"You didn't pick up chiggers, did you?"

"Pantyhose. I hate them."

"Why don't you take them off? You don't need hose at St. Patrick's. Or we can skip mass. Since the children are with Ellen, I don't mind."

"No, I don't want to miss church. I need to pray for

my mother."

"What's the problem?"

Sybil turned toward him smiling a crooked smile. "Her marriage."

"What's wrong with her marriage?"

"The same thing goes wrong with any marriage, I guess." With a smile she added, "You ought to know."

"I ought to," he said, "but I don't. The first thirteen years of my marriage were mostly sunny. Lightning didn't strike until we were well established in Memphis, and it came out of a blue sky."

Things had been going great. Ellen seemed to enjoy her job as a technician at the University of Tennessee, and at home, too, her mien remained cheerful. He had just won the Preliminary division on Jesse at the Knoxville horse trials; one of his French majors, a wide receiver on the football team, had been awarded a Rhodes scholarship; the students had given him the highest merit ranking in teaching; and he had been granted sabbatical leave in Geneva. Overwhelmed by his blessings, he could barely wait for the children to turn in.

"Sweetheart," he said, hugging Ellen in the living room, "I'm on top of the world. I've got everything. There's nothing else I could want."

"That's not quite true," Ellen said, freeing herself from his embrace. "You don't have me."

Hoping this was a joke, yet already beginning to feel numb, he said, "What do you mean?"

"I don't love you."

"I don't believe you," he said, catching her eye.

She looked straight at him. "It's a fact. I don't want you in my bed anymore. We can get singles."

Simon didn't believe her, but thinking that sleeping alone she might miss his company, he bought two double beds, setting them up on opposite walls. After staying in his own bed for a couple of weeks, often lying wide awake listening to his wife breathe, Simon couldn't stand the tension any longer. He watched Ellen undress, slip into the nightgown that she now wore, and pull the quilt up to her chin. Even in the dark, he could see her eyes looking in his direction. Kneeling on the rug near her head, he laid his hand on her hair, stroking it off her forehead. In the semi-dark that hid the growing hardness about her mouth, she didn't look any older than the day they had met.

"Don't touch me," she said calmly, pushing his hand off. "If you want to fuck, fuck me, but keep your hands to yourself."

Giving her space by sitting back on his heels, he said, "That's not what I want."

"What do you want?"

"I love you. I want to make love to you."

"You don't listen to me. I told you I don't love you."

~~~~~

"My whole family is steeped in divorce," Sybil's voice interrupted. I'm sick of it. Both sets of grandparents have a history of divorce. My father's mother was married to a bastard. He was mean to his wife even after their split.

I was glad when he passed away. The same year, his wife died, too. God rest their souls. My other grandmother divorced her husband when my mother was a child and married a lawyer twenty some years older who became a state senator. When I was four years old, my parents were divorced, too. Almost immediately my mother's parents sued for custody and got it. Piano lessons didn't pay her rent and support little me. It was no contest."

"That's the woman I met?"

"Yes, my mom."

"Why didn't your father help?"

"He was in med school at Johns Hopkins. He didn't have any money either. Anyway, I can't really complain. The senator was cold and aloof, and my grandmother was a drunk, but they clothed me and fed me. Don't get me wrong. My grandmother loved me, and I loved her. I still love her, despite everything." After a moment's pause, she continued. "Frankly, it was godawful, living with a drunk. And all the time, from the very beginning, I felt so sorry for my mother."

Simon glanced at Sybil's sculpted profile, realizing that though she made no sound, tears rolled down her cheeks. He used to think the worst that could happen to a child was never having known a parent. He wasn't so sure anymore. Being fought over by mother and grand-mother was no fate to be envied either. Now the little girl was pushing thirty, and the conflict hadn't been resolved.

Simon covered Sybil's fingers with his bony hand. For

a minute she was silent, then she said, "I'd like you to meet my grandparents. Gramme and Senator. She pronounced Gramme like the music award.

Not in the least ready to socialize with an alcoholic grandmother and a feeble old legislator, he said, "You think that's a good idea?"

"My parents and all my relatives, black and white, listen to them."

"They have money?"

"They're not wealthy." Sybil laughed. "Gramme thinks you're an improvement over the men I've gone out with." Noticing Simon's pleased expression, she added, "Don't flatter yourself. When I met you I was on the rebound."

"Who from?"

"A good man."

"Who jilted you?"

"On the contrary. He proposed."

Simon waited for details, but none came.

"Now that I've told you all about my family," she continued, "it's your turn."

"First I want to hear about your father."

"You know that his parents passed away. Before his retirement, his dad had been an insurance agent. His three sisters are married here in Memphis. One brother, also married, has a dry cleaning business in Nashville. His youngest brother sings in a blues band in Chicago. He writes his own songs. Of the entire family, I like him best. Actually, I like them all. You'll meet them."

"Sounds like you have a bunch of nice relatives."

"Sure do. How about you?"

"None. No family at all. My parents died before I was twelve, and I was the only child."

Sybil reached for Simon's hand on the steering wheel. "That must have been very sad for you."

When he stopped at the light on Danny Thomas, she dropped her hand onto his thigh and let it rest there.

"Were your parents good to you?"

"Very good."

"Well then," she said, "you have memories."

Simon agreed. Although by the age of six he had lived with several different "parents" and didn't expect the arrangement with Madame and Monsieur Philipe to be for keeps, it had worked out. They not only didn't beat him, they treated him kindly. In their late fifties, overweight, and childless, she suffered from asthma, he from a weak heart. But they owned a large house with a drugstore and pharmacy on the lower floor, and an apartment on the second. The boy called the old couple Maman and Papa, though later he realized they were more like sickly grandparents. Simon loved the big home, and from the very start helped in the store and delivered prescriptions in town.

During the nearly six years he spent in the Philipe household, neither parent ever hugged him, or tucked him into bed at night, as Sister had. The drugstore, even with the pharmacy and a soda counter, didn't make them rich but respected, prominent even. Although they employed a housekeeper, and a permanent assistant in the store, both parents worked six long days a week, sharing the selling, stocking, and the accounting. When the boy was in school, Papa, using the family car, sometimes delivered emergency prescriptions himself.

When Simon was eleven, Maman's breathing problems increased, and in early winter they became torture, not just for her, but also for her husband and the boy who witnessed her suffering. The first day of the Christmas vacation she lay on the sofa as usual, inhaling with a rasp. In the morning, she was dead. According to the doctor, she had died of rapidly deteriorating lungs, a disease that was similar to tuberculosis, he explained, although today he probably would have diagnosed it as emphysema. Poor Papa bravely coped without his wife for a few weeks, relying more and more on Simon's help, and then, on a cold January night, he died of a stroke.

As good as Maman and Papa had been to him the nearly six years he lived with them, Simon had never been very close to them. His heart remained with Sister. Sometimes he wished she would let him adopt her name, du Soulier. Simon Pièrre du Soulier had a nice ring. Like Sister's elegant Belgian French. To this day it was Elisabeth du Soulier Simon thought of as his true mother.

"My parents were sickly all their lives. Death came as a relief. I remember them fondly."

Simon could tell by Sybil's reaction that fondly didn't match the adverb she'd expected to hear. You remembered uncles fondly, and teachers, and maybe a dog. But they had arrived at St. Patrick's. Rather than squeezing the truck into a crowded parking lot, Simon stopped at the curb. Sybil rested her eyes on the boarded-up front entrance of the dilapidated downtown church, then raised them to the square belfry that had no bells but, Simon explained, was full of pigeon nests. And feces.

"Quite a contrast to an Episcopal House of God, isn't it?"

Simon took Sybil's hand and led her through the parked cars to a steel door near the front. Inside, with the homily already in progress, they filed along the benches on the wall, careful not to step on people's feet. Continuing around the rear they found seats next to a pillar, but Sybil refused to sit down. "That thing up there," she whispered, pointing at the Corinthian capital looming above her head, "looks cracked."

"Water damage." Simon nodded toward the folding chairs in the nave that stood clamped together in rows. "See any empty seats?"

Sybil shook her head and turned, preceding Simon into the darker area under the organ loft in the rear. Simon explained that the loft might be the least safe place in the church. No one dared climb up there anymore to play the beautiful organ. Which of course no longer worked either. Sybil said she didn't care to move elsewhere, so they remained standing against the wall.

The choir, occupying the front left of the altar, sang the Sanctus to guitars and a flute. Sybil thought that was beautiful, and Simon told her that the man with the flute played in the Symphony. She ought to come when the black singers joined the choir for a Gospel hoedown. Which rocked the building. He explained that the chairs in the nave came out for dances and flea markets and other fund raising occasions. That the priests, with the help of a couple of nuns, spent their funds in the neighborhood, working with children and youths, teaching the slow, organizing ball games, caring for the sick and the elderly, feeding the homeless. The whites who attended the church drove from various parts of the city and from some of the suburbs to get the chance to help the less fortunate in a practical way.

"A chance to love their neighbors," Sybil commented, "in the spirit of Christ."

Simon glanced at Sybil's face, but she didn't betray any sarcasm. "Actually," he said, "this church makes an effort toward social justice. That's one reason why I drag my children here."

During transubstantiation Simon knelt down on the floor. At the peace offering, when people in other Catholic churches discreetly shake hands, the congregation at St. Patrick's swarmed into the aisles, talking, embracing, kissing.

"This tidal wave of emotion is too much," Simon said, seeking refuge behind a pillar.

"I wouldn't mind a hug," Sybil said. Neither would he, Simon admitted, and clasped the woman in his arms. They were a perfect fit, and only reluctantly, they let go.

CHAPTER 20

The next time Simon and Sybil tacked up the horses for the trail, he picked her up and tossed her into the saddle, expecting her to shout in protest, but she just laughed.

"You're so full of it, Simon. First you tell me about your poor, sickly parents who died when you were a child, then you throw a hundred and thirty-six pounds onto the back of a horse. I'm more likely to believe that a couple of centaurs raised you."

Now it was Simon's turn to laugh. "I wish that were true. I like to believe I take after my Uncle Baptiste, my father's older brother, who shaped me to a large extent."

"I think I'd like to meet your uncle 'Buttiste.'"

"He'd love to meet you too. He had an eye for pretty women."

Simon mounted Snow Goose and led the way around the property heading south into the woods. Turning around in the saddle, he said, "You okay?" Sybil nodded, smiling. Soon the track widened and they rode side by side.

"Unfortunately, my Uncle Baptiste is no longer

among the living. He froze to death when I was sixteen. Sat down to rest on the way home from a beer joint and fell asleep."

"Are you making this up? If you are, it's not very funny. Freezing to death must be a horrible end."

"No. It's like falling asleep. If you're lucky, you cross the river in a dream. Uncle Baptiste was the kind of man who wouldn't drink for weeks, then suddenly, for no apparent reason, get stinking drunk. My uncle was in his seventies when he died. He'd loved life, although you couldn't call him a very lovable character. I first met him about a year before my parents' death. When I was ten. He showed up for dinner, his beard neatly trimmed, dressed like a logger, with tall lace-up boots over khaki pants and a red plaid flannel shirt. He smelled of beer and slapped my father on the back, but gently—he obviously respected him—and he gave my mother a one-armed hug from the side. He spoke in a deep, gravelly voice, and although he ignored me, once in a while he glanced my way. His gray, wavy hair fell down over his ears, and he kept brushing it back with his hands. Fascinated by the terrible scars under his left eye, I wanted to hear how the panther had attacked him, but all he asked about was the business. My father told him a hundred people owed the store money and, if he wanted one, a loan was out of the question. My uncle didn't say much after that until we'd finished dessert. Then he insisted on teaching me how to play poker. I still like playing poker."

"Speaking of dessert, I'm starving. Must be that horsing around. Aren't you hungry?"

The girl was right. It was past dinnertime, but they'd only been out for twenty minutes, and they hadn't even cantered their horses yet. "Let's run," Simon said, easing the Goose into a lope. This time, Sybil didn't scream as her gelding rocked into a canter. She laughed, wholly trusting Par who joined his sister floating side by side through a field of orange sage.

On the way home, Simon detoured to Tony's, where they picked up two large pizzas with all the toppings, causing so much excitement the two hungry children didn't seem to notice that their father had brought a black woman home. Even when he demanded their attention to introduce them to her, they said their Glad to meet you, Sybil, then hurried to set the table for this unexpected pizza feast.

And all during the meal and afterwards, when they played poker, neither Stefan nor Carolyn made a reference of any sort to Sybil's color, even when Sybil retreated to the kitchen to rustle up some snacks. It was Simon who finally cracked and said, "What d'you guys think of Sybil?"

"I like her crew cut," Carolyn volunteered. "She's real cool."

"Cool?" Stefan whispered. "She's spectacular."

"Yeah, and cool, too, like I said."

"Daddy's the one who's cool," Stefan contradicted his little sister. "He's going to integrate the hunt club."

That wasn't such an impossible task. The women in

the club had manners. And at the breakfast the men would bite their tongues, saving nigger jokes for duller moments in the field. Hell, it'd be an honor for the club to have a girl like Sybil as a member.

"Integrate what?" Sybil asked, entering the room with a tray of Fig Newtons, four glasses of orange juice, and placing it on the pile of poker chips in the middle of the table.

"The fox hunt," Carolyn piped up.

Sybil bit a Fig Newton in half, chewing it leisurely. Then she said, "You teach me how to jump Par Three, and I will."

Simon laughed. The son of a gun was serious.

CHAPTER 21

Ten o'clock was a late hour to meet Cat Morrison, the third member of the *ménage a trois*, but Sybil seemed in no hurry to leave the pickup. Judging by the strange vehicles parked on the street, she claimed, her mates had a guest or two, and they were probably smoking pot. Simon, still on a high from his children's casual acceptance of their father's black companion, was in no hurry to meet a bunch of potheads.

With a spurt of laughter, Sybil said his uncle hadn't done such a good job teaching him poker since Carolyn had won all the chips. Nodding in agreement, Simon said that the children were good at any kind of game, and he was happy that Carolyn, the youngest and least aggressive, had ended up the big winner.

"What else besides teaching you how to play cards did your uncle Baptiste do for you?"

"He became my second father."

"Really?"

After his parents' death, from age eleven to sixteen, Simon spent his summer vacations at his uncle's fishing camp. Only during the last two summers did he work a few weeks in logging camps. His uncle taught him everything else. He taught him to swim and shoot and fish. How to skin squirrels and rabbits and beavers, muskrats, an occasional bobcat or fox. Everything he needed to survive in the wilderness he learned from him.

"Like Tarzan teaching Boy?"

Sybil could laugh, but the uncle was a character. Take the way he burst into Simon's life the second day school was out. Some of the kids were playing poker in the sisters' den. For money, they used flat pebbles of various sizes and colors. Simon was winning for a change and had a large pile of white, gray, yellow, and some of the rare black 'coins' in front of him, when suddenly this hoarse voice behind him bellowed, "You know who I am?"

The children jumped to their feet so quick they hit the card table spilling the loot. A man as tall as a tree towered above them. His bushy eyebrows sprouted over piercing eyes; the left side of his face seemed even more disfigured by ugly scars. In the morning light, his beard looked so wild Simon thought it was spiked with twigs of pine. His long hair welled out from under a visored cap; gray curls pushed against the collar of his flannel shirt, and hair emerged on his wrists. The bottoms of his corduroy pants he'd again stuffed into his boots.

"You're my Uncle Baptiste," the boy stuttered, not knowing what to make of his uncle's unexpected appearance.

"*Oui*," the uncle answered in that stentorian voice,

"*je suis Baptiste Philipe, coureur de bois.* How old are you now, boy?"

"Almost eleven and a half," he answered proudly.

"Old enough to learn my trade," the uncle said, offering the boy his leathery hand. He shook it, trying not to wince, then followed the man to Sister Elisabeth's office without a goodbye to his playmates who stared at the trapper with open mouths. Obviously, the uncle had already consulted with Sister, because not only did she not raise any objections to letting Simon go, she helped him pack his things into a cardboard box.

Sybil's head had fallen against Simon's shoulder. Simon stopped talking, but she asked him to continue even though she'd closed her eyes. Her proximity was so enchanting and his uncle's spell so compelling that he just sat, not at all minding, letting the memories flow.

Elated yet puzzled that Sister was sending him off with a man who was hardly more than a stranger, a fear-inspiring stranger at that, Simon picked up the box with his belongings. Sister wrote her address on the outside in case he wanted to write to her, and stuffed the pencil in his pants pocket. "And you," she addressed Uncle Baptiste, "you take good care of *mon enfant*. I'm holding you responsible. He's a good boy."

"We'll soon see what he's made of," the big man grunted, an amused glint in his eyes. At the curb, his uncle introduced him to the driver of a new, dust-covered pickup, Horace Berthiaume, a middle-aged, somewhat puffy but jovial man with glasses. He lifted the boy's box into the back with the other bundles, sacks, and parcels, then crossed the street to the Papéterie Pelletier.

Monsieur Berthiaume invited Simon into the cab and questioned him about school. Learning that math was the boy's favorite subject, the man, who had seemed bored with Simon's praise of his nun teachers, said, "I might give you a job as a stock boy, if you're too squeamish to skin beavers in Paradise."

"Paradise?" Simon asked, a big question mark in his eyes.

"That's where we're going," his uncle explained, approaching from behind and handing him a paper bag with a writing pad, a couple of envelopes and postage stamps. "Now hop on top of the load."

On the way through town, Simon pondered about Monsieur Berthiaume who bore his enemy Guillaume's last name, wondering if the trader could be Guillaume's father. Leaning forward on the driver's side, Simon examined the man's profile through the open window. Mean old Guillaume didn't resemble this gentle-looking man. The paunchy trader couldn't have produced the vicious boy who pounced on him every chance he got. Though two years older than Simon and nearly a head taller, Guillaume never attacked without some of his buddies, usually out of an alley or from behind a parked vehicle Simon had to pass on his way home. If he weren't always wary, ready to run, he would be beaten regularly, not just on the rare times they caught him.

Guillaume was also the author of the graffiti painted

in red letters over the wash stand in the school's restroom: *SIMON LA FAUSSE COUCHE DE LA SOEUR.* The nun's miscarriage. To Simon's surprise, he'd even spelled it correctly.

"Monsieur," Simon asked, "do you have a son called Guillaume?"

Monsieur Berthiaume laughed, obviously with pleasure. "Of course, I have a son called Guillaume! The apple of my eye!"

This news cast a momentary shadow on the sunny day. At least he wouldn't have to deal with the monster until fall.

The pickup turned north, crossing the Saguenay River, heading toward the town of St. Ambroise, where they unloaded several boxes at one of the general stores owned by Monsieur Berthiaume. They continued the trip to Alma and spent the night in the apartment above the business headquarters. Through the window, they could admire Monsieur Berthiaume's summer home, a two-story house of red brick, more than a dozen windows on just one side of the building, two brick chimneys and other, smaller extremities rising from the tiled roof. It was a house even more ostentatious than the trader's winter residence in Chicoutimi.

Obviously, Monsieur Berthiaume was a prosperous man. A man with a leading role in the game of life, Sister would say. But not to worry, she would assure the little fellow; in the eyes of God, the star of the play is worth no more than a minor character or even an extra. Without the unimportant parts, there would be no play, and therefore no star. Simon understood that. Each played his role. Some were bigger, maybe, more significant, but not more important. And it was all right to admire the stars, even be in awe of them, as he was a little of the trader, despite his son Guillaume.

The next day Monsieur Berthiaume fitted Simon with wool socks and leather boots, a long-sleeved flannel shirt with red and black squares, denim jeans and a leather belt, a plaid wool jacket and an olive-green rain slicker, adding some cotton briefs and white, folded-up mosquito netting. They also loaded food supplies, mainly brown beans and green vegetables in tins, fairly filling the box of his uncle's pre-war Ford pickup that sat behind the store. Then Monsieur Berthiaume reached through the window and handed him a hunting knife in a tooled leather sheath. Immediately, Simon pulled out the blade, balancing it on his hand.

His uncle touched the edge. "It's a Bowie, sharp enough to cut through bone. Carry it with you always. It's more useful than a gun." This gift impressed Simon so much that he forgot to thank the man before the pickup lurched forward and they were under way.

After riding on washboard gravel for the larger part of the day, they reached the settlement of Notre-Dame-de-Lorette, where the road ended. Rubbing the dust from his eyes, Simon inspected the handful of small houses that made up the village. When his uncle stopped the truck at the largest building, a one-room garage and service station with a pump so faded he couldn't read the letters, he jumped out of the cab, happily accepting the bottle of Coke his uncle bought him. The talkative attendant pumped the tank full, checked the oil and cleaned the dusty glass, then they continued northeast on a dirt road through stands of black spruce interspersed with white birch, shimmering poplar, and slender aspen, jack pine and cedars, often crowded by alders and weeds and brambles, all reaching for the pickup, whipping the doors and the windshield, making Simon pull in his head like the turtle he'd teased in the sisters' vegetable patch.

Before long, Uncle Baptiste slowed down to turn left into an even narrower and bumpier track.

"How much farther to Paradise?" Simon asked, holding on to the dashboard, peering into the green, onrushing wilderness.

The uncle was too busy navigating the vehicle over the bumpy track to answer. When they reached the camp, a dog stood inside a board gate, barking furiously. Then, recognizing the pickup, it yelped and whined, jumping up and down, racing around the truck the uncle drove to the nearer of the two log cabins. A cruder structure without windows sat farther back on the left, and on the other side near the pole fence that surrounded the compound stood an open shed, just a roof on four posts, with boards and equipment underneath.

His uncle motioned to Simon to come out of the pickup, but the dog had now discovered him and started barking again. It threatened to jump right through the window into the cab. In looks and size, the dog resembled a German shepherd with ears that didn't quite stand up. Gray points peppered its brown and yellow hair. The dog dribbled from a big mouth and vicious-looking teeth.

Since Simon couldn't tell his uncle that the dog scared him silly, he gathered all his courage and said, "What's his name?"

"His name's Michel," his uncle said. "Don't show fear, or he'll tear you apart."

Simon wanted to laugh about the archangel who was a dog, but then he remembered the uncle's words to Sister, words he would never forget, that he would soon see what the boy was made of. Now it looked as if Simon would fail the test before he even set foot in Paradise.

It seemed Simon had to prove nearly every day what he was made of. The fact that the Philipes had adopted him didn't seem to matter. The kids still called him *fils d'une putain*, and worse. And he had to prove what he was made of by not striking back when struck. He had to prove what he was made of when adults felt sorry for him. Which made him feel worse than curse words. He even had to prove himself to the sisters in school who acted as though they would have preferred him stupid or lazy, or at least disrespectful and belligerent, traits they seemed to consider normal for an orphan. To be considered good, he had to do better than good.

The dog kept jumping at the window, showing its fangs. Think before you act, Sister had told him more than once. Obviously, an uncle wouldn't let a dog tear his nephew to pieces, even an adopted one. With a bang, he pushed the door open and stepped on the running board. "Bonjour, Michel!" he shouted at the animal, balling his fists and crossing his arms in front of his face, and hopped down. The dog jumped back out of his way, then approached with its ears laid back, baring its yellow fangs.

It licked his arms!

"Good dog," Simon said, as loud and firm as he could muster. He patted the dog's head and followed his uncle into the cabin, where the first thing that struck him was the absence of books. A home without books resembled a house without windows. He'd been surrounded by Sister's treasures that had opened a world of adventure and beauty. They had introduced him to the human soul, and the absence of his friends shocked him.

But the cabin's furnishings made up for it. On his uncle's bunk lay the pelt of a black bear; a crucifix on the wall above it was crudely carved out of cedar. The prize piece was the head of an eleven-point buck looking down from the opposite wall. Though glass, the proud animal's eyes followed him no matter where he went. Above the stone fireplace hung soot-blackened pots on hooks cemented into the rocks.

What impressed Simon most was the wolf skin his uncle used as a rug beside his bunk. Its head was stuffed, with its mouth open, its teeth fearsome. His uncle suggested he move the pelt to the far corner and use it as his bed. Chuckling, he said the wolf's head would make a nice pillow, though if he preferred he'd get him a stack of beaver pelts to use for a pillow, and an old army blanket to keep warm in the cool of the morning. And the mornings were cool, as he found out on the short walk to the outhouse, when birds greeted him, the new human in Paradise, with exuberant song.

A dock jutted out into a hoof-shaped bay on Lac aux Rats, with two boats tied to it, one on each side. Fishing boats with flat cushions on the seats that would accommodate three or four people. Simon looked out toward the western shore, barely a mile across, but to the boy it seemed immense. A sign over the entrance to the dock faced the water where the planes landed that brought the fishermen. The foot-high letters were burned out of sheet metal and welded to two wide angle irons attached to poles. Simon had seen a similar sign in a Western that said WELCOME TO TWINIHILL RANCH and was the home of Rex, the big stallion that saved the rancher's boy from death during an Indian attack; in his daydreams the same horse saved him from the persecution of mean old Guillaume. Uncle Baptiste's sign said *BIENVENU AU PARADIS*. And then, far out on the lake, a loon welcomed him with its loony, joyful cry.

"You know," Sybil said after a moment's silence, "I find it hard to believe that you were eleven years old and you couldn't swim. I learned to swim at the age of two.

Surprised at first that Sybil was still awake, and even more so that she'd picked on this minor detail in his story, Simon had to admit she had a point. "The nuns didn't teach phys. ed. Not even hygiene, really. There was no gym, no pool, nothing to keep you fit. If Guillaume hadn't chased me, I would have grown up fat and lazy."

"I'm curious how your uncle taught you. Did he throw you off the wharf?"

"He gave me an ultimatum. His main business, he explained, was hosting fishermen, Americans mainly, who rented his guest cabin, his boats, his skills as a guide, woodsman, cook, and wilderness character. If I drowned while fishing or setting traps, my uncle claimed with a grin, the old nun would have his scalp."

Sybil closed her eyes again.

At sunset the second day the uncle made Simon take off his clothes at the end of the dock. The old man took off his own, slapped his arms over his hairy chest, then stretched his legs to the rear, one after the other, like a dog luxuriating after a nap. Then, holding his nose with his left hand, throwing up his right, he jumped with a yell, disappearing in a splash of cold water that sprayed the boy's goose-pimpled figure. When his head surfaced, his long hair pasted over ears and cheeks and eyes, he snorted like a sea lion, waving for the boy to jump in.

"Did you?"

"No, but my uncle didn't seem to mind. Demonstrating various strokes, he explained that swimming was as natural as walking. He would hold me up, so I could start with the breaststroke. When I still wouldn't jump, he boasted that when he was my age, he would swim across the lake and dive like an otter. If I didn't learn, and learn quickly, I'd be useless to him, and he'd have to return me to my sissy sisters.

"I jumped, and swallowed some nasty water through my nose. I paddled like a dog with my arms and legs until I felt my uncle's hand under my chest. We swam in a circle. The old man glided like a seal, supporting me so securely that I soon relaxed. I love to swim. Compared to skinning the bloody critters I shot or trapped, swimming was a treat."

"What did you and your uncle do in the evenings? Did you play games? I mean it must have been kinda lonely for both you guys without books or TV. Especially for an eleven-year-old."

"We were too busy to be lonely. After dinner, we would sit by the fire. My uncle would smoke his pipe, and I would just stare into the flames. Once in awhile we'd exchange a word or two."

Not that they often talked around the fire. At least Simon didn't remember. "Thinking of the nun?" the uncle asked the boy one evening.

"No. Thinking about you. Why didn't you get married, Uncle Baptiste?"

The uncle struck a match and lit the pipe that had grown cold.

"Is it because you didn't meet the right woman?"

"The trapper blew a cloud of smoke, then cleared his throat. "The right woman was a lady." He laughed gently. "Paradise ain't no place for a lady."

"That's because you don't have books," Simon volunteered. "Ladies like to read books."

"You may be right at that," the uncle said. "There was a time, in the trenches in France, I read books, too. I was so cold and hungry and miserable and bored in the war, I even stuck my nose into the gospels." He grinned. "And don't you tell Sister!"

"Don't you miss reading?"

"No. I'm never bored here. And if I was, I'd be too tired after a long day to open a book. You know that yourself. You haven't even written to your nun."

When the sky darkened and the stars came out, Simon would get a bar of soap and his toothbrush and run down to the dock, drop his sweaty clothes on the boards, and, holding the brush between his teeth, dive into the cool water. There he would float, stretching his tired limbs, unbothered by mosquitoes and black flies. Standing in the water close to the shore, he would soap his head and body, and leisurely swim circles on his back, brushing his teeth. He would run by the outhouse, then cuddle up on the soft skin of the great she-wolf the uncle had killed years ago but would never talk about, just look at with an attitude almost of reverence. Simon would pull the army blanket up to his shoulders, squeezing the wolf's ears, gently stroking the face, running his nails over the teeth, feeling the fangs. Eventually he would lay his head on the beaver pelts and with his palms cover the green-gray eyes the wolf couldn't close, and close his own, as warm and safe as he'd ever been.

CHAPTER 22

Simon stretched his back, pulling out the arm that had fallen asleep under Sybil's weight, then turned sideways, moving her off his side, and straightened his legs.

"That's a wonderful story, Sybil said, covering a yawn with her hands. "I'm afraid I must have fallen asleep."

"You did."

"We'd better go in."

Simon felt even less like meeting strangers than he had earlier, but if he declined, he was only postponing the inevitable. Besides, he was curious about the other woman of this *ménage a trois*.

"Okay, for just a couple of minutes."

The smoke in the living room hovered so thick he had trouble identifying the four figures lounging on the floor, three men and one woman, obviously Cat, playing Scrabble. They sat up, peering at the newcomers, and one of the men, Justin Pott, rose, offering Simon his hand. "Hey, Simon. We expected you sooner. You missed a good party."

"Justin."

Slowly, still concentrating on the Scrabble board, the

others got up as well. One of the men was black, nice profile, muscular, named Kareem; the other had the soft black eyes of an Arab, or an East Indian perhaps, soft from top to bottom, with an exotic name that went in one of Simon's ears and out the other. The last to rise was the woman. The almond-shaped eyes she turned toward him had a hungry glint, despite the grass she must have smoked all night, judging by the odor in the place. Simon assessed her large breasts, hips and bottom, the strong legs. No beauty, but a woman with the magic of a Circe you wanted to delve into, for warmth and pleasure and comfort.

"I'm Cat Morrison," she said in a raspy voice, grabbing hold of his wrist with both hands, the stub of a hand-rolled smoke between her fingers, and pulling him toward the sofa. Their game was nearly finished, she said, and he and Sybil were welcome to join them for the next game. If he wanted to smoke, the makings were on the coffee table, and Sybil knew where the liquor was.

All except Justin smoked pot, passing the tiny joint so short now the Asian fellow put a pin through the end of it to get a last drag. The four settled around the board again and continued with their game. Kareem, a law student at Memphis State, by thirty-some points in the lead, had only two letters left, an I and a Q.

Simon followed Sybil to the kitchen for a drink. Pouring himself a glass of Jack Daniel's, he said, "How did you fit into this setup before you met me?"

"Same as now. It wasn't exactly "Three Is Company.""

None of us fits that script. We don't party every night. Once or twice a month. I don't drink much. I don't do grass. But I love Scrabble and good talk. I'm usually the first one to hit the sack." She paused a moment, obviously recalling some nights when she hadn't gone to bed early. Or by herself. As natural as that was for this feminine female in her lustful twenties, the thought drove him wild.

Sybil strolled back to the living room, and Simon followed. Settling on the couch, he stretched his legs and closed his eyes, listening to The Band, an album he'd enjoyed listening to ten years earlier, when he was these people's age. These days things changed so fast that ten years equaled a generation. What did he have in common with Sybil's friends? A recording? He'd grown up in a different time, a different culture. Lauralee had claimed that sex was the ultimate when she was stoned, as was dessert and music. Not for him. Downers dulled his senses.

Minutes later, the game was over, and Simon, to everybody's objection, said he needed to go home, he had an eight o'clock class. Sybil accompanied him to the curb.

"Cat turned you on, didn't she?"

"Why do you think so?"

"She's one of the sexiest women I know. If I weren't Cat's friend, she would have come on to you."

And he would have responded, Simon thought. How strange! Here was this wonderful girl he really liked and who obviously liked him and was by far more sensuous than Cat, and instead of making love with her, which he knew she expected him to do, and rather sooner than later, he'd considered wild sex with that cat woman. At least for an instant he had.

He laughed. "Men never grow up, did you know that?"

"That's part of their challenge," Sybil said, opening the door and jumping into the cab of the pickup. Laughing at Simon's surprised face, she explained she didn't want to go back to the house until the guests had left. Not unless he went with her. And since he wasn't going to do that, he'd better tell her the rest of the story.

"There isn't much more to it, except for the occasional guests from the States. And the wolf. I can't tell you about the wolf."

"Why not?"

"Because I'm embarrassed."

"In that case, don't tell me about the wolf. With me, you don't have to do anything you don't want to. Why don't you tell me about the guests?"

Simon laughed. Start with the guests and end up with the wolf anyway. But he didn't mind. Certainly not about the fishermen who would arrive in a charter plane from Quebec or Montreal that circled over the camp and hit the water with its pontoons so close to the shore the spray wet the bank as it turned into the bay, roaring boldly toward the dock. Fifty feet from it, the pilot would cut the engine and throw out an anchor. Two or three happy

Americans would shout greetings and drop their packs into the boat along with their rods and reels, cases of beer and fifths of bourbon or gin or rum. Usually half drunk already, and with much talk and laughter, they'd move into the guest cabin, staying three days, or five, or even a week.

In addition to rowing, opening beer bottles, and sometimes fixing broken lines or other gear, even climbing trees along the shore line to free a favorite lure stuck in the branches due to a poor cast, Simon helped Uncle Baptiste provide lunch. Around the lake they had spots with campfire facilities where they heated beans and peas, roasted potatoes in their jackets, and filleted the fish they caught, grilling them over the fire. While the men quenched their thirst with Labatt's or Molson's, Simon drank lake water. Not that he minded. It was cool and tasted as pure as from a spring.

Toward the middle of August—the beginning of the Canadian fall—his uncle drove to Alma with a load of furs to sell and to stock up on supplies, expecting to return in a day or two. Simon and the dog followed the pickup along the camp path out to the dirt road. While Simon watched the truck disappear around a far bend, Michel ran into the woods, yapping, as he always did on the trail of a fast moving animal.

Uncle Baptiste had been very specific with his order not to leave camp during his absence, and Simon was aware of it when he called the dog, yelling at the top of his voice. Michel heard him but didn't pay attention.

When the dog's hunting instinct took over, as he had already learned, nothing could stop it. Instead of letting the animal have his fun, Simon got angry and followed, breaking through the brush, bending under, climbing over, or pushing aside limbs and branches, heading toward the distant, now hardly audible sounds.

Though only a cur, Michel was relentless in pursuit. Given a chance, he treed raccoons and squirrels and chased rabbits. Sometimes, he caught a bunny and devoured it, crushing the delicate bones and leaving nothing but a piece of fur. Red foxes the dog pursued in the large circles they made until they lost him in a thicket, or they went to ground. The chase after gray foxes, more numerous in the area but not as sought after by Monsieur Berthiaume, offered the dog more fun. The grays ran in smaller circles, ins and outs and crooked lines, until they tired of the game and went to ground, or, like a coon, escaped up a tree.

The animal the dog hunted wasn't a fox. It was running in a straight line east, and Simon hustled after the dog's yapping as fast as he could. Before long, it got so weak he might have just imagined hearing it. But, like the dog, the boy had a relentless streak. And gradually, Michel's voice became audible again, and soon sounded as if he had slowed his pace or had stopped the pursuit altogether. His high yapping had changed to a deeper, belligerent bark. The dog had cornered his prey.

Then the barking stopped altogether, except for an occasional bellow. When Simon caught up with Michel, he was standing on a moss-covered outcrop, ears laid back, whimpering, and pointing to the far bank of the stream. There in the weeds stood a gray wolf, looking across, a tall, deep but narrow-chested animal, its shoulders slightly lower than its haunches.

That stopped the boy. Very cautiously, he advanced to join the dog on the rock. From there he could see the wolf's front legs through the partially trampled grass, the left one clamped in a steel trap. The leg in the trap was broken beneath the knee, pointing down at an angle.

"Good dog," Simon praised Michel, scratching his neck. Michel was trembling. The boy sat down on the outcrop and pulled the dog across his legs but never took his eyes off the trapped beast. He sat watching the wolf for a long time. The look in its eyes differed little from that of the she-wolf he slept on. Simon saw no threat, and no fear.

"Michel, I guess you have a right to be scared. We have no weapon, and we have what Uncle calls a situation. If we had Uncle Baptiste's rifle, we would send a bullet through the wolf's head, right between its tawny eyes. Then we would skin it and take the pelt home. Uncle would be proud."

On the other hand, since the wolf didn't seem to be suffering, he saw no reason to kill it. All he needed to do to free the wolf was to open the trap. The question was how. Simon had trouble opening beaver traps, and they were child's play compared to this killer trap. The first thing he ought to do, he eventually decided, was to knock the beast unconscious. Then he would worry about opening the trap.

Strolling along the creek to find a sturdy piece of driftwood, he soon weighed a five-foot rod two inches or better in diameter in his hands. Before proceeding, he tossed another rock. The wolf moved just enough to let it bounce off the steel with a clang. Now Simon took his heart in his hands and climbed down into the water where a paw print was still visible in a pocket of sand between the flat stones he stepped on.

On the other side, he waited a moment, gathering courage, and climbed the bank at a safe distance from the wolf who looked at him neither angry nor friendly. It was like the American fishermen, he thought, interested yet detached. About four feet from the wolf's head Simon raised his club. But instead of bringing it down with all his might, he froze and stood there like a statue. If the wolf made a fast move, he figured, it might break loose and be on top of him with one powerful leap, long before he had a chance to grab his knife. In his hands, the heavy club started to tremble, and still he just stood there.

Tilting its head, the wolf regarded Simon. Breathing hard, trembling from effort and dread, the boy lowered the club, stepped back, and hurried across the creek, where he threw himself down and clutched the neck of the dog, who was shivering harder than he. Hitting the beast over the head was out.

"Well, boy," he addressed the dog, "I don't know what

to do next. Let's think. You know what Uncle Baptiste says. Never give up. There is always a way." The dog just trembled, looking up at him.

"You're a big help," Simon said, and hugged Michel again. But soon he had another idea. He undid his boots, pulled out the leather laces, and tied his hunting knife to the straighter end of the rod. When the laces were tight, and the knife's tang was flush against the cut, he had a lance.

With the new weapon on his shoulder he crossed the stream once more, and again approached the wolf from the front. It didn't move except for pointing its ears. "You're a brave wolf," Simon said, talking to the beast mainly to give himself courage. He also hoped talking would distract the wolf so it wouldn't see him tremble even before he lowered a knee to the ground and pointed the spear. On his knee, the boy was shorter than the wolf, and the closeness to the danger made his hands sweat. The wolf, too, was hot. Its tongue hung out on the side, now that the day was warming up, and its head wobbled slightly each time it took a breath.

Having second thoughts, the boy moved back a few inches. Then, thinking of his uncle, he reached forward with resolve and laid the blade on the trap, the sharp edge against the fracture, and started sawing. One eye he kept on his work, the other on the wolf's eyes that were half hidden by lowered lids, as if Simon were scratching its back rather than cutting off its leg. He sawed patiently, not trembling anymore, and just as patiently, it seemed to him, the wolf waited for the job to get done.

Much more quickly than he'd expected, the blade cut through the bone. Immediately he pulled the spear back and jumped to his feet, keeping the blade pointed at the wolf's chest. But the wolf didn't jump. Slowly it straightened up and stood, blinking, stretching its body, even stretching one hind leg, as if waking up.

The weapon still pointed, Simon watched. The wolf licked the bleeding stump, then raised its head, looking at the boy. "You can leave now," Simon said, almost gently. When the wolf didn't move, just kept looking at him, he stepped back, away from the danger. "*Vas-y*!" he commanded. "Get!"

After another long moment, the wolf shifted its weight to the haunches and turned toward the trees, hopping three or four steps, then stopped, turning its head around.

"*Vas-y*!" Simon commanded for the third time, not shouting anymore, saying it almost with regret, then he slowly retreated across the creek and joined the dog on the outcrop. Michel growled deep in his chest but made no move to approach the wolf. Simon dried his feet with a fistful of grass, watching the wolf watching him, as if asking, "Now what?" While putting on his socks, Simon took his eyes off the wolf. Beside him, the dog stopped growling. When Simon looked up, the wolf was gone.

He just sat, staring at the spot. Then he unlaced his Bowie knife from the rod and slid it in its sheath and laced up his boots. The trap sat by itself now in the scattered leaves and dry twigs that had hidden it. The lower leg with the huge paw still hung from it. It wouldn't remain there long. Before nightfall, some predator would chew the meat off and suck the marrow from the bone. If he were the wolf, Simon thought, he'd come back and eat the leg himself.

On the long way home, the dog trotted ahead. Entering a stand of young maples, he chased the odd yellow leaf twirling down on the trail. Simon tried to think of how he would soon have to leave the woods and go back to school, but all he could see was the wolf. The way it had stood, looking as if it wanted to go with him, knowing it couldn't.

The woods were silent. No bird song, no buzz of insects. Even the falling leaves landed without a sound. Suddenly, the dog stopped. From the distance behind, a low, long howl ending in a high wail broke the silence. It wasn't a war cry, or a challenge. It was more a cry of despair that shook the woods, restricting the boy's heart. It was as if the pain in his own heart had found a voice in the wolf's howl. "We'll soon see what the boy is made of," his uncle had said. The soon was here now. Obviously he wasn't made of the stuff Uncle Baptiste expected. Instead of killing the wolf, he had set it free, although he knew perfectly well that a three-legged hunter couldn't run down the forest creatures it needed to survive. In the wilderness, even vultures struggled to find scraps. And yet, if he had killed the wolf, he wouldn't feel any better. Probably worse. No matter what he had done, or hadn't done, he couldn't have fixed the wolf's fate.

The air was still. No breeze. Not a whisper of a sound. The dog slunk to Simon, ears laid back, whimpering, keeping close to the boy's heels. Simon reached behind, patting the dog's neck. The leaves tumbling through the evening sun sparkled like gold. Simon's body started shaking, and he sobbed.

~~~~~

Sybil rested in Simon's arms, eyes closed. He lifted her out of the cab and carried her up the driveway and up the steps. At the door he let her down, and she reached into her bag for the key. Inside the house it was dark and quiet except for the whispering of a ceiling fan in the living room.

Standing in the open doorway, Sybil said, "Are you okay driving? If not, you're welcome to spend the night on the couch." She grinned sleepily. "Or in my bed."

Simon shook his head. "The children are by themselves." Lifting her arms, he kissed the back of her hands. "You didn't hear my story, did you?"

"Yes, I did."

"What happened?"

"The wolf broke your heart."

Simon laughed. "I don't know about that." But as far as he remembered, it was the first time that he cried. Probably more about his own fate than that of the crippled wolf's. As he turned to descend the steps, Sybil exclaimed, "Oh, I almost forgot. My grandparents are inviting you for lunch. Friday if you can. Can you?"

"I think so," Simon said, somewhat reluctantly, amused at this woman's practical mind.

"Good." She slipped inside and shut the door.

CHAPTER 23

When Simon arrived at his apartment, he was too tired to shower. He checked on the children, stripped, fell onto the bed, and promptly passed out. The noise that woke him came from far off. It took him a moment to realize that it was the ringing of the phone. The alarm clock showed three o'clock. The children were in bed, and if something went wrong with the horses, Mr. Crumb wouldn't be aware of it. It had to be a wrong number. Instead of getting up, he rolled over. But the ringing wouldn't cease until he struggled to the kitchen and unhooked the receiver.

"This is Cami Shriver," a woman's voice said. "Sorry to wake you at this hour, but I thought you might want to pick up Mark at Juvenile Hall. They wouldn't release him to me."

"Juvenile Hall? You mean Juvenile Court?"

"I guess so. Mark and my son Casper were arrested during a police raid on Overton Square last night. For possession."

"Possession of what?" Simon asked, suddenly clear-headed.

"Marijuana."

The woman explained that Mark had given the cops his mother's phone number, but they'd not been able to reach her. Simon thanked her and fought his rising anger, less for the offense itself than for the stupidity of two intelligent boys hanging out at a place notorious for drug raids. First he'd failed as a husband, now as a father.

Juvenile Court was a square building on a quiet midtown street with some trees in the yard, though Simon barely noticed. An officer asked him to sign a release form before opening a room with a sunken floor, more like a pit than a jail cell, where Mark sat on the elevated, wooden edge, dangling his feet. The boy looked pale, his expression defiant. The officer nodded, motioning with his finger for him to come out, and slowly Mark obeyed. He avoided both men's eyes, and Simon was grateful his son didn't notice the pity in his father's. Silently they walked down the stairs and out into the cold and climbed into the old Ford.

Mark zipped up his jacket and stuck his hands into his pockets, watching Simon slip on his brown cotton gloves and crank the pickup. Since the heater still didn't work, the fan blew cool air into the cab, and Simon directed it at the windshield.

"Aren't you going to yell at me?"

"What good would that do? I'm just sorry you felt so bad you wanted to be arrested."

"I guess you never did a stupid thing, did you, Daddy? You're Mr. Perfect! That's why Mummy hates you!"

From the mouths of babes? Nonsense!

"Just because I did stupid things doesn't mean you have to. If you can't stay away from the illegal stuff, don't flaunt it in public." He paused. "Better, stay away from it altogether, at least until you're of age and no longer my responsibility."

Again a dumbass remark. In his heart, his son would always be his responsibility.

"What did you do for kicks at sixteen? Get drunk?"

"I didn't smoke pot."

"That's because there wasn't any."

"True enough." He put the truck in gear and drove out into the street. "You can spend the rest of the night on the couch. In the morning I'll take you to your mother's place in time to get your books for school."

The boy made no comment.

"You're an A-student, president of the honor society, healthy, good-looking. What's going on, Mark?"

"I'm president of the math society."

"Whatever." Another dumbass thing to say. Being president of the math society was a big deal, and Simon was proud of him.

"You never care what I do in school. Or after. The only thing you care about is your horses."

Since his children attended classes for the gifted, it seemed a waste of time to worry about their academic progress. If one of them came home with a lone B among the A's, he'd say, "How come?" Not angry or disappointed, just curious.

"If you have a problem, Mark, you know I'll listen. Help if I can."

On the drive to the apartment, the boy remained silent. Simon thought of some of his students who smoked pot, like some of his colleagues, while his son got arrested for half a reefer in his pocket.

He had to call an attorney. But who? He knew a couple of lawyers among his fellow fox hunters. Swinging Lee Hansom, who specialized in injury suits? Or Gerry Cousins, a corporation lawyer with a more mature image? On the other hand, Mark might be better off with Sybil's friend Cat. As a public defender, Cat Morrison dealt with everything from shoplifting to murder; it'd be a breeze for her to cope with Mark's crime. If that's what it was.

Parking the pickup, he remembered Mark's reference to Ellen's hatred of him. Mr. Perfect? His son's opinion, not Ellen's.

In the warm living room, Mark flexed his fingers. A year ago the boy had bought a synthesizer, and sometime in the summer Ellen had started paying for piano lessons. With his ambidextrous hands, a musical ear, and the determination of a bulldog, Mark had learned the basics within days. He and Casper and a couple of other high school musicians met almost daily to practice their instruments together.

"Are you still studying piano?"

The boy shook his head.

"Did you give up on forming a rock band?" Simon

asked, rummaging through the closet to find a pillow and a blanket for the couch.

Mark had seemed calm when they got home, almost penitent. Now he was angry again. "As if you cared!"

"I do. I think you have a genius for science, but if you think your talent is rock, let it be rock. It's important to develop your true gift. That's what we're on this earth for."

"Did you ever develop yours?"

"Probably not," Simon answered good-humoredly. "I never had a talent I recognized as special. If they'd had marijuana when I was in high school, I'm sure I would have tried it, too. I tried everything else. I'm thirsty. Would you like to share a Dos Equis?"

The trace of a smile crossed Mark's face. "Is that legal?"

"In your home it is." Simon went to the kitchen, returning with a bottle and a glass. After pouring, he clinked Mark's glass with his bottle. "Santé!"

Simon still couldn't tell what was really bothering the young man. How did a father gain the confidence of a son who hardly ever talked to him anymore? A son in his care, if he was lucky, for half of the year? Was Mark seriously troubled, or was he just now old enough to begin establishing his own space?

"I know so little about your life, Mark. Like what motivates you. What pains you."

"You know a lot more about my life than I know about yours. I've always wondered why you left home as a teenager. Your parents weren't divorced, you had no cause to leave."

"My parents were dead."

For several seconds, Mark didn't answer. Then he said calmly, "Sometimes I think it'd be easier if you were dead."

"There are moments," Simon said, "when I think so, too."

"When you were a teenager, you must have gotten into trouble, too, or you wouldn't have left your home at sixteen. You didn't leave because you'd just lost your parents. They died when you were eleven."

"I left when my Uncle Baptiste died. To me, Uncle Baptiste was like a second father."

When Sister Elisabeth told Simon that Uncle Baptiste had been found frozen to death on a country road, she didn't have to tell him that the uncle had been drinking. Sober, his uncle would not have sat down in a snow bank to rest, and then fallen asleep. His body had been completely covered by snow.

On the morning of the funeral it was so cold and the wind blew so hard that Sister Elisabeth suggested they postpone the burial, but Father Lebas refused. "The old trapper won't mind," the father said to the sister, winking at Simon. Besides Simon and the father, only Sister Elisabeth and Sister Marie-Joséf braced the weather to the cemetery. At the grave, the sisters held on to their coat collars, their hoods flying. Simon tried to listen to the priest's words, but they, too, were carried away by the wind.

It was all right to shed a tear, Sister Marie-Joséf had said when Simon just stared at the coffin.

"Your Uncle Baptiste was a good man," Sister Elisabeth added, touching the boy's shoulder.

His uncle's death seemed to have robbed Simon of his joie de vivre. Schoolwork lost its challenge. Even Monsieur Berthiaume's offer of a summer job in the Alma store he accepted without enthusiasm. Compared to the outdoor adventures in Paradise, the confinement of the store felt claustrophobic. Yet at the end of the season when Berthiaume made the position permanent, raising Simon's salary from twenty-eight dollars a month to thirty-five, he quit school. A disappointed Sister asked him what he needed the money for. "To buy a car," he said. And move to the city, but he didn't mention that. Sister was fully aware that Simon had saved enough money in his bank account already to buy a car, but she was smart enough not to mention the obvious. She didn't even warn him about becoming greedy, always her pet beef.

Mark's glass was empty. Simon got another beer from the fridge and refilled his son's glass. Then he told him about that last weekend of October when the entire stock of rifles and shotguns had disappeared from the Alma store. With no evidence of forced entry, the local Mountie called the theft an inside job. He pointed out that Simon and Monsieur Berthiaume were the only people with a key, which made Simon the principal suspect. Simon argued that Monsieur Berthiaume's son, his old enemy Guillaume, also had access to the store. But it was unthinkable to Monsieur Berthiaume that his own son, who managed the store at St.-Ambroise and frequently visited Alma, could be a thief. He looked at Simon a long time without speaking. Then he shook his head and asked the boy to show him his bankbook.

In his savings account Simon had accumulated nineteen hundred and forty-nine dollars and thirty-seven cents. Simon showed Monsieur Berthiaume the first deposit of seventeen hundred and fifty dollars of four and a half years before, his share of the sale of the house and business when his parents died. Then the dozens of small deposits over the years earned by working after school, the summers with his uncle, and then the ten and fifteen dollar deposits from June till September, when he'd gotten a raise and deposited twenty. He would never bite the hand that fed him, Simon assured his boss. But the storekeeper said he couldn't ignore the evidence that pointed in Simon's direction. Only for his uncle's sake would he decline to prosecute. He would, however, expect Simon to make up the loss. He'd take nineteen hundred dollars as a reimbursement for the guns, leaving forty-nine dollars and thirty-seven cents in Simon's account. With the boy's reputation ruined, the usually jovial man added in a tired voice, he wouldn't find another job in this region.

Hurt enough to cry and mad enough to curse, yet smart enough to do neither, Simon packed his bag and looked for sympathy at the nuns'. Sister Elisabeth made him sit down in the old easy chair in the office where he'd probably sat a hundred times. Her face looked much older now, but her smile hadn't lost its kindness, despite a myriad of tiny wrinkles that framed her shining eyes, her firm, chiseled lips. When he finished the story of his dismissal, Sister uttered neither words of blame nor pity. She said Monsieur Berthiaume was a father. His feelings for his only child were surely as deep as hers were for Simon. Monsieur Berthiaume was not a bad man, just a weak man, whose love for his son impaired his judgment. She could forgive him that weakness, but not his greed. Taking Simon's money was almost as heartless as robbing him of his good name.

Leaning back in her chair, the nun smiled. "My theory is that God tests his favorites. The more he loves them, the harder He deals with them. And this Berthiaume affair is only the prick of a pin, hardly worth mentioning in the scale of things." To Simon's astonishment, the nun chuckled. "You must thank the Lord for the wonderful, exciting life you've had so far."

She'd produced a smile in Simon as well. At least the sister agreed that Simon was right about not finding employment around Chicoutimi. Eventually though, people would forget. People might forget, Simon argued, but he would not. He'd go to Trois Rivières and work in a mill. That's what his uncle had done when he was Simon's age.

"What about university?" was the nun's last word on

the subject, but even that wasn't said reproachfully.

He shrugged, trying hard not to betray his self-pity. His plans to someday attend university had never been cast in stone, or he wouldn't have stayed with Monsieur Berthiaume past the summer vacation. Nobody besides Sister Elisabeth expected an orphan to attend university, not even himself. Nevertheless, he was disappointed Sister didn't repeat her offer to send him to her relatives in Liège, to finish high school there, and maybe someday study at the Sorbonne. Getting to his feet, he said he would be leaving in the morning. Sister, too, rose, holding his wrists, her bony fingers squeezing his hands. He was amazed by how short she had become.

"You've grown, son," she said with a smile, touching his crooked nose, her eyes moist but without tears. "I've always known I'd have to let you go. Time for the little hawk to test his wings." With her thumb she drew a cross on his forehead. "Bless you, *mon enfant*. Pray for the old nun." Turning about-face, she left the office and didn't look back.

CHAPTER 24

"Is that when you left Chicoutimi?" Mark asked, opening his eyes wide. "This must have been a sad day."

"Not really."

Standing on the highway, facing the brisk November wind blowing from the northeast, wiggling his toes in his new leather boots and his fingers in the pockets of his parka, about to leave the only home he'd ever known, Simon certainly felt apprehensive but no longer sorry for himself. In fact, he was eager to start a new life. An aluminum pot tied to the outside of his backpack, his Bowie knife in the sheath hidden under his parka, he was prepared for bad weather, and for bad men. If the road got buried in a snowstorm, he would build a shelter and light a fire. And if he came across a crook who threatened him with a gun, he'd surrender the nine dollars and thirty-seven cents in his buttoned-down vest pocket. The two twenty dollar bills hidden under the insole of his left boot a robber wouldn't find. He carried more cash than he'd ever had on him at any one time, and he wouldn't hesitate to use his knife to keep it.

Simon chuckled. "Yes, I was one tough cookie, not

afraid of anything or anybody."

"Canada in the fifties must have been a friendlier place. Today I wouldn't hitchhike no matter where."

"Maybe. I got a lift to Quebec City, all the way downtown to Charlevoix Street in front of the Hotel Dieu. First I rented a room and then strolled up the hill to the Hotel Château Frontenac. That's an old, massive structure, still a tourist attraction today, but what really impressed me was the moonlit bay below, from where two hundred some years before *les Canadiens* had ventured and conquered the huge, beautiful land called Canada."

Awake for hours in his too soft bed, Simon had thought about the conquerors, imagining their hardships, their faith in God, and in themselves, and what a pity it was so much of the world these early Canadians had known was now settled.

The next morning he left town hiking north to the Saint-Charles River, and west through the suburb of Les Saules, intending to thumb a ride west on the north side of the St. Lawrence. If he couldn't get a lift, he figured, he might board a freight train. He had just traversed the village of Grondines and was already looking for a shelter to spend the night, when a fellow on a motorcycle dressed in black leather and wearing a coon cap with a tail stopped, offering him a ride to La Pérade, the next town a few miles farther along the river. Without a second thought, Simon hopped on, and the bike took off like a racehorse out of the gate even before he had found a place to put his feet. By pure luck he'd managed to grab the man's coat or he'd have fallen off. As they reached Pérade, the fellow switched on his lights and slowed down, stopping at the intersection where a road turned north. The way to Trois Rivières was straight ahead, he said. He himself was headed for La Tuque, a hundred miles north and about halfway to Lac Saint-Jean and Chicoutimi. He'd be glad to give Simon a lift. For one fleeting second, Simon was tempted. Get behind me, Satan, he almost said to the cyclist, but he just thanked him and jumped off.

Adjusting his backpack, he followed the highway through town heading west. As he reached the last building, it was so dark that he could barely make out the cars of a freight train standing on the tracks on his right, looking huge and forbidding.

As his eyes became accustomed to the dark, the silhouettes of the big iron wheels under the long, dark boxes became visible, and he thought he heard the faint picking of a guitar. He couldn't trust his hearing, though, when it came to guitar music. He could hear a tune at will, no matter where he happened to be. Climbing through the gap between two cars, he thought he noticed a light some distance beyond the train. Climbing on top of an iron coupling, he could see a small campfire, maybe a hundred feet from the train, partially hidden by leafless growth. A figure was moving near it. Another was sitting. Again the sound of a guitar riding the breeze.

He stood, watching, wanting to make sure he knew what to expect. The sitting man was indeed picking a guitar, the other, now squatting also, stirring a pot on the edge of the fire. Each had his shoulder covered with a blanket. Probably a couple of hoboes. One of them was a musician. Which was more than he himself was. Except for his outfit, he was no better than a hobo. Dishonored, without a job or prospects, considering riding a freight. Yet he was uneasy. He had a strong urge to climb back down to the highway and keep walking, build his own fire in a sheltered spot along the road. He could make tea and eat the remainder of the boiled eggs the sisters had packed, then sleep curled up to the hot embers.

Ignoring his unease, he climbed down the far side and walked through the low bushes, bending the supple twigs out of his way. The two men neither heard nor saw him, not until he stood over them, saying, "*Bonsoir.*"

"What the fuck," said the fellow with the guitar who was not much older than he. The other, of undetermined age but at least twice his own, only lifted his head but kept stirring the steaming liquid in a fire-blackened pot.

On the ground between the men lay two cloth sacks, a paper sack, a blanket roll, some potato peels. The man was stewing potatoes.

With a motion of his hand, the older guy invited Simon to sit. Discreetly checking the shadows, Simon hunkered down, a step farther back from the fire than they, keeping an equal distance from the tramps. Not that he was afraid, he tried to tell himself, just cautious. Simon had met some rough characters around the logging camps, but none had ever given him the creeps the way the pot stirrer did. Even squatting, he looked threatening, his broad shoulders pushing restlessly against the blanket. The black hat with the down-turned rim cast a shadow over his unshaven face and eyes but didn't hide the man's meanness.

The anglais didn't look trustworthy, either, despite the blond curls spilling out from under a brown wool cap that gave him a boyish look. Both men wore pants covered with patches of dark cloth, showing rough stitches of various thread, and worn lace-up boots. They cast furtive glances at his jeans and parka, his boots, and openly appraised his pack.

"Simon Philipe," Simon said.

"Where you headed?" the older of the two asked, apparently not about to introduce himself or his companion.

"Trois Rivières."

The light from the fire passed over the man's face as he turned, and something like a smile cracked the thin line of his lips, exposing teeth nearly as dark as the stubble on his chin. "So are we. If you like, you can stick with us."

"Ride the train?"

The man nodded, paying attention to his pot again.

With two trustworthy companions, Simon would have jumped at a chance to ride the rails. It might come in handy some day to know how the pros did it. The anglais, who hadn't said a word since the initial curse, laid the instrument down and handed Simon a soup can with the paper peeled off. From the sack beside him, he produced another tin, handing it to his partner, keeping one for himself, dipping it into the pot. Simon followed his example, filling half the can only to avoid burning his fingers on the quickly heating metal. The liquid tasted like tepid water. The morsels of cooked potatoes had no taste at all.

"It could use some salt," Simon commented.

In the field behind him, something fell to the ground. He turned quickly but heard nothing more, though he kept his eyes away from the glowing embers to get them accustomed to the darkness again.

"There's some goats back there," the older fellow said. "Maybe we ought to make a goat stew."

Then the French fellow asked his buddy to sing. Without answering, the young tramp put his can down, picked up the guitar, and began a negro spiritual. Simon listened, fascinated, determined to learn English so he'd understand more than curses and "Lord," a word the singer kept repeating. In fact, "Lord" was the last thing he heard before an explosion of stars left him unconscious.

Simon woke with a headache so throbbing he didn't realize for a moment he was lying in a ditch, buck naked, shaking, so cold he couldn't feel his fingers or his feet. A sticky mess covered his eyes. Opening them, he saw quarter moons rushing by, bobbing on their backs. At best, he had a cut on his head—the source of the dried blood on his face—or he was concussed. At worst, his skull was cracked. Since he'd come to and his memory functioned, he would live.

Just then, next to his head, a goat pushed its nose through the wire mesh, trying to reach the brown, frozen tuft of grass above his head. With great effort, Simon reached up, pushing his numb fingers through the mesh, pulling himself to a sitting position, hardly aware of the goat's tongue licking his skin. Two or three other goats approached the fence, joining their mate. If he didn't climb out and move his limbs and get to a warmer place, he might lose his fingers, or the toes he couldn't feel, possibly his nose and ears.

Next he noticed that the tracks were empty. The freight train was gone. On elbows and knees he crawled in the direction he knew the campfire had been, hoping to find some glowing coals left buried in the ashes.

The men had urinated on the fire. He could tell by the embers that were coated with a skin of ice and the scent rising from the still warm ash pile underneath. Before trying to revive the fire, he crawled around it, looking for clothes that the man who'd taken his might have discarded.

There were none.

Grabbing a stick he stirred the ashes as well as he could with his frozen hands, and sure enough, he uncovered some still smoldering wood. From around the edge of the ashes, he scooped up sticks that had escaped the flames, laying them on the coals in crisscross fashion, building a stack several inches high. Burying his hands in the ashes around it, he bent over the wood and blew.

Or tried to, because the pain of the effort was almost unbearable. And yet, when nothing happened, he blew again, and blew a third and a fourth time. The frosted twigs wouldn't feed a flame.

Discouraged, he crawled away toward the leafless bushes he had crossed on his way from the train, searching for clothes. The two moons bobbing on the edge of the sky didn't shine bright enough to help, but his knees and elbows were beginning to hurt, and that was a good sign. Shortly after, his hand scraped over something soft. Long johns! As he turned, feeling for more garments, flames rose out of the ash pile. His little stack of sticks had caught on fire. As fast as he could manage, he crawled to it, pulling the long johns along. Carefully he laid bigger pieces of wood on the little stack of burnt and half-burnt embers, and soon the flames warmed his skin and threw light on his booty.

The plum-red underwear was shabby, frayed on the edges, with holes worn into elbows and knees, and smelled half rotten, half smoky. It had probably never been washed. But Simon realized how lucky he was to have found it, regardless of its condition, and slipped into it. Then he sat by the fire, holding his feet close to the flames, rubbing the insteps with his soles and the soles with his insteps, slowly but constantly, stretching his arms toward the heat, rubbing his hands as well, and before long, toes and fingers began to sting, eventually causing pain so excruciating he wished he were dead. He should look for more discarded clothes, maybe the man's old boots, but until the agony in his extremities eased, he wouldn't budge from the warmth of the fire. It'd be just luck if he found more stuff before morning. If there were more.

By the light of the early dawn, the pain in his limbs became manageable, though the headache had worsened. Again he ventured into the bushes and soon found a pair of slacks, frayed and dirty, smelling of smoke, and slipped them on. Next, he crawled over a threadbare shirt with no buttons and, several feet farther, over a pair of boots with worn heels and holes in the soles. These he warmed by the fire, but his feet still hurt too much to pull boots over them even though they looked like his size.

Someone was wearing his boots and jeans, shirt and sweater, his parka, his double-knit wool cap, and they had surely divided the spare socks and shorts and long johns in his pack. The few books from Sister's shelves they'd probably sell. They'd share the cash, too, the twos and singles buttoned down in his vest, the handful of silver in his jeans pockets. The twenties folded under the insole in his boot they wouldn't find for a while. On second thought, they had probably found them already. It was the logical place to hide bills.

Suddenly, Sister's words about the Lord testing those He loved came to his mind. Was the beating he took and nearly losing his life a bigger test than losing his job and his home? Hardly. His losses were of small consequence. His body would recover. Money he would earn again.

Clothes and boots he would buy. The loss of his Bowie knife, that's what he regretted. The knife had become a part of him. Without it, he felt naked. But even the knife, in the scale of things, was nothing.

The clouds in the east turned as red as his long johns. He pulled on the old boots that had no laces and tried to stand up. After several attempts he succeeded and stood, legs apart. Slowly, putting one spread foot ahead of the other, with each step catching himself from falling like a drunk about to drop, he made his way toward the highway. Crossing the first track, he stumbled and fell, hitting the rocks with his face. He lay on his stomach, warm blood filling his mouth. Struggling to sit up, he heard a roll of thunder in the distance, then discovered the sun, a dozen suns risen suddenly, each bright as high noon, filing rapidly past his vision.

On the road below, a car screeched to a stop. He heard the engine idle but didn't have the strength to turn and look. Ahead, the suns were getting bigger, roaring nearer. The blast of a whistle shook him. Again, an even shriller blast. A train, he thought, lifting his head, as if waking from a dream. Then a wide hat bending over him. A Mountie. A thousand Mounties swishing past him, reaching out.

CHAPTER 25

Mark's glass was empty, and he seemed asleep. But when Simon stroked the boy's long, fine hair, he opened his eyes.

"You were really lucky, Daddy. Those tramps could have killed you. Did you ever come across them again?"

"No." That was lucky, too, Simon thought. For years he'd daydreamed about clobbering them to a pulp, one at a time, though he'd never hated them as much as he had Guillaume. These days his old childhood foe rarely crossed his mind, and when he did, Simon felt more gratitude than resentment. After all, if it hadn't been for Guillaume's lies, Simon might never have left Chicoutimi. And he would have lost his job anyway when general stores went out of business in the late fifties and early sixties.

"What were you looking for, Daddy?"

"Adventure. Love. Who knows? Years later I got the idea that essentially I was looking for who I was."

"That kind of introspection might have been okay for the ancient Greeks, like Plato, but it's hardly necessary for twentieth century people. Genes and environment

188

make us who we are."

Simon nodded. Papa and Maman had raised him in a proper middle class environment. Sister Elisabeth had shaped his morals. And Uncle Baptiste had given him the strength to persevere. So much he knew. But that was all shell. He didn't know his nucleus, and for a split second, Simon considered telling his son that he hadn't known his biological parents; therefore he truly didn't know who he was. Instead, he said, "When my uncle picked me up at the sisters' to spend the summer with him at his fishing camp and Sister Elisabeth told me that I was a good boy, my uncle said, 'We'll soon find out what the boy's made of.' That's what he said. And you know something funny? I still don't know what I'm really made of. It must take an earth shaking event to show you what you're really made of."

Mark laughed. "I don't have that problem. I know who I am. I more or less know which qualities I inherited from you, and which from Mummy. And I know what I'm looking for. Not adventures. Not love. Not yet, anyway. I'm looking for a perfect SAT score; I'm looking for a scholarship to the college of my choice; and then I'm looking for admission to the very best graduate school for gene research. In the long haul, the Nobel Prize. That's what I'm made of."

Simon's turn to laugh. "What about the pretty girl you bring to the house to play Dungeons and Dragons?"

"She's a friend. I can't get emotionally involved. A wife and a bunch of kids would interfere with my career."

Hardly able to keep his eyes open, Mark tried to smile. Uncertain whether Mark was pulling his leg, Simon again touched the boy's hair. "Don't knock love. Without love, life's hardly worth living."

"It didn't work so well for you and Mummy, did it?"

Mark closed his eyes. Simon moved the pillow under his son's head and lifted up his legs. Then he took off Mark's shoes and covered him with the blanket.

Watching the boy sleep, Simon regretted not having told him more about Sister Elisabeth. How the news of her death became a turning point in his life.

Four o'clock.

A dumb time for memories to rise into his consciousness, Simon thought, dragging himself to the bedroom where the window was wide open. He stripped and climbed into his now cold bed again. At six he had to be up to get ready for his eight o'clock First Year French class and to take Mark to Ellen's. Hardly worth going to sleep.

And sleep he didn't. Instead he watched himself getting home from the three-to-eleven shift at the mill, finding a tiny package at the door of his rented loft. It contained Sister's rosary with its carved wooden beads and silver cross, the framed photograph of a young Elisabeth proudly sitting her horse at her parents' estate near Liège, and a note in the shaky handwriting of Sister Marie-Joséf. He put the letter on the card table that was the centerpiece in his room, took off his coat, filled the kettle with water, set it on the hot plate, and only then did he read the message. Sister Marie-Joséf wrote without sentiment that Sister Elisabeth du Soulier had died in the night of February twenty-fifth. She was sixty-two years old.

He understood the words, but his heart refused to believe them. The third of March. She was already buried. The least Sister Marie-Joséf could have done was send him a telegram. He could have attended her funeral, as he had Uncle Baptiste's and those of his parents. A burial provided an ending. The smell of the earth at the open grave he'd found soothing, like the rhythmic Latin prayers of the priest and the memories shared by friends and neighbors afterwards over food and drink.

He turned off the kettle and, without putting his coat back on, descended the stairs and went out into the brisk, windy night, Sister's rosary crumpled in his hand. Instead of carrying it in his pocket, he hung it around his neck, stuffing the cross inside his shirt. He strode down the empty street, back toward the river and the mill, not knowing why exactly, probably just from habit. Passing a bar, he hesitated and listened to the talk coming out through the closed door. Having no desire for a drink, even less for company, he continued. At the mill, he headed straight for the loading dock, attracted perhaps by the smell of the timber that almost neutralized the overpowering odor of the pulp, perhaps by the river's black water, some of which came from home.

Simon was the only person on the dock, looking about the size of an ant next to a ten-thousand-ton mountain of timbers. He felt even smaller. This was the kind of blustery night it had been when Sister found him on her doorstep, a month less than seventeen years before. Once more he became the infant looking into the face of the kindly woman who bent over the Quaker State oil box, maybe saved his life, and watched over it always. He had a great urge to bawl, but at seventeen, you didn't cry anymore. Besides, he found it hard to breathe. He was practically gulping for air, like a bass removed from the lure.

On his way home he entered the bar and shared a fifth of Black Label with Gilles Pétard, one of his fellow dockworkers. At the end of the night Gilles invited him to drive to Windsor to pick up a diesel engine for his brother's garage. If they left early Saturday morning, they could watch a hockey game in Detroit that night between the Montreal Canadiens and the Detroit Red Wings. Simon, who had played hockey himself in school, was no passionate Canadiens fan, like Gilles, but just then he would have accompanied his co-worker to the end of the earth. He had never been farther west than Montreal, and the prospect of a six-hundred-mile drive lifted his spirits. Before going to bed, he made a couple of sandwiches and filled the thermos with hot tea. Pulling his new backpack from the closet, he dropped the provisions into it and, on an impulse, slipped young Sister Elisabeth's horseback photo in the outside pocket.

They left at three-thirty in the morning. There wasn't much of interest to see, even after the dawn broke. The trees along the slow-moving St. Lawrence River, from Cornwall to Kingston, and along the shore of Lake Ontario were still bare, but for years he remembered it as a green country. Except for downtown Toronto, which at the time was a gray, ugly city. After Toronto, they drove through London, then nothing but flat, boring land. When they finally rolled into Windsor, it was after six o'clock, and the warehouse was closed. At a gas station, Gilles called his brother's friend who agreed to meet them Sunday morning.

From Windsor to Detroit they crossed through the tunnel under the river. Simon felt weird having thousands of tons of water above him, and even weirder entering a country whose language he didn't speak, but the customs official only asked whether they'd been born in Canada. Then he gave Gilles, whose English was fair, directions to the arena located close by.

In their seats high up under the roof on the side of the Red Wings' goal, they found themselves surrounded by noisy, beer-drinking fans. Gilles and Simon, too, bought one Schlitz after another like the half dozen rough characters behind them who pushed their boots with shiny metal cleats on the pointed toes against the back of the seats. Like them, Gilles pulled a pint from his pocket, sipping Scotch between rounds, offering Simon his share.

Halfway through the second period the bottle was empty, but Gilles produced another. When Maurice Richard, the star of the Canadiens hockey fans called

The Rocket, broke through the Red Wings' defense, knocking a player to the ice and scoring the second goal for the team, the men behind them started cursing.

Simon didn't understand all the cuss words, but he certainly knew the meaning of the word frog. He had never minded much being called a frog, and still didn't. "When you fall in love with a Frenchman and kiss him," Uncle Baptiste had told him once with a wink and a grin, "even if he's as ugly as a frog, he'll turn into a prince."

Gilles, however, was insulted. He rose and whipped around, making an obscene gesture with his finger, yelling, "You motherfuckers, you meet us outside after the game. We'll show you who's a frog!"

Gilles Pétard's thinning, blond hair that he wore long, like some artist, gave him an effeminate look. That he wasn't effeminate you could tell by his mean gray eyes, even when he was sober. Once he had lifted the rear end of a Ford coupe away from the curb to get out of a parking space. But with a wife who was expecting her fifth child, he had no business challenging a bunch of tough hombres to a fight in a foreign country.

Either Gilles's speech had impressed them, or the fellows bided their time. They remained quiet until the Canadiens' next goal, when Gilles faced them again, pointing the middle fingers, cackling, "Up yours! Up yours! Up yours!"

"You're a fucking frog yourself, ain't you?" the big fellow behind Gilles said, and punched him in the mouth.

Gilles rocked against Simon, then hit back. Simon

stood up, trying to make peace, and promptly stopped a fist with his nose. Cursing in French, he retaliated, not doing much damage, being too full of beer and whisky. From nowhere uniformed guards appeared and threatened to clear the seats.

Wiping the blood off his face, Simon wanted to leave, but Gilles had other ideas. "The salauds insulted Quebec," he said. "They'll pay. We can take them. They're wearing boots. Who can fight in boots? You're not chicken, are you?"

Simon shook his head, trying to stop his nosebleed. He'd seen loggers fight in boots. They hadn't moved as quickly as men in rubber soles, but he'd watched a well-aimed kick break bone.

"Just cover my back," Gilles said, disgusted by his buddy's reluctance.

After the Canadiens' victory, the men with the boots remained quiet, but Gilles rose and spit at their feet, pushing out his chest and wagging his ass. Then he roared with his obnoxious laughter. "The frogs beat the shit out of the fat-assed Yankees! Eh! Eh! Eh!"

An absurd statement. The Red Wings players were Canadians, too, several of them French. Prancing like a drunken ballerina through the fast emptying seats, Gilles stared out to the empty rink, contemplating the cut-up ice. When he started shouting again, Simon was glad it was in French. "Who are the frogs now? Eh? Who are the frogs?"

Gilles lit a cigarette, holding it in one hand, and put

the other around Simon's shoulder for balance. The way out through the tunnel was by now empty of people, except for the echo of footsteps behind them that might have been their own. Passing a men's room, they pushed through the door. If they hadn't pissed with such exuberance, and if Simon hadn't had to spread his legs for balance, if he had stood straight like Gilles, holding on to the top of the urinal with both hands, croaking, "Look, no hands!" the attackers might have missed his testicles with the first kick, and he would have been able to fight back and escape, as Gilles did. But they didn't miss.

They kicked, and kicked. Simon doubled over, and his head hit the floor. Then they grabbed his upper arms and his pants, yelling, "That's how we kill a frog," and swung him headfirst into the urinal wall.

~~~~~

Simon's last thought before falling asleep was of Mark. He was sorry he hadn't given him a hug. In the morning, he would.

CHAPTER 26

Buried in a beanbag in the sunroom on an overcast afternoon, Simon wrote a comment in the margin of a paper on Molière's *L'École des femmes*. He'd always liked Molière's comedy about an old fart that made an ass of himself by falling for a young chick. The play had bite, so much so the French audience in 1662 had thought it wasn't funny but scandalous. Now it had lost some of its humor for him, too. He was tempted to identify with its hero, Arnolphe, who, afraid of mature women, was looking for solace in the arms of an innocent girl. Like Arnolphe he'd be ridiculed. Was being ridiculed already.

The reading of the papers went slow. Soon he wrote fewer comments, but perhaps kinder ones, feeling more empathy with the bourgeois pedant in the play and having more understanding for the students whose world was light years away from 17th century Paris. Like the world of Sybil, who ate at McDonald's and liked "concerts," and she didn't mean by the Memphis Symphony.

Carolyn approached, looking over her father's shoulder. "What does *L'École des femmes* mean, Daddy? School for women?"

"School for wives."

"Are you going to marry Sybil?"

"What gave you that idea?"

"She's so beautiful."

"Beautiful is as beautiful does. That's what Sister Benedicta told us in school."

"It would also be kind o' neat to have a black stepmother."

"Why do you think so?"

"I just do."

In many ways, Carolyn was most like himself. With good instincts. And Simon had to agree that Sybil would indeed make an interesting stepmother. "Even if I wanted to, I don't think Sybil has marriage in mind. Marriage is hard to cope with, even between two people who have everything going for them, like a similar age, religion, politics, social background, and definitely the same race."

On the other hand, it might not change his life much at all. As long as he stayed in midtown Memphis, anyway.

"Far too early to think about marriage, sweet pie." He laughed. "I haven't even kissed the woman yet."

"Oh? Is that important?"

"Sometimes, sometimes not." Considering any kind of permanent relationship at this time would be absurd. They first had to dump the garbage between them. Mainly his garbage!

Carolyn disappeared upstairs to play with her girlfriend, and Simon wrote a C+ at the bottom of the last page of the paper. Underneath, he added in French, "Before stating the absurdity of his characters when presented to audiences in the late twentieth century, you should have discussed Molière's humor within the framework of the mores in mid-seventeenth century Paris."

Actually, C+ was too good for this paper. C would have been more appropriate. But the way his colleagues inflated their students' grades, he couldn't afford to give C's anymore, or the French department would lose even more students to Spanish.

Digging deeper into the beanbag, he tossed the paper on top of the others on the floor and switched on the TV, hoping to catch the weather forecast in one of the news programs. Channel 13 advertised Monday Night Football. He would probably watch the game while correcting the quizzes.

"What do you see in this game?" Ellen asked him the very first time he'd watched football on TV back in Ottawa, the Hamilton Tigercats playing the Montreal Alouettes. "I'd rate football somewhere between hockey and wrestling."

"I like the way these guys hit. I couldn't take it."

The clash with the urinal wall had proven that. If it wasn't the most painful hit he ever took, it was certainly the most effective. Although he'd been concussed in Chicoutimi, and been knocked out on the road to Trois Rivières, it had happened at home in Quebec, not in a pisshole in a country whose language he didn't speak.

When he came to in that washroom, he knew he'd been out for some time. The air felt a lot colder than when he'd gone in. At first he couldn't remember what had happened. He thought he was in his bed, about to hear the alarm go off. Gradually the pain between his legs grew stronger, surpassing the hurt in his face, nearly matching the throbbing in his head. He was shivering, smelling piss and beer and vomit, hoping it was a dream. Then he passed out again and came to with the back of his head in the hole, his eyes open, but seeing nothing but darkness. He sat up and climbed to his feet, holding on to the top of the slippery urinal. He peed, shivering with cold, then zipped up his fly, grunting. Slowly he moved away from the urinals toward the sidewall. Overcome by dizziness, he lowered himself to the floor and sat, leaning his back against the wall, wishing he were lying on the tracks in Quebec, with a train roaring toward him, and a Mountie pulling him off at the last second. The memory almost made him smile.

His blindness, Simon suspected, was due to another concussion, just a temporary nuisance. He called out Gilles's name. No answer, just a hollow echo. Chances were that his buddy had gotten away. From the breast pocket of his shirt he pulled the pack of Lucky Strikes he had bought at a concession stand in the arena, stuck a cigarette in his mouth, then searched for the lighter in his pockets, all of which were empty. They had taken everything except the half-empty pack of cigarettes and Sister's rosary that was still hanging around his neck.

Leaving the smoke between his lips, he closed the zipper of his parka, and he stretched out. And despite the throbbing in his head and the agony between his legs he fell asleep.

Voices from outside woke him. The door was pushed open with what sounded like a bucket on rollers. A mop sloshed water on the floor, and someone was humming, pushing the mop, then squeezing it in the bucket. That's how he had cleaned the concrete floors in the mill when he started there. The same squishing noise, the same ammoniac smell. He thought it was Hébert, the other, somewhat older sweeper. "Hébert," he managed to utter with a croaking voice, wondering why the guy was mopping in the dark. "Hébert," he called out once more, and the squishing stopped.

The person who came around the wall with deliberate steps and stood next to him wasn't Hébert, a quick and agile fellow.

"Jesus Almighty," a woman exclaimed, lowering herself next to him. He smelled her perfume, flavored with the scent of ammonia. "You been shot, chile?" she asked, carefully undoing the zipper of his parka. "You covered with blood!"

"You speak French?" Simon asked.

"French?" the woman said. Quickly she rose and left.

He tried to get up, but moving his legs sent worse pains through his groin, so he decided to stay put. Even if he managed to stand up again, he wouldn't be able to find his way out of the place. He was relieved that the woman returned, now accompanied by a female with a lighter gait.

"Sacré bleu!" she said and continued in French with a coloration close to Canadien but not quite. She opened his shirt, wiping his chest. "No gunshot wound that I can see. You broke your nose! That's where all the blood is from."

"I'm glad. I thought it was piss."

"What's the matter with your eyes? Can't you see?"

"I think I have a concussion. I've had it before."

The two women talked in English, then grabbed him under the arms, lifting him. Groaning from the excruciating pain in his testicles, he spread his legs and they guided him to the sink.

"What's the matter with your legs?" the woman asked.

"They kicked me in the groin."

"First we'll clean your face, then we'll examine your balls," she said, chuckling.

At the sink he held on with both hands while the women washed his face and his neck, barely touching his swollen nose. They lifted his cigarettes out of his shirt pocket and mopped his blue flannel shirt with a wet cloth, then stuck the Lucky Strikes back in.

"We should call an ambulance," the French woman said.

"They took my wallet. I can't pay for an ambulance."

"What's your name?"

"Simon," he said, pronouncing it in French.

"I'm Thérèse. This is Mahalia. What if you don't regain your sight? What are we to do with you then?"

He liked Thérèse's throaty, no-nonsense voice. Her hands. The smell of her. "Let me rest in some corner," he said. "Couldn't you? If my partner's all right, he'll come back for me."

Again they debated. Then each held one of his arms and led him slowly along a corridor while he told them what happened, explaining he was French Canadian.

"Of course you're Canadien. I'm Cajun. We're cousins."

Walking with her, he suppressed crying out and barely grunted despite the pain. In the janitor's room they helped him get settled in a chair with his feet up on a box.

"Now," Thérèse said, "will you let me check your equipment?"

Simon blushed. "I'll do it myself," he muttered, but she was already opening his belt, and, unzipping his fly, carefully pulled down his shorts. "Mon Dieu," she said. "No wonder you can't walk. "Your balls are swelled up to horse size. Your cock is bruised, too. You'll have to be a good boy for a couple of days."

Then the big woman talked, and the Cajun translated. "Not to worry about your testicles, Mahalia says. She'll fix them." Humming, Mahalia broke cubes out of a metal tray onto the table, wrapped them in cloth, and laid them in his lap.

"Hold this package with both hands, and don't take

it off, even when it hurts," Thérèse ordered. "Mahalia and I have to go back to work. We'll return at eleven for lunch." Covering him with a blanket, she added, "That's my scarf the ice is in. Don't mess it!"

Gilles didn't show, unless he sneaked through the arena into the washroom without any of the cleaning crew spotting him, which was unlikely. Gilles Pétard didn't sneak. He announced his presence with bells on. Simon felt his concern for the fate of his compatriot fading. Gilles could take care of himself. It was his own predicament he needed to worry about. If his sight didn't return before the cleanup crew quit, he'd be in a pickle. Unless they'd let him stay in the arena overnight.

During lunch, the room filled with women. Thérèse asked him how he was, wrapped fresh ice in her scarf, and gave him a baloney sandwich and a cup of coffee from a thermos. The women chatted and laughed, probably joking about his swollen genitals, then left again.

Quitting time came, but not Gilles. Simon asked Thérèse to let him spend the night where he was. He knew he'd be able to see again before morning, and he'd leave quietly. Through a window, if they locked the doors. As the crew manager, she said, she couldn't let him do that. It would mean putting the cleaning contract at risk. If she didn't have a jealous boyfriend, she added, she'd let him stay at her place until he regained his sight. Simon argued that her boyfriend couldn't do anymore harm than the fans had already done, but the Cajun woman said he'd be surprised at the pain that man could cause. Mahalia would give Simon a bed for the night, and she herself would check on him after church in the morning.

Everything about the woman who took him home was strong: her arms, her voice, her language, an English quite different from that of the Americans he'd fished with, or the thugs who beat him. He hardly understood a word she said, and she didn't pay any attention to what he attempted to say. When the city bus stopped and the door flung open, she practically lifted him up the steps, then grabbed him around the waist, dragging him along. He winced every time his hip bumped a seat, some of which he could tell were empty. He tried to slow her, but she forged her way toward the rear.

Walking along the sidewalk to her home, Simon heard what sounded like dozens of children running, shouting, playing. He held on to the woman's arm, and she chuckled with her deep voice, shooing away the kids that surrounded them, asking questions and giggling.

Mahalia made him lie down on a Naugahyde couch and brought an ice pack wrapped in a towel. Simon opened his fly and laid it on his still tormented testicles. Soon the sounds of a radio entered the room, along with the smell of fried onions.

He was a sucker for punishment. On the road to Trois Rivières it had been his self-assurance, if not his arrogance, that caused the disaster at the hobo camp. Now it had been his drinking that made the beating possible. His pain was due to his own stupidity.

On the street, where the children were still playing with gusto, a car braked, the engine shut off, and a door slammed. Simon hoped whoever it was who entered the house wouldn't see him. The person shut the door as vigorously as he had the car and stopped in the middle of the room. In a resonant tenor, he shouted, "Who the hell are you?"

"My name is See-mon Philipe," Simon said, trying to cover his open fly, forgetting to give his name the English pronunciation.

Without an answer the man disappeared into the kitchen where a discussion ensued, the man doing most of the talking, the woman speaking only at intervals, but in a firm, calm manner. Later, Mahalia showed up and helped him off the couch. She led him to the bathroom, talking all the while. Standing at the commode, Simon asked her to leave, accompanying his words with gestures, and she did. When he came out, she led him to the kitchen where he sat down at the table, eating greens and cornbread and beans, all hotter than he'd ever tasted before.

For the night she gave him a pillow and covered him with a blanket, and despite the pain he had no trouble falling asleep. When he woke up, the icepack on his crotch had thawed, but the swelling had gone down, and he seemed to be able to distinguish shades of dark. In the bathroom he switched on the light. His image in the mirror was blurred, but he had regained his sight.

Thérèse, who showed up early, was as attractive as he

had imagined her to be, brown-haired and busty and bursting with energy. She smiled with relief when she realized he could see. Presently, Mahalia appeared in a scarlet robe with blotches of white magnolias, her skin as dark as the earth in Paradise.

Noticing that he could see, she flashed a broad smile.

A negress? Tall, broad in the hips, her lips generous, her eyes gentle. Maybe forty, maybe older. A magnificent female. No wonder her husband hadn't been happy to find a stranger on his couch. The two women talked, Mahalia mixing pancake batter at the table, and Thérèse frying bacon and eggs on the gas stove. By and by she told him not to worry about Mahalia's husband. He was just a little jealous. She laughed, adding that she didn't blame him for resenting a young stud in his house. But now that Mahalia had told him Simon would pay for room and board as soon he found his buddy, her husband had reluctantly consented.

Mahalia was clearing the breakfast dishes off the table when her husband entered the kitchen. He was shorter and thinner than his wife and looked older, but sinewy, with short, graying hair. The accusing look in his eyes reminded Simon of one of his fathers, who had hit his wife. The Cajun woman introduced him as Joshua Porter, but the man ignored Simon's hand, pulled a beer from the fridge and sat down at the table. Drinking from the bottle, he glared at him. Mahalia got busy at the stove, moving the bacon to the edge of the frying pan and pouring dough into the still simmering fat for more pancakes. Speaking French, Simon thanked the man for his hospitality. Noting the dour expression, he thanked him in English. Then he left with Thérèse to go in search of Gilles's van.

Even though it was Sunday, children dotted the street again, playing stickball, jumping rope, the bigger fellows tossing basketballs. They were colored all shades of brown, from high yellow to Mahalia's earthy black. Simon remarked to Thérèse that some of these children looked white.

"They may look white," she responded, "but they're not. They have their own vocabulary. Not unlike the Cajuns."

"Is that why you feel close to them?"

"I'm not close to them!" she protested, explaining that she tolerated colored folks because they worked for her, and she'd only come to Mahalia's house for his sake. No way was she close to her, though Mahalia was a good woman. Except for beating his wife when he was drunk, Joshua was a good man, too, as far as colored men went, or he wouldn't work at the Cadillac plant. A Negro had to practically speak white to get a union job.

Simon was hardly aware of any discomfort sitting next to Thérèse, who steered her Pontiac expertly. As they passed the Cadillac plant she'd just mentioned, he found himself wishing he could work on an assembly line, doing something significant, like lowering the engine into its compartment and connecting the driveshaft to the transmission and to the differential in the rear. Then, instead of keeping an eye out for the van, he looked at the Cajun.

"You must have gone to church early this morning."

She shook her head. "I skipped church."

Not everybody would have called Thérèse beautiful. She was probably pushing thirty. The boss of a clean-up crew, she was a woman without make-up or lipstick and with a worker's strong hands, but with eyes that assessed the world with humor and lips you would kill for. Lips, you knew, that would kiss you back.

"Are you sure," she asked, "you parked on Shelby Street?"

"Off Shelby, but we could see the arena from where we parked."

"From Shelby Street you could," she agreed.

But the van wasn't anywhere near Shelby Street or any place from where they could see the arena. Simon knew it was gone, long before Thérèse finally gave up. Driven, not towed. It would not have been in anybody's way on a Saturday night. Certainly not on Sunday morning. They hadn't parked in a loading zone or by a hydrant.

"What's that?" the woman asked, stopping the car and pointing at a dark bundle partly hidden by the weeds along a fire wall.

His backpack!

Now it was clear that Gilles had headed back to Canada. He'd obviously not wanted to explain Simon's property in his van. The discovery of the backpack eased his concern about Gilles, yet it angered him that the man had left him stranded. On the other hand, if Simon wanted to return to Quebec, he was old enough to find his own way. At this moment, he had no desire to report to the loading dock. In an odd way, Gilles's desertion gave him a sense of relief.

"Gilles is gone," he said.

"Your friend deserted you. Good riddance, I'd say. What will you do now?"

"Get a job."

"What can you do?"

"Trap and hunt."

Thérèse laughed. "They may need a dog catcher. We have enough strays in this town. What else can you do?"

"Fish."

"You're a regular Davy Crockett!"

"Just kidding. I last worked in a pulp mill. On the loading dock."

"If we have a pulp mill in Detroit, that would be a union job. My boyfriend is a union boss. I'll find out."

"Until I'm better, couldn't I join your crew? I can handle a broom. My first job in the mill was sweeping concrete floors."

She glanced at his crotch. "Don't you still hurt? Give it another day or two. Mahalia's happy to have you in the house."

"Did she tell you that?"

"She wants me to bring you back."

Simon didn't trust Joshua. The man was mean. Landing with a black couple in a ghetto was shocking enough. He didn't want to get caught up in a family squabble.

"Couldn't you let me sleep on the floor at your place? I don't believe the story about your boyfriend."

"You better believe it. My crazy Italian is liable to shoot you."

He thought of the shotgun hanging in Mahalia's hallway. "So is her husband," he said.

"You can't blame Joshua for resenting you. You're white. As soon as you've learned some English, you can get a job. Anywhere. Meanwhile, day after tomorrow you can join my cleaning crew. You won't need any language skills to pick up trash."

Thérèse parked the car south of the arena facing the river. Pointing to the left, she said, "A couple of miles from here there's an island in the river called Belle Isle. Farther north, when you get into Lake St. Clair just west of the Chrysler plant, there's Grosse Pointe Park. And on the Canadian side, a smaller island is called Peche Isle. I welcomed these French names when I arrived in the city."

A hundred years ago those names had meaning. Today, they were just names, butchered by the English tongue. He didn't need them. He needed the Cajun woman. The palms of her hands that now held his were calloused, like his own. They matched her face, lined about the mouth, wrinkled at the eyes.

"Are we kissing cousins?" he asked, pushing a hand into the woman's hair.

She laughed deep in her throat. Then she reached for his neck and kissed him tenderly, as if afraid of hurting or arousing him, both of which of course she did.

"Welcome to the United States, *mon cousin*."

CHAPTER 27

With the French papers corrected and neatly stacked on the floor beside the beanbag, Simon felt fair about his students' work. A couple of the papers earned an excellent, and two or three were solid B's. He also felt better about the age difference between himself and Sybil. To be frank, he resembled old Arnolphe neither in looks nor character, nor in any other aspect he could think of. The most conspicuous difference lay in the lack of wealth, usually a primary condition for a May-September romance. With child support and the maintenance of his horses, Simon scraped by with little or nothing to spare. He had health insurance, though, some freedom in scheduling classes, and the option to ride in the afternoon and work at night. That meant a mint to Simon but hardly much to Sybil for whom the daytime working hours were routine.

Simon's concern about looking old enough to embarrass a young woman like Sybil were valid only when he needed sleep. Rested, he moved with the vigor of an athlete in his twenties, with energy equal, he was convinced, to anyone's. In fact, with a rascal's glint in his eyes paired with Sybil's steady glance, they were perceived as just another couple, the age difference and, he thought, even the color, a non-issue. Indeed, in some ways, Sybil was the more mature. Like Mark, she knew who she was, and what she wanted.

That's the way Thérèse had been, too. Maybe that's why he'd been drawn to her. The Cajun ran her crew with an authority that didn't offend, that Simon welcomed when he was well enough to join her crew, scrubbing a union hall near the Chrysler plant. He worked every day that week, learning English, flirting with the handsome woman during breaks, falling in love. And although Thérèse pretended to be amused by Simon's attention, in his heart he knew that she liked him, too, was more than fond of him already. Optimist that he was, he expected the proud Cajun, though nearly twice his age, to fall hopelessly in love with him. It certainly never occurred to him, as it seems to have now, that love acknowledged age restrictions.

For starters, Thérèse played it cool, pretending, Simon thought, that Mahalia's attention to him amused her, the way it amused their co-workers. The only person not amused was Joshua, who was determined to get Simon out of his home and away from the reach of his wife. And Simon couldn't blame the man. Mahalia was practically floating through the house, humming spirituals.

"You watch it," Thérèse warned Simon when they got paid Friday night. "I've never seen that nigger so happy. When Josh goes on night shift next week, she'll jump into your bed.".

Simon laughed. "I hope not. I don't think the frame could stand two people's weight."

Thérèse sashayed away, humming a song, then turned about, raising her head, bending forward, giving prominence to her lovely breasts. "You wanna bet?"

Bet, he wouldn't, although he felt quite invincible with twenty-seven dollars and seventy-five cents in his pocket. "If there is any bed-jumping," he blurted out, blushing despite his efforts not to, "I'll do the jumping, and I'll do it into your bed."

"You wish!" she said, but then the light left her eyes and she quickly got into her car, followed by Mahalia. Simon, sitting in the back, thinking he had gone too far with his impertinent declaration, listened to the two women talk about shopping, understanding little of what they said, yet a whole lot more than he had only a week before.

At seventeen, he reflected, he should be in high school in Chicoutimi instead of in this giant city called Detroit. He should have a crush on a pretty girl, necking after a school dance, or even doing the ultimate, like Guillaume who boasted about it. But it hadn't happened, not even with plenty of chances when he worked at the mill in Trois Rivières. Sister's influence? Fear of repeating history, namely his own? Strange. Thérèse was the first woman with whom he wouldn't have any scruples.

Stepping out of the Pontiac in front of Mahalia's house, he tried to catch the Cajun's eye, but she didn't look at him, just waited till the two doors slammed shut, then gunned the engine, roaring off down the street, honking at the kids who ran screaming out of her way.

Mahalia shook her head laughing, unlocked the front door and headed straight for the bathroom. Simon heard the bath water running. When she appeared in the kitchen, she was wearing her scarlet robe. She cooked in it and ate in it, showing a splash of bust, a flash of thigh, always quickly covering it again. Simon grew increasingly uncomfortable, wishing Joshua were coming home for supper.

With no experience of sex, without even having seen an adult woman naked except in medieval paintings in one of Sister's art books, Simon couldn't be sure what those signals meant, or if they were signals at all. Nevertheless, he felt Mahalia was teasing him, or making advances, and he didn't know how to react. She was married with three grown children, was more than twice his age, half again his weight, and truly as black as the earth in Paradise. Her color bothered him least. Her blackness intrigued him. What bothered him, he thought, was the fact that she was married. But he wasn't so sure about that either. It wasn't much of a marriage. Not anymore, anyway. Maybe what bothered him most was Thérèse. The woman he daydreamed about. The woman he loved. With Thérèse his ignorance about sex wouldn't matter. He would trust her with his life, not just with his inexperience.

But watching the movements of Mahalia's body under

the gown as she stood at the sink washing the dinner dishes, he was so aroused he didn't dare get up. With both hands he grabbed the bottle of the Schlitz beer he was nursing and sat as if glued to the chair, and she didn't toss him the dish towel as she normally would but started drying, putting the cutlery in the drawer, glasses and china in the cupboard.

"Coffee?" she asked, placing the percolator on the gas without waiting for the boy's answer, then sat down at the table opposite him. "Too bad you don't understand me," she said, which Simon understood. After a full week in the U.S., he got more or less the drift of a query, or an order, and most statements that had to do with everyday tasks.

When the coffee perked, Mahalia poured it, adding cream and two spoonfuls of sugar. Sipping the sweet brew, Simon was tempted to ask her for a cigarette.

"You look tired," Mahalia said in her hoarse voice. "Why don't you go to bed, chile?"

Simon nodded and rose, turning quickly, dropping the empty bottle into the garbage can but leaving his nearly full cup on the table. "Good night, Mahalia."

"Good night, hon."

He brushed his teeth and crawled into bed, relieved yet disappointed, leafing aimlessly through a magazine he had taken from the bookshelf. Tired after all from the long day's work, he turned off the light. Thinking of Mahalia, then again of Thérèse, imagining the thrills of having her climb into bed with him, he drifted off to sleep. In his dream, the hall light was blocked by a dark figure, as beautiful and ominous as a thunderhead pierced around the edges by the sun.

"Move over, honey chile," the apparition ordered, shutting the door behind her. She chuckled deep in her throat, much as she had when he'd regained his sight. Standing beside his bed in the dim glow from the street lamp out front, she looked neither fat nor muscular, just tall and wide and firm, nor did the bed collapse when she lay down in it as he'd predicted to Thérèse. Moving against the wall, Simon tried to make himself thin to avoid touching the woman who started stroking him, unhurriedly, with lips and fingers, mumbling darkly, like distant thunder. And he let her grasp him, pulling him on top. Shy, almost stunned at first, his instinct took over, and soon he responded with abandon.

A couple of hours later, when Joshua came home, first slamming the front door, then the door of the ice box, probably reaching for a beer, Mahalia put a finger on his lips. Sliding to the carpet, she stood very still, ear toward the door, leaving Simon, whose body was still quivering, to wonder whom the betrayed husband would shoot first, him or his wife. But the noises in the kitchen stopped, and the man didn't appear at the door with his shotgun. Instead, he switched on the radio, listening to the play by play of a hockey game. Mahalia came back to the bed, whispering, "Sorry, chile," laid a hand over his mouth, bent over his groin, and finished in her throat what she'd begun kneeling over him.

When she left, closing the door quietly, Simon expected an explosion in the living room, but all he heard was the flushing of the toilet in the hall. Someone, most likely Mahalia, turned off the radio, and the house became still. Joshua must have passed out on the couch. Simon got out of bed, locked the door, and put the back of his chair diagonally under the knob.

He stared at the ceiling. Now he'd had sex. Not just with anyone, but with the woman who'd taken him in. He'd dishonored the man who'd offered him hospitality. Dishonored himself by not waiting for Thérèse.

Yet he'd enjoyed it. Thrilled to it! And even with his body drained, feeling strangely empty, he wanted more. The great woman could hardly have liked it as much. Zeus himself would have to mate with her, in the guise of a stallion perhaps. Sister was right. Sex was God's wonderful gift.

In the bathroom he washed, then put on his clothes, collecting his thoughts. The clock in the kitchen showed a few minutes past midnight. Although there were still nearly a couple of weeks left in March, he tore the month off the calendar, a scantily dressed woman with a leering grin leaning against the front fender of a Cadillac. He folded a ten dollar bill inside it, wrote "for rent" on the outside, and laid it on the table, weighing it down with the saltshaker. The money might delay an outburst of Joshua's fury for a few days.

From the kitchen, he stepped into the living room. Joshua was lying fully dressed on the couch, one arm folded over his neck, the other dangling to the floor, mouth open, snoring. Simon picked the blanket off the floor Mahalia must have covered her husband with, and spread it over the sleeping man. A few steps away, the open door of the main bedroom beckoned to him. He stared at it, then went to the hallway, took the double-barreled shotgun off the wall, broke it open, dropping out the shells, and hung it up again. In the kitchen, he opened the far cabinet, reached behind the stack of good plates, and, lifting a box of twelve gauge shells over the dishes, slid the two loose shells in it and dropped the box into the garbage can.

Outside the front door, he hesitated. It looked as if it was going to rain. Gusts of wind rolled trash along the curb, bits of paper, gum wrappers; empty cigarette packs tumbled in the breeze. Now he was on a doorstep again, after another birth of sorts, setting out for God knows where. Collar up and hands in his pockets, he strode along the familiar street, fighting the wind to First and Michigan, where he just missed a bus going east. Without blinking, he turned west, walking briskly, empowered by the knowledge of woman's power over man.

~~~~~

The room was getting dark. Then lightning lit it briefly, and an explosion of thunder announced an approaching storm. In a few minutes, Sybil would arrive, expecting to go to the barn for a riding lesson.

Mahalia. Now Sybil. Both black, yet as different as night and day. And yet, he'd come full circle. Or he would. Maybe.

CHAPTER 28

When the doorbell and the phone rang at the same time, Simon first let Sybil in, planting a kiss on her cheek, then ambled to the kitchen.

"You took your sweet time," Ellen said angrily. "Aren't the children there to answer the phone?"

When spoken to in that manner, it took some restraint not to say Screw you! and hang up. "Stefan's at the Pic Pac, sacking. Carolyn and Carrie are biking in the park."

"By themselves?"

"Together. They'll be back for dinner, before I pick up Stefan to go to the horses."

"Do you ever consider spending some special time with your other children?"

That was a sensible question. One that had often bothered him and still did. "Is that what you're calling about?"

"No. Mother just called. She wanted to make sure I had the leather chair and the footstool Daddy sent from Ottawa."

Simon paused. Trevor, as he called her father, had

222

sent that chair, along with the footstool, to Simon after the Joneses had sold the house in the Ottawa suburb of Rockcliffe and moved to a condo near the canal. The gray leather chair, scratched by the cat and dried out and cracked from old age, didn't look as inconspicuous in the condo as it had in the ambassador's large study, and her mother had wanted to be rid of it. Simon had grown fond of the two pieces.

"This is a joke?"

"Mother insists the two pieces remain in the family."

"Trevor wanted me to have them. You know he did."

"Why don't you let her have whatever it is she wants?" Sybil whispered, grabbing his upper arm with both hands and touching his ear with her lips.

Covering the phone with his palm, Simon looked at her. She was right. Stuff wasn't important. To Ellen he said, "If it's not going to rain, I'll deliver the chair and the stool to the house on the way to the barn. Otherwise you'll get them tomorrow."

He hung up. Sybil looked at him with questioning eyes. Simon explained about his former mother-in-law's wish.

"Her mom must have liked you a lot, or she wouldn't feel so much resentment," Sybil said. "Makes you wonder about Ellen, though. What did you do to her?"

"Do to her?" He paused, thinking about it. "I guess I got my way for the fifteen years we were married. We always did what I wanted, even when she had her heart set on something. Then, adding insult to injury, I got her pregnant three times."

"That was bad, unless she was the one who wanted the children."

"She said she did. I never asked her why. I think to please me, because she thought I wanted them. Which I did. A generation or two ago, French Canadian wives had housefuls of children. A kid a year. Like brood mares. The monk who married us was the youngest of twenty-four. All from the same mother. Women thought they lived fulfilling lives. Motherhood. Submission to God's will."

"That's more like abuse."

"In my case it wasn't. A year and a half after Mark's birth, Ellen said, 'It's time we had another child, don't you think?' And I, figuring we'd manage to provide for one more, said, 'Okay,' and our life continued as usual, except that Ellen stopped taking the pill, and a month later she said, 'You've done it again,' and I said, 'Let's hope it's a girl.' So Stefan was born, and we still managed financially, even though I was in graduate school.

"After Carolyn's birth, Stefan became the middle child. Ellen had read in some childrearing book that the middle child was destined to grow up miserable, so she wanted a fourth, preferably a girl. And I agreed. What the hell. The more the merrier."

"But there was no fourth child?"

"No."

It still saddened Simon that Ellen lost the fourth child in a miscarriage and decided not to have any more babies. Simon suggested he have a vasectomy, but, to his great relief, Ellen nixed that. Come to think of it, Simon thought, there was little he didn't agree with. It was rare, in fact, when they had to talk something out. They agreed with each other's thoughts before they even put them into words. Like a couple with one head and two bodies. And no arguments in bed either.

Without any warning, heavy raindrops pelted the kitchen window. Obviously, Sybil wouldn't want to ride in a cold downpour, nor would he want his Stübben saddle to get drenched. On the other hand, the rain came as a welcome change. The grass needed the water, and now that he was no longer looking for Jesse's tracks, Simon was quite pleased. He'd go feed the horses after dinner.

So noisy was the storm, Simon couldn't hear the kettle whistle. Sybil poured it over the teabag in her cup, adding a spoonful of honey. Simon nodded toward the window, "No riding lesson today."

"That's okay. I love a good storm." Picking up the cup, she preceded him to the den, lowering herself gracefully into a beanbag, crossing her legs. She smiled up at Simon, who for a moment was tempted to sit down next to her on the same cushion but stretched out on the one facing hers.

Sybil sipped her hot tea. Simon said nothing, listening to the rain, hoping that Carrie and Carolyn had been smart enough to find shelter at the Brooks Museum or the College of Art rather than under a big oak tree.

Setting the cup on the floor, Sybil said, "Since you

can't give me a lesson at the barn, how about teaching me some equine theory?"

"That would be Stefan's thing. He's the pony clubber and knows everything there is to know about horses."

"Well, how about telling me how the obsession took hold of you."

"Obsession? You think so?" Simon paused. "I admit, I always liked horses, as far back as I remember. The milkman's mare in Chicoutimi, the Percherons at the logging camps, cow ponies in the movies, most of all the photo of Sister Elisabeth as a young girl on her thoroughbred. That picture inspired me more than anything. But riding was always something I would do in the future."

"So how did you get hooked?"

Either the intensity of the rain had lessened or the den was more soundproof than the kitchen because they talked without raising their voices, and Simon enjoyed it. "When I was seventeen, I thumbed my way from Detroit aiming west." He shuddered. "The first two days it rained just like it's doing now. I got drenched to the skin, and I walked a lot. I walked through Chicago. It took me a whole day."

"Wow. I don't think that'd be safe today. Not even for a black person. Certainly not for a woman. But never mind, what were you doing in Detroit?"

Losing my virginity to a black woman, Simon was tempted to say. Instead he said, "Passing through. Two or three days after leaving Chicago I arrived in Sioux City, Iowa, and from there I got a ride to the Black Hills.

In a place called Custer I spent my last nickel for a cup of coffee."

Sybil laughed.

"It's funny now," Simon said, joining her laughter, "but it wasn't funny at the time."

The waitress at the café spoke some French. She mentioned the big money a man could make in Alberta's oil fields. Calgary, she said, was only seven hundred miles away, and spring was the best time to be hired. It was March, but it was snowing and cold, colder than any March Simon had experienced in Canada. Late morning, finally, an Indian family offered him a lift on the back of a pickup truck, an old Ford like his Uncle Baptiste used to drive. The others sat in the cab, five of them, piled on top of each other, and drove about ten miles into Wyoming, not on a big highway but a narrow road. Then they dropped him off and turned south on an even smaller track.

To keep warm, he walked. It started to snow harder, and the wind blew colder. It seemed he walked for hours. The powdery snow kept falling, the wind blowing. You couldn't tell where the side of the road ended and the grassland began, except for a barbed wire fence, and that was white, too. The whole world was white, and the world seemed immense.

The third or fourth time he hunkered down to rest, his back against the wind out of the northwest, he closed his eyes. Closing his eyes felt good. Not having slept much since he'd left Detroit, a nap would do wonders.

But he knew he couldn't keep his eyes closed, or he'd share Uncle Baptiste's fate.

Forcing his eyes open, he spotted a dark figure with a wide-brimmed hat riding toward him along the inside of the fence. The man was looking down, with his collar up and the rim of his Stetson shading his eyes. Simon watched him from a long way off and never saw the cowboy raise his head, but when he came within a few feet of him, he halted his horse and looked up. The lips under his mustache were blue from the cold. Bending to rest his elbows on the horse's neck, he said, "What the hell you doing on this godforsaken track?"

"I hitchhike to Calgary," he uttered, barely able to produce a sound, and got to his feet.

"Not on this road you won't. You'll sit here till hell freezes over."

If he had understood, he would have tried to laugh because that was happening already.

The rider pulled a metal flask from his sheepskin coat, unscrewed the cap, and said, "Warm your gut?"

Simon slid down the incline to the fence, unable to stop himself, hitting the wire just inches away from the horse that didn't even budge, but just slightly turned its head, looking at him. The cowboy handed him the flask, and he swallowed a mouthful. It was bourbon, and it made him cough. The man screwed the cap on and stuck the flask in his coat.

"Don't fall asleep," he said, "or you'll never wake up. You want to stay alive, keep walking."

Simon nodded, watching the rider move on. After about twenty strides the cowboy stopped his mount and waved to him, pointing at his horse's rump. Simon trudged through the drift and climbed between the wires, tearing his parka. The cowboy took his left boot out of the stirrup and held out his gloved hand. Simon grabbed it, put his foot in the stirrup, and the man swung him up.

Sitting on the bay gelding's back, practically on its rump, Simon held on to the cantle of a roping saddle while continually moving his icy fingers and toes to keep them from freezing. He wished he'd stayed on the road, walking. Later he found out it was twenty-some miles to the next settlement, a place called Wright, off on another road he would never have noticed, not even without the snow coming down. If the cowboy hadn't shown, it would have been a bad night.

Once in a while the man would halt to look at a crooked post, or he'd get off to nail a loose wire. Once he just got down to pee, and every time before he dismounted, Simon had to jump down first. By darkness, they pulled up at a shack with smoke rising from a chimney. Inside, two men sat at a table playing blackjack, and on the potbellied stove a kettle with coffee let off steam.

The next day when the sun came out, the sky glared so blue and the fields so white Simon had to close his eyes. Cattle dotted the snow as far as he could see. After a breakfast of bacon and eggs, burnt toast and black coffee, the cowboy, whose name was Rawlins and who was in charge of the line camp, took Simon to headquarters half a day's ride away, again on the back of his horse. At one point they crossed a river Rawlins called the Forch that turned out to be the headwaters of the Belle Fourche. The French had been in the high plains as well.

Toward noon, some of the snow had thawed on the gentle ridges. When they rode into the courtyard of the ranch house and jumped off, Simon slipped on the ice and fell. The fall plus the pain on the inside of his thighs from the two long rides made it hard to get up again. The rancher stepping out of the modest one-story brick home laughed. After Rawlins said a few words to him, the man introduced himself as Bud Hollister and invited them both inside for lunch. He asked all kinds of questions Simon couldn't answer. After explaining his presence in Wyoming with the help of Mrs. Hollister's high school French, her husband offered him a lift to Gilette, a town a few miles north, where, he said, he could catch a bus to Canada. Simon thanked him, telling him he didn't have money for a bus, and asked him for a job.

After the meal, Mr. Hollister told Simon if he wanted a job, he should follow him outside. Leading him to a stack of six-foot cedar trunks, he told him to split them for fence posts. As Simon regarded the man, not exactly understanding what he wanted, the rancher picked up an oversized axe and split one of the trunks in half, then each half into quarters. Handing the boy the tool, he returned to the house.

Simon knew this was to be a test. The rancher didn't

think he'd split one cedar trunk, much less a hundred or more of them, and he was right. Simon had handled axes, but this rail splitter wasn't exactly an axe; it was twice as heavy, and the handle wasn't very smooth. He started slowly. Soon he was sweating and blistering his hands. A couple of hours later when Mr. Hollister came to check on him, the stack of split rails was half as big as Simon had expected it to be, but a smile cracked the rancher's hard face. He took Simon to the bunkhouse, pointing at an empty bunk and at the woodstove in the middle of the room, and told him to build a fire.

In the morning, Rawlins explained he wasn't a cowboy but a wrangler, and offered him a hat and a pair of stiff leather gloves. He put him to work replacing lost nails on the tin panels that covered the bunkhouse and the sheds. In the afternoon, he split firewood, replaced a few broken rails on the corrals, and helped load hay on the flat bed truck that "the boss," as they called Hollister, drove out to the hungry cattle where Simon helped him dump the bales. It seemed to him he'd never seen such beautiful land. The wide-open spaces, the constant wind, swales with alders and aspens, all so lonely and wild. If he could ride one of those fleet-footed ponies, he thought, he would never want to leave.

~~~~~

Folding his hands behind his head, Simon stretched his back and his legs.

"Well," Sybil said, sitting up with a trace of impatience, "did you? Did you ride one of those cow ponies?"

She paused. "Of course you did. Otherwise there'd be no point to the story, would there?"

Simon laughed. "It was mean to bore you, but I wanted to feed you some background. Riding the 'cow ponies' was like dessert. They weren't really ponies at all. They were quarter horses. But not like the heavy, muscle-bound horses you see at Western Pleasure shows around here. The ranch ponies were more like small thoroughbreds. Agile and fast."

The first Sunday afternoon on the ranch, Rawlins had led the prettiest little mare into the yard. She was caramel colored with flaxen mane and tail. Simon had a crush on her before he knew what the foreman was up to.

"This is Tiger," Rawlins said, handing him the reins. "if you can stay in the saddle, she's yours."

Simon looked at the men lounging around, smoking, watching. Mr. Hollister sat on the front steps of the house, his wife peered through the kitchen window. "I can't ride a bucking horse," he said, while with his boot testing the muddy footing that would certainly soften a fall.

"She ain't no bucking horse. The boss wouldn't want any of us to get hurt," Rawlins said, grinning.

"Then what's wrong with her?" the boy asked.

"Get on her and find out," he ordered, stepping back out of the way.

The mare stood quite still, ears pointed, tail resting. Simon rubbed her forehead and stroked her neck. Then he patted her rump and put his palm over her eye. No reaction one way or another. So he took hold of the reins, grabbed the horn, and stepped into the stirrup. He swung a leg over her back and softly slid into the big saddle and sat. When nothing happened, he kicked her sides, gently he'd thought, but she shot forward so fast that she nearly escaped from under him. Rawlins, who'd bet that the mare wouldn't dump the boy, laughed, and the men who'd gambled against him cursed, but all in good fun.

That's how the riding lessons with Rawlins began. "Sit deep and straight," he would shout. "Don't lean forward. Never hold on to the reins for balance. Ride with your seat, not with your hands." And Simon learned, although Rawlins never said much more. The mare did most of the teaching, every day, even when they horsed around having fun. She was not just fast, she was quick, yet she stopped on a dime. And tireless, and willing, and eager. During the summer she taught him to cut out calves in the holding pen, a job she enjoyed. Showing her superiority over a lower species, Simon figured. More than anything both he and the mare loved herding cattle from one section of the ranch to another.

What Tiger thought of his attempts at roping and wrestling steers Sunday afternoons she never let on, but she did her best to oblige. She seemed to enjoy that as much as he enjoyed making a fool of himself competing against the pros at the rodeo Saturday nights. In retrospect, the little mare was the best buddy he had ever spent a summer with. At the end of August, when he boarded a bus for Calgary, it was Tiger he found hardest to leave behind.

"Maybe you shouldn't have left," Sybil suggested at the end of his tale. "Why did you?"

"Sister Elisabeth called."

Sybil raised her eyebrows.

"Well, Mr. Hollister didn't need extra hands during the winter. As it turned out, neither did the oil companies in Alberta. Did you know that in Edmonton, where I ended up, the average temperature in January was something like thirty below? I didn't care. I got a night job with a custodial firm, and in the daytime attended high school."

"Does Sister Elisabeth still influence your decisions?"

"Yes." Simon laughed. "Just now she's telling me to keep my hands off you!"

In mock fury, Sybil catapulted from her beanbag onto Simon, snuggling against his outstretched body, elbows on his chest, face an inch from his. About to bring his arms from behind his head, he hesitated.

The light in Sybil's eyes darkened. She pushed herself off, rising to her feet without apparent effort. Reluctant, Simon rose, too, trying unsuccessfully to match the woman's grace.

"That wasn't Sister Elisabeth keeping your hands off me. That was Ellen. What is it that brings her into your consciousness nearly every time I'm with you?"

"You, I guess," he said, annoyed, more with himself than with Sybil. "You are so much like her, it's absurd."

"How? I fail to see the slightest resemblance."

Simon grunted. "Ellen was beautiful. Almost as beautiful as you. She was intelligent, she was funny. Capable. Loving. And she was a great mother." And, Simon thought, she still was all of that.

Sybil remained silent. Then, getting the car keys out of her sack, she said, "You can call me tomorrow, if you want to."

Saddened by Ellen's renewed presence, and upset for having hurt Sybil, he didn't want her to leave. Perhaps he should reveal his vow to remain celibate until Jesse was found. Trouble was it hadn't been the vow that kept his arms from clasping her. Besides, a vow to St. Francis seemed a bit too unworldly to mention, even to him; it would look ridiculous to Sybil, if not absurd, although he couldn't be sure of that.

"How about going out after I feed the horses? For a beer, maybe to meet some of my friends at Alex's?"

Sybil shook her head. "I'm too tired to cope with strangers." Before she disappeared through the front door, however, she softly, very softly, pressed her lips against Simon's. Which, instead of lifting his spirits, depressed them even more.

CHAPTER 29

Still feeling low on the drive to the horses, Simon recalled the night he'd attended the final performance of a tragedy by an Ottawa playwright. It had received fair reviews, and Ellen's performance excellent ones. She had mesmerized the audience with her voice, steel wrapped in velvet. Simon was so impressed he crashed the cast party. Entering the author's house through the back door, he found Ellen in the kitchen slumped over an unclean table, stubbing her cigarette in a full ashtray and taking another from a Player's pack.

"Allow me," Simon said, picking up her lighter and flicking it. With a quick glance at him, she drew on the cigarette, blowing the smoke from the corner of her mouth past Simon's face. Then she lifted a bottle of Carling and took a swig.

"I'm Simon Philipe," he said, talking more and faster than he wanted to. "We met in the cafeteria. Well, we didn't exactly meet. But we've seen each other there."

"I know who you are. You and your girlfriend."

Simon was tempted to tell her his girlfriend had returned to France, permanently. Instead, he said, "Con-

236

gratulations. You did great. It takes talent to make a hundred pages of fluff come to life."

He bit his tongue, expecting her to say, "Who makes you a critic, asshole?" She only blew out smoke in her peculiar fashion. She looked so forlorn he wanted to take her in his arms and hold her. The end of the play, he realized, meant the death of the character she had lived and breathed. Now she had to be herself again, and apparently she didn't like it.

In the living room, a twist came to an end, and somebody began the Tennessee Waltz. Simon held out his hand. "Dance?"

At that instant voices shouted for Ellen. Two young men burst into the kitchen, took hold of her arms and lifted her off the chair. She stuffed the cigarettes into her purse, grabbed her beer, and was swept out of the room, but not before turning her head, catching Simon's eye. Then he headed outside and stood for a while listening to the sound of the cheers, still smelling her subtle perfume. He felt more alone than he had in a long time.

As always, the horses made him appreciate the present, and as Snow Goose bumped his chest, he asked himself what he'd ever seen in a depressed woman so different from the other women he'd loved, all of whom, beginning with Sister Elisabeth and ending with Sybil, enjoyed the world and faced it with gusto. No, when he met the young woman who later became his wife, she wasn't like Sybil, except perhaps for her beauty, and the character she played on the stage. Had he fallen in love with the heroine in a tragedy?

If the kids hadn't been waiting for him to come home and cook dinner, he would have swung himself on Snow Goose and galloped out into the night. It wasn't to be. His chores done, he waved an empty feedbag, chasing the horses into the back pasture, and hurried home.

During dinner, with Stefan and Carolyn relating the day's funny and unfunny incidents at their schools, Simon's restlessness disappeared, yet as soon as they were in bed, it returned with a vengeance. Again he considered asking Sybil out, but thinking better of it, climbed into the pickup and drove to Alex's, where Jonah Brown, Mitch Rouncreek, and Ludwig Stoppelfeld waved him to their table.

Surprised by the presence of his colleagues and pleased by their friendly welcome, Simon grabbed a glass off the bar and joined them. "What's the occasion?"

"I got my research grant," Mitch boasted, offering Simon a cigar.

"Poor sonofabitch is gonna spend a year in the jungle," Ludwig announced loud enough for all the patrons in the place to hear.

"Yeah," Jonah complained in his nasal voice, "we language teachers missed the boat. The only place I ever got a grant to was Oxford." He chortled. "Mississippi."

"Mitch is crazy," Ludwig said to no one in particular, shaking his head. "Who would want to spend a year in a jungle with no shower?"

"A year seems a little long," Simon admitted. "I

wouldn't mind a summer, though."

"Ludwig's exaggerating. I won't exactly live in a tree," Mitch explained. "The Franciscans provide room and board for me at the mission."

"You're gonna stay with monks?" Ludwig asked, pretending shock. "Won't they cramp your love life?"

"Now that I'm married, I rather welcome that."

"I hope you like mass wine," Jonah mumbled. "Pretty terrible stuff."

"Beats swamp water," Simon said. "When I was in the arctic, a glass of sweet wine at dinner was the highlight of my day."

"When the hell were you in the arctic?" Ludwig asked, disbelief obvious on his face.

"In college."

"You must be kidding me."

It seemed his competitive German friend found it hard to believe that he was capable of matching some of Mitch's exploits.

"It wasn't the North Pole," Simon admitted, "just the sub-arctic. An Eskimo settlement called Fort Chimo. It's located at the tip of Ungava Bay. From there the treeless tundra stretches north. I can show you an old map of the region at the office."

"Are you telling us you worked with Eskimos?"

"A little. I worked with a bunch of characters, carpenters mainly, who probably couldn't have found a job elsewhere."

"I know exactly what you're talking about," Mitch

declared, grinning.

"Why on earth have you never mentioned this?" Ludwig complained.

Simon shrugged. "You never asked me. It was a long time ago. I was only twenty-two."

"We're asking you now. Come on, give!"

Simon had wanted to hear about life in the rain forest, even though Mitch had apparently reminisced about Ecuador all evening and was talked out anyway, but now that Ludwig had flung down the gauntlet, Simon decided to pick it up. Whatever he and Ludwig did together, it seemed, turned into a competition, even shooting the bull. Well, let's see if old Lu can match this tale.

"In the spring of 1960, the Department of Northern Affairs and National Resources in Canada hired me as a supply clerk for a construction crew in Fort Chimo. I got the job mainly because I'd spent two summers in the North on a survey crew. I didn't spend much time taking care of supplies. I worked with the foreman and in the office with the superintendent, sometimes helping the carpenters. Sixty hours a week. I loved it. In the summer of '61 I returned as 'Assistant to the Superintendent.'"

"How far is it from Ottawa to Fort Chimo?" Ludwig asked somewhat impatiently.

"A thousand miles straight north. About the same distance from Montreal."

He'd had mixed feelings about flying north for nearly four months just two days after meeting Ellen, leaving her behind in a city full of potential lovers, but a job in the North was about the only place where a student could earn his full tuition during the summer months. Speaking mainly to Mitch who could identify with his situation, Simon admitted that when he boarded the turbo-prop, he was looking forward to seeing the old gang again. To working with Joe Walker, the foreman who'd become his friend, and playing pool with Charlie, an Eskimo boy Simon had sort of adopted.

Before the plane had leveled out, however, the flight turned rough, and Simon found himself fighting nausea. The Eskimos he shared the cabin with didn't seem to be bothered by it. Embarrassed and wanting to take his mind off his tormented stomach, he asked the teenage girl next to him where she was going. She said to Kangirsuk on the west side of the bay. The man across the aisle volunteered the information that he lived in Quaqtaq, a village even farther north than Kangirsuk. Since there was no regular transportation to those isolated settlements, the Northern Service Officer would take them to their lonely destinations in his cabin cruiser when things slowed in the fall. If not, a bush pilot would fly them home.

"Those Inuit names are a mouthful," Ludwig interrupted. Jonah and Mitch nodded, expecting Simon to continue.

Where his fellow travelers had been, Simon knew. When Eskimos flew south in the fifties and sixties, with very few exceptions they went straight to a hospital in the city of Hamilton, a polluted center of industry, to be cured of tuberculosis. To this day Simon hadn't figured out how the patients found a cure there, but they did. You could tell his passengers had spent time in the south by their new clothes, the absence of seal odor, the handful of English words they'd picked up, the tailor-made cigarettes they smoked.

The girl pointed at him, smiling, holding her tummy, then pretended to vomit. Simon tried to smile and shook his head. He wasn't going to provide the entertainment by throwing up. Leaning back hard against the seat, he pulled *The Hero With a Thousand Faces* from his bag and tried to read. Campbell's book was on the list for his comparative literature course he'd put off until his fourth year, but concentrating on the small print increased his nausea.

Before he'd expected it, the plane landed smoothly on the elevated gravel strip.

"Good to see you," Joe Walker said in his New Zealand accent, tossing Simon's gear into the back of a Chevy pickup.

"Nice truck," Simon said shaking hands and waving to the pilot and the happy debarking Eskimos. He was glad to see Joe, a man who never said a word too much. A man you could always count on. Simon could picture him as the boss of a construction crew in a World War II adventure movie in the South Pacific.

"How was the flight?"

"Rough. For the last hour I was on the verge of throwing up."

"It's rough going here, too. The new superintendent is a flaming drunk. Apparently the kids they're gonna send us this year are in high school. And McGhaw and O'Reilly are even nuttier than last summer."

"What kids are you talking about?"

"Sons of the department brass. They'll get here when school's out in a week or two."

The camp looked much the same except for some wooden frames for concrete slabs, the foundations for new cabins. The mess hall and the dorms hadn't changed. The Quonset hut again served as the superintendent's office. Before entering it, Joe told Simon that after lunch, when the super passed out, he would like him to work for him. Only if he wanted to, of course, but it'd be more fun than sitting behind a desk twiddling his thumbs in the super's office. He'd like him to drive the pickup and supply the men with material. In a few days Simon would fly north with a couple of men. To the Hudson Strait.

"How come?"

"You want overtime, don't you? You won't get any sitting behind a desk. And you know yourself you're not really needed here. The super agrees. Up there you'll put together a shed for a generator, a school, and a house for a teacher. All prefab. You'll be working day and night." He smiled. "You won't just make a lot of money, you'll be bringing civilization to the natives."

"Putting them on welfare."

Joe grunted. "If you can think of an alternative, tell

the Department."

The traditional Eskimo way of life was disappearing, if not already gone. For starters, blame World War Two, the American base in Fort Chimo. It was the Air Force that got the natives used to raiding garbage cans. And you couldn't blame them. Who would want to drive a dog team over the icy tundra chasing down food if you could scoop it out of a bin, already cooked?

Now Mitch interrupted. "Exactly. In Ecuador it wasn't the military. It was the mining company. But the same result exactly. Exactly."

"Interesting, the spread of Western ways to so-called primitive peoples, isn't it?" Jonah added. "If you had studied anthropology instead of languages, you could have profited by writing a paper on the subject."

"Stop interrupting," Ludwig urged.

Simon told how he dropped off his gear at the Quonset hut, and then Joe and he went to see the superintendent who was asleep on a bunk, an arm hanging down, the back of his hand flat on the floor. A clean-shaven man, wearing a tie. A gold band on his finger.

"Does he know the score?" Simon asked Joe outside.

"You'll find out tomorrow when you work with him. Now go find Charlie, he's been asking for you."

Charlie. The son of a single mother. Who didn't know his own age. Nine or ten, wearing a Yankees baseball cap, flannel shirt, faded blue jeans, and dirty white sneakers without socks. Simon had often played pool with the boy in the recreation shed on the hill late at night when his co-workers had finished. Not that these had been skillful games. The table was undersized, and Charlie didn't play well. Simon would have preferred to hit the sack instead, but the neglected boy moved him, and one of his smiles, when he sank a ball, made up for Simon's loss of sleep.

But instead of meeting Charlie, Simon came across the Mountie. Sergeant Michener, a tall man with glasses, who looked more like a professor than a policeman, seemed to lead a quiet, uneventful life in the only two-story home in the settlement. The summer before, Simon had seen him almost daily, always out of uniform, going fishing on the bay or coming back. Once, when Simon tossed some food scraps from the kitchen to the pack of starving Eskimo dogs that roamed the area, the officer gave him a bagful of fish heads. The Mountie himself kept his sled dogs in a wire mesh kennel in the backyard. They were fed char or whatever the Sergeant caught most of on a particular evening. If he didn't go fishing, the dogs were fed with fish from the walk-in freezer.

Simon nearly bumped into the man hurrying by the Quonset, carrying a rod in his left, a string of fish in his right, each nearly two feet long.

"Simon!" the Mountie exclaimed, breaking his stride. "Glad you're back. I'm told a child's been shot while I was on the water. You hear about it?"

"Sorry, Sergeant, I just got off the plane."

The Mountie nodded and hurried on in the direction of the Catholic mission, and Simon turned toward the construction site. The men laid down their tools, and in a noisy reunion they shook hands. Before Simon could ask whether the building they were framing would become the new school or the teacher's house, the men told him that the child who was killed was Charlie.

In disbelief, Simon stood, and the men related the incident. Poor Charlie had been killed accidentally because Gus, a young native, and Lebeau, a mechanic for the mining company, both lusted after a sixteen-year-old native beauty named Tilly. Tilly had repudiated Gus's advances, but the man wouldn't accept no for an answer. Lucky for Lebeau, his rival was drunk when he tried to shoot him, hitting Charlie who was riding on Lebeau's pickup with some other kids instead.

After dinner Simon joined Joe Walker in the shop to help build a coffin.

"I don't blame Tilly for refusing Gus," Joe said, as they moved a panel of three-quarter-inch plywood to the table saw. "There's no future with a drunk."

And you couldn't blame Lebeau for making out with Tilly, Simon thought. If he had to stay here longer than a few months, he would, too.

"Pretty clever for Gus to build a still," Joe, a nondrinker, commented, "but the poor bugger should have had more sense than to shoot at a moving truck."

Not with a bunch of children riding in the back, Simon thought, holding on to the roof of the cab, their heads sticking over the top like ducks at a shooting gallery.

The table saw roared, and the talking stopped. They

cut the boards for a box fifty-four inches long, twenty inches wide and twelve inches deep, fastened them together with eight-penny nails and made the cover stay in place by stapling strips of smooth pine on its lower edge. They loaded it on the pickup and drove to the mission.

Charlie lay on his back on the dining room table, wearing the same clothes he'd always worn minus the baseball cap. Simon hardly recognized him without it and his bright, black eyes closed. The bullet hole in the center of his forehead looked as harmless as a pink spot of missing skin.

"Looks like a twenty-two," the father said, coming out of his office carrying an old army blanket. The men set the coffin next to the boy on the table and shook hands with the priest. The father folded the blanket lengthwise, spreading it in the box, rolling one end to make a small pillow. Together, they laid the boy on it, forcing his already stiff hands over his belt buckle. Before they put the cover on, Simon tied the loose shoelace on Charlie's left sneaker and asked the priest for Charlie's Yankees' cap. The missionary hesitated a moment, then disappeared toward the back of the house and returned, handing Simon Charlie's cap with a smile.

Moments later, the Sergeant, wearing his hat and his red coat, stepped through the front door. Nodding to the three men, he approached the wooden box, felt its smooth corners and lifted the cover. He gazed at the body a moment and nodded again. "Thanks, Joe. Nice work."

"He's ready for the funeral," the reverend said. "In the morning would be a convenient time."

The Mountie shook his head. "We can't bury the boy. He's evidence. There will be a coroner's jury, and then he'll be shipped to Montreal together with Gus for the trial."

"To Montreal!" The father exclaimed. "How will we keep the corpse from rotting?"

"We'll store him in the freezer," the Mountie explained, "and when the time comes, we'll pack him in ice."

The following day, Sergeant Michener formed a coroner's jury, eleven rough men, a prospector, laborers, a bush pilot, carpenters, truck drivers, all of them fishermen and hunters on their days off. To the vociferous objection of a mining engineer, he made bilingual Simon the foreman. The jury's job was more a formality than a fact-finding investigation, but the eleven men followed Simon with obvious curiosity to the walk-in freezer to examine Charlie's wound. When they opened the heavy steel door, a steady drip of water, like slow-motion rain, was falling off the sides of beef and halves of pork and the fish hanging on iron hooks. As they filed in, bending under the leaking fish, the water dripped down their necks. Charlie's box sat on a stack of parcels of cut chops packed in white paper, also thawing, already somewhat lopsided, beneath a row of gray pike, hooked through their open mouths, dripping steadily on the wood. Simon lifted the cover, trying to shield the boy from the water drops. "Sonofabitch," the engineer behind him complained, punching at a thawing arctic char that had slapped his neck.

"It don't look like a bullet hole," a man said. "Looks more like he broke his skin, scratching, don't it?"

"This ain't the movies," another voice said. "No ketch-up running all over his face."

"It was a twenty-two, all right. Somebody check if it come out behind?"

"The Sergeant did. It didn't come out."

"That means Gus shot from a way off."

"At least three hundred feet, I'd say," another voice offered.

All twelve gun experts having examined the wound agreed that there was no point in staying any longer in the dripping cooler.

"He's swelled up a bit, ain't he?" commented Boston, a bearded bush pilot, as he helped Simon cover the box. To keep it from sliding off during the night and spill out, the two men lowered it to the wet floor and weighed it down with a quarter of beef in case the generator couldn't be fixed and the frozen meat thawed further.

That night McGhaw and O'Reilly, the two senior car-penters, as usual dominated the rehash of the events that had taken place during the day. McGhaw, a heavy-set man in his fifties, was a third generation Scot with thick glasses and called himself an Orangeman. The taller, somewhat stooped O'Reilly, red-nosed and gray-haired, claimed to be an Irishman, though his great grandfather had been born in Canada. His claim to fame was the time in his twenties that he'd spent as a trainee with the Royal Canadian Mounted Police. McGhaw considered O'Reilly a windbag, and O'Reilly said he had proof that in the forties, when the Scot worked in Michigan, he'd been a member of the Ku Klux Klan. Neither could ever say a word without having it contradicted or bested by the other, much to the amusement of their fellow workers who usually spurred them on, at least until the foreman put a stop to it.

There was a pause in the argument now, and some of the men were already snoring.

"You know," O'Reilly started up again, "this ain't the first time Lebeau got into trouble. He was involved in a knife fight about some broad last winter."

"How d'you know that?" McGhaw asked sneeringly. "From your contact with the Mounties?"

"It's true," a sleepy voice in the far corner uttered. "They cut each other up over Rainbow Liz."

"That slut?" McGhaw spit in disgust. "The French! They're no better than the sled dogs. When they ain't fucking, they're fighting!"

"Yeah," O'Reilly said, laughing, for once agreeing with his adversary. "That's because they have a prick for a brain, and you, you impotent old fart, you're so frigging jealous you're about to explode!"

"Shut your face, you sleazy old queer!"

"Hey," Simon interrupted, "if you want to talk like assholes, go to the john!"

The crew, already half asleep, grunted in agreement, except for O'Reilly who cursed with Jesus and Mary and half the saints until he choked in a fit of coughing.

CHAPTER 30

"I love those guys," Mitch declared, calling for more beer.

Jonah shook his head. "Poor Charlie. That's unreal."

"Poor Gus!" Ludwig huffed into his beer. He ever go to jail?"

"I don't know. I don't think so. Four months later, when I flew back to Ottawa, Charlie was still in the freezer. Gus, meanwhile, had been exiled to Baffin Island."

"That's typical," Jonah said. "I'm always amazed that the bureaucracy manages to get anything done at all. I'd rather depend on a drunk than a bureaucrat."

Simon shrugged. He wouldn't, although he had liked Superintendent Yancey, the only alcoholic he ever had to deal with on a daily basis. The balding, bespectacled, forty-year-old civil servant had a gentle disposition. He never got angry at the slowness with which Simon's two index fingers typed the letters he dictated. Of course they were meaningless progress reports, confirmations of deliveries, requests for paychecks, answers to queries from the ministry; nothing that needed to be dispatched in a hurry. And Gerald, as Simon called the superintendent, was never in the least embarrassed about his drinking. He openly poured three or four fingers of rum into his coffee, sipping one cup after another, until about eleven when he retired to his bedroom.

In regard to the "kids," Joe had exaggerated. When they finally arrived, the playfulness of the half dozen high school boys contrasted favorably with the stolid temperaments of the tradesmen, most of whom were in their fifties, coping with rheumatism and hemorrhoids and various other aches and pains resulting from their life-long labors in a harsh climate. True to his word, by early June Joe asked Simon to pack for the project in Ivujivik, a small Eskimo settlement on the Hudson Strait, where his official job would be to cook and assist in the construction of the buildings he had mentioned. What the foreman didn't reveal was the identity of the carpenters. When they turned out to be McGhaw and O'Reilly, Simon told Joe that those two alone in the tundra would kill each other.

Joe grinned. "That's why Gerald is sending you, to keep them from killing each other. We can't send one of the youngsters to do that."

"You could replace either McGhaw or O'Reilly with another man."

Still grinning, Joe said, "Why would I do that? I've had it with those buffoons."

Simon grinned back. "You'll regret this, Joe. If you make me work with those assholes, I'll work all right. I'll work sixteen hours a day."

The fighting between the carpenters had started before they boarded the plane and continued while they were waiting for take-off at the far end of the gravel-covered runway. Simon had a hard time stomaching the Irishman's attitude, especially his repetitive boasting about his career as an undercover agent with the Mounted Police and, in that capacity, his conquests of all the "delectable asses" that included a pathetic male informer. But at least O'Reilly's boasting made more sense to him than McGhaw's bigotry.

"Gimme some room, you goddam papist!" McGhaw shouted at O'Reilly who sat next to him as the pilot started the engines.

Simon, who sat ahead of the carpenters right behind the pilot and had been watching his actions, didn't know what had brought on the outburst and tried to ignore it. Raising his voice even higher to outdo the roaring engines attached to the wings overhead, McGhaw yelled, "It's a fact! I'd rather be ruled by Krushchev than the antichrist!"

The pilot turned around to Simon and said, "*Quel salaud*!" Then he shouted for all the passengers to hear, "Let's all pray we get this overloaded crate into the air!"

The heavy, twin-engine seaplane was easier to put into flight from land than from water, but as it raced down the elevated strip, its nose wouldn't lift. Mentally helping the pilot pump the pedal that moved the flaps on the wings to lift the plane off the ground, Simon rushed through an Ave Maria. The other six men who'd come along to help unload the cargo and set up the camp and then return to Chimo held on to their seats, anxious eyes glued to the front. A hundred feet from the bluff at the end of the runway, the plane was still running on wheels. Then it shot out over the edge, dipping and veering left, with the tip of its wing seemingly low enough to scratch the top of the ten thousand barrels of kerosene left by the American Air Force. While Simon, watching the sea of silver barrels rush by below, visualized instant death in a gusher of flames and prayed they'd make it, McGhaw threw up, and for once O'Reilly sat quiet, his face dripping sweat.

"That was close," the pilot shouted over the noisy interior as the plane straightened out and roared a few feet above the quiet water of Ungava Bay.

"We could have been fireworks," Simon said, taking a deep breath but not yet easy, since the plane hadn't begun to rise.

"You wouldn't have felt a thing," the pilot said, laughing and lighting a smoke. "What you guys got in those toolboxes, anyhow? Lead?"

The toolboxes the pilot referred to weren't standard equipment you could buy at Sears and Roebuck. Between five and six feet long, two feet high and nearly three feet wide, the solid steel containers held every possible carpenter's tool, including a vise, iron clamps and all available electrical gadgets, from circular saws and drills to sanders and jigsaws. It took two strong men just to lift one corner of a box, four men to move it.

As the airplane gradually rose from the Bay, McGhaw wiped the vomit off his chin with the sleeve of his parka. "It's not the tools," he said. "It's that goddamn generator! What the fuck do Eskimos need a generator for?"

The pilot, who didn't know McGhaw, commented in French, *"Un vrai salaud."*

"Yeah," Simon agreed, "a real sweetheart."

"You know," O'Reilly said, having caught his breath, "that was nothing. I tell you what. When I was with the Mounties, we had an emergency landing in Yellow Knife that makes this take-off look like a kiddy-ride at the fair."

"Shut up, you windbag!" McGhaw spit, about to be sick again. "Or I'll barf all over you!"

On the approach to the village, the plane skimmed over a cliff. Then, plunging into the water, it plowed half-submerged through the choppy sea, balanced only by a couple of slender pontoons hanging from the wing tips that spread from the top of the body. The Eskimo settlement didn't come into view until the pilot turned the plane. Maybe two dozen tents and a wooden building, one roof topped by a spire, made up the settlement. The population assembled on the gently rising shore, men and women and children in colorful, hooded cotton shirts, scruffy dogs yapping, and, off to the side, like patient crows, two men in black. The missionaries. An old brother, and a younger, vigorous priest, Frère Robert and Père Gagné. Simon went straight to the two reverends, introducing himself and his two companions.

A young woman stood behind them, some distance from the other natives. Although he glanced at her quickly, not wanting to appear too curious in front of the two churchmen, he was aware the girl was pretty, with white teeth and dark, almond eyes. Apparently the only native, Simon noticed, not wearing a colorful cotton parka. Instead of a hood, a gold-colored, embroidered wool cap sat on her head like a crown. A rather slender female for an Eskimo, Simon thought, even in the bulky, earth-brown sweater and loose, dark-gray skirt long enough to reach the tops of her mukluks. Though their eyes met for only a moment, it felt like a challenge.

The friendly welcome in the village didn't quite make up for the barren landscape, the rough sea behind them, and the dark cliffs surrounding the bay. The pilot seemed nervous, in a hurry to unload the cargo before the receding tide stranded his anchored plane. The crew they'd brought with them from Fort Chimo borrowed a flat-bottomed boat from the mission and together with the help of young Eskimo volunteers unloaded the equipment. Standing in the water, the men lifted the pallet with the generator that must have weighed a ton into the boat, then pushed it up onto the gravel bank, lifted it out and half-dragged, half-carried it to a shed attached to the mission house to keep it out of the weather.

The Father suggested they set up their tents halfway between the mission and the creek that would supply their water, but the two carpenters had other ideas. To have the opportunity to vent their dislike of each other without interference from the natives or the missionaries, they insisted on erecting the two tents, one for living and one for storing supplies, on a rise that seemed like a quarter mile from the village. Simon didn't mind the distance between their camp and the tents of the natives and the all-pervasive smell of seal blubber, but he wasn't happy about lugging water that far. Still, he shrugged, and erected the tents and dug a latrine with a couple of the Chimo people while the rest of the men and a dozen strapping natives carried the supplies up the hill, stacking them at the campsite. The whole operation took less than a couple of hours. When the men put down the last box, the pilot started the engine.

The plane with the Chimo crew boarded rode out toward the distant cliffs, turned about, and plowed through the white caps, becoming louder and bigger, taking to its wings just moments before hitting the shore, roaring over the village, as dogs and children scampered for shelter, and disappeared south over the tundra.

When the plane was gone, a moment of loneliness touched the three men on the rocky slope. Dejected, the two carpenters retreated to the tent and set up the card table and two of the metal folding chairs and began a game of cribbage. Simon unpacked the Coleman stove and fried the char steaks they had brought with them, warmed a couple of cans of green beans, and made coffee. By the time they had eaten, it was evening, although you couldn't tell by the sun still high in the sky.

Refreshed and in higher spirits, they piled the supplies into the tent. There were no brown or black bears this far north, nor would the polar bears come this close to a settlement, where they'd be shot on sight. But Simon didn't trust the starving sled dogs, and he double-checked the pegs, drove some of them deeper into the hard ground, and asked O'Reilly and McGhaw to help him barricade the inside of the door with one of their heavy tool boxes. McGhaw scoffed, calling the precautions a waste of time, but O'Reilly agreed and even helped him tie and knot the screened window openings. When the food was secured, they leveled a spot for their sleeping bags, removing all the jagged rocks, and spread their ground sheets. They undressed, and the carpenters went to bed. Simon brushed his teeth outside, and checked on the supply tent one last time. It looked safe, the sea was calm, the village quiet.

Despite the late dusk and the snores of his companions, Simon fell asleep and slept well. He didn't hear the pack of dogs tear down the storage tent, ripping open every can of food in their six-week supply till the animals started a fight, growling and yelping. Simon jumped out of his sleeping bag and in his bare feet slapped his coat against the feasting canines. It didn't deter them, so he grabbed a broken tent pole, swinging and stabbing, but the dogs just ducked and slunk out of his way. By the time the carpenters emerged in their long johns, bare feet stuck in unlaced boots, the dogs were circling the tent through the can and debris-strewn battlefield, wary eyes on Simon's staff.

"What the fuck!" yelled McGhaw, peering at the destruction through his thick lenses.

"Sweet Mary o'mercy, O'Reilly cried, stepping rednosed into the bright morning sun. "This is your doing, McGhaw! You stupid bastard! You're the one wanted to camp seven miles from every livin' soul!"

"My doing?" the Scot wailed into the wind blowing from the sea. "Like hell it is, you crazy sonofabitch!

What do we do now? Hunt rabbits and cook fucking rabbit stew? I wished I never set foot in this curse of a country!"

"Rabbit stew?" O'Reilly spit. "By the blue Jesus fuckin' Mary, where would we find a rabbit on this moonscape, you motherfuckin' excuse for a human bein'? You're more likely to find green fuckin' cheese than fuckin' game. And if there was rabbits, what the fuck would we shoot them with? You didn't pack your gun, you braindead prick."

McGhaw threw a right at O'Reilly, missing, and nearly crashed to the rocky ground.

"Thank your lucky stars you missed, you fat-assed clown, or I'd've punched your dentures down your cocksuckin' throat!" the Irishman shouted, trying to kick the panting Scot with his open boot, losing it, hitting the rough ground with his bare foot, crying out in pain. Simon wasn't amused by the childishness of the two middle-aged craftsmen, but he didn't mind their bruising each other a little.

At the bottom of the slope, the Eskimo population had gathered outside their tents, men, women, and children in their green or maroon or brown or yellow or blue or red cotton parkas. And now the missionaries, the crusty old brother, his bald head reflecting the sun, and the quiet priest joined the spectators.

"Cut it out!" Simon shouted. "We'll borrow food from the mission till we get fresh supplies. Maybe we can eat there, too."

"Me," the Scot shouted, "break bread with those pagan papists? I'll starve to death first!"

"Pipe down!" Simon warned. "They can hear us."

"You sick prick of an Orangeman, if the father's grub ain't fuckin' good enough for you, sweet Mother o' Jesus, go beg the women for stinkin' blubber!"

The Scot lunged forward. The Irishman stepped sideways to avoid contact, but McGhaw tripped, hitting O'Reilly head-on in the belly. Both lay there on the rocks, groaning, then struggled to a sitting position, panting hard.

The missionaries retreated to their cabin. A small boy started clapping his hands, and several others joined in. The carpenters turned their faces toward the Eskimos, who continued clapping, white smiles on their dark faces.

A wooden box that contained flour, egg powder, and sugar had not been torn completely open by the dogs, but some of the contents had been spoiled by the fruit juice that ran out of the punctured cans. The only thing the dogs had spared in the storage tent were the metal tool boxes that had been carried up the hill on the shoulders of eight men, four on each side as though they were coffins.

Graciously, the missionaries invited them to share their table. For the first dinner, the carpenters shaved, donned clean shirts, dusted their coveralls and brushed their boots, and McGhaw wiped his thick glasses and greased down his three strands of hair. Upon entering the mission, he trod stiffly, his hulk hunched over, and during grace, bowed his head. The food of the missionaries came out of cans also, except for the fish which was fresh, as was the bread the brother had baked. The pièce de resistance was a glass of altar wine the brother poured for each setting. It tasted sweet as nectar, and even the Scot tried it. Unlike the Irishman, though, who babbled constantly, the Scot kept quiet, for which the company was grateful.

Simon was impressed by the priest's clean exterior and the daily routine he had maintained in the twenty-five years he'd been stationed at the mission. A routine, Simon knew, no one held the priest to except himself. His simple eating habits and the equanimity with which he seemed to accept what this primitive life gave him, made Simon doubt whether he himself would be able to spend a quarter of a century without the distractions that Canadian civilization offered in the south. There was no newspaper, much less a library. No TV. Even the radio was strictly for business, for relaying news, reaching out to ships sailing the strait, to captains in trouble. Ships passed so far away he couldn't see them, though he lived in the land of the midnight sun.

Simon asked the reverend how many converts he had made during his twenty-five-year effort. "Not many," the priest answered gently. "A handful." To Simon this seemed like failure, but Père Gagné explained that proselytizing didn't necessarily mean making converts. It meant being a friend to people in need, regardless of whether they were or wanted to be Christians. He was, you might say, proselytizing by living a Christian life. This live-and-let-live attitude reminded Simon of his Uncle Baptiste.

Three days later when the freighter with the building material for the planned structures still hadn't arrived, Simon attended mass in the little church, not expecting much of a congregation at six a.m., but a couple of Eskimo men lurched toward the front, nodding to him as they passed. Then some women followed, one with a baby strapped to her back. During the service, the woman nursed the child by pulling its head over her shoulder and lifting up her breast, a long, slack breast that the child grabbed hungrily. The altar boy, his jeans covered by a white robe, mukluks crossed, rang the little brass bell with abandon, obviously enjoying the noise.

Simon concentrated on the home-baked wafer the reverend raised above his head. Silently he asked the Lord to forgive his sins and to bless their stay at this primitive camp. Then the priest raised the chalice with the wine, and again the little brass bell tinkled. It tinkled like the bell he himself had rung in the chapel in Chicoutimi, as young if not as innocent as the boy at the altar.

Just then the girl with the yellow cap walked past Simon's pew, head erect, looking neither left nor right. Without bending her knee, she slid into the first pew and knelt, apparently watching the father cover the chalice and turn to his missal. Her hair was dark, with an auburn hue in the candle light of the windowless chapel. A wide braid fell down her back over a dark, hand-knitted wool cape she had folded over her shoulders. She again wore a long, ample skirt, also of a dark cotton and, like the altar boy and every other native in the settlement, mukluks on her feet, tall boots handmade of sealskin with soft soles, the fur on the inside, folded over at the top, and laced with leather strings.

Simon watched her rather than the proceedings at the altar, hoping she would look back and show him her face, but she didn't turn. During Communion, she waited till Simon walked to the front, kneeling down on the pine floor next to the mother with the nursing child, receiving the Host in the shape of a broken bannock, the unsalted Eskimo bread baked in a pan over a wick burning in blubber. On the return to his pew, he concentrated on the Host he had just received. As he knelt down, however, he noticed the girl receiving Communion, too. When she rose and turned, her head was bowed, the tips of her fingers coming together over the bridge of her nose, hiding most of the face, as women and children often did in prayer. In the pew, she knelt again, showing Simon only her back.

At the end of the mass, the father and the boy left the chapel, followed by the handful of Eskimos. Simon stayed, wanting to see the girl who was still kneeling, head bowed. Minutes passed. Finally she got up to leave, walking as she had on the way in, head up, the gold-colored cap sitting on her head like a crown. Simon made no bones about watching her, wanting to see her face, a pale, oval face with a wide forehead, a delicately carved chin, full lips with a near pout, a crook in the nose, and not quite almond-shaped eyes, set wide. Passing him, she kept her head high and straight, but under lowered lids, and half hidden by her lashes, her pupils moved, looking him over.

Quite unexpectedly, the father invited Simon to have breakfast at the mission. Figuring it wouldn't hurt the two carpenters to mix their own egg powder, he accepted. As he did during dinner, the brother set the food on the table and poured the coffee that, he pointed out proudly, came from New Orleans. Eating his oatmeal sweetened with molasses, Simon asked about the latest news regarding the arrival of the building material. The brother shrugged, explaining that in the arctic the wheels of business turned only as fast as the props of the ships that sailed an often unfriendly Baffin Strait.

"What did you think of our princess?" the father asked, refilling their cups with that delicious chicory brew.

Simon knew exactly what the priest was talking about, but not wanting to betray his fascination with the striking girl, he just looked at him.

"Don't tell me," Père Gagné said, smiling, "you didn't notice the pretty girl?"

"I noticed her," Simon admitted, thinking that even a blind man would.

"An arrogant female," the brother said in his sullen voice. "She doesn't believe our men are good enough for her. Not even Umilik, the man she is promised to."

"Like Sleeping Beauty," the Father said, regarding some point in the distance, "she's waiting for a prince to wake her.

Simon had met Umilik, an imposing figure of a man, who spoke a bit of English and had been giving directions to his fellow natives during the unloading of the generator and the tool boxes. Checking his watch, Simon asked to be excused. He thanked his hosts and headed toward the tent, wondering how the carpenters had gotten along. As he was leaving the village, the tall girl stepped into his way, raising her cape she held with both hands over her shoulders, flashing white teeth and sparkling eyes.

"Hi," Simon said, keeping his hands in the pockets of his parka.

"I'm Kanguk," she said in French, jutting out her chin.

"I'm Simon," he said, suddenly aware of how boring his own name must sound to the girl.

"Would you like to go fishing, Simon?"

Almost rendered speechless by the girl's beautiful French, he stuttered, "With you?"

The girl nodded.

"When?"

She reached toward the sun with her left arm, bringing it down to her right shoulder, then broke into infectious laughter.

"You mean tonight?"

She nodded. "Seven o'clock Eskimo time. That means whenever we're ready." Smiling brightly, she turned, head high. Swinging her arms without letting go of the blanket, she disappeared between the tents.

"About time," McGhaw said, playing cribbage with O'Reilly. "You're not gonna make scrambled eggs again, are you? I can't eat that powdered shit even one more time."

Still mesmerized by the encounter with the Eskimo beauty, Simon said he could make pancakes with the flour and lard Brother Robert had given them. They'd have to do without butter or jam, but the dogs had spared some of the bottles of maple syrup. He was pleased the two men were tolerating each other for the moment, but wondered what they'd tire of next, since he'd made scrambled eggs just twice. Maybe he should accept the brother's offer of a case of Spam, of which the mission had a year's supply.

"The brother," he said, "has offered us a case of Spam."

Both players brightened. "Yeah?" O'Reilly said, looking up. "We can fry it for breakfast. Beats powdered eggs, eh, McGhaw?"

Starting the batter, Simon told them he would explore the coast this morning. And after supper, he'd go fishing.

"Fishing?" O'Reilly asked. "Where?"

"In some river, I guess. The girl who invited me didn't say, and I didn't ask."

"What girl?" McGhaw asked, lighting a new cigarette on the burning butt.

"I bet I know," O'Reilly declared. "The movie squaw. The beauty with the braid. Jeez, does the good shepherd know you're about to deflower his prize lamb?"

Having considered all kinds of possibilities himself, Simon said somewhat embarrassed, "We're going fishing."

O'Reilly laughed. "That's all right. You know, when I was stationed at Frobisher Bay, the Eskimo women would kneel with their elbows on the floor. That's the way they wanted it. Sweet Mother o'God, how they loved it!"

"You disgusting pervert!" McGhaw spit.

Simon jumped to his feet, and left the tent without a word, heading toward the mission where he asked the father if he needed a rifle to explore the country. The reverend said that nobody had sighted any polar bears lately, and there was no other game Simon had to worry about. If he was lucky, he might come across some birds and small rodents. He should make sure he didn't get lost, and that was done by not straying too far from the shore. If he followed the shoreline, he would always find his way back.

And that's how Simon started out, climbing over the rocks in and out of the various little bays that made the going interesting but slow. Eager to cover more ground, he turned inland toward the distant hills, counting on the position of the sun to find his way back. After a few minutes he changed his mind and headed back to the shore. No point in risking getting lost without a compass.

If there was wildlife in the endless hills and vales, he didn't see it. No birds, no rabbit, no fox, not even a rat or a mouse, nothing but pale moss and sparse, pale, short grasses. The land seemed as deserted as the moon that hovered on the edge of the immense sky. What wonderful country to discover on horseback. Marching on he no longer noticed the details of the tundra but imagined himself on Tiger, his Wyoming ranch horse, galloping toward the rising, ever changing horizon.

After an hour's brisk walk he stopped at a sheltered cove where the icy water felt a touch warmer and a bluff slowed the wind off the Strait. Simon stripped and dove in, planning to swim out to the nearest white caps, but couldn't stand the cold. After just a few yards he hustled back to the rocks and dried his shivering skin with the cotton lining of his parka, wishing for a hot shower to wash off the salt. Still, he returned to the settlement refreshed.

Before meeting the girl to go fishing, Simon asked Father Gagné for tackle and rod. He wouldn't need any equipment, the reverend explained. Angling was a group effort benefiting the whole village, including the mission. Simon should enjoy it, he said, provided he could stand cold water. He asked him about the name Kanguk, and the priest explained that it meant Blue Goose, or White Goose, or Snow Goose, take your pick, but that he had baptized the girl Marie-Louise. Her father was the navigator on a Norwegian whaler stranded at the village seventeen years before. A fellow with red hair.

"She speaks a beautiful French."

"Yes. She's well educated." The father smiled. "I taught her everything I haven't forgotten, including Latin."

"A great deal of good the language of Caesar will do her on this forgotten pimple of the world," Brother Robert muttered. "She now thinks she is special."

"That she is," Father Gagné agreed.

During the hike to the river where the net was anchored, the girl stayed close to his side, touching his arm, stroking locks from his face. They talked and laughed together as though they were on a date by themselves. Then Simon noticed the amusement of the men and women around them, and he was glad when they reached the tent on the bank of the narrow but rapid river. Big Umilik, just a few years older than Simon, asked him to remove his parka, roll up his sleeves and get into the boat with him and two other men where a net, fastened to heavy rocks, had been spread across the stream. Reaching into the water for the net and holding on to it with one hand, they detached the fish with the other.

The strong current tipped the boat hard, threatening to sweep it downstream. The icy water wetting his rolled-up sleeves, Simon held on, tossing the fish he freed from the net into the boat. Pulling the craft slowly across to the other shore and back again, they harvested nearly twenty arctic char that flip-flopped about his legs. Meanwhile, the women boiled water in the tent for tea, then scaled and cleaned the freshly caught fish. Kanguk massaged Simon's cold arms, buttoned his sleeves, and helped him back into his parka. Then she handed him an aluminum cup with hot tea and a plate with slices of raw char. Kanguk made him open his mouth, stuffing a piece of pink fish between his teeth, a tender morsel that tasted like a cocktail treat, and offered him the tea to wash it down. With nodding and laughter the company approved his "initiation into the Eskimo way" as Umilik put it. Kanguk rolled a couple of smokes, lit them, and stuck one between Simon's lips.

Every morning after breakfast Simon packed a lunch and took off, exploring the moonscape in a different direction, over and over again amazed at the beauty of this unexplored world. Toward noon he would head toward the coast, searching for a sheltered bay, take a dip in the salty liquid, scrubbing his shaking body thoroughly, wiping it with his hands, then stretch out on a smooth, flat rock, letting wind and sun dry his skin. The carpenters, who couldn't understand his obsession with hiking through the barren land, just shook their heads. If he had asked himself why he was wearing out his boots, he couldn't have given an answer. Maybe because he expected an adventure, like finding an animal, any kind of critter, no matter how small. Or, along the shoreline, discovering a spectacular cliff, a cave, maybe sighting a school of whales. Maybe he walked for hours to be too tired to imagine making love with Kanguk.

It was in the middle of the second week when, after pulling himself out of the water onto the outcrop he had dived from, he discovered his clothes were gone. The high rock he was standing on was only one of several similar outcrops in the shoreline, but from where he stood, all those other places were clearly visible. His clothes were gone. The wind, though brisk, wouldn't blow them off the rock. And no animal was large enough to carry them away all at once. Unless it was a bear. Umilik had the pelt of a polar bear in his tent that he'd killed along this shore. An animal so huge it could carry off a bunch of clothes with a man in them.

To return to the village, Simon didn't need his clothes. It was probably no more than a good hour's hike. The wind and the overcast sky made it a good day for walking. But he needed his boots! Without some sort of foot covering he'd tear up his feet. And the water was too cold for swimming that far. Examining the higher bluff farther up the shore, he was puzzled why an animal would steal his clothes, every stitch, without dropping at least a sock. No living thing in sight. Trembling with cold, he started moving, not across the gravelly tundra, but along the shore, sticking to as many of the smooth and slippery outcrops as he could.

A high whistle stopped him. He looked up at the sky, expecting to see a hawk circling above, as hawks had done in the skies of his youth. Another whistle made him turn toward the bluff, and there, on the highest point, stood four women waving his clothes in the breeze.

"Hey," he shouted, starting to climb toward them.

The tallest of the four, Kanguk, gathered his clothes in her skirt, folding the bundle over her belly and, exposing her long legs, climbed boldly down the rocks toward him. She was grinning, flashing her white teeth, a mischievous glint in her slanted eyes, well aware of Simon's discomfort at his nakedness. She dropped his clothes at his feet, grabbed her plaid wool skirt and started to rub him down, from his black curly head to his big feet. On the bluff, the others had disappeared, then showed up on a ledge a hundred feet away, covering their mouths to hide their giggling.

With a quick wave of the hand, Kanguk dismissed her companions. Simon watched them disappear in the direction of the settlement, but that was no guarantee they had actually left. No longer shivering but aroused, he regarded the beautiful girl who'd settled herself on a boulder a couple of steps away, staring out to the sea. Following her eyes, Simon scanned the horizon for movement but saw nothing.

Still turned seaward yet fully aware of his turmoil, Simon was sure, Kanguk started to roll a couple of cigarettes, and he put on his clothes. When he was fully dressed, she lit a cigarette, stuck it between his lips, struck a match to her own. Exhaling, Simon watched his smoke mix with hers, then drifting toward the sea.

"What do you see out there?" Simon asked.

Tears wetting her cheeks, she said, "Freedom."

~~~~~

Simon paused, wondering why he hadn't asked the girl what she meant, rather than just assuming he knew. Jonah said, "That water must have numbed your nuts."

"More like his brains," Mitch added with a laugh. "The poor girl wanted you bad. To deny her, that was mean."

"Yes," Ludwig stated, shaking his head. "The nuns did you no favor."

The waiter brought another pitcher, and they refilled their glasses. "Is there a point to this narrative?" Ludwig asked, tapping his foot on the floor.

"Fuck the point," Mitch chortled, pouring more beer. "I love it. You're talking about my kinda life!"

There was a point to the story, but it was between himself and his relationship with Ellen. And maybe with Sybil, too. "Ludwig is right. No point, not anymore."

"I'm with Mitch," Jonah confessed, "I like the carpenters, too. Tell us more."

CHAPTER 31

Except for mealtime breaks, the carpenters lay on their sleeping bags in the tent, snacking, smoking, arguing, and cursing Joe Walker, who had selected them for this project. Not that they minded getting paid for sixty hours a week without hitting a single nail. They minded missing out on the overtime their colleagues in Fort Chimo were making. The absence of overtime bugged Simon, too. He needed the cash for his tuition, but he kept too busy to dwell on it. He hiked and swam and fished with Kanguk and company. He cooked breakfast and supper, read plays for the Renaissance literature course he still had to take in his senior year, and he'd spend an occasional evening at the mission, talking to the father about the long, dark winters. Once the priest made a reference to Kanguk.

"Marie-Louise," the father said in his detached way, "disregards the marriage proposal by Umilik. Who's a good man, as men go, but not good enough for her. If I could, I'd send her south. She knows enough literature, history, science and math to attend university. Perhaps when she contracts TB, and I hope she will," he added with a sad smile, "she might find her prince charming at the hospital in Hamilton. An encounter with an intern, maybe."

"You're cynical, Father." And Simon didn't just mean his reference to tuberculosis to which so many natives became victim. A white man's disease, just one of many. The price the Eskimos paid for a generator.

"I'm not cynical, just factual," the priest said. "I love this girl like a daughter. What is this intelligent creature so full of life to do? Marry Umilik and chew the soles of his mukluks to keep them soft? Which in the end, she probably will."

Simon smiled uncertainly. Was it possible that Eskimo wives still played slaves to their men? Not to men like Umilik. The Father was being dramatic. Umilik's dark face with the deep-set eyes inspired trust, despite the long, black, unwashed hair, the black mustache hanging over his lips, and the few hairs on his chin that had given him his nickname "bearded one." At first sight a scary man, like one of Captain Hook's pirates. But at twenty-six, the undisputed village leader.

To Simon's disappointment there had been no hunting so far, just stories Umilik told in his tent on those late sunny nights while he carved sea lions and whales and polar bears from junks of gray soapstone, and men spearing them. "Eskimo art" that the Northern Service Officer collected when he dropped in with his cruiser in the late fall. The carvings were eventually flown south, numbered and identified as genuine rather than Japanese copies, and sold in licensed stores in cities throughout Canada.

Mostly Umilik told hunt stories, but once he also mentioned the sun goddess and the moon god, for whom he had more respect than for Jesus. And Simon listened, smoking his pipe, drinking tea and eating bannock. In the French language, he told Umilik, the gender of the fertile sun was not feminine but masculine, while the sterile moon was feminine, and the Eskimo found this hilarious. To the Inuit people who lived in the cold it made sense to deify the source of warmth. More sense than to worship a man born of a virgin who asked his disciples to eat his flesh and drink his blood.

At the end of the fourth week of Simon's arctic exile, a radio message from Fort Chimo informed the father that the labor dispute which was holding up the shipping of the building material would not be solved in time to accomplish the project this year. A plane would arrive the next day to pick up the crew.

"Happy?" the father asked, pouring coffee for Simon's early breakfast at the mission.

Simon shook his head. Except for the overtime he'd be able to make down in Fort Chimo, he thought. Or so he hoped.

The priest said that he himself had no second thoughts about leaving this lonely outpost for a year's sabbatical in August. Saddened about Kanguk's future, Simon suggested the father take the girl with him to France. Slowly, the priest shook his head. It was not possible.

Depressed, Simon hung around the tent, watching the carpenters play cribbage. The imminent return to Fort Chimo, to their buddies, to better food and to overtime had apparently created a cease-fire, however temporary. O'Reilly invited Simon to play the winner, but he declined. Instead he would hike along the shore for one last swim.

Usually with the wind blowing from the north, Simon marched into it, in order not to have to buck it on his return to camp. Now he traveled south with the wind, not caring about the harder way back to camp. And an hour later he found a bay that looked more inviting for a swim than any he'd come across before. It was a circular basin, about a hundred yards in diameter, with only a small opening to the rolling sea. Without delay he stripped and jumped in, stroking hard to circle the pool before the cold numbed his body. Then, right behind him, there was a splash. A second later, the snout of a seal popped out of the waves beside him, ahead of him another. A group of seals were playing around him, some of them nearly twice his own size, eyeing him curiously, playful, unafraid.

Hustling back to the village to announce the good news, Simon suddenly had second thoughts. When Umilik stopped him, however, inviting him to spend his last night in his tent, Simon changed his mind and betrayed the seals. An excited Umilik immediately lumbered away, returning with his rifle, an old, inefficient looking twenty-two with a rusty barrel, and a dented tackle box full of long shells. Together they dragged the priest's rowboat into the water and clamped a small Johnson outboard to the back. While Umilik opened the tank to check the gas, Simon tossed in a couple of oars, and they puttered off, traveling south along the shore, bouncing over the whitecaps, lowering their eyelids against the salty spray.

The seals were no longer in the sheltered bay. Umilik kept going farther south, more slowly now, eyeing the waves for the elusive animals. Fifteen minutes later when they still hadn't discovered them, he steered the boat away from the shore, heading out into the sea toward Mansel Island, thirty miles west. After about a mile he turned north, cruising toward home. With as few words as possible, reinforced by the simple sign language that was easier to understand than spoken words above the noisy outboard and the waves splashing across the bow, Umilik explained that the seals were probably swimming out into the ocean where he wanted to intercept them. He motioned to Simon to take over the engine, and he moved to the front. Grinning under his drooping mustache, Umilik pointed his fingers at his eyes and then across the bow, meaning he had more experienced vision.

Before long Umilik yelled, stretching his arm forward. Simon immediately cut the speed, lowering the tip of the boat. They were now rocking wildly, being sideswiped by the wind blowing offshore, but even Simon could see the seals, bobbing also, less than a hundred yards ahead, heading out to sea.

As Umilik began feeding the magazine of his rifle with shells, Simon didn't have to be told what to do. Gently accelerating, he steered toward the swimmers, and soon his companion started shooting, rapidly discarding the spent shells. Within seconds, he had the gun reloaded and emptied again, without apparently hitting any of the diving targets. Simon thought he never would. To hit a gray snout that appeared for a split second in the silver comb of a gray wave would have been difficult from firm footing on the shore. From a fiercely bobbing boat it was surely improbable. More than half the shells were gone, but Umilik kept shooting. More slowly now, but still aiming, Simon noticed in disgust, at any snout that came up for air. Simon thought the Eskimo should concentrate on just one seal, the big bull, apparently the only male in the bunch, by far the largest animal of the lot. Then with only a few shells left in the box, Umilik scored a hit.

The Eskimo put his rifle down and waved the boat forward. Raising his body high, he flung a small harpoon into the back of the mammal. Simon, now idling the engine, grabbed the rope to help Umilik pull the animal into the boat. They had half the body in when it revived, struggling to get away, pulling them forward. Simon had visions of Captain Ahab and the great white whale. But like Captain Ahab, Umilik wouldn't let go no matter what.

Soon, however, the cow, that measured ten feet in

length, ceased its struggle and died, and together they dragged it into the boat. Umilik took over the engine, and Simon sat in the front, his back to the wind, the pretty, very feminine head of the dead seal between his boots. Every time he caught Umilik's eyes, the fellow grinned, even when the Johnson began to sputter and stalled. Umilik poured gas into the tank from an old Coleman can, trying hard not to spill all of it into the rough sea. Then he pulled the starter cord, over and over, but the motor wouldn't crank. If the Eskimo, with his superior strength and experience couldn't get the motor going, there was no point in Simon's trying. Instead, he put the oars into the guides and started rowing.

All around, it seemed, there was nothing but wild, black waves, relentlessly pounding the side of the boat. After a while, the puddle of water in the boat started rising, and the seal rolled against one foot and then the other. When Simon's arms tired, Umilik took over the oars. The waves now hit the left side of the boat, tilting it each time, making it difficult to dip the face of the oar into water. As they were rowing through the arctic dusk, some of the waves lost their white caps, and the boat moved faster.

The starved sled dogs must have smelled the carcass before they saw the boat. They barked and howled and yapped, waking the village. As the keel scraped through the gravel, Umilik let out a triumphant yell, and almost instantly every living soul, including the missionaries, came down to the shore, milling around the boat, eager to relieve the hunters of their prey. The men dragged the big animal through the sandy gravel, just far enough so the tide wouldn't reach it, while others lit oil lamps or sharpened knives.

The first thing Simon did was to relieve himself at the back of the mission. As soaked and cold as he was, he didn't go to the tent to change but again joined the crowd, surprised by the praise both men and women heaped upon him, accompanied by smiles and nods, although he didn't understand more than a few words. He couldn't believe the joy the seal had brought to the settlement, and he was curious as to what they were about to do with it. Even happier than the people were the dogs, barking and jumping around the men skinning the seal. Slinking between them, they were frequently kicked back, yet without malice or anger, simply to let them know it wasn't yet their turn. The dogs didn't growl at the men. They took out their frustration on one another, snarling, biting and screeching, and again and again trying to snatch a morsel.

Finally stepping back from the center of the action to wander up to the tent and change his wet clothes, Simon found himself facing Kanguk. Her arms and hands were hidden under a blanket she had wrapped around herself, and she was not wearing mukluks but moccasins. She stood very still. Simon noticed her bare knees and shapely calves, even a slice of thigh where the blanket was split. He also noticed the sheen of her long hair that enveloped the sculptured face in the magical twilight, the intensity of her eyes.

"Come," she said, her hand appearing from under the blanket and seizing his. Looking over his shoulder as if reluctant to leave the colorful scene, but mainly to check whether Umilik had noticed the girl leading him away, Simon followed.

Walking briskly, the loose blanket allowing her to stride, Kanguk led him along the shore to a set of outcrops. She climbed up without letting go of his hand, then sat and slid down into a hollow, sheltered on all sides from the wind and from curious eyes. All pebbles and stones had been piled at one end, leaving clean sand.

"Welcome to my upluk," said the girl, sitting down and pulling him down beside her.

"Ooplook?"

"My love nest."

"For Umilik?"

"No, silly. For you."

A dog's cry of pain startled Simon. Trying to rise to peek over the edge, he was stopped by Kanguk who reached for his parka and started to pull the zipper. Around the fire the dogfight got fiercer, distracting Simon.

"Don't mind the dogs," the girl said, now pushing back his hood and pulling on his sleeve. "Eskimo dogs are used to fighting. It's their nature."

"I don't care about the dogs," Simon said, which wasn't true. He liked animals, even these half-wild sled dogs. Maybe especially these unloved, uncared-for creatures. Besides, the activity of the whole village around the fire a stone's throw away, and especially the proximity of Umilik, the girl's beau, his friend, gave him little comfort. "Kanguk," he said when she'd gotten his parka off and laid in the sand, "I'm leaving in the morning."

"I know," the girl said, sliding the blanket back over her shoulders, pointing two firm breasts at him.

Touched by the smell of Ivory soap that had replaced the girl's scent of seal, and suddenly overcome by a wild passion, Simon tore off his clothes. Still wet and cold, he wrapped her blanket about them, and the world of order faded to the edge of his consciousness along with the possibility of his creating a child, a quarter-Eskimo creature so far from his own kind it might as well be born and raised on the moon.

Around the fire, the dogs were still yapping, people talking, occasionally shouting, though the dusk was about to turn into dawn. As the two sat up, facing each other, Simon was shocked by the splotches of blood the girl was wiping off her thighs and off his parka with a corner of the blanket.

"I guess I'm a woman now," Kanguk said, smiling. "Your woman."

"Jesus!" Simon said, covering her with kisses, then folding her in his arms. But it wasn't sympathy the girl desired. Her passion was just awakening. She wanted more, making love with a fire and yet a gentleness, matching Simon's abandon as if it wasn't the first night, but the last.

Which it was.

When they climbed the wall of the "bird's nest," peeking over the edge, the lights were out. The men cutting up the seal were gone, along with the spectators. The meat for eating had been divvied up, the blubber for stoves and lanterns stored in cans and locked safely in the mission shed. Only the dogs still lingered. Still hungry, still pawing the gravel for a drop of spilled blood.

Without a sound, the girl flung her arms about his neck, pressing her body against his, trembling violently. The sudden breakdown of her reserve so surprised Simon that he simply stood, holding her just tight enough to let her breathe. Before long, Kanguk's body relaxed. She leaned back, regarding Simon with luminous eyes and traced his bearded face with her hands the way a blind girl might. She had shed the image of a wild spirit and become Marie-Louise, the girl the father had baptized into the church, a gentle, caring, loving woman.

"I like your face," she said. "I shall remember it always. In the fall, when you watch the geese fly south, will you remember Kanguk?"

Controlling his urge to climb back into her upluk, Simon nodded. The girl wrapped herself in the blanket, and strode away, the loose hair flowing down her back. Before she disappeared between the tents, she looked over her shoulder, flashing a smile.

Simon waited, then circled the tents, away from the water. He also looked over his shoulder, but he did not smile. He remembered that fellow Gus in Fort Chimo who had tried to kill Lebeau over a pretty girl and shot poor Charlie instead. Umilik had needed a tackle box full of shells to kill a seal. If he was awake now, watching, he wouldn't be tossed on the waves, shooting at a bobbing target. He would stand on terra firma, aiming coolly at a broad-shouldered man walking up an incline. Umilik would not miss. For an instant outside the tent, Simon almost welcomed a bullet, but it never came. Only the sun pushed out of the sea, painting the village red.

CHAPTER 32

"A fairy tale," Jonah huffed, relighting his pipe.

"Yep," Ludwig said, "from the middle ages, called Le droit du seigneur."

That was a bit of a stretch, Simon thought, but he wasn't about to start an argument.

Mitch asked whether Simon had ever seen Snow Goose again, and Simon shook his head. The following day, he explained, he'd flown back to Fort Chimo, grateful that the girl hadn't come down to the shore to see him off. He didn't mention how sad he'd felt as the plane roared over the village and the slender figure stood on the hill, without the golden crown, hair streaming in the wind.

"You were luckier than me," Mitch said. "At the end of the first summer when I had to leave the forest, my woman threw a fit. The whole damn village tried to run down my jeep."

The men laughed.

"It wasn't funny," Mitch said grinning, and rose. "Not that Consuelo was a dog. She was as pretty and sexy as any young paisana. When I got back the following year, she had a child. A little girl, half Caucasian. Unfortunately, or fortunately, I guess, Consuelo was a popular dish. An intern at the mission laid her, and one or two of the mining engineers, too. Still, if you want to know the truth, the child might have been mine."

Mitch left. Jonah shuffled to the restroom, then excused himself also. Over Simon's objection Ludwig ordered another pitcher.

"You've got to be pulling my leg about this arctic goose."

Simon shook his head.

"Come on! A sixteen-year-old native virgin who's not only beautiful and intelligent, but educated?"

"You forgot sensual and loving. Her father, the Norwegian navigator, must have been some stud. The opposite of her phlegmatic mother, anyway."

"What did she look like? I mean, really."

"Like the carpenter described her. A movie squaw. In a fifties Western, I guess he meant. Honey-skinned. Lovely."

"Was it a racial thing? Is that why you left her?"

"I don't know. I don't think so. What would you have done in my place?"

"Examined my feelings. Then either brought her south, or not."

"That would have been hard to do, even if I'd had the means to hire a bush pilot. Things might have turned out differently if I'd stayed in Fort Chimo. I nearly did. Snowstorms delayed my flight south for ten days. If I'd spent the winter up there, who knows what I might have done. Still, I considered myself lucky to be able to return to civilization."

Ludwig took a long draft, half watching the TV.

"It was an odd experience, returning to civilization," Simon said. "When the plane finally got to Ottawa and I stepped onto the tarmac, I felt like an alien landing on earth."

"Mitch said something similar the last time he returned from Ecuador."

From the airport Simon had taken a cab directly to the campus, asking the driver to wait. Confirming his registration for the fall semester should have been a mere formality. But since Simon had missed the deadline by a week, the registrar wouldn't let him enroll for a full load. The rules allowed for two courses, provided the professors agreed. Simon could of course appeal to the admissions committee whose chairman was Professor Olsen, the head of the English department.

The administrator let his eyes wander up and down Simon's outfit, making him suddenly aware of his lace-up boots, khaki slacks, the red flannel shirt that showed prominently under the open army-green parka with gray fox fur framing the downed hood. His beard was unruly, his long, wavy hair reminiscent of Uncle Baptiste's mane.

As an honor student, the registrar continued with a sneer, Simon should have been more prudent and booked an earlier flight.

Simon ran to the Arts Tower to call on Dr. Olsen, who was also his adviser. Not that he had much faith in the man's will to help. The popular professor's velvety delivery mesmerized students, yet when Simon read over his notes, he often found little substance. Even before knocking on the door, he knew that he was wasting his time.

"Ah," Dr. Olsen greeted him, opening the door wide and spreading his arms without intending to embrace him. "See-mon! So glad to see you. We've missed you."

Simon launched into an explanation for his belated arrival, and the professor shook his head, professing deep regret. He was the chairman of the admissions committee, that was true, but they were too busy to meet this week. Besides, it would look like nepotism if he, as his friend and adviser, talked up his case. Anyway, he personally would love to have him hang around an extra year.

"Professor Olsen," Simon said, trying to sound calm, "I'm nearly twenty-three years old. I'm tired of being a student. I need to make a living."

"My friend, things have a tendency to work out for the best."

"As in Candide?"

The professor nodded, grinning.

As frustrated as Simon felt, he nearly grinned, too. Voltaire's hero, who believed he lived in the best of all possible worlds, wasn't so wrong. Simon had always loved the world as it was, with its beauty and ugliness, joy and misery. A world that Sister Elisabeth called God's testing ground. Yes, assholes like Olsen and the registrar were God's creatures, too. Like the black flies in Fort Chimo.

On the way down, Simon stopped at Professor Friedman's office. Gustave Friedman, a Swiss immigrant with a degree from Yale, was the head of the French department. Dr. Friedman assured him he could enroll in two of his courses, and, with his language skills, easily minor in French.

When he climbed into the taxi to find that the meter had run past the ten dollar mark, Simon got angry. He was an honor student and had been treated like a panhandler begging for a favor. The closer the cab came to the apartment on Argyle Avenue, the more he felt like chucking a B.A. degree and going back North. To work with men.

At the house, Simon tipped the driver and hurried up the three stories on the outside stairs. The apartment was locked, so he reached into the rain gutter above the door and pulled out the key. Then he entered the old haunt, bending his head to keep it from bumping into the slanting ceiling.

Wellington Kelly, who shared the apartment with Simon, wasn't in. Wellington's room looked neat. Too neat for him to be in town. The bed was made, and even the records were stacked. His roommate usually drove home for the weekend. He had probably played poker all night Sunday night with his father, a hard-working country doctor, and some of the other leading citizens of

Smiths Falls. If Simon had arrived a week earlier, when he was supposed to, he'd have gone with him. Wellington would be back tonight, still hung over.

Simon's own room smelled musty. Without sheets, his mattress looked like a discard from a Goodwill store, which it was, as was the flimsy card table by the window with its rickety chair, now covered with dust. Dust on everything: the lamps, the books, the shelves made of red bricks and unpainted boards. Dust on the dresser, on the manual typewriter he'd put away in the closet, on the framed picture of Sister Elisabeth as a young woman on horseback sitting crooked on its top, her rosary hanging on the wall above it. The Carleton student who'd spent the summer in his room had been a worse housekeeper than himself.

Simon opened his duffel bag and pulled out his clothes. Unraveling a bundle tied with the sleeves of a shirt, he unveiled a carving Umilik had made for him, a cross with the body of Jesus nailed to it. Lifting it up, he was amazed at how effeminately the Eskimo had carved the Savior, the tilt of the head, the limp arms and legs and body. Not Simon's image of the Christ, of God who was man, muscular and gritty, tougher than any man he'd ever know. Umilik, a warrior himself who created nothing but scenes depicting struggles to the death, didn't see the struggle in Jesus, only the kindness. He'd carved a Christ as soft as a seal.

After a long shower, the first hot one in nearly four months, he opened a bottle of O'Keefe's from the fridge, spread a pad and sheet on the mattress, and lay down. He ought to go out for a drink to celebrate his safe return, or to drown his disappointment at having to study an extra year to get his degree. But drinking was a social ritual, and he didn't want to round up his buddies to help him cry in his beer.

The October sun that flirted with the dirty window lit the silver cross on Sister's rosary. Simon studied it for a while, then jumped off the mattress, stuck the empty bottle in the carton, and rummaged in his closet. Instead of the heavy flannel he'd worn all summer, he put on a white button-down shirt and a vest. In a tweed coat and cotton slacks he headed out into the cool, bright afternoon.

In the loafers that fit like moccasins instead of the heavy boots he'd worn for months, he felt so light-footed he had to make an effort to keep from floating. He walked along Elgin Street, stopping at the bank, then on toward Confederation Square, which, because of the traffic tie-ups around the circle and war memorial, was known as Confusion Square. It was the heart of downtown Ottawa, along with the Parliament buildings, shops and restaurants, the railroad station, and the old, grand Hotel Château Laurier.

If Wellington were in town, they would have had a few beers, put Brubeck on the hi-fi, and talked. Then they'd have eaten out and gone to a Western, munching popcorn and cheering on the Indians. It would have been good to talk. He hadn't had a real conversation since he'd left in May.

Leaning his back against a shop window, he watched the traffic on the square. A bus lumbered up to a stop. Several of the disembarking passengers glanced at him, and a young woman with bare legs and an attractive smile turned her head before disappearing into Sparks Street.

He hesitated a moment, then walked in the tracks of the pretty woman, just to have a purpose. Strolling along the busy street, he was astonished at the large shopping crowd on a Monday afternoon. When he passed a barbershop, a rather fancy salon, he went in for a shave and a haircut.

~~~~~

As Simon poured more beer, he noticed that Ludwig was no longer listening but watching the television set high above the bar, though the sound was too low to hear the words. Simon struggled to his feet and lurched to the bathroom and back to the table, where he leaned heavily against the back of the chair, also turning toward the screen which was depicting shoppers on a New York sidewalk. It was like waiting on the bench in the Ottawa barbershop, he thought, watching shoppers pass by the window, wishing he had a home to go to.

In that barbershop, he'd closed his eyes, thinking of his mother. Who surely was still alive, a musician, a singer, perhaps popular, even famous. The picture of his mother he carried in his mind at that time was that of a pale woman with dark hair. Sometimes he saw her performing in a concert hall. Then again she played in the band at Lafitte's beer joint on the road to Alma, stamping her foot with the rest of the musicians, laughing lustily at the ribald jokes.

As Simon opened his eyes, a woman looked into the barbershop, and for a moment they locked glances. A middle-aged woman carrying a guitar, her hair was parted in the middle and clasped in the back. Brown hair with streaks of gray. Large hazel eyes. Simon sat petrified as two young ladies joined her, one with a violin, the other holding an instrument in an elongated case, possibly a flute, both laughing. Then all three vanished from his view.

He could have followed them and addressed the woman. And been ridiculed. It couldn't be his mother. They were musicians going to rehearsal. Or coming from it.

Civilization. He was back in civilization.

The barber, bald and friendly, offered him a seat and flung a sheet around his neck. He sharpened the razor on a strop, soaped his beard, and started to shave him with short, precise strokes. Grateful that the man didn't talk, Simon again closed his eyes, thinking, despite himself, of the woman he'd seen regarding him through the window.

In the North, he hadn't thought much about his mother. And that was good. Because dealing with his mother's desertion wasn't getting easier, though you'd think his own mistakes would make him less judgmental.

Too bad she hadn't died when he was born. Her death

would have absolved her of guilt. But when he kept pestering Sister Elisabeth about his mother, she eventually told him that no woman of child-bearing age had died in the city that week, and none was admitted to the hospital to be treated for any birth-related complications. No, his mother and her two companions had simply stuffed him into the cardboard box and driven off.

All his life he'd been nagged by the fear that she had abandoned him because she couldn't stand the sight of him. That she had hated him for interfering with her music, her pleasures, her career, her selfish life. And a fear even worse, that he, too, might have his mother's callousness. Was his callousness the reason he'd abandoned Kanguk?

But what if his mother had been depressed? Believed that giving up the child was the lesser of two evils? His poor fucking mother. What the hell! Poor fucking Simon. What could be worse than rejection by one's own flesh?

With his long hair trimmed and brushed and a smooth chin smelling strongly of aftershave, he wandered back the way he'd come. Outside Yousuf Karsh's photo studio he stopped as he always did to have a look at the famous man's latest work on display. He'd hung out three pictures. On the left a portrait of Albert Einstein, with that rascally glint in his eyes, bright fuzzy hair against a dark background. Slightly above, a man in an easy chair, a politician or a business man, judging from his cynical eyes. A frank, unflattering study. On the right, at eye level, a picture he couldn't make out because the reflection of his own face obscured it. Stepping aside, he immediately recognized the broad forehead framed by silken hair, the big eyes, never quite in focus, the somewhat heavy nose contrasting with the fine lips, turned downward at the corners.

Ellen Jones!

What a contrast to his own face reflected next to hers! His tanned forehead and nose and cheekbones dark as leather, topped by his dark hair, which, despite the trim, was still unruly. More odd was the shaved lower half of his face with its unhealthy pastiness. At least, he admitted to himself, his eyes weren't weighed out of focus with sadness. It must have been Ellen's eyes that had compelled Karsh to photograph her. Besides being an ambassador's daughter.

Simon had the sudden urge to call the girl whose party he'd crashed four months ago. Years, in a young woman's life. She was on a first-name basis with the prominent sponsors of the Little Theatre. She met a dozen new people every week at her father's cocktail parties, including foreign diplomats. How long did it take to fall in love? A second? A split-second? She wouldn't remember him. Why was he determined to embarrass himself?

After one last look at her troubled eyes he turned, ambled again down Sparks, and entered Woolworth's bargain store. In the semi-darkness of the soda counter, he ordered coffee and a banana split, taking his time, enjoying the treat, lighting his pipe. Then he leafed through the book at the pay phone, put a nickel in the slot, and without a clue whether or not this was her address, he dialed the number of T.P. Jones on Buena Vista in Rockcliffe, where many government big wigs and diplomats resided.

"Yes!" a man's no-nonsense voice said.

Surprised to hear a man answer in the middle of the afternoon, he responded, somewhat hesitantly, "This is Simon Philipe. I'd like to speak to Ellen."

"Ellen doesn't live here anymore."

Simon's hopes vanished. He was too late. The girl had gotten married. Still, he spoke up, even raising his voice. "Could you give me her phone number, your Excellency?"

His Excellency took his time coming up with his daughter's number. Simon was surprised how easily that title had passed his lips after the months in the north. But he and Wellington had been in and out of the homes of their friends in the diplomatic corps so often that using absurd titles had become second nature. It's like being an extra in a nineteenth century operetta, Wellington said, after he'd called on the short-sighted daughter of an Austrian count.

"Who did you say you were?" Mr. Jones asked.

"Simon Philipe."

After another long pause during which he was either checking a pad or deciding whether to tell him, the ambassador obliged, and Simon wrote the number onto his left palm and thanked the man. Back at the counter, he relit his pipe, and sipped the lukewarm coffee.

If he could have borrowed Wellington's car, he would have crossed the river to the Gatineau Club. He could have a couple of drinks and take in the show, then pick up a woman there. Maybe one of the dancers. A night of sex. But that was not what he wanted. He wanted to make love. Love with every fiber of his being.

After ordering another coffee, he put a nickel into the slot and dialed the number he'd printed on his palm. On the fifth ring, Ellen answered.

"Simon Philipe," Simon said. "How are you?"

"Out of breath. I just came through the door."

"I saw your picture this afternoon."

A pause, then, "Ah! The one on Sparks?"

"Is there another?"

She laughed in her low, clear voice. "I'm glad you're back. I thought you'd flown the coop. Where have you been?"

"Up north."

Almost stunned at the ease with which they talked—like old friends, though he'd only exchanged a few words with her at the party he'd crashed—he told her about the arctic and asked her to have dinner with him in the Grill at the Château Laurier.

"There are more reasonable restaurants," she suggested.

"I've been eating out of cans all summer. Can you meet me at the Grill around seven o'clock?"

"Yes."

By seven, he was pacing around the pillars in the lobby, wondering why he had suggested such an ostentatious place, why he had made a date with a girl he didn't know. Then she pushed through the revolving doors, approaching with a firm step, smiling with closed lips. Fine, flexible lips. A contrast, he thought, to the strength in her legs, her strong, wide hips. And her eyes, so somber in the picture, were smiling, her silken hair bobbing on her shoulders, some of its wisps touching the pearls around her neck. Everything about her looked strong.

No peck on the cheek, as there would have been with a French girl. A nod of the head only, a soft hello with her low voice. Not that Simon was more demonstrative. He also nodded with a smile, appreciative of her brown, unobtrusive yet elegant autumn dress, suddenly conscious of his secondhand tweed coat, the worn trousers, his scuffed loafers. At least his silk tie was new and his loafers shined. He considered offering her his arm. To a French girl he would have done so. He, too, he realized, had adopted the cool ways of the anglais.

They ordered Scotch, he on the rocks, she with water. He suggested she try the arctic char, but she preferred snapper, and Simon asked for a T-bone. The conversation was slow starting. Though Ellen had spent the summer in the cultured heart of the capital while Simon had lived in the tundra, she apparently found it just as hard to find words.

"How was the North?" she asked when the waiter had taken their orders.

It took Simon a moment to come up with an answer. He thought how he'd loved the land of the midnight sun, the work, and the men. How on the Hudson Strait he'd felt at home. And he thought of Kanguk, and suddenly felt so sad he closed his eyes. When he opened them, Ellen offered him a cigarette from her Player's pack, and as he accepted it, he saw Kanguk. And indeed, he realized, there was a great physical resemblance. Probably a mental one as well, he thought, giving her a light, then lighting his, elated at the discovery.

"It was a good summer," he said, blowing a cloud of smoke that mixed with hers. "And yours?"

"I worked as a filing clerk at Freiman's department store. On the first of this month I moved into an apartment on Gilmour."

"How did your parents take it?"

"They're helping me out, actually."

"I talked to your father today. He gave me your number. There was a moment, I think, when he considered not to."

"I doubt that. If my father met you, he'd like you."

"Why do you think that?"

"As a student he also worked in the North. Northern B.C."

Just then the waiter brought their drinks.

"*Santé*!" said each. Ellen blew smoke from the corner of her mouth, and tasted her Scotch. Simon asked her about her studies and learned that she was a philosophy major.

"As an actress, I expected you to study English."

"Except for a couple of his plays, I don't care for Shakespeare."

Simon, who considered Shakespeare the greatest writer of all time, was surprised. "Why?"

"The language has changed, and so has the Christian ethos."

"Are you a Christian?"

"I'm as Christian, I suppose, as our culture allows."

Years later when Simon asked himself why he fell in love with Ellen during that dinner, he thought it was because she didn't ask questions. Because she accepted him as he was. Would accept anybody, he felt, as they were. He'd have felt comfortable introducing the carpenters to her.

With dessert, they ordered coffee and cognac, then went outside, circling the Square to Elgin Street. Ellen slipped her left hand lightly into his elbow, and they walked to her new pad in a red brick house on Gilmour, not far from his own place. She preceded him down some steps to a basement efficiency with only one tiny window in the kitchen.

Simon glanced at the dishes in the sink, the half-empty cardboard boxes stacked in one corner, the pile of clothes in another, the crooked stack of books and papers on the one chair.

"Are you shocked at the mess?" she asked, turning off the ceiling light and pulling the chain on the bedside lamp.

He was surprised, but figured she was still rebelling against a too-orderly parental home. For an answer, he drew her to him and kissed her, and she kissed him back, slowly, exploringly, and only gradually with passion. Then, as if on some silent command, they shed their clothes, adding them to the general disorder on the floor. Ellen stripped the quilt off the bed and switched off the light.

When his first ardor was gone, she offered him more. She met his hunger with humor, going out of her way to please, and Simon felt he'd come home.

In the morning, when his lips brushed her belly in the pale light from the kitchen window, Simon suddenly stiffened.

"Stretch marks?"

She nodded, her eyes enormous.

"Where's the child?"

"Gone."

"Dead?"

"Adopted."

Thunderstruck, he sat up at the foot of the bed, leaning away from the woman's body, as though she'd become too hot to touch. Ellen, very much aware of his reaction, pulled up her legs, holding her knees, lying bowed and drawn in the middle of the narrow bed.

"Was it a boy?" Simon asked, having regained his calm.

"A girl."

"You must get her back."

"I can't. It's not possible."

Of course it was possible. "When did you . . . ?"

"Last fall. There's no way I can get her back."

"Why?" he asked, though his question sounded more like, "How could you?" He bit his lips.

"I wasn't given a choice," Ellen said, sitting up now, pulling the sheet over her knees and reaching for her Player's.

Everybody was given a choice. He watched her pick up the lighter on the nightstand, watched the smoke obscure her face. She blinked, her eyes now void of the luster that earlier had brightened the morning. Since the little girl had been adopted as an infant, the parents would love and treat her as their own. Maybe never tell her she was adopted. And if the child did find out, and wondered about her mother and her father, she'd have to grin and bear it. Like him. The one suffering now was not the baby, it was the childless mother.

Ellen switched on the lamp, dressed and sat on the edge of the bed, smoking. Kneeling on the rug in front of her, Simon tried to catch her eye, but she wouldn't oblige. Her eyes were directed toward the kitchen window, tawny and detached, like the wolf's, Simon thought. Only, what this woman had lost was worse than the severance of a leg.

Deeply regretting his first reaction, Simon took the cigarette from Ellen's hand, stubbed it out in the ashtray, and took her in his arms. He wanted to tell her that her child would be all right, that he, too, was adopted, had never known his mother, and yet he'd loved his life. But he didn't, just hugged her harder, wiping his tears that threatened to wet her hair.

Banging the counter with a bottle for the second time, Alex offered his patrons a last round. Simon joined Ludwig in a long yawn, waving the waiter off. Maybe for the first time ever it occurred to Simon that quite possibly his marriage had failed because he hadn't been able to heal Ellen's wound, although he'd been so convinced that he could and would.

"It's terrible to be in love with two women," Ludwig said, yawning. "Especially for the women."

"In all fairness, I don't think that's my problem."

"Maybe not. But I know what your problem is. Having grown up Lutheran, it's a problem I used to have myself."

Ludwig yawned again and seemed to have lost the thread of his thought.

"Well, are you going to tell me? I'm curious now."

"You sleep with a broad once, and you feel obliged to commit yourself. That's your problem."

Simon shook his head. Not with Ellen, Simon was certain, though it was hard to tell so many years later. On the other hand, Ludwig's assertion about Simon's attitude toward sex and marriage wasn't completely off the wall. Sister Elisabeth still ruled. That's why he hadn't touched Sybil, not because of a promise to St. Francis. He had to smile. That promise, too, was Sister's doing.

"Times have changed, Simon. This is the seventies.

Nineteen seventies, not eighteen seventies. Or is it Sybil's color that stops you from giving her her dues?"

"That's funny, but I'm too tired to laugh. Tomorrow's a long day. And I'm meeting Sybil's grandparents for lunch."

"Grandparents? She a ghetto kid?"

"Her grandparents raised her, but they're white. She grew up in one of those large homes with park-like yards on South Belvedere. And we're having lunch at The Four Flames."

"Grandparents in loco parentis. How long have you known this girl? Three weeks, a month? Isn't it a little soon for an engagement?"

Simon got to his feet. "Sybil wants me to meet her grandparents because they don't disapprove of our relationship, and they have influence among her relatives."

"What's the matter with her relatives? Prejudiced against honkies?"

"More the twelve-year age difference. Still, I feel odd. This luncheon reminds me of the time I had to meet with Ellen's parents. It's like history repeating itself."

Rising, too, Ludwig said, "That's what history does. It's its nature."

The two men waved to Alex and the few remaining drinkers, and steered out into the sobering night.

CHAPTER 33

Having double-parked outside the downtown high rise where Sybil worked, Simon cranked the truck and drove off before she'd snapped her lap belt, all the while throwing admiring glances at the girl gracing the seat beside him.

"If I were an Englishman," he said, "I'd say you look smashing."

Sybil crossed her legs and smiled at him. "I'm glad you like me in skirt and sweater. It's what I usually wear at work."

"I like these because they're as muted and soft as the colors of the Southern fall."

"Gramme will be happy to see me wear the sweater. It's a gift from her." She pronounced Gramme like the music award.

"Are we really meeting with the grandmother who abused you as a child and now consumes half a gallon of bourbon a day?"

"You can't hold grudges against the sins of the past. Certainly not against a person who couldn't help herself. Despite her drinking, Gramme and Senator have a

307

pretty good marriage, considering."

"Considering what?"

"Senator's from an old Southern family. My grand-mother comes from pioneer stock. Rough and tumble. A touch above white trash."

Sybil's frankness was refreshing. Obviously her grand-mother wasn't white trash anymore. As a senator's wife, she must have acquired generations of respectable ances-tors.

"At eighty-five, Senator's still mentally alert. Still writing. Giving talks about the Civil War. He's also an expert on the Boss Crump era. Back in the thirties, when he was elected to the State Senate, he was a lawyer for Mayor E.H. Crump."

A man who kept the blacks in their place by buying their votes. At least he hadn't stonewalled their demands as Mayor Loeb had the garbage workers' when Martin Luther King was shot. If the mayoral dinosaurs in the city of Memphis represented the politics of her grandpar-ents, he would have to bite his tongue.

"You don't mind their politics?"

"They have theirs, I have mine."

"Why do you think the old man puts up with your grandmother's drinking?"

"Most days she doesn't start until after lunch. On good days not until before dinner."

"Let me warn you. I'm not like the senator. If you should start drinking, regardless of whether it's me who drives you to it, I don't think I'd put up with it."

Sybil laughed. "You're the one who keeps buying me wine."

Simon remained quiet. It all seemed a little more than he'd bargained for. Indeed, history repeating itself. Then again, it wasn't the same. With Sybil he was stepping in with both eyes open.

As he thought he had with Ellen, of course. Going to parties, the theater, movies, discussing books they'd read, playing Scrabble with each other, or bridge with fellow students, making meals for each other, and love. Always love.

"I don't know why I'm doing this," she said the second night they spent in her apartment. "I'm a sucker for punishment."

"If you get pregnant, we'll get married."

"And what will we live on?"

"Love," Simon said, laughing. If he suddenly had to support a wife and child, he would find a fulltime job. He always had. If push came to shove, they'd move to the town of Sudbury in northwestern Ontario and he'd work in a mine for a couple of years. The money they'd save would make an existence in that desolate area tolerable, especially if he could finish school by correspondence.

What a glorious time they'd had at Carleton together. What optimism about a future that beckoned with possibilities of riches, joys, children, adventures. So unlike the present. Now that he'd been picked for the department chair and was about to buy another house, his future was laid out, so to speak. An unsettling thought. Unless, of course, he got serious with Sybil. She'd create challenges of a different sort.

Squeezing into the parking space at The Four Flames put idle thoughts on hold. In the doorway he glanced back at the four torches burning on pillars in the middle of the day. It was probably these oversized gaslights that gave the midtown restaurant its reputation.

Inside, the decor was simple enough not to detract Simon from his hosts already seated at a window. He shook the trembling hand of Mrs. Bolton, Sybil's Gramme, whose first husband had sired her mother, and went around the table and offered his hand to the frail old man whose gray suit had become too loose for his emaciated body, but who rose from the chair and shook it.

"Glad to meet you, Senator."

"I understand you are a professor," the senator said with a weak but clear voice, and a twinkle in his eyes.

"At Brinkman."

"*Eh bien! danse maintenant*," Mrs. Bolton declaimed, quoting the last line of La Fontaine's fable *La cigalle et la fourmie.*

"*Ah, vous connaissez La Fontaine*," Simon answered, amused yet impressed. "*Le poète est un de mes auteurs favoris.*"

The old lady, who looked as worn and as bitter as a French Canadian matriarch with a house full of children, smiled. "I just told you all the French I know. It's what my grandfather used to tell us when we misbehaved. He was a teacher in a one-room schoolhouse in Pueblo, Colorado."

"One of my teachers, Sister Benedicta, made us memorize 'The Cicada and the Ant,' and several other fables. For her, La Fontaine, or Aesop, I guess, since they were really his stories, competed with the Bible."

"What was it that your grandfather told you, Gramme?" Sybil asked, looking over the rim of the menu.

"Aren't you sorry now you took German instead of French?" her grandmother said without much humor.

The old man came to Sybil's rescue. "It means," he said, turning his head slowly toward his granddaughter, "instead of working and storing food, the cricket sang all summer, and when winter came, and the singer was starving, the busy little ant told her to eat her songs."

"I'm not sure I agree with La Fontaine," Sybil said, putting the menu down. "A person ought to use her talent."

Not at the expense of other people, Simon thought, but he didn't voice his opinion. He was there to be checked out, and he wasn't interested in involving himself in a pointless discussion. "Pueblo," he said, "must have been a primitive place when your grandfather lived there, Mrs. Bolton. Were you there when he taught school?"

"No, but my father was. I'm a descendant of a long line of pioneers."

"Gramme's a Daughter of the Revolution," Sybil said,

probably to bring the conversation back to the present. And she said it with the same kind of pride with which she might have announced that her white grandmother was a member of the NAACP.

"In Canada," Simon said, "I believe there's an organization called Daughters of the Empire."

"Ah," the old lady said. "Don't tell me your mother belonged to the Daughters?"

"I'm afraid not. My mother was a working woman."

"How do you like Memphis?" The senator forestalled his wife's response, adjusting his hearing aid.

"It's a good place," Simon said smiling, "if you own a horse."

Not sure what to make of this reply, the old man nodded, turning to the waitress, poised beside him, waiting for his beverage order.

All except Simon, who wanted a bottle of Dos Equis, said just water, which was already on the table. For the entree, Senator ordered salmon, Gramme shark, Sybil grilled lamb chop with creamed spinach and steamed potatoes, and Simon asked for trout.

During the meal, the grandmother steered the conversation back to Simon's family. As a retired lawyer, she considered herself a working woman, too, and wanted to know what kind of work his mother had done in Chicoutimi. Simon explained about the drugstore, and the summers spent with an uncle in the woods. He smiled at Mrs. Bolton. "A pioneer type."

"It's too bad about your parents. I must say you yourself look the picture of health."

"On the whole, that's true. I guess I inherited my Uncle Baptiste's constitution," he lied without blinking, and wondered whether he'd done it because of his involvement with Sybil, or whether he was getting to believe that Baptiste was his real uncle. In either case, he resolved not to make this claim again in the future.

"So your uncle is still living?"

"No, he's passed away, too. I have no living relatives."

"You're alone in the world?"

Simon shook his head. "Far from it. I have two sons and a daughter, and two horses, and a job I like." And maybe Sybil, he thought, laying his left hand on her right.

While they ate they chatted little. During dessert, the senator invited Simon to his cottage on Horseshoe Lake sometime. Simon thanked the couple for the lunch and excused himself to get back to the college and his two o'clock class. Sybil rose from the table and accompanied him to the truck.

"You think they approve?" Simon asked.

"Gramme approved already before she met you. She maintains that a relationship with a mature man stands a better chance."

A chance for what? Simon wondered, but he only said,

"And your grandfather?"

"He doesn't care, as long as I like you."

"You like me?"

313

"Yes, I like you."

As he backed out of the parking lot, Sybil watched, smiling brightly, then returned to the restaurant. Simon, on the other hand, didn't smile. His stomach felt heavy, the fish wanting to come up. Had he ordered trout to make a good impression on the old couple that wanted to pass judgment on him? His breath smelled fishy, too. His hands. It was symbolic. Getting caught in the net again.

Not that Simon had considered himself caught in the net when he and Ellen decided to get married. Not even when he called on her parents that December night to ask them for their consent. Her mother opened the front door just enough to look at Simon in the beam of the entrance light, parka hood up, hands deep in his pockets. Before she had a chance to speak, Simon introduced himself. Mrs. Jones asked him to step inside where she left him standing in the hall and hurried up the circular staircase. Simon had pushed his hood off and was deciding whether to unzip his parka, when Mrs. Jones came down again, followed by the ambassador, who descended the stairs three quarters of the way and stood, holding on to the rail, looking down at Simon.

"You know who I am," Simon began, since Ellen had informed them of their marriage plans.

His listeners stared at him as though they didn't have a clue what was to come. Looking from one to the other, he blurted out, "I've come to ask you for your daughter's hand in marriage." Then he closed his eyes, swearing under his breath, trying to speak in a less stilted way. "What I mean," he added, opening his eyes wide and un-zipping his parka, "Ellen and I would like your consent, and your blessing."

"Well," the ambassador said, straightening up, letting go of the rail and descending the rest of the stairs, "nice of you to ask us, but Ellen's of age. If she wants to get married, she can do so."

"Nevertheless," Simon replied, "we want your blessing."

Her mother's dark eyes glistened. With a smile, she said, "You have our blessing."

The ambassador nodded, holding out his hand, and Simon shook it.

~~~~~

Well, the lunch with Gramme and Senator had gone well. Without much significance, of course. Hardly comparable to Simon's meeting with Ellen's parents. The real test would come when he met Sybil's father, the "Masai warrior" she'd called him. That, he hoped, was a few weeks off. He'd deal with her father when the time came. Or rather, if the time came. As he would deal with her other black—or white—relatives. Tomorrow was Saturday. Fox hunt! And the following weekend, the Nashville Event. First things first.

CHAPTER 34

On the rise at the north end of the valley, Simon sat Snow Goose listening, watching. Usually Stefan accompanied his father, but today the young whipper-in was riding with Hugh Huffman, master and huntsman, who was now combing the wooded ridge, encouraging the hounds with occasional high, short puffs of his horn. Some of the dogs drifted out of the covert, tails high and noses to the ground, circling through the browning bermuda, then drifted back into the trees.

Suddenly they hit the scent on the far side of the ridge and hustled off in full cry. Below Simon, the field emerged from the trees, crossing the grassy plain in a hand-gallop, aiming for the coop over the barbed wire fence that separated the grassy plain from the woods. A coop—two wooden panels made of oak boards spread wide at the bottom and nailed together at the top to cover the barbed wire—is an inviting fence, but this one was fronted by a ditch, offering the horses a challenge.

Lily Terrell, the young field master, jumped her big bay hunter across the ditch, took one stride and floated over the coop, disappearing into the trees. Gerry Cousins, at sixty no longer the most agile rider, uttered a shout as his gelding popped the fence, lifting him a foot off the saddle and coming down hard. One or two of the big horses flew across the trench, bouncing the panel, but most of the riders made their horses drop in and scramble out of the ditch, then took a stride or two before jumping the coop.

Melissa Banion's red gelding, that tried to leap across, didn't make it. His front hooves hit the bank, and he landed on his chest, throwing the girl over his head, and she plowed face first through the churned-up weeds. The last rider, a pony clubber named George, held his horse, looking around for help. Simon spurred the Goose, within seconds arriving at the ditch. He jumped off and threw the reins to the boy. The gelding had risen to his feet, shaking himself, but the fallen rider lay motionless. As Simon touched the girl's shoulder, she lifted her head, face bloody, covered with dirt.

"Don't move," he said, kneeling down beside her. "Relax a minute."

Over the ridge, the sound of the fast moving hounds was fading. A few moments later, Melissa rolled onto her back, and stretched out.

"My face hurts. And I think I broke my wrist."

The young woman, probably still in high school, gave him her right arm, slowly moving her wrist and her fingers.

Simon pulled her up. "You got bramble scratches, but your hand's not fractured. Do you think you can jump this coop?"

She nodded, but the pony clubber shook his head.

"Hounds have gone away," Simon said. "We can try to catch up, or you two can ride back to the clubhouse together. Your choice."

"Catch up," both said decisively.

Simon gave Melissa a leg up, mounted, and led the two in a canter down the valley. Approaching an easier coop at the lower end of the field, Simon asked them to follow close to Snow Goose, who floated over these coops easily, dispersing whatever doubts still lingered in Simon's mind about the Nashville horse trials only a week hence. George's bay mare hesitated but jumped, and so did Melissa's gelding, both riders gaining confidence on the next panel, downhill out of a black locust stand where they had to bend low to avoid the spikes on the branches. The girl's chestnut seemed to have fully recovered from his fall. During the descent to the iron bridge that lay crumbled on the far side of a sandy stream bed, Simon commented on the gelding's gleaming red coat that reminded him of his stolen Jesse, a loss Snow Goose's performance made easier to bear every time he rode her. More to pass the time than to satisfy his curiosity, he asked the girl what high school she attended.

The young woman laughed. "I'm twenty-three years old. I'm a college graduate, married, and pregnant."

In that case, Simon suggested, they shouldn't jump anymore, but Melissa assured him she wouldn't fall again. She talked about her husband, who was a lieutenant in the Navy stationed at the base in suburban Millington, and about her job at Union Planters Bank, where she assembled collateral reports on loan applicants.

"Sounds like a lot of typing, he said, and Melissa nodded.

Just the thought of typing gave Simon the shivers, even when it came to using a computer's keyboard. He never could figure out why. Perhaps because Ellen's first job after the wedding was in a typing pool. Simon had been stunned the afternoon he walked into her place of work, seeing four long rows of women at tables no larger than school desks, so many he couldn't find his wife among them. A supervisor floated up and down the rows of women of all ages and sizes, all pounding away on huge, black manual typewriters.

Waiting in the doorway in the rear, impatiently glancing at his watch, Simon wondered how a person could do finger gymnastics eight hours a day without getting cramps, and admiration for his tough, talented wife swelled his heart. Then a bell shrieked, the drumming stopped, and the women rose and started moving toward the rear door. Standing in the middle of the opening, Simon ignored the females filing past as though he were a rock in a stream. He finally discovered his wife coming toward him, purse and coat hanging from her shoulder, smiling, the corners of her mouth up.

"I get claustrophobic," he said, grabbing her hand and hurrying her down the stairs, "just looking in at the place."

"It's a job. Until I find something better."

Having her beside him in the Corvair, sitting back, lighting a smoke, and laying her hand on his thigh, he felt happy. And powerful. Not only because the automobile cruised safely through the rush hour traffic, passing the cars crawling on the snow and ice covered streets, but because he had a wife, a partner who'd mastered a job he himself couldn't do, who could obviously master anything she set her mind to. Both his full-time job teaching English in Hull at the Institut de Téchnologie and two First Year courses of French at the university were going okay, too, and he could see the end of his studies. The world out there was beautiful, with a hundred options, all beckoning. Simon picked up her hand and pressed the palm against his lips.

"What's that for?"

"For letting me love you! I'm so rich it's hard to bear!"

"Huh?" she said, but she smiled.

Although their one-bedroom apartment on the top floor of a three-story brick home on Renfrew was as modest as their furniture, Simon felt they were living in a castle tower, a love nest safe from the demons within, secure from the enemies without. And when he left his fortress, he no longer had to stand in the wind at the bus stop; he drove a new car, loving it. With the traction of the six-cylinder rear engine, he easily traveled the hazardous streets to and from his two jobs home to his wife, who normally took the bus, and who had dinner ready on the candle-lit table.

Shortly after Ellen had accepted a position as a writer with the Royal Canadian Mounted Police, Simon picked up a black kitten in an alley in Hull, nearly starved to death. Ellen called it Lumumba after the first African leader of a free Congo, who'd just been assassinated. During the day, the kitten ventured into the world by descending the fire escape to the backyard, returning through the window at dinner time. One evening it jumped into the car with Simon when he drove to the university, and followed him from the parking lot through the busy hallways into the elevator and to his office.

"Odd," Professor Friedman said. But the professor didn't mind the black cat stretched out on Simon's desk, watching him read papers, cross out words, and scribble between the lines. When Lumumba sharpened his claws on the wooden legs of the desk, almost in slow motion, his tail up, his long back stretched to its limit, Simon reached down, stroking the silken fur. "You're not odd," he said. "You can feel the woods in me, as I can in you."

One night, Lumumba dashed as usual into the apartment ahead of Simon, jumping up onto the arm of the couch at Ellen's elbow, who stroked the cat with a knitting needle.

"You guys had a good time?" she asked with a sly grin.

"Lumumba chewed on a student's quiz, and my first

class wasn't so hot."

Ellen rested the knitting in her lap, watching Simon in the hallway take off his coat and his boots. Coming back to the living room, he said, "What's up? You look like you've swallowed the proverbial canary."

"You've done it!"

Simon regarded his wife's peaceful yet excited mien and the large ball of sky-blue wool beside her. "Are you knitting what I think you are?"

She nodded.

"How do you know it's going to be a boy?"

"It feels like a boy." Again, the knitting needles clicked softly. "Or would you rather have a girl?"

He took off his tie and sat down beside her, reaching across her lap to pet the cat that pushed its face against his palm, purring its deep, rumbling purr. With the other hand he touched Ellen's belly, stroking it gently. All of a sudden his wife had become a vessel, an almost holy creature that would bear a child, and he was at a loss for words.

"You want some dinner?" she said, kissing his hand.

"I had a sandwich on campus."

"You feel okay about my being pregnant?"

"It's wonderful. And you? Are you as happy as you look?"

"Except for my job. I'll lose it. Women are obliged to quit at the end of their first trimester. And I like my job!"

Simon had expected better from the Mounties. But

by the end of the summer he'd have his degree and he'd get a raise. Education policy was changing in Quebec, the Church slowly withdrawing from the school system. With a B.A., his salary would increase fifty percent. They'd manage.

"Do you want to play Scrabble?"

"No, I think I'll turn in."

"You aren't sick to your stomach, are you?"

Ellen smiled, shaking her head, and held out her hand. Simon pulled her up, lifted her into his arms, and waltzed the laughing woman to the bedroom.

~~~~~

"I think I hear hounds," the boy said, bringing his horse alongside. "Can you hear them?"

Simon raised his head. They were walking through a herd of white-faced Hereford cattle grazing on an incline, close enough to the highway and the subdued roar of passing eighteen-wheelers.

"I think what you hear is traffic. Sounds like the distant bay of hounds. If you open your mouth and relax, you can tell better."

"You're right," the girl said excitedly, pointing northwest, away from the highway traffic. "That's hounds, isn't it?"

"Sure is."

He led the way through a grove of oaks with low hanging branches toward a weathered panel in the fence line, so close to the steep bank the horse couldn't risk more than half a stride after landing before it was forced to turn sharply right and slither down a narrow, nearly vertical descent to a web of roots, with a four-foot drop from there to the sandy bottom. Usually the ditch at this "wailing wall," as the hunters called the notorious crossing, held only a few inches of water, but even some of the experienced horses had second thoughts before dropping into it. On the other side, the bank was steep as well but more manageable. Riders just had to watch that they didn't bang their knees in the narrow gap between the sweet gums at the top.

"Hold on after you land and the horse makes that sharp turn," Simon advised, remembering Jean Rienzi, who'd lost her balance, tumbling down the twenty-foot bank. There was a foot and a half of water in the sandy bottom that day, softening the plunge, so she'd only fractured a collarbone.

After taking the coop and sliding down to the roots, Snow Goose hesitated a split second before she jumped, splashed through the brown liquid, and started up the other side.

"Grab mane," Simon shouted, holding on himself as the horse scrambled to the top of the nearly vertical bank. Almost immediately, the boy pushed through the brush behind him, followed by the girl, both glowing with excitement. They rode up the incline between the paddocks of McPeters' barn now, causing the horses inside to gallop in circles. Leaving the horse farm over a rail near the stadium course, they cantered through tall, orange sage, crossing a freshly trampled path. They stopped, examining the hoof prints, all pointing north-east.

"Is that where the field went?" the boy asked, eyes beaming.

"Looks like it. But we won't follow them. We'll take a shortcut to the left. That's where Mr. Coyote will show if he circles."

Cantering to another ditch crossing, Simon asked his companions not to follow too close. If his horse fell in this rough stuff, they needed room to stop. Snow Goose leapt more than cantered through the grass and reeds that reached above the riders' heads.

At the next fence, they jumped into a pasture with a large herd of Angus yearlings, all approaching the three riders like a black wall. Simon trotted toward the very center of the herd, cracking his whip and shouting, "Get." For a long moment the animals stood as if frozen, then turned about-face, moving off to either side like the parting sea. Flowing together again behind the hunters, they stood with raised heads.

"Can you hear hounds?" Simon asked.

"That way," the boy said, pointing southwest.

Cantering away from the beeves, they soon came to a rickety bridge made of oak boards laid over telephone poles that spanned the ditch full of overflow from the lake they were approaching. Snow Goose, staring at the wide cracks, refused to tackle the weathered boards.

"You think one of your horses will give us a lead?"

The two shook their heads.

Simon dismounted. Handing the girl his whip, he asked her to tap his filly on her rump when Simon stepped on the bridge leading her. But Snow Goose didn't need Melissa's encouragement. She followed voluntarily and calmly, unlike George's mount that crossed the bridge like a scared cat, not knowing which side was a greater threat to her life, and Melissa's gelding acted similarly. As they mounted again, a large, crooked V of Canada geese flew south, straight over their heads, gossiping.

"They've come a long way," Simon remarked, following the birds with his eyes until they disappeared.

What was wrong with him? First he groveled in the halcyon days of early marriage, then Kanguk beckoned him. "I won't have it," he said out loud, kicking the filly, and she shot forward, high stepping over holes and roots on the slippery ground along the lake shore. Farther down at the overflow ditch, the water reached to the rim, and there was no bridge. Without any comment, Simon spurred his horse into the muddy liquid, lifting his legs high to keep the water from filling his boots. Getting wet up to her neck, Snow Goose didn't need much encouragement to plow through and climb the soft bank on the far side. Both of the other horses followed, first the bay, then the chestnut.

"The water's run into my boots," the boy said.

"Mine, too," the girl complained.

Simon laughed. "You're certified fox hunters now."

Meanwhile, hounds' voices had become louder, more

to the north than the west. Galloping along the big lake, Simon looked over his shoulder. The huntsman emerged from the distant covert, unmistakable on his white mare, followed by Stefan on Par Three. And then a red coyote came bobbing down the slope.

"Tallyho!" Melissa shouted, pointing forward.

Holding up his hand, Simon halted. "Let's not turn him," he said. "Wait for hounds."

Within seconds, the entire pack appeared over the hill in full cry, tails high, noses to the ground. The coyote turned north into a fenced pasture, attempting to lose its scent among the half dozen Hereford bulls lazing in the lush fescue grass. If it didn't hurry, the distraction of the bulls wouldn't help. Hounds would hunt it by sight. But the coyote didn't dawdle. Turning east again, it crossed the ranch road and disappeared into the cedars.

"Did you view?" the huntsman asked, coming up with Stefan and riding past, expecting them to follow.

Simon described the route the coyote had taken.

"Any idea where the field went?"

"No. When Melissa crashed, the field left her behind, so she and George rode with me."

Noticing the scratched-up face of the young woman, her wet horse, breeches and boots, the master graced her with a rare smile. "I guess you better ride with us. Everybody got left behind."

Except Lucy Harnett, who was approaching fast on her tireless Anglo-Arabian, trailed by an outrider a quarter mile back. While the whipper-in was catching up,

Simon cantered beside Stefan, who told him how far he and the master had gone, and how they had always just missed a view.

Hounds picked up the coyote's line again and ran north in full cry. The small group of hunters galloped after them, Rockford's white mare in the lead. And then from the south, spread out and in full gallop, the riders of the field appeared.

Simon asked Melissa, who seemed very pale, how pregnant she was. When she said four months, he tried to slow her down. The way this wild dog was running, losing the hounds, then letting them find it again, it was obviously playing with them, and the hunt might well last another hour. Or longer. He offered to accompany her to the clubhouse, but Melissa declined. Somewhat disconcerted, Simon shrugged. It was probably all right for a pregnant woman to ride on the flat, but jumping ditches and coops?

Not that Ellen had borne her pregnancies wisely either. She'd smoked, and drunk at parties. Nobody had told her she shouldn't. Nicotine, maybe just the mechanics of smoking, seemed to make the morning sickness more tolerable. So did her work for the Mounties. Even at the end of the third month when Ellen was forced to resign from her job, she remained active in the theater. In fact, very little changed during her pregnancy. She shopped, cooked, and made love. If she felt discomfort, Simon wasn't aware of it. But he was aware of the creature developing within her. A boy, she was convinced by the way he kicked.

Almost seventeen years before, he'd driven Ellen to Grace Hospital, which was run by the Salvation Army and reputed to be the best birthing place in Ottawa. At two a.m. the wind blew so hard through the empty streets it rocked the car. The heater blew lukewarm against their legs. As always, Ellen claimed to be all right, though the labor pains were obviously becoming torture. Simon was cold, worried about making it in time, worried about the care at the old facility, the actual birth, the loneliness of his wife in the hands of strangers. As they approached the hospital from the rear, the inconspicuous structure looked deserted and he wondered whether they hadn't made a mistake by not choosing a facility with bright lights inside and out.

The slowness of the clerk at the desk where he signed a form and handed his wife over to the care of a nurse made him feel even worse. After Ellen disappeared around the corner, the woman dismissed him with a gesture that came close to being contemptuous, as if he were a schoolboy who'd knocked up his girlfriend. Driving home through the darkly lit brick canyons, he felt he'd abandoned his wife. Letting her give birth in a strange place seemed as cruel as leaving her in some jungle. He visualized Ellen birthing a son with his help in Paradise, bedded on the wolf skin, a fire roaring in the hearth.

Simon didn't have to see his wife's exhausted countenance the next morning to realize what she'd been through, though now, with the little boy suckling on her breast, fiercely, shaking his tiny hands, she looked at peace.

"Greedy little bugger," Simon said, touching the fine, dark hair on the baby's head, making an effort to consider the miracle of his son's birth as routine. He was walking on a cloud, yet felt guilty, and he swore to share the arrival of the second child.

And two and a half years later when Simon was a graduate student at the University of Kentucky, it really looked like he would have more luck in that Southern city than he'd had in Canada's capital. Ellen's doctor informed him that if he and Ellen took a course together in prenatal care, he'd be allowed in the labor room when the time came.

The large number of young women in various stages of pregnancy in that course, all trying to stay limber, relaxed Ellen. Simon was not thrilled by the slide show of a naked woman shortly before giving birth. The close-ups showing the stress the maturing fetus causes on the mother's body were graphic. He began to understand Ellen's desire to get the birth over with. The obstetrician cooperated. Unwilling to change his vacation plans, he induced her delivery a week early. Seeing Ellen's swollen feet, Simon suppressed his objections.

In contrast to Grace Hospital in Ottawa, St. Joseph Hospital in Lexington was a busy, bright place. As Simon escorted Ellen through the door to give birth to their second child, the tremors that vibrated through her body shot through his hand and arm like electricity.

Within minutes of her admission, a nurse led them to a dimly lit cubicle, asking Simon not to panic when his wife yelled a little.

In the semi-dark of the windowless chamber Ellen lay on a single bed, covered by a sheet. Simon could barely make out her features. It didn't matter. He was glad that he couldn't see the strain on his wife's face when the pain came, only feel it through the grip of her hand in his. The pains quickly became more intense and slowly, very slowly, more frequent. Ellen's body trembled, then shook, and she screamed. And no matter how he held her, and what he said, nothing he did could help her.

Simon pressed the button. The nurse who witnessed similar scenes every day took her time before she came. When she eventually showed up, Simon pleaded with her to give Ellen a shot. She couldn't, she said, showing no pity. Labor pains, she probably figured, were the price woman paid for the miracle of birth.

Witnessing his wife's agony, Simon would have given anything to switch places. Yet he breathed a sigh of relief when they wheeled her and not him away to deliver the baby.

And again it was morning before he got to hug his wife in the room she occupied with a woman fast asleep.

"You want to see Stefan?" she asked, chipper and smiling.

"Stefan?"

"They pressured me into coming up with a name. Since we'd only discussed girls' names, I was at a loss.

At Carleton, you and I liked the name Stefan. The priest told me there was a saint called Stefan."

Simon laughed. "If not, there will be one now."

At Carolyn's birth, two years later, Simon was an instructor in the French department at Transylvania University, a liberal arts college just a few blocks north of the University of Kentucky in Lexington. When their neighbor called his office, he was editing the re-write of his dissertation on François Villon, the fifteenth century vagabond poet who'd barely escaped the gallows but never lost his lust for life. Simon's secretary, a boy on the work-study program, sat at a desk beside his, typing furiously.

Janie, the neighbor, told him that Ellen had driven herself to the hospital, and would he mind coming home to take care of his children. She needed to do some shopping. Simon glanced through the last typed page, laid it on top of the growing stack, and added the title page, "François Villon, Sinner and Saint." Switching a briefcase full of books and papers from one hand to the other, he jogged the fifteen minutes to their rental apartment on Short Street.

After changing Stefan's diaper, he spent a few moments playing fish with four-and-a-half-year-old Mark, and then, standing by the stove stirring spaghetti sauce, he corrected the day's quizzes. As soon as the children were in bed, he took off again. The May night was so pleasantly cool that running to St. Joseph's he didn't even work up a sweat. He found Ellen dozing with the bedside lamp on, an open book resting upside-down on her chest.

"Is it a girl?" he asked, removing the book.

She nodded, smiling, reached for the metal stand, and picked up a photograph. "That's her."

Simon held the color Polaroid shot under the lamp. A baby with a wide forehead and light-colored, wide-set eyes. "She's beautiful," he said, pressing her hands against his lips.

"I must admit it's nice to have a girl. A child who looks like me."

"Both boys look like you. Very much so. I'm not a very pre-potent stud."

This made her smile.

"My dissertation is due Saturday. You'd better get some sleep. You won't get much when you come home."

"I'm fine. Don't forget the car. It's parked on the right in the last row."

"Janie will keep an eye on the boys while I teach tomorrow. I'll come back to see you when they're in bed. Is there something you need?"

"Strength."

"You've got plenty of that. You're my hero."

Ellen squeezed his hand. Simon became aware of the woman in the other bed who seemed to be waking up. Time for him to return to the children who were by themselves, asleep, he hoped. If they weren't, they'd have to cause quite a racket for Janie to hear them in that solid old brick house. He fidgeted with his watch, wanting to tell his wife how much he loved her. Words were so inadequate. He stood there, holding her hands, not wanting to let go.

~~~~~

It seemed Señor Coyote had given hounds the slip in the woods, a good half dozen miles north from where the three riders had met Stefan and the huntsman. Some tired hounds slunk out of the trees into the fallow bean field, looking up at the Master, but others stayed in the covert, not yet ready to quit. Huffman, afraid they might cross the nearby highway, blew his horn, calling them in, and gradually, in ones and twos, they trotted out of the woods.

On the southern horizon, the riders of the field approached, walking their tired mounts. Simon turned to Melissa, whose face looked ashen between the black eye and the dried blood along the scratches. "What's wrong?"

"Nothing, I hope," she said with a strained expression.

"Let me ride to the clubhouse with you."

Melissa nodded, unsmiling. Simon talked to the master, and he and the pregnant woman rode off, entering the woods.

"My kingdom for an armchair!" she said, groaning.

"Would you rather lead the horse?"

She shook her head. "I don't think I could."

Simon, suddenly feeling tired himself, was glad they could open gates and wire gaps instead of jumping fences on their way to the October cub hunt brunch in the clubhouse. He wouldn't mind a soft chair himself right now, not to mention a beer.

On the parking lot, Simon jumped off Snow Goose's back and tied her to the trailer. Melissa hesitated before dismounting. Grabbing her reins, he watched her drag her leg over the chestnut's rump. Supporting her hips with both hands, he let her slide to the gravel, then removed her tack.

As Simon helped the woman load the compact little gelding, the members of the field arrived, the riders talking and laughing, exhausted yet exhilarated from the day's wild chase. Beyond the road, the huntsman blew his horn, indicating to the initiated that he had returned with the entire pack of hounds, and all was well with the world as he knew it.

CHAPTER 35

Crawling in the bumper-to-bumper traffic through the suburban sprawl, Simon fought sleep. Tired from the day that had started before sunrise, and full of the hunt brunch's lasagna and a heavy Cabernet, he regarded his son beside him, leaning against his jacket suspended from a hook. He touched Stefan's shoulder. The boy turned his head, tired also, but smiling. The best young rider Simon had ever seen. From the first moment the nine-year-old boy had climbed onto the back of Par Three, he looked like a pro. Instead of giving the boy pointers in the arena, they rode the horses out on the trail where they not just walked and trotted but cantered. And the sweet, three-year-old gelding acted as though he knew he was carrying precious cargo.

At least until a dog dashed out of the bushes. Then Par leapt sideways, dumping the child, who landed head-first inches from a stump. He wasn't unconscious. Nor was he crying. Before Simon had stopped and turned his horse, Stefan had risen to a sitting position, holding his wrist, blood running down over his left eye.

"How's your head?" he'd asked, parting Stefan's hair

to check on the cuts and abrasions, and wiping his fore-head with the tail of his T-shirt.

"My wrist hurts."

It didn't seem to be broken. Simon helped him get back on the horse. At home, they put band-aids on his forehead and wrapped the arm with ice.

"Do you remember your first trail ride?"

"You mean when a cur dog jumped from the bushes and I banged my head?"

"Absurd the way we tempt fate. Melissa Banyon, who fell today, is four months pregnant. But I can't fault her. I did worse. In Las Cruces I let Mark share the seat behind me on the motorcycle, and you straddled the gas tank in front of me."

"Mark and I loved it. Too bad Mummy didn't like living in the desert."

"Your mother was raised in the capitals of the world. She feels at home in a city."

As much as he'd liked Southern New Mexico, Simon hadn't regretted his move to Memphis. He did feel an occasional twinge of regret for coming to this sprawling metropolis where the humidity rivaled that of a rain forest's, the mercury was liable to burst the thermometer in the summer, a cold snap bust the pipes in the winter, and addicts didn't just break down your door and destroy the sanctity of your home. If you happened to be in it, they were liable to shoot you.

He recalled the summer day when Ellen made the announcement at the dinner table that from now on the boys had to lock the front door.

"Nobody on our block has been broken into," Mark observed.

"Things are changing. There was a break-in on Sheridan yesterday. Another on Vollintine. And a bad one in Dr. Mason's house on Jackson. There have also been burglaries in Hein Park."

"It's a good thing we have a dog," Carolyn said.

"Yeah," Mark scoffed, "a sweet Dalmatian wagging his tail!"

"Let's say grace and eat," Simon suggested. Taking a hand on either side, he prayed, "Thank you, Father, for our blessings. Make the thieves see the harm they do, and help the victims overcome the hurt. Bless this food. Bless us. Amen."

"What's with this anxiety all of a sudden?" he asked Ellen, who sat across from him at the round oak table. "What's happened?"

"I was robbed on the bike. This boy on a ten-speed came up from behind and ripped my purse from the carrier. I chased him north on Watkins to the public housing where he disappeared."

"I'm glad you didn't catch him," Simon said. "Your purse isn't worth getting shot for."

"What was in it?" Stefan asked.

"Stuff. A couple of twenties. My driver's license. Do you know how much trouble it is to get a new driver's license?"

"I think it's great you chased him," Mark said.

The others grunted in agreement. And the picture of Ellen furiously pedaling through the projects after the elusive robber made Simon smile.

"Catching the little bastard would have taught him a lesson," she said. "I felt violated. Imagine how the woman across the street feels who was raped last week."

"What woman?" the children asked in one voice.

"Linda Vaughn. The pretty blonde with the three girls. I wouldn't have mentioned it, but after what happened to me today, I thought maybe I'd better. The rapist was only a teenager, like the boy who took my purse, but he had a gun, and he's already raped three other mothers in the neighborhood."

"What would you do, Mummy, if a man held a gun to your head?" Mark asked. "Would you let him?"

"It won't come to that!" Simon broke in.

"It's a good question," Ellen continued, ignoring Simon's signals. "What would you do if a fellow threatened you with a gun?"

"Is Mrs. Vaughn going to have a baby now?" Carolyn asked.

"No. This boy demanded oral sex."

"A blowjob?" Mark said coolly.

"Fellatio's the term," his mother corrected. "No matter how you rape, it's a violation of a woman's body. Of her soul."

"Let's continue this discussion after dinner," Simon ordered. "And I don't think you ought to bike to work anymore. It's not safe."

"I bought a hiking belt for my wallet."

"I'm talking about the traffic."

"You let us bike to school," Mark reminded Simon.

Biking to work was the only way she got her cardio-vascular exercise, Ellen declared. She didn't have time to run when she came home, like him. She had to cook. And in the morning, she got the boys ready for school.

As usual, she was right. She kept on biking until early July when the temperature passed ninety-five. Then she took the car to work, and found out how she would react with a gun pointed at her head. Actually, the big fellow in the Medical Center parking lot aimed it at her chest, just as she was reaching in her purse for the key.

"Gi' me your purse," he said, waving the little gun from a couple of feet away, a glazed, mean look in his eyes.

"You can have my money," she said, extracting her wallet, "but I won't give you my purse. I don't have the time to stand in line again for a driver's license." She handed him the bills, crumpled up in her fist. "Here!"

The fellow stuffed them in his pocket along with the gun and took off running.

"And you didn't catch him?" Simon asked, causing some laughter, even from Ellen. "Next time," he said, "for the sake of your children, and for my sake, give up your purse." In his heart, however, he was proud of her. It was what he imagined he would do. Unless, of course, he kicked the revolver out of the robber's hand and wrestled him to the ground.

"Jesus!" Simon exclaimed.

"What's wrong?" Stefan asked, opening his eyes and sitting up straight.

"I was thinking about crime in Memphis."

"Did I tell you that Victor's family's moving to Germantown? Blacks are sick of crime, too."

"The other day I looked at a place in Cordova. A three-bedroom home, a barn, and twenty-some acres of pasture."

"Can we afford that?"

"Not really with one income."

"Well," Stefan said, rubbing his eyes, "we're doing okay, though, aren't we?"

"Sure we are. We're doing super."

CHAPTER 36

Next morning Simon woke early to a clear, cold morning. This being the Sunday before the Nashville horse trials, he drove to the barn after breakfast and worked Snow Goose on the flat. It wasn't she who needed the work. He did. By the time he got home, the sun had come out, and the two children were ready for church. A quick shower, and off they went to mass at St. Patrick's, picking up Mark on the way. To reward his brood for attending church, he invited them to lunch at the Pancake House, then took them biking in Overton Park. By midafternoon, tired and happy, the kids were back in their respective homes. By the time he settled in the beanbag to read French papers, he had to switch on the lights.

Ellen had picked Stefan up for a dress rehearsal with the Snowden School string quartet, and Carolyn was upstairs playing Dungeons and Dragons at Carrie's with a couple of her friends. Carrie's mother would feed her. He himself would do with a leftover potpie he'd eat on the way to the barn.

Diligently, without any distractions, he worked away, hoping to get through in case Sybil showed up to go jogging in the park. However, when Sybil came in the door at five past eight, he had neither fed the horses nor finished the corrections.

Despite a bulky, gray sweatshirt with faded blue letters advertising Amnesty International, Sybil's appearance stopped his breath. A blue sweatband that was absolutely unnecessary with her cropped hair enhanced her sculptured features, and as he stared up her long, shapely legs ending in short, white shorts, he said with some effort, "I'm a slowpoke. I'm not done with my papers, and I haven't fed the horses yet either."

"Why don't I go feed the horses while you finish your papers? Then we can relax." She held out her hand. "Keys? I didn't bring my car."

"They're in the pickup. Sure you want to?"

"If I'm to become a horsewoman, I'd better start with the basics."

She headed toward the kitchen and went out the backdoor. Simon put the potpie into the toaster oven and continued his work. By nine o'clock, a few minutes after Sybil's return, he was finished. He changed into his black shorts, T-shirt, and running shoes, then phoned upstairs, telling Carolyn he was about to go jogging with Sybil. She could finish the game if she wanted to, and not to forget to brush her teeth before hitting the sack.

Heading out the front door, they met Stefan coming in, carrying his violin, and outside, Ellen's car was stopped at the curb, the left turn signal blinking. There were two more boys in the back seat of her car. Ellen waved through the windshield. Simon nodded, and Sybil waved back. While Ellen waited for the line of cars to let her pull out into the traffic, Simon and Sybil jogged north, easing into a run.

"Ellen's a good woman," Sybil said, lengthening her stride, forcing Simon to increase his speed. "I wish we could be friends."

"I don't see why you couldn't, given time. Do you have white women friends?"

"I have more white friends than black. Due to my job, I guess. And probably because I'm more white than black. Sometimes I think that the only thing black about me is my color, and even that isn't very black."

Enjoying her long stride, and at a loss for an appropriate comment, Simon remained quiet.

"I am black, of course. To a majority of people I'm just another black female, not bad looking, no, a nice piece, but when you come down to it, I'm just another nigger. Ergo, whether I like it or not, I'm more black than white. Which means I'm black. *C'est la vie.*"

Simon laughed, grabbing her arm to slow her pace. Ellen's car had made it out into the traffic, now passing them. Two intersections ahead, it turned left to drop off the boy who played the cello. She would have to drive the viola player over to Hein Park. Then she would drive home where Mark, he was sure, had built a fire in the living room.

"The guy who proposed to you, is he black?"

Instead of answering his question he thought he'd had

no business asking, Sybil said, "Carolyn tells me you marched for Dr. King."

"One time. On the first anniversary of his assassination." Simon would never forget the Memphis cops who lined the downtown streets and stared with such censure at Ellen and him leading three small children, he feared for their safety, and he was glad to be shielded by black folks.

They now ran on the short, soft grass of the park, and Simon switched to a higher gear.

"What did your acquaintances say when you joined that march?"

"Martin Luther King was Ellen's hero."

"Ellen's? And not yours?"

"I don't have any heroes. Not since my teens, anyway. When I worked in the Alma store for Monsieur Berthiaume I did admire Rodrigue, the protagonist of Paul Claudel's drama, *Le Soulier de satin*. The play, *The Satin Slipper* in English, was one of my favorite books."

"What is this play about?"

"Rodrigue is an adventurer who falls in love with a married woman. Rather than getting involved in a sexual relationship, since she's married, they renounce it and seek fulfillment in a mystical union. But even for that, they pay. She dies, and he becomes a slave."

"A slave? When did this melodrama take place?"

"During the time of Columbus."

"I can tell you one thing right now. My love wouldn't be fulfilled in a mystical union."

"Obviously neither would mine. All I have in common with Rodrigue is his Catholicism. Or I did, before the divorce."

"Come to my church. Episcopalians don't reject sinners."

Simon laughed, tempted to mention King Henry the Eighth and his syphilis that, in the final analysis, caused the split with the Pope.

They were approaching the zoo. Stepping from the grass onto the broken asphalt of the parking lot, she grabbed his hand to slow him down.

"I like to see where I'm going," she said.

"You mean in regard to me?"

"I mean I don't want to sprain an ankle. Yes, in regard to you and Ellen, too."

"I thought you understood my connection to my ex-wife. The stress on ex. Even if I hated her, I'd be tied to her through the kids. It's natural that I love and admire her for what she's achieved, raising three children, putting up with my selfish ways. But I'm not in love with her. I'm in love with you. I know I never told you that in so many words, but you know it."

They'd been running in the bus lane, and now Sybil slowed to a stop, facing Simon.

"Okay. I agree with what you're saying about being connected to Ellen. About your being in love with me, that's another story. I don't think you're really in love with me. I'm probably just another challenge to you. Another adventure. You're intrigued because I'm black. You want to show your colleagues, your friends, your neighbors, this racist town, how progressive you are. Maybe, in some twisted way, you want to punish your ex-wife for dumping you."

"Maybe. There's a grain of truth to every motive you've mentioned. And there's one more point. I believe you could be the woman to create another loving home for the children."

"Huh! Become your live-in maid." She laughed. A cheerful, friendly laugh. "As wonderful as your children are, I bet they can be a handful. You really think I could handle them?"

"Yes. You've got a mountain more patience than I. They do test my patience, especially Mark. He's a tough kid. Always was. His slender build and long hair are deceiving. When I was a Scout leader a few years back, I watched him play football with the troop at Little Flower. Mark was in the fourth grade, practicing with the big boys on the gravel parking lot, no pads; knees and elbows bare. On the first play as a lineman he sacked the quarterback, recovered the fumble, and scored a touchdown. And in camp, when he kept making snide remarks and some of the bigger boys cornered him in the woods to beat him up, he pulled his Scout knife and looked so threatening they left him alone." Simon grinned. "Mark does have a smart mouth. Smart enough at times, Simon thought with regret, to make him lose his temper.

They were standing at the edge of the bus lane, the dark forest beckoning at Sybil's back.

"Three kids," she said in almost a detached way. "Children need lots of love. I don't see how you can spare much love for other people. I'm a person who needs tons of love."

Simon grabbed her hands, then moving his palms along her arms and shoulders to the sides of her head, he began covering her face with kisses, and Sybil responded in kind. He was about to lead her into the woods, when the howl of a wolf broke the stillness of the night.

"What was that?" Sybil asked.

"I'll be damned. That was a wolf."

Sybil pushed Simon back, trying to read his face. "Are you serious?"

"There must be a wolf in the zoo. I heard it once before, two, three weeks ago."

"Does it make you homesick?"

Touched that she had really listened to his wolf story, Simon shook his head. "Midtown Memphis is my home."

"I'm glad," Sybil said, moving away from the edge of the woods and starting to jog in the direction they had come.

Reluctant, yet somehow relieved he hadn't dragged her into the bushes, Simon followed. He'd dodged a bullet. Or had she? The idea made him laugh.

"What's so funny?" Sybil asked, still running in front of him.

"Me."

"Yes," she said, reaching back for his hand, "and I love

you for it.

CHAPTER 37

When Simon packed his gear for the Nashville horse trials, Stefan suggested once again that he compete with Par Three instead of Snow Goose. He again insisted that the cross-country course in Percy Warner Park wasn't safe for a young horse, mainly because, to earn his B-classification with the Pony Club, he'd had a refusal at an airy feeder without a ground line. He still hadn't forgiven the technical delegate for allowing that obstacle.

The fact was that Stefan didn't trust Snow Goose. He believed his father expected too much from the Anglo-Arabian who was only three and a half years old, as Ellen believed he was always asking too much of his children. But from the very beginning, Simon had taken it easy with the foal. He'd put a halter on her at the age of two or three weeks and led her in the field with the mare in tow, always petting the foal as a reward. Before long, she'd learned to stand still to be brushed and have her hooves trimmed. On a sunny spring day, Simon had dusted off the old cavalry saddle, spread a Western blanket under it, and approached the long-legged yearling filly while she was eating. The Goose turned her head a fraction, regarding the object that touched her side.

Talking to her, he moved the saddle back and forth, letting the heat-hardened leather rub her skin. Then lifting it, he gently lowered the saddle over her back. The filly stopped chewing and brought her nose back, trying to grab the blanket with her teeth. Simon reached under her belly to straighten the girth, pulling it up and fastening it loosely on the billets. The McLellan fit her back perfectly.

"I guess you've seen enough saddles on the other horses," he said, leading her out into the paddock. Holding the lead rope, he asked her to move forward but she spread her legs, then bucked, landing hard, shaking her head. Simon laughed, stroking her neck, and asked her again to walk. This time she did. He led her a couple of times around the paddock, then removed the tack, watching the filly run around the enclosure, bucking wildly.

He'd used long lines and lunged her in the spring she turned two but didn't ride her until that fall. It had been an unexciting moment. Once he'd climbed into the saddle, Snow Goose wouldn't move. She stood inside the paddock gate like a statue until Stefan teased her with a can of feed. After that she walked and trotted, obviously hardly bothered by the nearly two hundred pounds on her back, and she'd listened to Simon's legs.

Then, against Stefan's advice, he took the horse to the bottomlands. "Wow!" he said, sitting deep in the saddle, loving her soft canter on the rutted road. Out in the field he let her gallop. Approaching the shore of the beaver pond, he tried to slow her down, but the Goose, excited by the wild run, took her time responding. Hopping high over the eroded ground, she stopped a foot from the edge, threw up her butt, and tossed Simon in a high arc into the pond. The water wasn't very deep, just enough to prevent his breaking his neck. Rising and shaking muddy water from his eyes, he got a glimpse of the filly galloping the way they'd come, reins and stirrups flying.

Half laughing, half cursing, he sloshed to dry land. Opening his belt and the zipper of his chaps, he shook himself, then took off his running shoes and emptied them, getting ready for the long hike to the barn. He had hardly walked a hundred feet when a white flash dashed through the distant trees and then, pounding the ground at breakneck speed, came galloping toward him. The Goose bounced to a halt inches away and threw up her head, whinnying.

One rein was gone, and a stirrup was missing, probably torn off in the woods. They were worn leathers and reins and had easily broken.

"You nutball," Simon said, stroking her neck. "Horses don't return to the scene of the crime. But thanks." He checked her mouth and kissed the soft spot behind her only lightly blowing nostrils. Grabbing the one rein, he swung himself into the saddle.

Snow Goose had only been hunted a couple of times, but she had never refused a fence or a ditch. She'd even jumped barbed wire with his jacket laid over it.

"You don't really believe in jinxes, do you?" Simon asked, tousling the boy's hair."

Stefan shook his head, grinning. "I'm just jealous. I'd like to compete on Snow Goose myself."

"You will. I promise."

CHAPTER 38

At the office early Friday morning, his secretary, who'd gotten there even earlier, told him he'd received a call from Sergeant Pryor of the North Precinct. Simon phoned the precinct.

"I don't want to get your hopes up," the policeman said after a quick introduction. "I found out today from the Sheriff's Office that on Saturday morning four weeks ago, a lady on Benjestown Road—that's near Shelby Forest—reported a loose horse eating the honeysuckle in her yard. Shelby Forest's a long way from your barn, but if you want to check it out, I got the lady's number."

Saturday four weeks ago? That was the morning after the horse was stolen. To get to the northwest corner of the county, Jesse would have had to cross the northern half of the city traveling for miles on blacktop, go through traffic lights, cross a bridge over the Loosahatchie River plus all the smaller bridges over creeks and run-offs.

"I don't see how it could have been my horse, but I'll check it out. It's a lead. The first one, in fact."

The officer gave him the woman's name and number, and Simon called. Yes, Mrs. Miller said, it was a sorrel mare. Yes, she was sure. She was eating the honeysuckle on her fence and went to the bathroom on her lawn. Simon asked if he might drop by and talk to her. He could be there by ten o'clock, possibly a little earlier, and she said of course.

He'd almost put the loss of Jesse behind him. Ancient history. Now it hit him again with a vengeance. And again he rehashed his feelings of guilt. How it wouldn't have happened if he'd kept Jesse at a show barn in Germantown instead of a rundown place in a crummy neighborhood just because it was convenient. And now he was wasting time because of some woman's say-so who probably couldn't tell the difference between a bay and a sorrel or a mare and a gelding. Wasting the time driving to the distant northwest corner of the county instead of going through his lecture with Ludwig, who had volunteered to deliver it for him in his rusty French while he and Hector were off to Nashville.

At least the drive to Shelby Forest was pleasant. The steaming heat of summer had been replaced by a dry coolness, and the lush green foliage was changing to muted yellows and browns and reds. Simon envied the folks who lived along this reserve that reminded him of the woods of his childhood.

Like other homes he'd observed on the way, the outside walls of Mrs. Miller's house were built of cinderblocks. Pink geraniums decorated the window-sills. She invited him inside, but he declined, not anxious to waste more time with chitchat. A quick glance at the thick, brown bermuda lawn showed no hoof prints. And he couldn't tell whether or not a horse had indeed eaten honeysuckle off the chain link fence that separated her yard from the next-door garden, fallow except for three beds of greens and some okra stems. The fence was fully covered with vines.

Of the several hoof prints on the edge of the driveway he discovered only one that was distinct, and although the shoe looked like the size and type Jesse wore, the evidence was far from conclusive. Nearly every farrier in Shelby County used mass-produced shoes. Simon was fairly certain, however, that the horse that had walked there wore shoes in front and back.

"Are you sure, Mrs. Miller, the horse you saw was a mare?"

The woman smiled. "I'm sixty-seven years old. I ought to could tell a male from a female."

"What color was she?"

"Sorrel. Red mane and tail. No markings that I noticed."

"A small horse?"

"No, tall. Tallest I seen in these parts."

"Sounds like my horse, all right," he said, excitement lending timbre to his voice.

The woman gave him a dubious look. "I hope you're wrong. The mare I saw was in pretty bad shape. Cuts on her chest and legs, bare patches on her sides, still bloody. She must have fell on the road and cut herself on wire. Pretty deep in places. She was lame, too. I noticed it when I chased her off."

"Which way did she run?"

"North. She didn't run, exactly. She limped away."

Simon thanked the lady, got back into the pickup, and slowly drove north. Which was pointless. It'd been four weeks since the mare had eaten Mrs. Miller's honeysuckle. If Jesse had only traveled half as far each day as she had the first night, she was through the next two or three counties already.

He drove as far as the bank of the Mississippi, which made a sharp bend west along the county line, and left the truck. Dirt paths among saplings and brambles, some patches of grass, more orange sage than green fescue, and occasionally steep, narrow descents to the river. Not a bad place for a horse to recuperate. Too bad she hadn't stayed there.

Recuperate she would. Probably already had. The nights were cool, and even in the daytime flies were rare now. The skin would have healed, the hair grown back, and the cuts would have closed, if she was lucky, without infection. There would be scars. If the lady was right, ugly ones. That didn't matter. Worse was the lameness. If it was due to an injured hip, it might take a while to heal, if it healed at all. But Jesse recuperated fast. She was probably as sound as ever by now.

Back at the office before eleven he called Sergeant Pryor, mentioning the horse's injuries and the apparent route of her flight. The officer promised to get in touch with the Sheriff's department in Tipton County and ask them to keep an eye out.

"Don't give up," the officer urged him cheerfully.

"I never give up," Simon answered, making an effort to match the sergeant's bouncy voice, fully aware he'd given up on Jesse already.

CHAPTER 39

Despite the busy morning, Simon met Hector Hollenbach at his barn by one o'clock, loaded Othello, Hector's old gelding, and they headed off for Nashville. Always in the market for a new woman, Hector announced first thing he'd had a premonition about a rich prospect. On the other hand, he added laughing, he'd be happy just meeting a cutie-pie like that Sissy in Birmingham the summer a year ago.

Snow Goose traveled well by herself in the two-horse trailer, but it didn't hurt having Hector's horse along. The Ford pickup was cruising at fifty-eight miles an hour, only three miles over the limit on the Interstate. That wasn't fast, but Simon glanced at the side view mirrors every dozen seconds or so from habit, checking on the trailer and the traffic.

After some idle chatter, Hector suddenly burst into laughter, and Simon, who knew he was going to hear a joke about the French, or God, couldn't help laughing with him. "Let me give you my friend Philip's definition of Heaven and Hell," Hector said.

"Heaven," he started, still laughing, "is a place where

the Swiss are the administrators, the English the police, the Germans are the engineers, the Italians the lovers, and the French are the cooks."

Another burst of laughter, and he continued, "And hell is a place where the Swiss are the lovers, the English are the cooks, the Germans the police, the Italians the administrators, and the French are the engineers."

Simon thought the joke missed the mark in regard to the French, who, after all, had created the Concorde, but Hector's laughter was infectious. Hector told a few more jokes, none funnier. Then Simon started a Hank Williams tape in the cassette player he'd attached to the underside of the instrument panel with speakers in the rear corners of the cab, and Hector, who would have preferred Lieder by Schubert, asked him about life in midtown, confessing that he, too, had been raised near Simon's apartment.

"A shame the area's gone down. Big Foot get you yet?" Hector asked and yawned, tilting his head back.

"Yeah, he did."

The burglar, already a legend in the neighborhood, had kicked in the wooden door, breaking the frame. Stefan, tired from sacking groceries, had been napping in the bedroom at the time and hadn't even heard the uproar. After that, the landlord installed a steel door and window bars. These were no guarantee against burglaries, but they'd slow the thieves down. Simon liked the neighborhood. Whenever he returned from a weekend away, he welcomed the sight and sounds of the children strolling home from school. Even the teens with their boom boxes blasting rap. It meant there was life in the street.

"I still drive through your neighborhood Sunday mornings," Hector boasted with a grin. "On my way to church."

"What church?" Simon asked surprised.

"Unitarian. The only church a self-respecting atheist would want to be caught at."

Simon turned toward his friend who was chuckling at his own humor. That was the Church on the River. A jewel of contemporary architecture with glass walls offering an unspoiled view of the Mississippi.

"You still attend that ghetto church?" Hector asked.

"St. Patrick's, yes."

"You ought to come to our service sometime. Did you know Ellen's a member?"

"Not of your church?"

"Yes. In fact, I've considered asking her out."

Ellen and Hector? The idea wasn't as odd as it first struck him. According to Mark, Ellen was playing the field. Her latest beau was a lawyer who brought Mark candy. Would Hector be next? The picture of Ellen in bed with other men didn't exactly amuse Simon, although he wanted to believe that he had adjusted to the loss of her as surely as Ellen had adjusted to single parenting.

"I wish you luck with Ellen," Simon said, but his words were drowned out by the roar of a passing eighteen-wheeler.

At the rest stop along the uninhabited stretch between the Natchez Trace and the descent to the Tennessee River, they stopped to use the bathroom, and Simon checked on the horses. Opening the escape door, he rubbed the filly's face. Her large, luminous eyes viewed him curiously, and she tried to push her head beneath his arm. Being tied, she managed only to twist her nose under his armpit. "We're more than halfway there," he told her and walked around to the other side of the trailer to pat the twenty-six-year-old black horse, who looked more like an Uncle Tom than a Shakespearean hero.

"Well," Hector said on his return, yawning, "I think I'll close my eyes for a while. Are you okay driving?"

"Sure," said Simon, suppressing a yawn himself. He inserted a Mozart symphony into the cassette player, and pulled out into the Interstate. After crossing the Tennessee River, they would soon pass by Waverly and the farm that Ms. Baugh had used for her equestrian school four and a half years earlier when he'd taken Jesse there to be bred. He'd liked the valley, despite the closeness to the traffic on the freeway that divided it in half. There had been horses everywhere, some being lunged out in the unfenced pasture, a few getting worked over jumps in the stadium, others under saddle in the dressage arena, ridden by young women wearing helmets, breeches, and boots.

Ms. Baugh, the owner and director of the school, was a lady Simon guessed to be in her sixties. She wore breeches and boots as well, but no head cover, and her long hair was tied loosely on top of her head with gray strands falling over the dark eyes that appraised the world severely. In her left hand, veined and big-knuckled, she was twisting a dressage whip. Not to calm her nerves, Simon thought but to flex her claw-like fingers. A no-nonsense woman, tough but probably not unkind. She had to be tough to cope with the string of young women who daily handled and trained what looked like a couple of dozen horses.

She had helped him open the back of the trailer, stepping aside as Jesse backed out eagerly and threw up her head, shaking her short, red mane. She pranced and snorted, bossy and curious.

"Thoroughbred?"

Simon nodded.

"Let me show you our senior stallion. Afire Two."

Ms. Baugh grabbed the lead rope and led Jesse toward the main barn beyond the paddocks. After putting the mare into a box, she proceeded along the hallway to the other end. Behind him, Jesse whinnied so fiercely it was almost like a human cry.

"She'll settle down," Ms. Baugh said, "once you're gone." Implying, Simon thought, that he'd spoiled her. "There are plenty of horses and people to keep her entertained." Opening the door to the last stall, the woman exposed a dappled gray Arabian with a long mane and tail, stepping lively right up to them, sniffing for a treat. She produced a carrot from her coat pocket, and the stallion sucked it gently from her hand, crunching it between his teeth.

Simon was now cruising past Ms. Baugh's farm, surprised at the changed look, wondering whether the woman had closed her equestrian school, and if so, what she'd done with Snow Goose's sire. Black and white spotted Holstein cows stood in the pastures where horses had grazed, all the way up the slopes rising into the wooded hills. The big barn still stood, but the paddocks had been removed. Under a pole barn that was new, round bales of hay were stacked, probably fescue, judging by the still deep-green pastures. A couple of the sheds were new, and the two-story house on the hill had had its natural cedar clapboards replaced with aluminum siding.

The thought of Jesse, for the second time this day, moved him with sadness. He could only hope that some kind soul had found the mare and was taking care of her. Reaching into the paper sack beside him, Simon pulled out a carrot. Crunching hard reminded him he had good teeth, good appetite, and a lust for life that tended to drive depressing thoughts away.

"How's your new girlfriend?" Hector asked, half opening his eyes.

"Who told you about her?"

"Lee Hansom saw you with a woman at the Danube Café. He said you were so smitten you were dead to the world."

Wondering whether that was all that Lee, a prominent member of the hunt, had said about his date with Sybil or whether he had commented on her color, Simon remained silent.

"Well, who is she? Do I know her?"

"I doubt it. She's black."

"So? I know black people," he burst out, quite offended. "Our best designer is black. What's the woman's name?"

"McLellan."

"McLellan? Not Sybil McLellan?"

Surprised, Simon nodded.

"Good Lord!"

"What?"

"The original Ms. Luscious!"

Luscious wasn't Hector's bag. Hector liked the Barbie type. Neatly coiffed, with delicate features, but nonetheless he'd uttered the word with a tinge of admiration.

"I met her when she went out with one of my black employees. About a year ago, I guess. Did you know that her grandfather's a retired state senator? White, of course. But I guess you know that."

"Small town," Simon said, annoyed he had to find out through Hector that Sybil's old boyfriend—if it was the latest one—had been a black guy.

"The McLellans are an old Memphis family; more tradition than wealth. Still, I think the girl's a keeper."

Simon laughed. "She isn't a horse, Hector. And I haven't got a clue where this relationship is heading. I have my doubts about her willingness to commit."

"Commit to what?"

"Something more than a one-nighter. Not that I blame her. I have my own barriers."

"Yeah, like not forgiving Ellen for dumping you."

"I could forgive her for that. What I have a hard time accepting is the destruction of the children's home. And another consideration is the Church. I'm not sure I want to do without the Eucharist for the rest of my life."

"That shouldn't be a problem. You get an annulment for a few hundred bucks."

"Annul three kids?"

Hector laughed, his eyes now wide open. "If I were you, I'd say screw the Church and join a more forgiving denomination."

"Like the Unitarians? It's a thought. Your church's view of Old Man River alone would be worth it." He paused a moment, turning more serious. "You know, Hector, whether we like it or not, the Catholic Church is the roots of our civilization." Not to mention the roots of Sister's life. Certainly his own.

"If it's one thing I give Pope John Paul credit for," Hector replied, "it's his consistency. The old fart hasn't changed one iota of the Church rules that would embarrass the hell out of a living Jesus."

Simon expected Hector to blame those rules for the population explosion and its disastrous results among some of the world's poor countries, but he didn't. Instead Hector predicted that for its survival the Church would eventually have to ordain both married priests and women priests, as it'd done in its beginning. Then, unscrewing a jar of salted peanuts, Hector stuffed his mouth.

The exit down to Highway 100 came shortly. It curved downhill, turning into a narrow road. Simon turned off the music, concentrating on the directions to the stabling site. Once there, they unloaded, picked up their information packets, then led the horses to their respective stalls. They spread the shavings and filled the water buckets and the hay nets. Hector declared he was going to check out the prospects, and Simon returned to Snow Goose's box, where the filly greeted him with a friendly nicker.

CHAPTER 40

On the way out of the barn, a woman's voice with an English accent hailed Simon from the shadows. A tall figure wearing black boots stepped into the slanting afternoon sun, the leather worn thin and scuffed and oiled a thousand times, yet still a perfect fit on the long legs in breeches that had an old-fashioned flare. She was dressed in a faded black coat over a white shirt with a stock tie, and her intense eyes were shielded by cheekbones tanned a leathery brown and topped by a bird's nest of gray hair. For a split second, when she called his name, he'd felt anxious.

"Ms. Baugh!" he managed to utter, recalling her name mainly because an hour earlier he had passed by her former riding school. "Good to see you. Are you competing in the event?"

"No," she said with an undercurrent of contempt. "Unless you show up with a groom and a coach and a seventeen-hand horse trained by a professional, you don't stand a chance. If you ask me, the sport has become as snobbish as the hunter ring."

This unexpected condemnation of eventing hit Simon

as strange, although he supposed he would have felt even more so if the old lady were still galloping over solid cross-country fences.

"The sport for people like us, who love horses, is endurance riding. I saw the mare you just stabled. With that deep chest and sleek body she could win the Tevis Cup."

Simon raised his eyebrows.

"That's a hundred mile race over the Sierras. But you don't need to go west to have fun. We have endurance rides right here in Tennessee. And we don't stay in motels. We camp outdoors, enjoy nature. Too bad. Your mare would have made a great endurance horse."

Half noticing the odd tense she used, Simon imagined trotting Snow Goose along rocky ridges, racing over sandy plains. About to remind her that his mare was her stallion Afire's daughter, and wondering why the woman hadn't noticed the filly's resemblance to her sire, he suddenly realized Ms. Baugh was no longer there. He shaded his eyes with the back of his hand, but saw nothing but the empty tunnel running through the barn into the setting sun. Was he hallucinating?

Shaking off the silly thought, Simon got into the truck and drove to Percy Warner Park to walk the cross-country course. Squinting against the bright disc of the sun, he felt lucky to be riding at eleven twenty-six the next morning, not at eight-thirty or nine like the Preliminary horses. He wouldn't want Snow Goose to canter into the rising sun that created shadows at some of the obstacles, making them tough to gauge for a novice horse. Walking the course twice, then jogging it in the twilight a third time, he memorized each obstacle, the approach to each, the speed, the turns, getting a feel of the terrain.

Back at the barn he decided to do the braiding for the dressage test. Of all the chores, braiding a horse's mane was the one he liked least. Standing on a hay bale, combing the filly's short mane, he used a sponge to wet down each narrow section, then braided a three-foot piece of black yarn into the damp strands. He made slow progress, but Snow Goose calmly accepted his clumsy work, and mentally he reviewed the sixteen jumps on the cross-country course.

Just as Simon started the slippery hair of the eleventh braid, Hector showed up with a young woman in jeans named Sharon. Simon nodded, glancing at her, not letting go of the mane. A somewhat stout girl with sandy hair, light eyes, refined features.

"What a gorgeous animal!" she said.

Simon thanked her, nodding, then Hector walked Sharon to her truck. To prove to himself that he wasn't superstitious, Simon started a twelfth braid, making the forelock the thirteenth. As he was snipping off the yarn ends, Hector returned, and they drove to Nashville for dinner.

At the steak house around the corner from the Days Inn, where they had booked a room, Simon ordered a rib eye, a baked potato and a green salad with Italian dressing. Hector, apparently not in the least concerned about his growing waistline, ordered the same plus chicken livers and onion rings, and talked about Sharon, whose family owned ten thousand acres in the Mississippi delta.

"Imagine," Hector said, heaping sour cream on his potato, "what a man could do with ten thousand acres of row crop land."

Simon was tempted to warn him not to count his cotton before it was baled, especially since Sharon, who was barely twenty, probably still had a vigorous father. He wouldn't part with his land to a son-in-law.

"Why are you looking for a woman with money? Your business doing so well, you don't need it."

"In this country, everybody needs more money. Unless you gross a million a year, you're nobody." Hector laughed, and they both ordered more beer.

~~~~~

At six in the morning Simon drove to the barn to feed Snow Goose and Othello. By seven, he was back at the motel. Hector was up, shaving.

Wearing boots and spurs, black coats and white stock ties, the men drove to McDonald's for a breakfast of orange juice, coffee, and pancakes with scrambled eggs, all served in plastic containers they stuffed into the garbage can already overflowing early on a Saturday morning. Somewhere in the back of his mind, Ms. Baugh emerged, condemning eventing and the motels and restaurants that went with it, calling him to endurance rides and camping in the woods.

"They call this the information age," Hector said, "but as far as I'm concerned, it's the age of plastic. Dishes, diapers, razors, pens, televisions, computers, cars. Everything is throwaway. Think of the sanitary inserts," he added, chuckling. "Billions of them. I wish Sybil had come with you. We might have double-dated."

Simon laughed at the triggers in Hector's mind. But why not? If Hector was still friends with Sharon at the next event, and Sybil stuck, she might even compete herself at a spring event.

Snow Goose's thirteen braids, rather than the traditional twenty plus, were obviously too thick, but they didn't take much away from her elegance. Though old, his tack was clean, as were his yellow breeches, white shirt and stock tie, and the black coat he'd used on the hunt before becoming a whipper-in. His helmet had seen its days, too, discolored with splotches of purple and gray, the little bowtie at the back missing. It had been his very first hard hat and had become part of him, much like the old field boots he wore for eventing. He should have blackened the worn spots of the fine leather with dye, but leather preservative was healthier for them and kept them supple. The judge, a retired colonel from Virginia, appearing rather stern with his steel-rimmed glasses, would have preferred that he wear dress boots.

In the warm-up area Snow Goose trotted and walked and cantered as if she were at home, and suddenly number 83, the rider that preceded him, was finishing her test, steering the dark bay horse on a long rein along the rail toward the exit. Before she was completely out, Simon began circling the arena at a walk, passing in front of the judge's trailer, pleased that the mare didn't shy at the flower decorations, switching to a rising trot back toward the entrance at the letter A. The dark bay before him had done one of the better tests, if not the best one so far. Again Simon circled the arena, staying with the walk. The walk was the mare's weakest gait. She tended to be high-headed when she was fresh. Finally, at the end of another circle, the judge's scribe shook the little bell.

After a big turn at the front, he entered the arena in a rising trot down the center, coming to a halt, greeting the judge by taking off his helmet. He put it back on and continued, tracking right, keeping his head up, paying no attention to the colonel, concentrating on his line, his aids, the transitions, his own calm. And Snow Goose responded. Her walk was as relaxed as it had been in the warm-up, her head forward and down, much like a Quarter horse at Western Pleasure; the transitions to the canter, and again from the canter to the trot, were balanced, a feat he hadn't always achieved even with Jesse. It was as if she knew she was expected to move with effortless grace, submitting softly, being one with the rider.

After the test, Simon loosened Snow Goose's girth, then led her to the open field, checking on Hector.

"You did fantastic," Hector said, looking down from black Othello, who tried to rub his nose on Simon's sleeve.

"How about you? Othello seems calm."

"Too calm. I'm kicking like hell to make him go."

After Hector's test, which Othello performed "without being on the bit," as the judge commented on the sheet, the two men walked their horses back to the stables where they removed the tack. They filled the water buckets and fed them only a thin section of hay, not wanting them to have full stomachs for the cross-country phase.

On the scoreboard, with thirty-two and a half penalty points, Patricia Dupont was in first place. Pat was a freelance writer, fox hunter, and a friend. Beating her would take some doing, even though Snow Goose was fourth, just three and a half points behind.

It was pointless to speculate. The hard stuff was yet to come. A refusal in the cross-country phase added twenty penalty points to the score. A stop in the stadium, ten, a rail down, five. For both men a satisfactory start. Nonetheless, on their return to the stables, Simon was glad not to come across Ms. Baugh.

CHAPTER 41

An hour and a half later, having changed his black coat for a blue polo shirt and the dressage saddle for a close contact, Simon jogged Snow Goose to the warm-up area of the cross-country phase, pleased with the cloudless sky and the still cool air. For fifteen minutes he trotted the filly, then tightened the chinstrap of his jump helmet and cantered her over the warm-up fences. An official called his number, and he steered the Goose toward the starting box, halting twenty feet from it.

While the starter counted down from fifteen, a portly woman in breeches and paddock boots said to an equally portly rider on a seventeen-hand Hanoverian, "Remember, trot the first bench, and use your spurs to make him canter over the second. And remember to trot the bridge, too. Urge him on, but trot!"

Not good advice, Simon thought. The benches were the fourth and fifth fences at the steeplechase track, slightly uphill from number three, a log parallel over a ditch called a Trakehner. The woman was right about trotting the bridge, but over the uphill fence he planned to canter.

Now the Hanoverian was off, loping toward the first fence, a vertical rail decorated with greenery. He cleared it and aimed for the airy table. His long-striding canter looked almost like slow motion, making the obstacle appear small, but then, instead of gliding over it, the big warmblood stopped in his tracks and lowered his head, letting his rider slide headfirst down his neck, depositing her on the tabletop. Throwing his head high, reins flipping like the cord of a whip, the horse swung around on his hocks and came cantering back toward the warm-up area. Several people on foot, grooms and trainers, reached out for the trailing reins, trying to stop the giant, but he weaved right on through them, gaining speed, galloping toward the distant stables.

"Don't do like the big horse," Simon said to the filly, stroking her neck. Walking his mount in a large circle, he tightened the girth another notch. As he entered the starting box, Hector rode up with his new friend Sharon, Hector winking and crossing his fingers. The starter counted down the seconds, glancing back and forth between his stopwatch and Snow Goose, making sure she didn't step over the line before he gave the command.

Calmer than the rider, the Goose stood still, moving only her head, and her eyes, not quite knowing what to expect. Behind him, all was normal again, voices advising circling riders, a horse knocking down a pole on the oxer. The big warmblood must have reached the stables by now, his rider, unhurt except for her pride, well on her way there too, with truck and trailer. Once more he turned his head toward the schooling area, for a moment thinking he'd seen Ms. Baugh on a high spot watching.

"Go!" the man said, nodding encouragingly. Simon turned out his toes, and the filly trotted forth, easing into a canter. She met the first fence in the center where he had pointed her, and jumped it. On the approach to the table, he sat back, driving her forward, shortening her stride. The horse's head rose. Now just two strides away, Simon let her feel the dull points of his spurs. One more stride, a split-second of hesitation, and over she went, higher than needed, but landing softly, heading toward number three.

"The game is half won," Simon said to the Goose, touching her neck. The filly cantered easily, light on her feet, continuing north inside the steeplechase track. She hopped over the pole with the ditch beneath, approaching the first bench. "Up we go, girl!" Simon said, floating over, landing and shortening her stride across the track, and clean over the second bench into a left turn southeast, now going past the grandstand, empty of spectators except for some kids chasing one another up and down the weathered benches. The judges at the drop and the helsinki, two of the easier obstacles, were probably bored, but Simon almost envied their chance to watch the pretty horses meeting a challenge, often despite a poor rider.

Now just past the halfway mark, he turned sharply right, crossing the track uphill toward number eight, a simple post and rail, after which he held her back to maneuver a hard turn downhill, and then the filly's hooves drummed over the bridge. Heading uphill again, he was approaching fence number ten, a low vertical, and the first element of an in-and-out. The second element was flagged for Training. Pre-Training riders were to turn around it. There being no penalty for taking other fences on the course, and this one being in a direct line to the next obstacle, Simon pointed the filly at it. She lifted off, landing on grass, and next brushed through the bullfinch.

By this point the horses had established a rhythm and gained confidence as had the riders. Nonetheless, the last few obstacles were impressive enough, especially the feed trough, placed downhill with bushes hiding the approach. Snow Goose flew over it, cantered on toward the water jump, approaching it at a trot. One split-second the Goose hesitated, but Simon's bat whopped her hard and, eager to please, she dropped into the pond, plowed through it and hopped out, dripping water. Almost immediately she regained the same measured canter, without hurrying, jumping the last fence, a log pile, in stride. Then she passed between the finish flags, quickly slowing to a halt. Simon jumped off, leading Snow Goose off to the side, stroking her neck and kissing the soft spot behind her barely blowing nostrils.

They'd made it. Maybe clear, maybe with a refusal. It depended how the jump judge had seen the split-second hesitation at the water. It didn't matter. The Goose had done great. The stadium phase still lay ahead, but those fences didn't maim or kill the way the solid beams on the cross-country could. They collapsed when hit. A horse could knock down every fence in the arena and probably not show more damage than some bruises and cuts. And if the rider fell, he wouldn't likely break his neck. The dangerous stuff was behind them.

The Memphis crowd wanted to celebrate. Everybody was in line for a ribbon with the exception of Hector Hollenbach and Longfellow Cohen, a commodities trader and also a hunt member. Hector's Othello had jumped the table and all the other jumps, but a mediocre dressage score kept him out of contention. Longfellow was so high on uppers that he was singing along the entire course, completely unconcerned, steering his trusty mount into the fences, and old Firebrand, a former Preliminary horse, just gently glided over them. Lucky until the end, he passed the finish flags on the outside, hollering still, and kept going, ignoring the calls to come back, eliminating himself.

During dinner, mostly burgers and fries, Simon wondered why he hadn't taken Stefan out of school to join the fun with the pony clubbers and their proud mothers at the table behind, enjoying their children's success. Not just for the boy's sake, but for his own. Stefan would have given him the confidence Simon lacked every time he faced a stadium ride with judges, stewards, and fellow competitors looking on. About to rise, Simon felt a pair of hands on his shoulders.

"Did you know you're in second place?" Patricia Dupont asked, starting to massage his neck. "The third-place horse had a refusal on the cross-country, and the second-place rider withdrew with a lame horse."

Simon pulled the woman down to a chair. "Martini?"

"I've already had my share. Me and this jump judge. But what the hell."

You couldn't tell about the drinks. Patricia spoke with ease and looked at Simon with a steady eye, and Simon looked back at her, wishing he'd met her years before when they both were single. He still admired her slender but strong figure, the bold yet feminine chin. A handsome female with cool blue eyes that could easily warm, even without a drink.

"Where're you staying?"

"Days Inn, with Hollenbach. You?"

"Holiday Inn."

The waitress brought their drinks, and they cheered each other, aware of the possibilities that would never materialize. Her husband, Brendan, practiced law and had little use for horses but tolerated the passion of his partner. Rising, Simon offered her a lift, and told Hector to find his way home with someone else. Hector grinned, nodding, winking at him. Patricia laughed, winking back.

Despite the martinis, Pat gave Simon precise directions, and within minutes he stopped at the entrance to the Inn. When she made no move to get out, he cut the engine.

"You're in first place," Simon said. "What's wrong?"

"The paper rejected my article on the Hunt. The second rejection this month. I'm losing my touch. Never mind me. What's bugging you? Your girlfriend? I hear she's a beauty."

"Have you ever loved two women at the same time?"

She laughed. "Not really my cup of tea. But I've loved two men at the same time. Three, counting you. Perfectly normal."

"I'd like to think so, too," he said, cranking the engine. "But now I'm tired, and when I'm tired, I'm betwixt and between. It's like a curse."

Patricia laughed. "That's par for the course, too. You'll sort it out. What we both need is a hug," she said, and he laughingly obliged. "I'll tell you a secret," she whispered. "Ellen's a wonder, it's true, but she's gone. Love the new girl."

After Patricia disappeared into the lobby, Simon drove back to his own motel, feeling better. Stretched out on the bed he pushed the power button of the remote, checked out the cable channels, and settled down to watch the football game between Notre Dame and Tennessee.

Tennessee, again overrated this year, was losing as seemed to be their habit in a big game. The Volunteer in him wanted the Big Orange to win, the Catholic the Irish. What he liked about Notre Dame was the name. Every time he heard it, he recalled the village of Notre-Dame-de-Lorette, probably changed beyond recognition since his days in Paradise.

The tight end of the Big Orange fumbled on the three-yard line of the Irish. Disgusted, Simon switched off the TV, changed to his warm-up suit and sneakers, bent and stretched his limbs, then jogged down the busy street. He circled about ten blocks, hoping that Hector might be back, ready to gossip and keep his unease at bay. However, Hector hadn't returned. Simon showered, shampooed his hair, and vigorously rubbed himself dry. To offset the silence in the room, he punched the remote and found an "Austin City Limits" repeat of a blue grass band. Turning the sound down until he could barely make out the words, he climbed under the sheets, and closed his eyes.

CHAPTER 42

The show jumping started at ten o'clock with the two sections of the Open Preliminary division. Counting the course changes that took several minutes each, as well as an award ceremony with music and a victory gallop at the end of each section, not to mention unforeseen delays, Simon probably wouldn't ride before one.

He was sitting upwind on the edge of the warm-up area holding Snow Goose's reins, letting her graze on the sparse, dusty grass around him as he reread the high-lighted passages of Camus's *La Peste*, a novel about the plague raging in North Africa.

"The waiting's the hardest test of all," a middle-aged woman said to him, strolling by with her horse in tow.

Junior Training was about to finish. Senior Pre-Training began next. Since they rode in reverse order—the rider in last place jumping first, the one in first going last—Hector was the seventh competitor and Simon the eighteenth, indeed in second place, as Pat had predicted.

At the warm-up fences, Al Graham, one of the few pros in the competition, was assisting a couple of his students over the vertical. "Keep his head straight," he shouted to a teenage girl on a dark thoroughbred. "Stay up! Keep your legs on!" The horse jumped late but clean. "Good release," the instructor called after the girl. "Keep your position, keep riding him, keep riding your horse all the time, even on landing."

It was more profitable to watch a pro instructing at a fence than the stout ladies yelling at their charges. Those women couldn't balance on the back of a horse if their life depended on it. They might have ridden as promising teens before marriage and children and chocolate cakes added the pounds. Then, never realizing their potential, they became instructors, like some of the English profs at Brinkman, would-be-writers who hadn't made it and settled for teaching jobs instead. However, though the women's constant, high-pitched bellowing might not make much sense to their young charges, their mother-hen presence was comforting, boosting the children's confidence. Again Simon listened to the pro, and at the same time he kept an eye out for Hector's arrival, and Patricia's, who was probably at Percy Warner's, warming up her spirited mare by galloping around the cross-country course.

While a dozen strong men and women lowered the fences under the supervision of the technical delegate, Simon stuffed the book into the inside pocket of his tweed coat, tightened the girth, mounted, and trotted a few times around the warm-up area. He eased into a canter, jumping the crossbar a couple of times. Then he aimed for the vertical, still set for Training height, which the Goose took in stride.

Simon dismounted, handing the filly's reins to Hector, who had appeared leading the old gelding, and headed into the arena to walk the course. As he rejoined Hector, Patricia jumped out of the saddle and threw him the reins of her lathered mare, making Snow Goose raise her head. Even Othello perked up, stepping away from the thoroughbred that laid her ears back.

"About time," Simon said. "I don't want to win by default."

"That'll be the day!" She laughed, urging Hector to come with her into the arena to check the course. Simon had his hands full trying to control Pat's restless mount who didn't bother with Othello but tried to bite Snow Goose. The old gelding was quite at ease, enjoying the scuffle of the two horses whose future, unlike his, still lay ahead of them.

Not that horses were aware of their future, though they were conscious of their past. Pat's young mare, who'd been bought off the racetrack, had obviously had a more stressful life than the Goose. Besides her difficult birth, Snow Goose had been through few traumatic incidences. Her past was no different from the present with which it merged, a present she was acutely aware of. She knew Simon was agitated although he wasn't touching her. She felt the vibes through the air, through the reins hanging loosely between his hand and her rubber snaffle.

Patricia returned and led her mare away. As if to show her pleasure at the removal of the nervous thoroughbred, Snow Goose bent her head, nuzzling the gelding beside her, and the old gentleman pressed closer without moving his feet. And standing in front of the two horses, Simon gradually relaxed, too, checking out the course once more through the enclosure, following the route he would ride. The announcer asked the competitors to clear the arena, and the presiding judge, flanked at the table in the stands by his two associates and other event officials, blew the whistle. Number 91, the last place horse in Simon's group, entered the arena at a walk, facing the jury. Halting, the rider bowed his head, cantered a circle in front of the starting line, and jumped the first fence, an inviting brush. The announcer called the man's name and the name of his horse, adding the number of penalties so far in the event.

Hector asked Simon if he'd seen Sharon, who'd been eliminated on the cross-country course. She wanted to school the table and the bridge when they were done with stadium. Was that okay with him?

No, it wasn't, Simon thought. It had been a long day already, and when the competition was over, he wanted to get home. Sybil was making dinner, and he'd promised the children to take them all roller-skating in Raleigh. He also had to look over his notes for Monday's lecture on Camus.

"I think I have a chance with Sharon," Hector continued.

There was his friend, dressed perfectly in his stock tie and Scottish tweed, yellow hunt breeches and black boots, worrying not about the imminent stadium round but about ten thousand acres in Mississippi. So Simon promised to wait for him and Sharon to school some jumps after the show. A half hour longer wouldn't matter. While the two were riding, he would read.

All of a sudden, it was Othello's turn. After watching the old horse carry his rider over the nine obstacles without as much as a nick, Simon clapped his gloved hands, joining the applause of the Memphis contingent, and Hector acknowledged it with a tip of his helmet. Of the next two riders, one had a stop in the in-and-out and had to repeat the combination, and the other knocked down a rail at the oxer. About two minutes to go. Simon mounted, trotting the horse in a wide circle around the practice jumps, making her sidestep and bend to loosen up; then he jumped the vertical and the oxer from both leads.

By the time their names were announced, Simon Philipe on Snow Goose, thirty-six penalty points, he had already saluted, circled, and taken the brush, approaching the white gate. The Goose took it in stride. Like her rider, she always looked for the next fence. Her rhythm remained regular, unhurried, and she seemed to know when to lift off without much help from her partner moving with her on her back. Before Simon realized it, he was facing the final obstacle, a plain white wall with red-roofed spires on each side. Simon tried to shorten her stride, but Snow Goose retained her easy pace, just raised her head a fraction, and jumped it, landing softly, cantering through the flags of the finish line, circling to a halt.

Aware of the applause, Simon heard the announcer's voice over the speakers. "Clean round. No time penalties." He was still in second place.

Pat and Arizona, her high-strung thoroughbred, quickly gained everybody's attention. The accomplished horsewoman was struggling to control the mare before she even completed the circle to the first fence. The liver chestnut rushed the fence, despite the rider's effort to hold her, but jumped it clean, and again rushed forward, clearing the big oxer two feet higher than necessary. The distance to the woodpile gave Patricia time to slow the horse enough to manage the hundred and eighty degree turn to the combination. As wildly as she went, the mare hopped both elements, took the wall straight up, like an elevator, then galloped toward the exit, making the rider pull desperately to keep her mount from running through the finish and out of the arena. At the last moment, she managed. Heading away from the exit, the horse slowed, taking the ladder and the gate along the stands, leaping the fan hugely, turning toward the last fence, the wishing well with the red-roofed spires. She lifted off, clearing it, then, with the applause already starting, kicked with her rear legs, knocking the top section off.

Groans among the spectators. Simon rode forward,

blocking the way of the disappointed friend who had handled a difficult horse well. "That was a great ride, Pat," he said, and for one fleeting moment he wished she hadn't had the knockdown.

Patricia smiled vaguely. "You've got the better horse."

Simon wanted to hug and kiss the Goose when the stadium steward hooked the blue ribbon on her brow band. He felt like raising an arm, shouting. Instead, he stroked the filly's neck.

When the first bar of the march sounded, Simon led the victory gallop around the arena. Looking over his shoulder at the horses with the colorful ribbons fluttering from their heads, he saw that all the riders were smiling, including Pat, in third place now instead of first. Every pair behind him was a winner, as were every horse and rider that had finished the three phases, overcoming mishaps and setbacks, fear and disappointments, and never giving up.

The grim old woman might have sneered at eventing, but it was a sport like no other. In dressage it took months and years to bring out the gymnast's skills that are latent in a horse. And for the endurance phase, exercise at the trot and canter had to become routine. The rider needed patience and skill and courage to teach a horse the trust necessary to leap over an immovable obstacle of scary shape or color, often without seeing the other side. To drop off a bank, fly over ramps, plunge into a milky pond. And, last but not least, in the stadium, that carefully planned confusion of airy hurdles bedecked with greenery and flowers, it was again the skill of both horse and rider, in a more refined way perhaps, that decided the competitor's fate.

Some of the Memphis friends came up to congratulate him, to pet the Goose, who seemed to know what was happening. She showed fire in her eye and just a touch more spring in her step, as if ready to go again. He reached forward, pulling the ribbon off the bridle, rolled it up and stuffed it in his pocket. A young woman approached, asking for his bridle number that was still in place on the horse's brow band, and tried to unhook it.

"She's got a long neck," Simon said, detaching the number.

"Why'd you remove the ribbon?" Hector asked, still mounted.

Simon shrugged. Some of the air had already gone out of his balloon. The taste of success never lasted long. More satisfactory was the work, the effort to achieve.

They loaded Othello into the trailer with his tack on, the Goose without, and drove to the cross-country course. Sharon, already there and mounted, waved to them.

"She isn't a bad-looking gal," Simon said, unloading the two horses again. Nice complexion, pretty mouth, and a friendly, though somewhat cold disposition. Quite a fringe benefit to go with ten thousand acres. If he were Hector, he'd court her, too. But he wasn't Hector. He wanted to go home and share the success of the day with his children. With Sybil.

"Don't forget," he called after Hector. "Half an hour!" Hector waved.

The Goose stopped munching hay from the net and raised her head, eyes following the departing Othello. Simon climbed into the pickup, leaving the door open, took off his tweed coat, and pulled *La Peste* from his pocket.

CHAPTER 43

Suddenly in no mood to deal with stark realities, he stuffed Camus' novel into his bag, jumped out of the truck and lay down in the grass, enjoying the warmth of the afternoon sun that caressed his face. A stone's throw away, riders still sloshed through the water hazard. Farther on, a couple of eventers schooled the Pre-Training table that looked deserted without the flags and the jump judges. Other horses cantered along the slope beyond the track. That's probably where Hector and Sharon were, playing at the bridge.

The half hour slid by, and Hector didn't show. Another quarter hour passed. The Goose nickered. Simon sat up and regarded the boots he was still wearing, the spurs. He rose, wiped his palms on his breeches, stretched his neck and his limbs, and looked for the bootjack. Snow Goose nickered affectionately, reaching toward his side. He went to her and rubbed her nostrils, and she laid her lips on his head, rubbing his hair.

"You want to go home, don't you?"

The filly whinnied lustily, spraying saliva.

"Shall we find Othello?"

With his open hand he brushed her back, rubbing her sides and belly, amazed at how little dried-up sweat blew off the silken coat like dust. He rubbed her face and stroked her legs, not feeling any bumps or cuts, and tacked her up. The humidity was so low that the saddle blanket had dried. He put on his helmet, mounted and walked the horse to the west side of the track where Hector had said he'd be. A big bay horse came barreling over the Training jumps along the mountain slope, clearing the helsinki, now approaching the big rail that led straight to the bridge, running at a good four-hundred-fifty-meter-a-minute clip, rattling over the bridge, making the Goose lift her head. She wanted to follow. Simon watched the rider turn into the combination to the inside of the track, then head south toward the obstacles within the bend of the longer steeple chase track.

Curious where this fellow had come from, Simon cantered uphill, jumping the helsinki from the back side, coming to a couple of drops, like giant steps that led up to a rail. The Training competitors must have taken the rail from the other side, dropping down over these banks.

"Let's climb the stairs," Simon told the filly silently. "Then we'll go farther north, and find out what's in the woods."

Like most riders, he communicated with his horse by thought, which, instinctively, was transferred by touch. And the Goose understood. Pointing her ears, she cantered uphill toward the two banks. Power surging through her muscles, she jumped and stepped and jumped and stepped, then hopped the rail and, a spring in her stride, approached a picnic table, leaping over it with perfect economy, neither too high nor too low. Downhill she aimed for the big footbridge, jumped, and slowed her pace, waiting for Simon to guide her. Ahead was the north bend of the longer track, and in the trees on his left, some tall, vertical rails, but he let the horse canter downhill, heading for the trailer.

Neither Hector nor Sharon was back. Simon dismounted, undecided whether to quit or whether to school a couple more jumps. Reaching through the driver's door, he picked the yellow envelope off the dash that held the cross-country maps and studied the Preliminary route.

"Okay, wonder horse." He swung himself on the Goose's back, raised the stirrups one hole, and tightened the girth another notch. "We'll jump the Preliminary course. Are you game?"

The filly didn't whinny a yes, but she twitched her ears and energetically trotted away from the rig that was her home away from home, toward the starting box. Passing it, Simon asked for a canter as they approached the first fence, a curved rail that she glided over, heading toward the steeple chase brush that was no longer in the best shape but still taller than anything she'd seen so far. Simon was prepared for a leap over the six-foot cane, as green horses might, but, like an experienced warrior, Snow Goose aimed at the top of the wooden box, jumping through the leafy stalks. Next came the coffin, out of sight until they had circled an old corral, turning north on the road between the inner and the outer track, a hard-packed dirt and gravel surface heading downhill. Facing the high pole barring the way to the pit, the filly raised her head and pointed her ears, looking beyond the bar at the gaping hole in the ground. But feeling Simon's spurs, his will to move on, she jumped, leaped across the trench, and in two short strides out over the second pole. Now they traversed the track uphill toward and over the footbridge, around the trees to the right, downhill toward two post and rail verticals.

Always wary of fences on a down slope, Simon shortened the horse's stride, taking the two verticals like stadium jumps. Next he faced the picnic table again, now from the other side, and once more she floated over it. According to the map, a ramp going downward was next. Simon didn't notice it until he'd gone past.

Cantering on, he approached the top of the banks he'd taken earlier from the bottom, jumped the rail, hopping down as if they were tiny steps, then to the big drop above the bridge, more scary to him than the horse, making him lean back in the air, catching the impact of the landing with his bent knees and heels flexing in the stirrups. From there, rushing down to the log bridge, he had to hold the Goose hard to keep her on track. She leaped across, turning up the hill again, and around through a large window frame. This series of obstacles wasn't difficult. If they had been taken more slowly with the horse in balance, almost any Training competitor could have jumped them.

Diagonally down the hill and across the south end of the steeplechase track, he approached the tiger trap. A ramp built of seven-foot poles with airy spaces in between, rising to optimum height, with a downhill landing. Snow Goose attacked at a good clip. He tried to check her speed, but she wouldn't listen. Keeping his eyes up, he couldn't tell exactly where she lifted off, a yard and a half, two yards in front, but lift off she did, nearly leaving him behind, flying like a bird, the arctic goose whose name she bore. While in flight, Simon wanted to shout for joy, but there was still the drop to earth, which he hardly felt. "Good girl," he said, slowing the pace, heading toward the water.

You could tell by the number of riders schooling the pond that if there was one obstacle on a cross-country course that competitors worried about, it was the water. Few people had the opportunity to school a water jump at home. Not many builders had the skill to construct a pond with a level bottom that was firm and durable yet soft enough for horses to safely land on and jump out of. Snow Goose liked water. On the hunt she'd crossed sandy streams with belly-deep currents, and she walked far into lakes for a drink.

The Preliminary rail at the water that Simon was heading for came close quickly. It wasn't a big fence. About three feet, with a drop of four to the water, five to the bottom. It was built at a forward slant, two rails stacked on the ground, a single pole on the top with a gap between. An inviting fence. The other three sides of the square pond had no in or out obstacle. For one instant, Simon thought of circling to the level entry on the side, where he'd dropped in during the competition, but at the moment of his approach there was a pause in the activity, and he decided to take the fence. Shortening her stride, he kept the filly's energy up to discourage her from thinking about the jump or the water that she could see over the top as well as through the gap. Four, three, two more strides, and they were there, her head up, ears pointed, and then, just before lift-off, Simon could feel her rear legs slip on the mushy surface that had been splashed on by the competitors the day before, and again all afternoon by the horses sloshing through the pond.

But she jumped. Behind her a tug and a crack, like a shot. The horse landed in the water, and stood still. Simon turned his head, checking the rails. They were still in one piece. Yet something had made that awful sound. Then the blood drained from his head. The Goose was holding her right hind foot above the water, broken above the fetlock, cut and twisted. "Easy, girl," he said, patting her neck, but she wasn't moving. Again he regarded the fractured limb, astonished there was so little blood. Then he looked at his field boots with the laces on the instep, and at the fourteen inches of water, and for a second he was at a loss. Swinging his right leg over the filly's neck, he slid down her left side into the pond. She turned her head, looking at him with her trusting eye as if asking, "What now?"

Simon stroked the filly's head, wondering how to get her out of the water on three legs, though he realized that horses, like wolves, could walk on three legs. Eventually the milky water that was filling his boots encouraged him to take hold of the reins and to start walking. Willingly the horse followed, hopping with the one sound hind leg, holding the injured limb up.

At the edge of the hazard, facing the low wall and the duck blind beyond which he would have jumped next, he climbed out, pulling on the reins and, looking over his shoulder, asked Snow Goose to hop out of the water. She scrambled out, banging the injured leg against the hard edge, making her companion groan. The contact had further damaged the fracture. If saving the leg had seemed dubious before, it looked hopeless now. The filly stood very still, three-legged, the injured limb up, even the tail unmoving. Her head lowered, balancing her weight, she looked at her friend.

At the trailer across the tracks, Hector was tying his old gelding; then he ambled toward the hazard.

"Christ!" he said, paling.

Simon asked him to go call for a vet at the ranger station.

"Right," Hector said. He hesitated, turned, and walked away briskly.

Simon pushed the stirrups up on both sides, undid the girth and pulled off the saddle and laid it on the ground.

Then he removed the bridle.

The mare nudged his arm wanting to stick her head under his shoulder. He put his right arm under her neck, holding up her head. Obviously, Snow Goose wasn't in great pain. The two poles that had fractured her leg must have cut the nerve, much as the killer trap had cut the nerve in the wolf's so long ago. With his left hand, he reached for the bowie knife in the leather sheath on his belt. He was surprised it wasn't there, although it hadn't been there for more than half his lifetime. Cutting her foot off wouldn't do any good. A three-legged horse was even more vulnerable than a three-legged wolf. He wished he were eleven years old again and could leave the scene, trekking home with his dog.

Beside him, horses were still dropping into the hazard, sloshing through the water, hopping out on the opposite side. A hundred yards beyond the scraggly bushes, Sharon was loading her horse. Hector wasn't there, so he had to be looking for a vet. That would take awhile. The situation wasn't an emergency. In an hour or two, the horse's condition would neither improve nor deteriorate. So the vet could take his time. At her trailer, Sharon waved, climbed into the big rig, and slowly drove away, her stoplights flashing on and off as she braked over the bumpy terrain, soon disappearing from sight.

There goes the ten thousand acres, Simon thought. It was like a joke. He'd give up his job not to have jumped the killer rail. Have his own leg broken to see the horse's whole again.

More than an hour passed before Hector returned. He announced sadly that the only vet he'd found would come to Percy Warner's Park as soon as he could but couldn't make any promises. Simon thanked him and suggested he look after Othello.

Gradually, the riders stopped schooling the water. One by one the trailers left. In another hour the sun would disappear behind the hill. The Goose stood three-legged, like a horse at the hitching rail outside a saloon, her head resting in the crook of his arm long since sore from supporting the weight. He couldn't hold her much longer, or bear the trusting way she looked at him. He knew she expected him to wrap her legs and lead her into the trailer. To fill the net with scented hay, tie the old gelding beside her, and take her home. There he would unload her and let her out into the pasture where Par Three would prance up, tossing his head, and the two of them would lead the rest of the herd in a trot around the field.

His thoughts were interrupted by the approach of a pickup with a gooseneck trailer. Patricia Dupont's rig, unmistakable with the oversized Hettinger emblem of fox hunters, a red fox mask against a black cap on a green background, painted a foot square on the doors of her white truck. Patricia stepped out of the cab, coming toward him with the athletic stride that only enhanced her femininity. "So sorry," she said, making an effort to sound matter-of-fact. "Can I help?" When she saw the dangling foot, however, she blanched under her tan, saying no more.

"You can get me a gun," Simon said, more to himself than to her.

She didn't blink. Turning about-face, she headed back to her truck, reached inside, and returned with a brown paper bag. Handing it to him, she said, "My Saturday night special."

Simon removed his arm from under the horse's neck, and Snow Goose, now unsupported, lowered her head almost to the ground. After stretching the arm that had fallen asleep and rubbing his elbow, Simon extracted a tiny .22 caliber pistol. "Loaded?"

"Small shells. Do you know where to aim?"

Simon handed her the paper bag and put the gun in his pants pocket. "I guess we'd better move the horse away from the pond." He nodded toward the tall grass and low bushes on the trackside of the water. Hector offered to go get a halter, but Simon shook his head. He took hold of her short main and slowly led her away from the water, just far enough for a backhoe to have easy access for loading the carcass into a dump truck, or whatever Davidson County used for the removal of dead horses.

Again, the filly wanted to push her head under his arm, but Simon gently scratched her forehead, trying to establish the point where the diagonal lines from the base of the ear to the eye would cross. Through that point, the old man in the turnip greens had told him just four weeks ago, the bullet was sure to enter the brain.

"This won't hurt," Simon said, releasing the safety and putting the mouth of the pistol against the fatal spot. His two companions took a step back, but he didn't pull the trigger. Leaning forward, he laid his lips on the horse's left eye, feeling the tremor in the closed lid. In seconds, he relived the dawn of Snow Goose's birth with the excited horses circling, seeing again the wild foal he'd gentled and groomed and trained, taken out for midnight gallops with Par Three, and finally ridden, hunted and evented. And loved, like no other horse before. Then he applied the gun once more, setting the barrel at a right angle, and pulled the trigger.

The shot was less loud than the crack of his hunt whip. Snow Goose collapsed upon herself, quietly, almost in slow motion. She rolled to her side, crushing a sapling, and lay still. Simon reset the safety and handed the weapon to the woman who returned it to the bag. Then he knelt beside his friend and closed the eye that still seemed to be looking at him, expecting him to help her. He rose and picked up the tack.

"Don't," he said to Patricia, who was about to touch him. "Don't come near me!"

CHAPTER 44

Neither of the two men spoke, cruising west on I-40. The sun was so low on the horizon that Simon drove squinting. On the stretch before Bucksnort, the sun squatted on the highway, fiery red, expanding at the bottom like a balloon filled with water, as it had, Simon recalled, when he'd been searching for Jesse.

He remembered the emptiness he'd felt after the theft of his mare. As if part of himself had been ripped away, leaving him crippled. And now he'd lost another creature he loved. Again they passed Ms. Baugh's former land where the cattle in the field grazed as peacefully as they had two days earlier. Again speeding cars zoomed past his rig. Semis struggled by. Yet nothing was the same. There was absolutely no doubt in his mind that Snow Goose hadn't just accidentally broken a leg. He'd murdered her. She lay in the weeds, fifty or sixty miles behind, already stiffening.

Jesus.

When the bone had cracked and the filly landed in the water and stood, three-legged, he'd been stunned. Odd, he thought, for a man who prided himself on his reflexes. He'd moved as if in a dream, slow and unreal, only gradually able to accept the unacceptable.

"I wish it'd happened to Othello," Hector mumbled, his mouth full of chicken livers he'd bought before they hit the Interstate. It took Simon several moments to respond to the presence of his companion. "It's kind of you to say so, but I'm glad it didn't." The black gelding was old. That was true. This might even be his last horse trial. But that wasn't the point. Old creatures wanted to live as much as the young.

These words didn't quite correspond to Simon's feelings. He was angry; tempted to tell Hector that if he'd spent only the half hour with Sharon that he'd promised, he wouldn't have tacked up. They'd be home now. But that wasn't fair. If he needed to blame somebody besides himself, he'd have to blame the jump designer. If the ground hadn't been slippery, the leg wouldn't have gone between the poles. But damn it, around a water jump, you expect it to be wet. You don't create gaps for a leg to slip through.

Against his will, Simon was working himself into a minor fury. While another semi passed the pickup, making conversation difficult, he took a few deep breaths. When the big rig had moved into the right lane ahead of him and switched off the blinker, Hector said, "You've got to sue!"

"Sue who?"

"The Middle Tennessee Pony Club, the organizer, the county. Everybody. Talk to Lee Hansom. His firm specializes in injury cases."

"I can't sue the Middle Tennessee Pony Club. It isn't exactly a profit-oriented, to-hell-with-the-victims corporation."

Simon thought of Job, who lost his health, his home, his children, but somehow never his faith. In the end, of course, like the heroes in all good stories, he was rewarded with double his wealth and a set of new children. New children, Simon would argue, no matter how wonderful, could never replace the first crop. As no other horse would replace the Goose.

Simon tried to look ahead, but his thoughts pulled him back to Percy Warner Park, where Snow Goose rested in the weeds. Would lie there until Monday or Tuesday, when this unusual October heat had swelled the sleek horse to double her size. Then some detail from Public Works would be sent to the park. A backhoe would lift and drop the body into a dump truck, and the driver rumble on over to the landfill, raise the box, and let the carcass slide down the hill of the day's garbage where it would barely be noticeable except maybe for the legs sticking out, the broken foot from the right hind hanging at its sad angle. A day or two later, even the legs would be buried in stinking refuse.

"I've done some stupid things, Hector. All the way back to my youth and childhood. Risking my life to no purpose. Breaking up my family. And here I am, almost forty years old, and I kill my horse."

"You're too hard on yourself, Simon. One time or another, everybody screws up. It can't be helped. It's how we deal with teh mess we make, that's what counts. Anyway, Sybil will love you for it."

"Why do you say that?"

"Women love a man with feet of clay. Just look at me!" Hector threw his head back and laughed.

Simon didn't laugh. He obviously wasn't a man whose life had gained an even rhythm, as he'd believed. A force in him played havoc with his good intentions, dangerous to his own person and everyone he touched. But then Sybil knew that. She had sensed it the very moment they measured each other at the Gospel meeting. And she had accepted him.

As they crossed the Tennessee River, going up the steep incline on the west side, Simon put the pedal to the floor, and the old truck responded, gaining speed with a roar. At the top, he had the feeling the rig was rising still, making him airborne. He switched on the lights, almost expecting the beams to hit the clouds.

He had felt numb; now his mind was sharp, impersonal, as if it were separate, regarding him from above. And he was amused at his somber expression. He burst into laughter, and almost instantly the weight lifted from his chest and escaped through the window, fluttering like old rags.

First thing he had to do was tell his children. The news of Snow Goose's death would be hardest on Stefan, but being a horseman himself, the boy would accept the inevitable. It wouldn't upset Mark too much. Mark loved dogs. Poor, sweet Carolyn would be the one to shed a tear. And she'd beg her father not to jump solid obstacles anymore.

Simon, of course, couldn't make that promise. No question, he would get another mount. A thoroughbred gelding. Some big powerhouse.

Hector remained quiet all the way to Jackson, where they left the Interstate on a circular ramp, heading south under the highway, and pulling into the nearest service station. Simon filled the tank, washed the windshield, and checked the oil. Then he dragged Hector into Shoney's across the road and ordered not only a large coffee to go but a cheeseburger, onion rings and fries. Hector, inspired by Simon's craving, loaded up as well.

Changing bills for a handful of silver, Simon found the pay phone and called his apartment. He expected Stefan to answer but it was Sybil.

"Sorry about missing dinner," Simon said, trying to sound normal. "Would you tell the kids I'll take them roller skating tomorrow?"

"Ellen took them skating." Sybil's voice sounded excited. "Where are you?"

"Seventy miles from home. We're at Shoney's in Jackson, loading up with junk food."

"You won!"

If he hadn't been standing in such a public place, Simon would have broken down and bawled. Instead, he said, "Yes, we won," wanting to add that Snow Goose broke a leg, but Sybil didn't give him the chance.

"Oh, that sweet Goose! I had an idea you'd win. That horse would do anything for you."

"She did. But afterwards, when I schooled her over some big jumps, Snow Goose broke a leg."

"Broke a leg? Is it bad?"

"Yes." He hesitated, then steeled himself. "We had to put her down."

"Oh my God!" Sybil whispered into the phone. "I'm so sorry. How terrible for you. Please, come home. Please!"

Holding on to the wall, Simon burst into tears, groaning, dropping the phone. Hector hung it up and put a hand on his friend's shoulder. When Simon turned, he had recovered and appeared to be his old self again. "Let's go," he said, leading the way. "Let's go home."

Printed in the United States
48109LVS00001B/5